TWENTY~FIVE CENTURIES WITHOUT
You

Viktória G Duda

TWENTY~FIVE CENTURIES WITHOUT
You

Addison & Highsmith

Addison & Highsmith Publishers

Las Vegas ◊ Chicago ◊ Palm Beach

Published in the United States of America by
Histria Books
7181 N. Hualapai Way, Ste. 130-86
Las Vegas, NV 89166 USA
HistriaBooks.com

Addison & Highsmith is an imprint of Histria Books. Titles published under the imprints of Histria Books are distributed worldwide.

Library of Congress Control Number: 2023948272

ISBN 978-1-59211-380-4 (hardcover)
ISBN 978-1-59211-401-6 (eBook)

Dedicated to

the Librarian,

with eternal gratitude

for your help and cooperation.

According to Orphic legend, at the beginning of the universe, there was love. The original creative mind, which permeated all the emptiness, split into gods and goddesses whose desire was to feel desired by the Other.

One night, when the stars were born, Dionysos and Diona embraced high up in the sky. The Titans, full of evil and jealousy, threw themselves on the couple making love. They tore out their limbs and roasted them, devoured their flesh, and swallowed their entrails. Before they could eat the hearts, however, Zeus saw what they were doing. Outraged, he killed and burned all Titans with a single bolt of thunder.

Athena took the still-beating hearts of the divine lovers and placed them inside alabaster statues she created using the ashes of the Titans.

Then she gave them breath and placed both on a still barren Earth. Those effigies became the parents of the first humans.

And all the gods went up on the Mount of Olympus, because they liked a good story to unfold: it was most captivating to watch the struggle of the humans, whose titan-infused bodies never let them fully experience the love their divine hearts were always longing for.

Their brave vulnerability soon touched the gods, who sent down rain on the barren land, sunshine to ripen the crops, and made their eternal promise:

Those humans who are willing to enter the wheel of rebirth again and again, forever and ever, as long as it takes to purify away the titanic part in them, and find each other in love, will themselves become gods:

Almighty. Immortal. Infinite.

PART ONE

Chapter 1
Thanatos

A tenacious thought kept recurring in my mind, the meaning of which I could not decipher. It was also quite melancholic and wistful to attend. So, each time I let it dissolve and pass by like a fleeting cloud on the horizon. Yet, it came back ten thousand times and allowed me no rest.

It was the thought of a woman who walks into a museum and falls in love with a statue. She takes a glance at its faultless ancient splendor and from that moment on wastes all her heart, all her passion and care on a man who died twenty-five centuries before she was born. Day in, day out, she returns to the same hall, and seats herself on the same bench, just to be near him.

Most certainly, such a thing was not my kind of thought — I shuddered at the futility and utter despair of her desire. Still, I could tell, this was a story wanting me to follow it up, even though I insisted that I did not wish to.

Until one night I unexpectedly found my way back to the Eternal Library. That is not a place to which one can easily travel. Like Plato's world of ideas, it has its place among the stars. Only in a dream, that magical kind of dream in which we can access other worlds, or when our consciousness takes its nightly flight away from the body, can we reach it — and only if we are awakened or lucky enough can we afterward remember that we have been there.

That night I dreamt that I had died and traveled to the Eternal Library in a realm between realities. The library was floating among the stars. It had no ground, no walls, and at any given time, only parts of it were visible. Even though it held the world's most alluring books, scripts, and scrolls, only those shelves manifested which one needed. The rest of the library remained a potentiality. As soon as I took a seat in one of those grand armchairs that were hovering there in mid-air, the librarian approached me.

"Do you want to know what happened to that lady and her sculpture in the museum?" she asked me straight away. Up there, in that mystical place, such a question carried great weight.

"Yes!" I exclaimed.

"Shall I give you a book in which it is all written?"

"Yes! Yes, please." Enraptured, I imagined reading a book in the Eternal Library would be the treat of a lifetime. Surely, it must be different from reading on Earth. Perhaps after reading a few pages, the printed letters would dissolve into a myriad of little silver threads, to then gain color and form a new reality, so maybe, just maybe, I could step into the very story...

The beauty of the book, which the librarian thereupon collected, certainly suggested such magic: there was something alluring about its velvety crimson color... or was it rather the pendant it featured? The pendant was on its cover as a high relief: it consisted of a black obsidian stone in a silver frame, which had the form of a lyre. I opened the book with great expectations, but to my shock found all of its pages — empty!

"Why are the pages empty?" I demanded from the librarian.

"I'm sorry," she said while she glanced over to the book through her silver-framed glasses sitting on top of her nose. She looked quite enchanting, with a be-witching little curl of hair falling onto her forehead, but the words she uttered sounded severe. "The writer whom we sent the idea to must have chosen not to work on the book. It appears to us that she had little faith in the story, thinking it was sad and senseless for a woman to fall in love with a man of by-gone days — although I assure you, the story would have actually ended with their love being fulfilled."

"Who is that writer?" I asked, aghast, and she left to check their eternal files. Soon, she came back with an answer that shocked me.

"It was you."

Distressed, I asked her, "Can I still make up for it? Can I have another chance to write it?"

She took her glasses off and stared me in the eye, with a strange look, like a feathered serpent.

"Yes, you may have a chance or two more," she said with a barely visible nod. "You aren't dead yet. This is just a dream."

There and then, in that space of eternity, I vowed that once I'm back on Earth, no matter the circumstances, I will make the book happen. It cannot be my fault that something which is meant to be, never comes to realization — but I needed the first piece of the puzzle to return with.

"Can you... tell me her name?" I asked.

"Her name is Sofia because of the wisdom she has accumulated over the ages. It is all quite simple, really."

"Can you show me her face?" Pushing my luck a little, I tried to ask another question, but I knew my time was up — the view of the library had already begun to fade back into darkness.

"Yes, I will, but later." I heard the librarian saying. However, with every word her voice sounded more distant. "You must go now, as you're not welcome here until you fulfill your mission."

By now I strongly felt the cosmic pull taking me away from the scene, the image of the Library looked smaller and smaller, darker and darker... on my way back the words fulfill your mission... your mission... mission echoed in my ears, leaving an indelible imprint on my mind.

The first time I caught a glimpse of Sofia's face, it happened in the shower. There she was... washing her hair with some fine, rose-scented shampoo. As I began to see her slim but strong body, I sensed that she was not a figment of my imagination. This was perception. Aided by the librarian, this was my perception of the miraculous.

As my mind tuned in to her, I could even penetrate Sofia's skin and skull, go into the microscopic depths of her brain, and see her thoughts firing. Ghastly, persistent images were coming to her mind, which she could hardly ban, images of men so gaunt as if they were coming out of a death camp, flashbacks of skeletal remains, severed limbs, and severe injuries, not from accidents but from that ancient curse we call war. She wasn't just casually washing her hair, she wanted to get rid of all the mud and blood from a whole decade she had spent saving lives near detonating bombs, amidst government curfews, and in besieged cities. She deeply inhaled the scent of roses, hoping that it would mask the madness. Today, she was longing for some beauty, pure human warmth, and affection. This was the first day of her sabbatical year, which she took in hope of balancing her life a bit back to normal.

Sofia had powerful resilience and great ability to transform. By the time she got herself dressed, her dark curls fell with rich volume onto her shoulders. Her eyes, which had seen the terror, now held a secret spark. There was no sign left that she did not come out of a spa or a gymnasium but spent years in some of the most horrendous war zones of the world.

"You look lovely, my dear," said Cynthia, the little old housekeeping lady whom Sofia inherited from her father, just as she inherited all this work they'd been doing for the United Nations. "Surely, you'll have good luck today. I've done your horoscope."

Sofia found herself smiling. Wouldn't it be easy, if all the magical-mysterious ways of life were really so simple as a chart drawn from the stars?

But this time, Cynthia seemed more serious about her suggestion than ever. She opened her eyes stunningly wide and pulled down the tip of her pointy nose. She looked like an owl. Her voice deepened, as she continued to speak:

"You have seen the titanic destruction humans are capable of, but there is also love. A beautiful thing is written in the stars for you, my dear. Tonight, you are going to meet your soulmate."

Later, Sofia was still chuckling about these words while she took the train out of London to go to the hospice, where she had been invited for a volunteer work interview. Only much later would she understand how right Cynthia was this time with her prediction.

From the outside, the hospice building almost looked like a small garden center, in front of which someone grew lavender and exhibited potted plants for sale. Yet, from the inside, the place had a dreary feel to it. Its energy felt sticky, like an old bachelor's greasy cupboard, full of cups of forgotten disappointments and plates of censored, yet unquestioned beliefs. Nothing could cover up the sadness lingering on within this building: none of the aroma lamps placed everywhere, none of those bright wall colors picked by psychologists, none of the guided relaxation sessions offered by volunteers. The hospice remained gloomy.

Sofia began to find her way through its corridors when she heard a disturbing cry. She recognized the sort immediately. It was this labored sound, powerlessly struggling itself through the vocal cords like a distress call from beyond the realm of the doomed. This was the voice of existential despair which occurs when an uninitiated is first confronted with the primordial, empty solitude of eternity, unable to comprehend it.

Sofia rushed through the open door from where the sound came and found an old lady, in agony, trying to sit up in bed. Professional habit quickly prompted her to check the patient's datasheet at the end of the bed and tend to her without further delay.

"Doctor." The lady reached out to her. "Are you a doctor?"

"Yes, Mrs. Windworth, I am," Sofia said, as it was her profession, even if she did not work here, or not yet.

"Doctor." With eyes stuck wide open, the old woman prepared to ask her the same question she had been repeating for weeks now. "Tell me, tell me... what will happen when I die?" To the question, which came up from the deep anguish of her soul, none of the doctors or workers at the hospice had given an answer so far. Quickly, they always deflected it, some even told her not to talk about such silly things, she was not going to die just yet.

Sofia, however, gently grabbed the lady's shoulders, helped her into a comfortable position, and sat down with her. She answered in a compassionate, at the same time professional, way.

"When you die, your consciousness separates from your body. It will feel like you are floating, as you will no longer be using your physical senses. But your consciousness will remain intact, like now."

The patient grabbed Sofia's hand and pleaded, "Do you really believe that, doctor?"

"No, I don't believe that," Sofia said, "I know that." Then she placed her other hand on the heart region at the lady's chest. A wonderful warmth emanated from Sofia's hand, which made Mrs. Windworth calm and serene.

"You know, doctor, I've been seeing my dead husband and mother all day long. I thought I was going crazy."

"No, you are not going crazy," Sofia said with the power of conviction. "It's natural when death approaches that one perceives both worlds. Soon you may talk to your husband and mother like you are talking to me now, and then you will no longer be talking to me."

"If it's so," Mrs. Windworth looked dreamingly into the sunbeams glittering through the folds on the window, "I'm looking forward to that."

"If people knew what death was," Sofia said, slowly letting her hand go off the lady's chest, "they would not be afraid of it. They would merely look forward to birthing again into another realm."

As Sofia and the old lady looked into each other's eyes, invisible sparks of gratitude traveled between them. The more Mrs. Windworth looked at Sofia, the more elevated she felt by the cosmic reflection in her eyes and the more Sofia looked at Mrs. Windworth, the more she felt that her decision to leave the war zone for now and instead work with people who are dying naturally, was right. When the doctor on duty finally arrived in the room and wanted to administer the usual tranquilizers, Mrs. Windworth said that she no longer needed them.

The interview was held at a long conference table. Some grave-looking ladies sat behind it, most likely doctors, nurses, and caretakers, who appeared to Sofia like minor liminal deities, guarding her entry into the world of servicing the peacefully dying.

How much, Sofia wondered to herself, have these women seen of the physical as well as the non-physical worlds, to really understand the significance of their vocation? Would they understand if I told them about my memories?

Even as a baby, Sofia did not feel like a newborn: more like a cosmic traveler who was aware that this life came out of a previous death and that death came out of a previous life. At night, she used to lay in her crib with full adult consciousness, thinking her way into the dense darkness, wondering how she got here. She even had some vague, shapeless remembrance of a time, many lives, many deaths ago, when she may have found an exit from the wheel of birth and rebirth, but somehow, she could not access it. She only felt that there was some curse or doom or misfortune which had prevented her from using the portal...

"Dr Erato." Sofia was brought back from her musings, by the voice of the hospice director, a corpulent woman with a round, bittersweet face. "You have quite an impressive résumé here. Truly extraordinary. You seem to have a whole collection of academic qualifications: doctor of medicine, summa cum laude, another doctorate in metaphysics, and even a bachelor of arts in archaeology, all before the age of twenty-seven."

Sofia didn't like the enlisting, it sounded a bit like an accusation. She always thought there was something wrong with someone who had two PhDs before the age of twenty-seven.

"And you speak Japanese!"

"Yes, my father was Japanese," Sofia put a story to the fact, as if she had to take away the edge from all her skills. "He met my mother — who's English — in Vienna while working for the United Nations."

"Is that how you ended up working for the UN Peacekeeping yourself?"

"Yes."

"As a doctor?" a meager-looking woman from the panel asked, lowering her head so she could look from above her glasses.

"Yes, as an emergency field doctor. And a forensic archaeologist."

"Archaeologist?" She now took her glasses off in surprise. "Doing what?"

There was a long pause, as everyone waited in anticipation of what on earth a medical doctor had to do with archaeology.

At the same time, the door opened, and a young man came in. He had a pleasant face and was wearing a cozy-looking caramel sweater.

"We were digging out mass graves," Sofia said softly while looking at the man. "Gathering evidence for genocide."

While saying that, her gaze followed the young man further as he took a seat at the panel. She was curious about him and wanted to take a longer look, but the director already posed the next question.

"What would you say is your greatest strength?"

It stunned Sofia yet again, like on many occasions before: how deaf and blind people remained to the sufferings of the world! They never asked more questions, instead, always ran back to the well-known patterns of social habits and protocols as soon as they heard her mention the graves. Such things were permitted in the evening news but seemed utter taboo in the living reality of our fine lives.

"What would you say?" the director reminded her of the question.

"My greatest strength?"

"Yes."

My greatest strength is irrelevant, Sofia thought to herself, what matters is the patient. Yet, she knew she had to reply something.

"When I am in hell," she said, "I keep going."

Yet again, no one asked her about the hell, but Sofia noticed the young man was studying her while she said this. The man's face was an intriguing blend of a young, boyish look with a little stubble and a hint of mischief. He smiled at Sofia, like someone who understood.

"You went to the room of one of our patients before," Sofia now heard another doctor taking over the interrogation. It was the one who had come into Mrs. Windworth's room.

"Yes, I heard her cry for help in the corridor, when no one was around," Sofia said, puzzled as to why she had to justify herself.

"No, that's great. And you calmed her down remarkably well. I'm just curious what you said to her."

"She asked me what happened when we died."

There was another great, one could say, deadly silence in the room.

"And what did you tell her?" the director of the hospice wanted to know.

"I told her that our consciousness leaves the body in the moment of — "

"But, Dr. Erato," she interrupted, letting out a small laugh. "We must not force our beliefs on our patients. That's against the policy of our institution."

She said that like a teacher correcting some nonsensical idea of a pupil, not expecting the conversation to continue. Thus, she was a bit startled when Sofia thought long and deep to tell, "With all due respect," she said, "you are doing just that."

"Doing what?"

"Forcing your beliefs on your patients. You believe so much that the question of life after death is a matter of religion or superstition that you utterly fail to investigate it. As a result, you leave your patients completely without information, which causes so much fear in them that your policy amounts to a kind of psychological torture."

All the grave-looking gatekeepers looked shocked and dismissive. Only the young man, who now looked right at Sofia, smiled with a hint of pride.

"Interesting view, Dr Erato," the director said, yet her words echoed only polite emptiness. "I shall think about that. Anyway, pleased to have met you. We'll inform you about the results of your interview by the latest in two weeks."

Back in one of the empty corridors again, Sofia paused and closed her eyes for a moment. By simply holding still, she could bring herself to a portal between the worlds of mind and matter: a place where invisibly, but surely the ten thousand things of creation were resting in the ineffable ocean ground of consciousness. From there, Sofia felt like she had to linger on in this building for a little while longer.

As she opened her eyes, her gaze fell on a picture hanging on the wall. It was a framed poster of a lonely lake at sunset, on which a wooden causeway ended in the middle of the dark waters.

What a horrible image to show to the dying, Sofia thought to herself. It is peaceful and serene, yes, but at the end, it depicts a path leading to nowhere. Urgently, this ought to be replaced by a stairway leading into the stars at the end of which the celestial city awaits — or something like that...

Pondering like that gave her time to stay longer, until she heard a male voice from behind.

"I can't stand that picture, either." Sofia turned her head and saw the young man from the interview panel approaching.

"It sounds like you are reading my mind," she said.

"Maybe... maybe I just read your non-verbal expressions." The young man smiled and extended his hand towards Sofia and introduced himself as David Carter.

"Did the doctors find a good excuse to get rid of me?" Sofia asked bluntly and without delay.

"Yes." David laughed. "Immediately, they did. You're overqualified. In fact, not to blow my trumpet, I was the only one suggesting to take you on board."

"Overqualified...," Sofia mused. "I never understood that type of excuse. If one is capable of doing more, one's capable of doing less too. Argumentum a maiore ad minus."

David smiled. Sofia looked at him, with her head slightly tilted and wondered, "Are you one of the doctors working here?"

"No, I'm a social worker, meanwhile promoted to my highest level of incompetence. Now I work for the government, coordinating and supervising all these social institutions. Sometimes this makes me feel like a spy...," David said with another laugh. "Listen, don't be bothered. People tend to be scared of anyone who knows more than they do."

"Maybe..."

On the spur of the moment, David stepped in front of Sofia and thought of something.

"Do you want to come to the museum with me?" he asked.

"To the museum?!" Sofia was taken aback. Normally, she didn't think much of museums. She saw them as just another attempt in the human project to fool away death, to preserve olden days, and counteract the experience of impermanence, which most people simply couldn't handle.

"Oh!" David exclaimed as he saw her surprise. "Yes... you see, I like to go to the museum after work. The coffee is very good there. Fine arts, fine coffee. So, I just thought, some fine conversation there might cheer you up after these dreary doctors."

Sofia looked at David. Good coffee sounded inviting, but foremost, there was something familiar about this man's company, as if she had always known him.

"All right," she said, curious about him. "Why not? I haven't been to a museum in a thousand years."

Soon, they found themselves not just having a cup of coffee but strolling amidst some of the grand marble columns of civilization. There they were, walking amidst sarcophagi and mummies from a time in which death was still held sacred.

"I imagine the ancient Egyptians would not have rejected me as a doctor, just because I dared to talk about the afterlife," Sofia remarked. "They showed respect to things which are eternal."

"Yes, and we don't." David nodded while looking at a perfectly preserved crocodile body that had endured five thousand years. Everywhere around them, there were mummies: corpses of cats, birds, and humans.

"No, we don't," Sofia agreed with him. "Look at how we have put these mummies on public display! It's a disgrace, especially since they come from a people who knew the dead must not be disturbed."

Their mood had turned dark in this hall, but a sign in front of the next door suggested something more enlivening:

Come on in, here are the gods, it said.

Sofia and David stepped into a hall full of ancient Greek statues.

"All this beauty!" Sofia exclaimed as if she had stepped into a magical forest. "Now that I see this, I notice how much I was longing for something like that, David. A time in history when beauty prevailed!"

As she said these words, they came to a halt in front of a white marble statue depicting close-up the accomplished nobility of the Greek physique and art.

"Beauty, yes, but I believe there was also hardship," David remarked. "Their time surely was not as easy as their artifacts are on the eye. Look at the caption."

It read:

STATUE OF A GREEK SLAVE
ATHENS, CLASSICAL PERIOD

"He was a slave," Sofia whispered and shivered at the thought. There was something horrific, yet at the same time strangely captivating about that. "He was living, breathing, thinking, feeling, yet owned by an Other."

She couldn't help but look at the statue and wonder how he had been treated. My god, he still looked so alive! His pose was not that of a statue, but rather of a human being calling, inviting someone. Yes, inviting the lover: the intent of the statue was clearly to seduce. It was begging you to glide and lay your careful hand on his shoulder, bring forehead to forehead, lips to lips, skin to skin. It wanted you to taste that alluring little vein visible on his neck through which blood pumped into moving muscles once upon a time. The whole statue silently asked to be awakened, not only to life but to love, that enchanted experience that can only be initiated by the metamorphic touch of the Other.

"Someone must have loved him, don't you think," David said, "having such an exquisite statue to immortalize him?"

"Certainly…," Sofia heard her own voice saying. She could not hold back. Any alarm which now may sound be damned!

Sofia lifted her hand and with her thumb, she gently caressed the alluring cheekbone of the statue.

At this moment, the miraculous happened. There was nothing to see. The statue did not move like in a fantasy, nor was Sofia's vivid imagination at play, but she felt it so strongly that there remained no doubt about it: as she caressed the statue, the statue caressed her back.

Chapter 2
The Acquisition of Pasión

Ancient Greece, 416 BC.

Before he was sold, Pasión lived his whole life on Melos Island. Ever since his childhood, he spent days on end crawling on this gigantic stone relief crafted by the wild artist, the volcano and his helpers, the wind and the waves. During the years he grew up, the island revealed more of its secret to him than to anyone else, alive or deceased. Pasión had become the eternal, natural artist's human apprentice. At times, he received intuition where to dig or dive for splendid minerals to provide colors for his brush, so that he could paint wondrous frescoes all over his parents' house. At other times, he heard the soul of a rock calling and began to chisel it free — that is how he created his first statues. On certain days, as an artist, he felt like the creator himself. Yet, at other times, he appeared desperately insignificant: standing on top of a cliff and seeing the waters below him in the deep, he knew it wouldn't take nature much to blow him away and destroy him. It was on these days, in the shadowy thought of death, that he needed to remind himself of the tiny flowers that grew on the rock giants at the sea. The flowers could utilize grains of sand and drops of dew to sustain their existence, thereby beating the odds against the greater elements. While the volcano, the wind, and the waves randomly created yet destroyed again what they had formed, the flowers brought forth petals in pleasing patterns to counteract the chaos. The flowers also grew seeds to catapult their patterns into the future, beyond any destruction that may come to them. Matter, as Pasión learned, will eventually destroy matter, but the consciousness of life eternally knows how to renew itself.

Humans, in the large scheme of things, remained a puzzle to him. While Pasión always had friends and lovers, he never felt quite at ease with his own kind. Humans seemed to possess a great potential to create flowering harmony but were driven by some unquenchable ire that blinded them to truth and beauty, they were only too seldom using it.

Like in these last two months, humans regularly unleashed horrific, titanic size destruction upon each other, which worried Pasión more than any raging of volcanoes and storms at the sea.

This time it was the Athenians, who led their arrogant mission to spread democracy against the will of the peoples. When the Melians showed no willingness to pay tribute to their confederacy, the Athenians seized their city. Day by day, week by week, month by month, the siege lasted and lasted: the paradise island gradually turned into a pot of hell. The sacred homes of the people became their prisons. The sloping streets, where once the healthy bloodstream of the community used to flow, deteriorated into mad hunting grounds. Heroes mixed there with traitors as well as the desperate who would do anything for a handful of barley or a single drupe of olive. To survive these days, no means seemed too strange, no measure too extreme, no belief too bizarre.

On the last day of the siege, Pasión was walking with his mother and his older brother, Moris, in search of some food and maybe some news. Many people were out on the streets, their horror suppressed by necessity.

At the plaza, a monstrous image of Athena was set up, made of straw, covered by wax, and bound to four spikes of an inescapable wheel. The Melians, ready to torture the effigy, grabbed whips and heated spears to pierce through the protector goddess of their enemy. A great Melian speaker stood on a makeshift podium towering over the entire scene, holding a beautiful little statue of Dice, the goddess of Justice, in his hands. The orator raised his voice:

"The Athenians told us it is law that the powerful extort what they can, while the weak suffer what they must." There was a quiet but bitter uproar coming from the gathered crowd. "But we will show them that it is law: what you do to others, will be done to you!"

A large, cloaked man, who stood next to the crowd, lifted a spear and began to throw a frightening incantation over the straw and wax effigy.

"As this figure of Athena will now be tortured and burned, so will the city of Athens be tortured and burned. In the end, it will be humiliated and besieged, its people will betray themselves and go mad with pain."

"Don't even look there," Pasión's mother, Anisa, said to her two sons as the people began to throw spears. The smell of molten wax and smoking straw reached their nostrils.

"Why not?" Moris, Pasión's big brother protested. "These Athenian dogs have been starving us out like rats; nothing should be spared to bring them down!"

"But this is black magic," Anisa said in a soft voice against the barking shouts of her giant son. "Putting curses on people will always backfire."

Pasión shuddered at hearing this because he was sure his mother told the truth. His whole life, Pasión had observed it. His mother, Anisa, knew magic: not the theatrical kind that uses tricks and builds on people's superstitions, but real magic: she knew about the invisible, yet powerful hidden structure and workings of the universe. Still, at this moment, Pasión's anger grew against his mother's wisdom, and he also cried out in hurtful desperation.

"Backfire?" he repeated. "But, mother! We did not start this belligerence. The Athenians made themselves our enemy, not us!"

"You never know who your enemy is," his mother continued to talk in her quiet and mysterious ways. "Someone who seems to be your enemy, may turn out to be your greatest friend."

"Mother!" Pasión objected but regained his usual soft-spoken and affectionate voice. "They are destroying our homes and our lives. You turned as thin as milk's skin because they cut off our supplies. They clearly are the enemy."

"Damn right!" Moris said. "I will now go and throw a spear into that Athenian poppet, too, just to make myself feel better."

"No…," Anisa said weakly, but Moris was gone. Pasión looked at her and thought that she shouldn't be out on the streets. Her legs trembled, and it looked like she was going to fall, so Pasión lifted her famished and feverish body and carried his mother home. She weighed nothing. Even though Pasión himself was drained from malnourishment and all the fighting, she felt but a feather in his arms.

At home, Pasión laid his mother's hollow bird body on the sofa and tried to give her some water, but she refused to sip.

"Pasión," she insisted instead, "you must promise me something."

"Anything, mother, anything," Pasión replied hastily while he arranged some pillows behind her head, trying to make her comfortable. He caught her scent, which he remembered so well from his childhood. He always loved to breathe in her milky flavor of coconut and mystical herbs, while his mother — his magical, cinnamon-eyed mother — told him unusual stories about Kronos, the god of time, eating his own children, and Orpheus, the artist, descending into the underworld. His brother Moris never listened, rather ran off boxing and wrestling late into the night. But Pasión hung on to every word she ever uttered, for her tales suggested there was more to life than was made out by the ordinary senses. They prompted Pasión to stay connected with the world of inspiration: he learned to play the lyre exquisitely, carved reliefs and statues, and painted frescoes until no inch on the wall was left untouched.

"Promise me," this time Anisa's voice, which had told him a thousand and one tales, said, "that you will never take your own life!"

"Why would I do such a ghastly thing?" Her son backed away, aghast. Everyone acquainted with Pasión knew, let alone his own mother, that no one ever loved this terrible, terrifying, beautiful miracle called life more than he did.

"Just promise me," she repeated.

"I promise," Pasión said, upon which his mother did something she had never done before.

Around her neck, Anisa was wearing a pendant. Never ever did she take it off: no matter how much Pasión begged and cried as a little boy, she never gave it to him. The pendant had the silver form of a lyre which framed a black obsidian stone. The obsidian was formed here on the island from volcanic lava, but the silver came from Attica.

Now she removed the very same pendant, which had mystified Pasión his whole life, and placed it around his neck.

"Make sure that you always, at any given time, wear this visibly and that you never, under any circumstances, part from it."

Before she could say more, Moris burst into the house. He was carrying a bundle of raw meat under his armpit, which he quickly chopped up and threw on the hearth to grill. Moris had been clever and canny to obtain food in the midst of famine, but it was mostly meat he brought home, which their mother never ate.

The two hungry brothers gulped down that which had been roasting. They had given up lying down for supper like civilized people do since their father died. After killing hundreds of enemies in dozens of battles, he had been one of the first to fall during this present siege. Since his death, family rituals had become obsolete.

"What is this meat?" Pasión asked, chewing, suspicious of its source. "Where did you get it from?"

"Stolen, all right?!" Moris barked back. "I lied for it, killed for it, so you don't go hungry. Shut up and eat!"

The meat didn't taste bad, yet it made Pasión's stomach churn; he didn't quite know why.

"Mother, you must eat some too," Moris said, while in his half-open mouth he turned a chunk of meat around, which was still quite raw and dripping with blood. "You must get some strength! Want some?"

As the brother said that, an unfathomable feeling of horror came over Pasión, even before his brain registered what it was. It was more than the anger towards his brother who knew very well that their mother would never eat meat yet kept offering it to her. It was a deeper feeling of irrevocable loss, like knowing a treasure had just fallen into the abyss, never to be retracted.

"She doesn't even answer me. Mother!" Moris exclaimed, as he also noticed something was not right. "Mother!"

He went over to her and shook her body. It was lifeless.

"Oh, fuck!" Moris yelled as he realized their mother had just died. "I told her she should eat!" In his anger, he picked up a chair and broke it by throwing it against the wall and vehemently ran out of the house.

It was a blessing that he left: everything became calm and peaceful. A sacred silence descended onto the house. Pasión began to witness something ineffable: he could feel a great, upward-spiraling vortex opening up in the room, which then lifted his mother's consciousness up into realms where he could no longer follow her. First, Pasión shed tears of joy for his mother to journey towards such miraculous dimensions, then tears of grief for himself, left behind, abandoned to the whims and cruelties of his fellow men.

While he buried her in the garden, Pasión thought about what his mother used to say about life. She always said it was but a dream from which one day we will awaken. In that moment it will not matter what we had in life or who we were. It will only matter what choices we made: whether we developed the courage, curiosity, and creativity to expand or remained in the cages of the cowards; whether we followed the path of compassion or remained in the swamps of hatred; whether we succeeded to turn all our evil into things of nobility so that the gods will respect and welcome us as one of their own. Pasión planted a fig tree on Anisa's grave and hoped over time it would expand to the full beauty of its being. Else, he left the spot unmarked.

Then he went off, just to wander the streets of Melos aimlessly: which once was a dream, had now become a nightmare. Something in town had changed again, as he hardly saw anybody. In many houses, doors and windows were left open carelessly, as if nothing mattered anymore. Inside one house, Pasión saw a father stabbing his two young children: a crawling toddler and a little girl of only a few years of age. The mother stood by without saying a word. At other places, people were hastily tying together some bedlinen to form ropes and hanging themselves. Pasión remembered his promise not to commit suicide and wondered what was going on. He sped up his steps.

Eventually, he reached the siege line. At first glance, it looked like a miracle: somewhere close to the sea, the fortification was broken. But no! This was no liberation, this was terror.

Lost in his grief, Pasión failed to notice the unspeakable: Melos had surrendered!

Suddenly, he heard a loud, unpleasant but familiar voice calling him from somewhere above.

"Pasión! Brother!" It was Moris. Pasión usually found his bullying brother hard to deal with, but now he ran towards his call. It should be good to have some ally in the midst of this growing madness.

He saw Moris standing on a cliff high above the sea. Pasión knew this spot. They'd been here before, but this time they weren't alone. A large crowd had gathered. Many of the locals were running up a sharp ridge a little further away from the shore.

"Watch out! Behind you!" Moris yelled at him. Only as Pasión looked back, did he realize what was unfolding here. The Melian crowd wasn't gathering: the people were being hunted! Like wolves surrounding the sheep, the Athenians corralled all the locals into groups. Women and children were tied together to be sold as slaves. Men, they ushered up that steep hill. There, against the breathtaking beauty of the turquoise-blue Aegean Sea, the most frightening sight of their time awaited them. Soldiers were standing in a hoplite phalanx row, complete with shields and spears longer than two men's height. The spears pointed precisely forward and impaled all who were forced to run towards them. Pasión and Moris saw the first of their unarmed, starved, and defeated countrymen die at the blades of the victors. Then they noticed that at least a dozen soldiers were already closing in on them too.

The two brothers looked at the massacre, looked at each other, looked at the sea, and then nodded. Perhaps for the first time, but in an instant decision, they agreed on something. They started a mighty sprint away from the others, accelerated their bodies into a curved flight, and jumped from the precipices deep into the waters below.

Once upon a time, it was Pasión who found out the truth about this lethal-looking spot on the island. It happened on a rare occasion when he and his brother went for a walk together and they happened to stroll along this very cliff. Now lost in memory, it may have been their mother who prompted them to try and be friends, but Moris only used the time to tyrannize Pasión by calling him a coward for never taking part in any fights.

"It doesn't make me a coward that I have better things to do than punching others," Pasión told him.

"Yes, but how else would you prove that you're not a chicken?" His brother laughed at him.

By then, all the bullying had started to penetrate Pasión's very soul and poison him from within. He knew he had to act against it. At that moment, a voice emerged from the innermost depth of his being. It was a voice that, so far, he had only known from his dreams. Yet, it was a voice that always spoke the truth, and following it had never led to a bad decision. It was the voice of Chairon, his centaur mentor, whom Pasión's mother had taught him how to meet in dreams.

This time, Chairon's voice came while he was awake. In his kind, rich baritone he exclaimed only one word: "Jump!"

Pasión, who trusted Chairon unconditionally, looked at his brother.

"How about jumping off this cliff?" he suggested.

Moris looked startled, but Pasión did not leave him time to think: with one leap, he disappeared into the abyss.

After that, things were never again the same: Moris, who went home thinking his brother had died, never dared to call him a coward again, and Pasión, who learned that it was indeed quite possible to survive that dive, remained forever connected to the ethereal wisdom of Chairon. More than a decade later, it was Pasión's single act of brave discovery about a dangerous-looking, yet safe spot to jump, which saved them both from the worst massacre in the history of Melos.

Even though the Athenians had sent a flock of arrows after them, Pasión and Moris were no longer in the sea. Promptly, they had swum into a cave under the rock which was not visible from above. As they emerged out of the water in the safe cavern, despite being ice-cold, they exchanged some hearty laughs, arising from the unexpected euphoria of being alive!

This was their last best chance to escape for good, by going into hiding. Pasión was on friendly terms with some wild folks, who secreted themselves in the mountains, loathing not just the Athenians, but any government in power. They believed someone who wanted to be fully free had to learn how to survive as part of nature. These people camouflaged themselves among the thousands of little caves buried away in the thorny, rosemary-scented valleys of the island. Pasión knew that they were the ones who would never be found by the intruding forces, so it would have been only reasonable to join them. But in life, a man does not tend to follow reason. Instead, he follows, unknowingly perhaps, any path that leads him to the innermost labyrinth of his own heart, where he can find forgotten hopes, forbidden desires, and forsaken fears to remind him of his highest destiny. This is how Pasión, instead of saving himself, went — home.

He went home to water the fig tree on his mother's fresh grave, to finish the scenes he was painting, and the alabaster statue of Aphrodite he was forming in the garden. What a relief it was to arrive back! Everything was there: all he had to do was to pick up his brush and chisel again. There would be a way to overcome grief — tomorrow. For now, an invincible tiredness wrestled him down into a deep, dreamless state. It left him unaware of what Moris was doing, but most likely, his brother must have fallen asleep somewhere also.

Pasión had lost his sense of time. When he awoke, he had no idea for how long he had been dormant — was it already the next morning? He had woken up to a brilliant, bright light — was that perhaps the sun rising to a glorious new day?

It took him a surprising while to recognize what it was. We are all wired to expect the expected, so when the unexpected happens, it may cause surprising delays. Pasión saw the burning arrow that was shot into the room, but only when the wooden beams in the room caught flames did he recognize that his house was on fire. Even then, he was so hypnotized by the fiery dance that for long moments, he just watched it. As the flames started licking his own paintings on the wall, he felt simply amazed by the great and surprising artistry of the fire. The flames changed the hues he had used and brought some scenes truly to life. Pasión found this fire to be a great artist and also a superb teacher of impermanence: it only worked in the present moment, never to repeat itself. The artwork Pasión could admire in these mad moments was never to be seen again by anyone. Look, there was Orpheus, who descended into the underworld, to retrieve his lost love. Now his beloved, who had made the fatal mistake of looking back, could be seen on the wall consumed by those fires of hell…

Finally, Moris screaming brought him out of his curious reverie.

"Get out of the house NOW!" he shouted.

Suddenly, Pasión's body took over: without allowing the brain to think another thought, it moved his legs and made Pasión jump out of the window just a blink of an eye before the flames were to catch his limbs.

He bounced straight into the trap: on the spot, Athenians caught him with a net. Promptly, chains were put around his neck — this wasn't the military. These were scavengers, a couple of odd-looking slave merchants, who tried to make as much fortune as they could from the destruction left behind. They rented spaces on merchant ships to bring their human stock to cities where they hoped to obtain a better price for strong, young male survivors than they could for crying children or malnourished women.

The waiting was the worst. For a few days and nights, Pasión was left chained at the harbor with his brother and some others until a willing ship would come and take them. The nights were icy cold. He could hardly, if at all, sleep, and so found no escape from the misery. During the days, he watched the enemy taking possession of all the Melian properties. How could he be so naive to ever think he could reclaim his home? Melos has become a colony of Athens.

"Hey, you!" One morning Pasión was made to look up by a jab delivered to his shoulder. "What can you do?"

Pasión noticed a ship in the harbor. The same two men who captured him and his brother now towered over him, apparently ready to take them on board. One looked like a rat, he thought, and the other like a lanky scarecrow.

"What can I do?" Pasión quietly repeated the question, letting it roll on his tongue and on his mind. In his tired confusion, he didn't understand: surely, shackled and chained, there was nothing he could do right now.

"Yeah," the rat-looking trader snarled at him. "What is it that you can do? Do you have any skills?" he demanded while jerking Pasión up and forward by his upper arm.

"Oh!" came out of Pasión's lips. Of course, it was only logical, too horribly logical: this man was gauging him as slave material! "I can … read and write," Pasión slowly brought it out, while he was made to stand and tried to keep his balance.

"Really, uh? Read and write?" The rat-face leaned in close to him as if he wanted to sniffle something interesting there. Repulsed, Pasión drew back: the handler smelled of piss and sweat, mixed with some fine jasmine scent, which he must have gotten from a lady he bought or raped. "Can you read and write well… or just a little?"

"Well."

"Very well or just well?" the trader asked again and began to feel the skin on Pasión's cheeks, who pulled away from this nasty touch as much as he could.

"Very well," Pasión admitted.

"Ah! And can you perform what you are reading?"

"I can… perform," Pasión said, but with difficulty. The trader now played with his hair, rubbing his gentle curls between his rude fingers, assessing its quality. Although Pasión wanted to make a favorable impression, he found it utmost disturbing to be touched by a coarse man like this. Touch had always been very important to Pasión: while nothing comforted and strengthened him more than being in the physical proximity of someone he loved or felt attracted to, he couldn't suffer being handled by such a nasty and hostile, inside-out ugly person. So, he struggled, but kept his voice firm, as he said: "I can perform epic and lyric poetry, I can perform the lyre and the cithara…"

"Oooh, niiice," the rat opened his eyes into a large gaze. "We'll make a good deal with this one," he said to his colleague, the scarecrow. "Has silky hair like a cat and skin soft as a pussy. We'll sell him to some rich motherfucker: he will look pretty as a boy or a girl, whatever boss wants. Exquisite! I bet we shall make 300 Drachmas on him or more. Let's ship him to Athens."

Athens! Wasn't it always his greatest dream to go there: to see the sculptures, to meet the sculptors! Yet, Pasión's heart sank, hearing the words of the trader now. He feared rape. It was one of the many horrible memories his father left him with: one night, when he was growing up, his father summoned up the slave boy, who had become Pasión's favorite playmate, into his bedroom. He heard his cries from the corridor and saw the next morning that his little friend found it painful even to walk. He said it hurt more than any whipping — of which he received plenty anyway. On this occasion, Pasión resented his father the most — even more than for refusing to buy him marble, as the father, ever so rich, thought so little of art. Sometimes he wondered how his mother could be such a blessing and his father, such a curse…

"And what is it that you know, giant boy?" Pasión's thoughts were brought back into the dire present as the slave trader attended to his brother.

"What I know?" Moris said in a provoking voice, which certainly did not rouse the rat to come closer to him. "I know how to escape, and I know how to take revenge. I know how to take care of my family in times of a siege. I know how to kill an Athenian soldier and use his grilled flesh to feed my family." He looked at Pasión with a diabolic laugh which chilled not only him but shocked even the hardened slave traders.

"Useless," the rat-faced man concluded, once he caught himself. "Off with him to the mines."

Pasión wanted to scream out in protest, but ice had already formed around his heart. Mercifully, this numbed the horror he just learned about, but it also sealed his throat. As they embarked, his brother was taken to another part of the ship. Neither of them said a word. Their ways were parted.

As Pasión looked back once more at his island, he saw thousands of glittering golden sun fairies dancing on top of the azure and lapis lazuli patches of the sea, but the wind was already blowing it all away from him. He forced himself to look forward instead; a part of him was even strangely relieved to be taken away from the hell this island had become and sent into the unknown.

In the belly of the ship, he found himself cramped between merchandise and many other slaves from other shores, other wars. Eventually, he closed his eyes and tried to find a good thought. His mother always taught him that the quality of one's thoughts was more important than circumstances — but now it was hard to remember anything reassuring; everything in his past was shadowed by grief. If he thought of his beloved colored rocks at the sea, it came to him that he might never see the moon-like landscape of Melos again. Thinking of his mother's face brought the chilling realization that she was now dead. The thought of home came with distressing images of fire and his own destroyed artwork. Finally, to bring himself some sense of spaciousness, Pasión entertained thoughts of the sky and his dreams of flying, as the sky was something he had not lost. But it was hard to maintain thoughts of celestial skies when one of the fellow captives — all freshly taken out of their silken lives — always started to wail, until reminded by the crack of a whip to remain silent. The worst troublemakers were lined up and shackled by their ankles to a long, robust stock in the middle of the ship. As the night grew more silent, their moans grew louder, as the forced positions over time turned into torture.

Surviving one's position was tough even without being at the stock. The sea became stormy and Pasión felt his stomach making the same waves as the sea. He got so overwhelmingly bilious that the sickness squashed his gut, his brain, his heart into one confusing mess of pain. It was enough to override his disgust and make him curl up in the fetal position, down on the foul, infested floor, waiting for this mad, terrible mother of a ship to birth him into some new life, sometime, somewhere, somehow.

It woke him up from this distant, nightmarish state of nausea when suddenly the chief merchant of the ship appeared at the entrance. This large, muscle-bound man addressed the whole miserable congregation with one roaring message of doom:

"The first rule is: Know thyself!" the voice of the slave driver rolled down heavily from above the stairs. "Know your place! I don't care whether you have been a king or a queen before, from now on, you are a slave. You are a tool. An object. Tomorrow you will become the property of another. You will use yourself for nothing else but to service whoever has paid your price. Forget that you have been a person before. You are no person, no longer. Tonight will be your last great opportunity to ponder upon that."

Pasión knew this was not just merely some business to discipline them, but a diabolic ritual to prepare the prisoners that not only their bodies but their souls would be taken too. He understood this was a time of great peril! Therefore, during the night, he followed this one order of the chief merchant to the strictest degree and took the gloomy opportunity to think deeply. He brought to his troubled mind all the wealth of wisdom his mother, Anisa, the centaur, Chairon, and nature ever shared with him. He made no mistake about it: to allow fear, resignation, and distress to take hold of his mind in this hour would inevitably lead to the worst of human fates. A slave, who becomes a slave also from within is a doomed thing, he had seen it. Pasión had to find the good medicine: the highest vision, which was diametrically opposed to the misery he currently found himself in.

So, he found out he was longing for freedom to love and pursue his fine art. He was longing for a deep connection with life and an Other he could embrace. Although he was as far from it as possible, he was longing for human warmth to shield him from the madness of the world. He was longing for closeness which would reach straight into the soul, for an invitation to explore the depths of our existence, and to find a way not only out of slavery but to end all suffering. It was a high aim, the highest perhaps for a human — still, in that darkest night of the soul, Pasión made a vow to make it into his highest vision and never give up on pursuing it.

"No matter what anyone will say or do, no matter how they will treat me," he vowed to himself, "I will live this life truly worthy of a human being. I will remain true to myself and the truth I know, to my dreams of flying and my dreams of creating art. I will never let people, cruelty, or any other evil stop me from reaching out for truth, beauty, and love."

As he thought like that, hot and liberating tears began to flow down his tormented face. Through his vow, he was setting invisible, yet real, forces into motion coming to his aid and protection. Magic, as his mother would call it.

The next day, he may have broken down if not for the vow he had made to himself: the inner sightings of the slave market whacked him with feelings he never thought he would ever have to experience. Standing on a stage, amidst other slaves, some lethargic, others hysteric and being punished, Pasión was grabbed by the most brutal and primordial of all fears. His heart began to flutter in his ribcage like a trapped bird, and a crazy inner current ran through his nerves hitting straight between his legs like a tiny bolt of lightning. This was worse than any of the battles he had had to fight before. Deprived of using his agility, muscles, or intelligence, he now found himself thrown in front of the worst predator in this world: the innately insane species of humans.

And who would that human be whose mercy he would soon be left with? Pasión looked at the row of people standing by the podium, all potential buyers who could become his master in a matter of hours or even minutes and have life and death power over him. The faces he saw brought him close to fainting! In the crowd he could see it all: the same cold stare his aunt Suha had, the sister of his father, who used to punish a slave girl by rubbing ginger into her eyes night by night until she lost her sanity. There were savages like his own father could be: these were worse than lions, who would enjoy tearing you to pieces and only nurse you back to health so they could start over again. Finally, Pasión detected a gap-toothed man who looked the worst: a skull-head, who wouldn't stop at your skin, but would tear into your soul, tear after tear, until you believe what the merchant said yesterday: that you are nothing but an object.

Even so, Pasión remembered his vow. He tried to focus on it with all his might, but he was about to lose consciousness. Even though he did not fall, the world around him began to blur. Suddenly, he felt no more air going into his lungs, no more blood going into his brain, as if his body went into protest, wanting to give up on this insufferable reality.

This is when it happened. For a moment, it seemed as if time came to a halt and in Pasión's perception, all movements seized but one. The sounds of the bidding muted and the market scene with the slaves and the buyers faded into shadow. At the same time, Pasión's vision became impossibly sharp in one spot. He saw a man walking by in the middle of the crowd. Although he was far away, Pasión saw every detail about him, like in a dream: the shoulder-length, wavy black hair and the silver rings on his fingers as he lifted a hand to neaten the tunic draped over his left shoulder. His whole being exuded beauty and elegant strength. In a strange and mysterious way, Pasión knew that he was here just at the right time, at the right place, as long as he could see this man. Truly, he found him so intriguing and magical that he became at once frightened that he might lose him out of sight.

And he did.

His attention was drawn back violently to his panicking body, as his ears heard the intolerable: the traders were now putting him on offer! They were praising his skills and his looks, advertising him as an excellent possible *pedagogos* or *pornoi*.

Pasión noticed his body was shaking, seized by uncontrollable, anxious tremors. The bidding began. The price went quickly above the wildest hopes of the merchants: skull-head was soon leading the auction with 490… then 530… 560 Drachmas.

"Mother!" Pasión found himself praying, screaming inside. "Mother, please help me! Do something!"

It was an angry, alarmed prayer. Full of terror. The world be damned, if he had to stay alive only to be thrown in front of the pigs! Damned if he had lost his last best hope for a worthy life! Damned if he had to live in fear…

But in truth, there was no reason for anger and no need for prayer anymore. In the distance, even if Pasión couldn't see it, the mysterious man, who had long black hair and silver rings, had already turned around. He was now walking back towards the stage to stop the skull-head from buying Pasión — just in time.

"One thousand Drachmas," Pasión heard a voice rising as clear as a carol above the crowd. At the same time, the crowd gave way for the man who was the winner of the auction.

Pasión felt immense solace and gratitude as he saw that it was him — and he hadn't even noticed yet that the largest of the rings on this beautiful man's hand was formed like a lyre around a precious stone, just like his own last property, the pendant of his mother.

Chapter 3
The Obsidian Pendant

"C'mon. How can this be legal?" Pasión thought to himself. He had been taken backstage to a scribe — another slave — who crafted a document on a papyrus roll documenting his new master's ownership over him. "They don't know my name, they don't know my father and my mother, they can't even identify who I am, yet they pretend to be able to register me as someone's property?!"

Nasty as this was, he aimed to dull the experience by simply staring down at the dry, gravel ground under his feet. Yet, his attention was brought back violently as his captors launched a new attack against him. They wanted to remove his mother's pendant! It was futile to plead, and being in shackles, Pasión could not protect the last valuable he still owned. Fear, the same enervating, heart-pounding fear as before overcame him once again.

However, at that very moment, his new master arrived on the scene.

"Don't touch that stone!" on the spot, he said.

Pasión was taken by another surprise: if there was anything more inviting about this beauteous man than his looks, it must have been his voice. It sounded like a skilled instrument used not merely to communicate, but to set vibrations into motion, invisible potentialities, and waves to affect mind and matter. The rat-faced handler, however, noticed none of this and was dumb enough to argue at first.

"But you see, sir," he spoke in search of excuses. "This jewelry does not come with the sale. It's only an accessory — decoration, so to speak. We always put it on our prettiest slave on display. The pendant is ours, not his."

That was too much to hear! Pasión could not hold himself back.

"It's mine!" he burst out. "My mother gave it to me before she died."

"This slave is lying," ever so impertinently, the seller pushed further. "Shall I get him whipped for you, to teach him some manners? Doesn't quite know yet how to behave, I'm afraid. He's a first-time slave, fresh from Melos."

Pasión's new master looked startled as he heard the mention of Melos, but continued to speak in his calm, yet commanding, hypnotic voice.

"You've presented me a boy with a pendant, which I bought," he asserted. "If you fail to hand me over the same boy with the same pendant, I shall take you to court for deception and get you whipped."

His tone suggested that he would easily do such a thing, and the seller backed off.

"No need, sir, of course, no need," he hurried to say. "You shall receive what you wish."

"Very well then. We'll go. Take off his shackles."

The merchant raised his black, bulging eyes.

"Are you sure, sir?" he asked carefully. "Perhaps you should keep those on until you arrive at your house. He can walk all right like this. Otherwise, he might try to run away."

"If he attempted to do that," the master said, and for the first time looked at his new slave, and he looked him straight in the eyes, "the guards of Athens would catch him and crucify him on the spot. I'm sure, at this point he thinks it's a better idea to come home with me instead."

Pasión — still very much used to being a free man — withstood the gaze and even got himself lost in it. He felt ravishing rays of personal interest coming towards him, which he found intoxicating. Along with the words *come home with me*, this left a much greater impression on him than any threat of punishment. What sort of magic was this? Truly, there was no need for shackles; this man himself was dangerously and darkly magnetic. He awakened Pasión's slumbering curiosity, his all-time favorite feeling. This came to his rescue as now he did not mind following his new master as he was ordered, even though he had to walk on his left, one step behind him and was at no time allowed to utter a word unless asked.

In that manner, they walked through the tightly-packed lanes of the Agora. There, a mouthwatering aroma hit Pasión's senses, which came from a stew cooking outdoors in a bull-shaped cauldron: oh, that ambrosial scent of roasting sesame oil spiced with saffron! How much it reminded him of his great hunger! How he wished his new master would stop for them to eat! But instead, they walked deeper into the mad masses of merchants and artisans, where the place started to feel more and more oppressive and confined. From one side, dead fish stared back at him with muted eyes of frozen desperation. Elsewhere, smelly corpses of birds lay row after row on wet clay tablets. Goats, still alive, were bleating here and there, which sounded to Pasión like the cries of lone children abandoned in a hostile country. He wanted to get out of here as quickly as possible, but no! Instead, he was led to the most narrow shop, which poured out volcanic heat and the smell of burned charcoal and molten metal. It was the workshop of Hephaestos.

"Come, I must take you in here," his new master said to him. His voice sounded gentle but still, a surge of nerves hit Pasión as he looked inside the dimly lit shop. An enormous blacksmith stood next to his forge, handling tongs and hot iron sticks glowing orange in the fire. Surely, the Athenians were not branding their slaves, or were they?

"Good day, Melaneos!' his master greeted the smith like an old acquaintance. "Meet my new slave I bought this morning."

"He looks like quite a find," the smith approved with a grin. "Congratulations, Master Laurin!"

Laurin, the beautiful man's name was Laurin! Pasión was thrilled every time he learned a new detail about him, even though now, in all this heat and smoke, he could hardly breathe and was frightened of him too.

"He surely is quite a find, yes," Laurin nodded. "And there is something you could do for me with him. Look, he has this pendant. Do you think you would be able now to fuse the silver chain around his neck, so that it can never again be taken off?"

"Yes, I suppose it can be done..."

Pasión stood amazed.

Laurin stepped behind him and told him to hold still. He took the pendant between his silver-ringed fingers and experimented with its length. "Like that." He showed the craftsman that he wanted it quite short, leaving almost no space between the chain of the pendant and Pasión's neck.

"Make sure you do this carefully, not to burn his skin. Absolutely, I won't have any scars on him, nor tolerate disfigurement."

"Ay, ay, boss. Pretty boy slave, ha?" The smith smirked with a dirty kind of smile, but Laurin's face remained serious. He stayed skin close to Pasión throughout and held up his hair while the smith placed a protective layer of leather on his neck and fused the chain.

Afterward, Pasión caught himself feeling sorry the procedure was over: Laurin's touch had felt silky and full of ease on his skin. Once outside the workshop, he whispered a heartfelt thank you to him, which Laurin acknowledged with a nod, but then continued his silent walk, like before. This time, Pasión followed him with a secret feeling of homecoming, as it sank into his soul that he would never part with the pendant, along with the certainty that he now irrevocably belonged to Laurin.

He dared to look around a bit more and noticed the statues! They were everywhere out here on the streets of Athens, yet Pasión could find little delight in them. Like Athena, towering over the Acropolis, they were all colored too brightly, wearing clothes as if they were humans of flesh and blood. With their painted eyes widely open, they appeared as if they'd been watching every detail of life flashing by them. What did they see, Pasión pondered, when they looked at him: did they admire Pasión, the artist, or were they mocking Pasión, the fool who could not escape slavery? Statues were intimidating, of course, as they were — in their own way — immortal, and who could stand calm when scrutinized against eternity?

And eternity it was that Pasión suddenly stared at in the very next moment. If he'd only looked at the statues, he would have seen nothing, but now he took his first glimpse at the city's brand-new temple, built after decades of devastations, which the Athenians had suffered from the Persian enemy. It was the Temple of Hephaestos, rising high against the Aegean sky, with its perfectly aligned multiple marble rows of fluted columns. Pasión didn't notice that in his awe, he stood still and failed to follow his new master.

Laurin, nervous as he no longer heard his steps, turned around. There he saw his new slave transfixed by the beauty of Doric architecture at its best.

"Last week we inaugurated that temple," he chose to tell him, with a bit of Athenian pride in his voice. "What do you think of it?"

"Divine, so calm and elegant," Pasión said softly, delighted to have been given a chance to speak. "The statues of your city scare me. Their colors are too spicy for my eyes. But this temple… looks exactly like in my dreams."

"In your dreams?"

"Yes, ever since I was a boy I have wanted to learn from the great sculptors and artists. I always dreamt of coming to Athens one day," he said, upon which, against the odds, master and slave smiled at each other.

Pasión glimpsed one more time at the eternity represented by the temple. He had no idea that the temple indeed would still be standing here in thousands of years to come, as would the statues, scattered all around the world. They will have lost all the paint and thus time will reveal their pure beauty of marble white. Even less did Pasión know that events would lead to the making of another statue which would mysteriously and forever link his consciousness to a woman who was not born yet, who would not be born for another two and half thousand years — a time span the human mind may be able to measure, but will not be able to ever fully grasp.

As they entered the master's home, Pasión was led through a carefully land-scaped, harmonious courtyard straight into the kitchen. Inside were two women: a gorgeous young slave girl Pasión did not dare to look at, only glimpsed that she had golden hair as long as a river. The other was a crooked crone called Medea, who immediately took the newcomer under scrutiny. She seemed to be part of the house like inherited furniture, taking up space, but impossible to move.

"No, I wasn't planning to buy him," Laurin explained to her upon a rain of questions. "Yes, we may have a welcoming ceremony for him, but not tonight. Maybe at the symposium? Yes, when the guests are here."

Yet, Laurin was short of any answer when the old woman asked the new slave's name.

"Yes, what is your name?" Laurin turned to him.

"Whatever you would like it to be, Master," Pasión said. "My own name I sadly lost days ago, with everything else that was my life."

For a moment, Laurin looked startled and sincere: he must have felt the pain behind such words, as well as the rejection, but then breathed in a sigh and let the issue be.

"Well, then. Medea, give our little prince whatever he wants to eat. Feed him well! He's starved, yet I need him back to full strength as soon as possible."

Instantly, Pasión regretted not having said his name. Why was he being so arrogant? In truth, he was longing for nothing more but a genuine human connection, to be seen as a person with a name, not some object of the house. His pride be damned: Laurin was already leaving the kitchen, without even looking at him a second time.

Medea dutifully said, "Yes, Master," and asked Pasión, "What can I get you?"

"Anything, thank you so much," Pasión said, trying to sound more respectful, while he stared with brutal hunger at those appetizing olives and barley bread, goat cheese with honey, and vegetables waiting on the round kitchen table. "Anything, as long as it is not meat."

This answer caught his master's attention, who looked back from the threshold.

"Meat, you won't eat?"

"No, Master. Not since…"

"Not since… what?"

"Not since…" Pasión lowered his voice, "not since the siege of my island, during which — unbeknownst to me — my brother fed me human flesh."

Hearing this, a dark cloud passed over Laurin's face for a moment, but it seemed as if he was trying to look beyond that and peer into nicer landscapes of Pasión's past.

"Your mother," he finally said in a serious, quiet voice, "didn't eat meat either, didn't she?"

"No, she didn't." Pasión was stunned to hear. "But how would you know?"

"Because I don't eat meat, either," the master said, and thereby left the room. Only afterward did Pasión realize that this didn't exactly answer his question.

For the day, the old woman gave him some peaceful tasks in the garden, after which he got permission to take an early rest. His body felt grateful, as he was no longer tormented by hunger and could finally sleep. A quiet little slave room was assigned to him at the end of the corridor, which was clean and comfortable enough. Yet, his still tormented mind could not fully unwind, and as soon as he drifted away, Chairon appeared in his dream.

Pasión was delighted to see him, but the face of the centaur suggested concern, even reproach.

"Do you remember what I taught you about being an artist?" Chairon warned him. "You will not become a great artist by merely having learned the craft of chiseling and drilling, or even all the finesse about harmony and colors. If you ever want to create something that is artistically relevant, you must leave the course of ordinary action and step into the scary, wondrous magic of life."

"Yes, I remember that, Chairon." Pasión sighed. "I remember everything you ever said, but what use is that for me right now? You can see that I'm no longer an artist, merely a slave: a tool in someone else's garden."

Hearing this, the centaur jumped into a frightening rear on his strong hind legs and wildly trumpeted out loud. His eyes, usually full of sparks of civic kindness, now sent bolts of anger toward his student.

"I heard the vow you made on that ship." He sounded like a wrathful deity. "And I am now holding you accountable for honoring it!"

With that, the centaur came back to all his four legs and continued to speak more calmly.

"Being an artist does not depend on the whims of life and what others do to you. But it depends on one singularity: your willingness to turn suffering into beauty. Stop doing what feels so sad and safe! Get out of this sorry room and do what feels dangerously exciting! Be a man, Pasión, follow what your heart desires…"

That moment he woke up from his dream, but Pasión still could hear the words clearly and loudly echoing all inside him, all around him: "Get out!"

He stood up and slipped out into the corridor again, like a cat on soft paws going on his nightly adventure. The whole house seemed asleep. Only a little, dim light streamed out from Laurin's study. Pasión knew if a slave attempted to disturb his master or simply snuck around at night like a thief, the consequences could be dire. He was quite afraid, like on the day he jumped off the cliff, but as then, so now, he did not let fear get in the way of the charm. He stopped at the threshold of the study and peered in: Laurin was immersed in something strange, walking up and down in the amber glow of a single oil lamp, he murmured words and occasionally read from a scroll laid out on the table.

Yet, he quickly noticed that his new slave was standing there at his door. Pasión's knees began to shake a bit as he made his master suffer an interruption, but it still felt liberating and so good to have his attention.

"Yes?" Laurin questioned him as he looked up from his scroll. However, he did not appear displeased to see him.

"Forgive me." Pasión walked a tiny step in. "I mean no disrespect, Master, and would not want to disturb you, but…"

"But?"

"I… I must ask you a question. Please, I cannot live if I may not ask you."

Laurin looked at the boy incredulously but sensed the gravity of the plight and gestured for Pasión to come in.

"And what would that question be?"

Who are you really? Pasión thought to himself. Just another Athenian slaveholder, a member of the enemy clan, who will hold me captive for the rest of my life? Or someone magical, as I sense, who would let me into a new world, to live through things I have never seen before?

"How do you know about my mother?" out loud, he only dared to ask.

Hearing this, Laurin's expression softened. He came closer and focused on Pasión in a manner which was impossible to decipher. He slowed down his breathing and took some time as he began to feel his way behind the simple words.

Then the miraculous happened: Laurin answered the question, Pasión's hidden, unsaid question, without even saying a word:

He stepped close to Pasión's shivering body, carefully touched his shoulders, and pulled him into a protective embrace. He held him and allowed the moment to linger on forever, giving a new lifeline to Pasión's starved body and frozen soul. Slowly, the ice around Pasión's heart began to melt and run down his cheeks in the form of hot, salty tears. Laurin let him cry: he didn't hush or judge, just caressed him, and suddenly, Pasión felt safe to pour out all the shock and terror that he was forced to keep inside so far. Neither of them minded the tears: there was no shame, there was only joy over the moment they shared.

Later, after the tears came so strong that they began to shake Pasión's body with violent force, Laurin laid him down on his back, on a small bed in the corner and placed his hand over his heart.

And Pasión, born a sensitive, who could feel all the world's pain and pleasure a thousand times more than the common man, immediately perceived it. He had never known anything like this before, but a hot current entered him from the touch. It eased his pain, and his crying was swiftly soothed away beneath Laurin's healing hand.

***

Soon, Sofia found nothing more soothing than to return daily to the museum. Day by day, she drank that good cup of coffee with David and didn't emerge from their talks about life and death for hours on end. Afterward, she loved returning to her favorite statue, sitting alone on that little bench next to him. There, she could let her thoughts run free like wild horses: fast, rebellious, oftentimes dark, they always raced away from the rigid and numbing confines of habit. Sofia needed to think from many perspectives as she sought to make sense of all the hell she ever witnessed. Conventional explanations left her hunger for truth unsatisfied: when her colleagues, those doctors of psychiatry, talked about post-traumatic stress disorder, it just felt to her like mushy baby food thrown in front of a lion who craves fresh, raw meat. Sofia knew that post-traumatic stress disorder was nonsense, as the trauma was never in the past, it always was in the present. She has seen how resilient human beings were when going through the greatest of horrors; the trauma will wait and catch up later, when things are back to relative safety. Feeling the trauma — in whatever crazy way — was never a disorder, merely a natural reaction to the unthinkable. The social failure of reflecting on the horror, that was a disorder: expecting soldiers to return from war and assume life without addressing the enormous pretense inherent in our world. As she had seen children and beings of nature being murdered, Sofia sensed at the depths of her core that there was something fundamentally, structurally wrong with the entire human conception of reality. Everything seemed to be based on fallacious and distorted assumptions, while love — the true panacea — was overlooked as a mere sentiment, when in fact it was the single organizing power in the universe that could counteract the basic, entropic tendency of matter to drive itself towards ever-increasing levels of chaos.

Strangely, it was in this seemingly lifeless museum hall that Sofia's bewildered isolation was ever alleviated. Here, she began to feel that somehow, somewhere, there was a group of people she truly belonged with. Whenever she looked at the statue of the once-upon-a-time Greek slave, she felt a mysterious connection. Despite the impossibility of her unexplained, yearning desire, she wanted to find him so badly it hurt. Time and time again, she looked at the statue's endearing face and wondered: Where do I know you from?

***

"Your mother and I," Laurin finally said, when Pasión was no longer crying, "we belong to the same mystery school."

Upon this, Pasión pushed himself up on his elbow and looked at Laurin. His heart was fluttering with dream-like wonder and excitement.

"Did you know her?" he asked without delay.

"No, I don't think I've met her," Laurin said. "I cannot recall seeing a female member from Melos."

"How would you know then?"

Laurin brought his hand back to Pasión's chest and lifted up his obsidian pendant. This was when Pasión noticed that the largest of Laurin's rings had a silver frame in the form of a lyre, too, surrounding a stone, although his was not black obsidian, but amber.

"These are the signs of our order," Laurin said, gliding his long, slender fingers around the pendant and the ring. To Pasión's relief, he began to explain more. He spoke in a quiet and calm voice, which sounded like it could tame beasts, and soothe all fear and confusion in the one who listened to him. "You see, I did not go to the market this morning to buy a slave; nothing was further away from my thoughts than such a thing. I went to the market because I received intuition that I needed to walk across the Agora. When I saw you on that stage, it became immediately clear that I had come for you. Your pendant was shining straight at me like a light tower for a ship in the night. At first I thought you were a member, as only members are ever permitted to wear the sign... but then I realized it was your mother. She gave you this pendant because she knew it would save your life: there is a code of honor among us to rescue each other in times of peril."

Pasión felt a powerful presence was enveloping him into a sphere of protection much grander than he ever thought was out there. In these moments, he understood that the magic his mother and Chairon had taught him was around at all times and reached out to him to save his life from degradation. His heart felt overflowing with gratitude.

"But if only members of the order are allowed to wear the pendant...," he began to say, and Laurin finished his thought:

"Yes, you will need to be initiated. Especially, if you don't want the order to kill you as it does with usurpers." He smiled at Pasión, who was a little bewildered as to whether Laurin was teasing or frightening him.

"Who will initiate me?" Pasión asked, eagerness in his voice, but Laurin didn't mind: he was fond of seeing passion and curiosity in him.

"I will," he said, to Pasión's amazement. "When you are ready. Something tells me it will be sooner rather than later, but first, you must heal." Again, he placed his hand over Pasión's heart, who yet again felt that healing current flow through him. "Anyone would freeze from witnessing the devastation and horror that happened on your home island, but you in particular have a soul that is bound to feel everything deeper and higher than others. You must heal before you can be as whole again as required for a mystical initiation."

"How can you touch me like this?" Pasión's rousing and rousing curiosity led him to more questions. "How can you read me so well?"

"I am an initiate," Laurin said. "With our initiation, each of us receives some gifts, develops some talents. I have life force energy concentrated in my body. If I touch you, I transmit it to you. If you touch me, it flows into you. Simply being close to me, being touched by me, will heal and restore you."

For a moment, Pasión wanted to ask no more. He just let himself feel the pleasure of this sheltering and enchanting touch. By now, he dared to look at the man who had become his master. He was wondering but couldn't guess how old he was: Laurin's body looked youthfully vigorous, yet his face carried the patina of wisdom which comes with the experience of many, richly lived years.

"Why are you so good to me?" Pasión asked yet another question. Perhaps, he was hoping that Laurin sensed something in him also, which was more than respecting members of the order. Perhaps, he was just longing to hear his voice again.

"We have lived a thousand and more lives. This is not the first time we have met," Laurin said and looked at him. His eyes drew Pasión in: miraculously that felt as if he was traveling outward into the starry sky. Inside Laurin's eyes, he could discover planets, milky ways, and galaxies. The words as within, so without came to his mind, even though he could not recall where he had heard that. Then he listened attentively to every word Laurin spoke.

"It is fate that in this life you became my slave and I was made your master. In another life, it might well be the other way around or completely different. We may not yet understand the workings of fate, but we learn by playing the roles. Make no mistake about it, I can be a tough master. If you ever disobey or turn against me, I will come hard and punish you. But our souls — and this is what matters — are very old friends. You must not fear! I will never harm you: I will never break your skin or bones and most importantly, I will never break your soul. I am here to help you grow into and thrive to the fullest of your own unique and beautiful nature. So, stay respectful and beautiful, but be not afraid. Relax."

Being in Laurin's proximity was like standing at the most majestic, scenic spot on earth, where the world of humans meets the divine. Laurin's healing touch and words of wisdom brought the long-forgotten good life back to Pasión, reawakened his soul, and let love flow back into his veins.

"Laurin," Pasión whispered, while his body — now feeling safe and sound — finally began to crave sleep. "May I stay here with you tonight?"

"Yes, you may," Laurin said. He laid himself down next to Pasión, pulled him close, and laid a blanket over them both. Pasión, giving in to his tiredness as well as to a wordless, magnetic attraction, twined his arms around him. Laurin sensed him fast falling asleep.

"I waited for you my entire life," he said as if to himself. "Of course, you may stay."

But one more time, his new slave, before finally drifting off into the trust of a deep, dreamless sleep, opened his eyes.

"My name..." he said last. "My name is Pasión."

Chapter 4
Training with the Enemy

Death had many faces. Sofia had seen them all, but it was the face of fear which distressed her the most. David told her that Mrs. Windworth was the last patient who died peacefully in the hospice. Ever since the management rejected Sofia's application, fear again dominated the expressions of the dying. For a long time now, Sofia had been observing such people who gazed with unspeakable terror into that good night and raged against what they believed was the "dying of the light." She often wondered why they allowed fear to infiltrate their mind and body so much that it supplanted curiosity, creativity, and the sacred quest for divinity. When was it that most people missed the call of their soul to gather wisdom and learn about the dawn that follows every night?

"My heart goes out to these people who die with fear in their eyes," Sofia said to David, as they sat together in the museum café again. "Like children, afraid when the lights are turned off for the night, they cannot yet comprehend the morning of the next day rising. Someone ought to teach them about death and eternity. I was thinking of opening a school for dying — or something like that."

David looked at her with affection. He knew things about Sofia that she herself had forgotten and came into her life to help the remembrance. He knew that Sofia, at the very least, was capable of giving hidden knowledge to those who want eyes to see the invisible, ears to hear beyond sound, and sense things which are undetectable to the body. But he also knew that she was capable of a lot more.

"You could do so, yes," David said and impishly added: "or… you could find out what it is that eternity wants to tell you."

Sofia had no doubt he was referring to her secret desire: the statue.

"Yes." She nodded. "I sense the past wants to tell me something. Part of me just wants to study whatever I can find out about this statue. Yet, it feels so selfish," she sighed, "to follow an impossible obsession when so many in the world are suffering and need help."

"It's a paradox," David retorted, "but those who turned their back to the world and followed their own secret and impossible obsessions ended up contributing the most to humanity."

Sofia found there was something sweetly provocative about David today. Like a trickster, he seemed to be luring Sofia away from being serious, wanting her to play and follow the quiet call of her heart. He was wearing glasses, which was out of his character, contrasting the naked, natural look of his face — all that was attractive and infuriating at the same time.

"Here in the museum when I see the statue and when I talk to you, David," Sofia began to open up, "I feel so much closer to something I do not recall, yet painfully miss. Even as a baby, I was aware that I came from somewhere else. Thus, I also knew this reality was not the only one. I had some vague memories of lives bygone and even of afterlife realms. There was this one pure land... such a magnificent place! Once I seemed to have access to it, but I cannot recall anything more about it — how I wish I could!"

David also wished he could tell her more, but as a member of the Order he was bound to only reveal as much as the listener was ready to receive. Sofia herself needed to slowly but surely lift that ancient curse still lingering before she could remember who she was.

"I guarantee you," he only said, "you will never regret a single moment you spend with your statue or learning more about him."

Sofia looked dreamily past David and his words.

"He is so beautiful," she whispered, "that it can even be painful to look at him."

David closed his eyes. Yes, he remembered: Pasión's beauty could indeed be so striking that it cut into your heart, reminding you of... impermanence perhaps? But then, they all loved each other so much that it always eased every pain. It was always a pleasure to be around Pasión, always a joy, always good to be around him.

***

In the morning, Pasión awakened next to Laurin. Still wrapped in bliss, he cautiously moved his hand towards the noble Athenian. He drew his own body closer, but slowly. He sought closeness, and his cheeks wanted to feel Laurin's skin, but also, he was afraid to infringe. Thus, he felt grateful when Laurin turned to him and with a touch like silk, seized his shoulder.

"Some people are born slaves, as it is their fate to learn through service," Laurin said to him. "You are not one of them. But perhaps it gives you consolation that I always wanted someone like you at my side: someone with the faculty of deliberation, who can learn how to be mine and would come with me everywhere I go."

"Yes, master," Pasión said, relieved that they would not part during the day, but only until Laurin spoke again.

"I am a trainer in the Athenian military," he said. "We shall go to the gymnasium, and you'll train with us."

"Oh, no!" Pasión exclaimed involuntarily. How dizzy he became at the prospect! Already, he felt like a traitor solely for being so attracted to Laurin, but the idea of joining the Athenian military at training was impossible! "Surely, I cannot do that."

"Yes, you can," Laurin assured him. "You can because I am not giving you a choice."

Pasión knew he had no more say in the matter. Yet, he wished for something to hold on to, any word or detail which would ease his circumstance. Luckily, Laurin revealed to him something later, which did.

It was after a hearty breakfast of barley bread with olive oil and figs that Laurin let Pasión walk at his side as they headed back to the Agora. Cats and dogs, straying around on Athens' streets, children rich with noise and dust, all ran after Laurin as they saw him walking by. He was different and interesting: his tunic was dark blue and silver-lined, not simply white, like most. Laurin smiled and petted all the little folk, but after they crossed the small stream of Eridanos and left animals, children, and laughter all behind, his face turned serious.

"There is something I want to tell you," he said to Pasión. "Not in order to justify myself, but rather as you are bound to wonder… You know, in this polis, we have democracy. We vote on everything."

"So I've heard…"

"I was there when the assembly voted on Melos," Laurin said in a dark sentence. "I'm a full Athenian citizen, so I too cast my vote."

Pasión started fidgeting. Will he now have to hear that Laurin was the enemy after all? He was hoping he would not have to hate him... Fortunately, Laurin said, "I voted against the aggression on Melos. Also, I want you to know that I'm not a soldier," he added. "I train with the youngsters, but I never engage in any attack or aggression. I have never ever participated in war and never will."

"How is that?" Pasión was back in his mood of curiosity.

"Being a higher member of our Order obliges me to non-violence."

"Yes, Master, but does being a citizen of Athens not oblige you to join their wars?" Pasión looked at him incredulously.

"I'm exempted from military service," Laurin said, "because I am a member of the chorus."

Grabbed by fascination, Pasión thought back to last night. So, that is what Laurin was doing in his study by the amber glow of the lamp: studying for a new play! Oh, how magnificent his magical voice must sound on stage. Oh, how much Pasión wished to go and see him perform! He had to doubt that he ever would, as slaves were not allowed in the theater — but neither were they at the gymnasium and still, that is where they were heading.

"Master." On the way, he asked one more of his never-ending questions. "If you don't go to war, why would you train to fight?"

Laurin halted and stepped ahead. Behind him, Pasión could already see the long column row of the stoa which belonged to the gymnasium.

"If a man does not fight because he can't," Laurin answered, "he is merely a coward. If he can, but chooses not to, then he is an adept."

With these words, Laurin ushered Pasión through the entrance of the gymnasium. In the dressing room, they were alone. Laurin ordered him to remove his clothes like everyone else, which gave Pasión immense relief: slaves were always required to keep some attire on, and getting naked saved him from being exposed as one.

"Today will be tough on you," Laurin told him before they entered the training grounds. "Your body is still weak from the famine, and your mind irate from the atrocities you suffered. Yet, I want you to hold your ground out there. You must do this, not only for me but for yourself. Everything from now on is preparation for your initiation, including your physical training. Initiation requires the utmost strength. Don't waste a single moment. And give up the concept of an enemy out there!"

"How on earth is that possible?" Pasión gasped. He remembered back at Melos, how startled he was when his mother said a similar thing on the last day of her life.

"On our mystic path, we learn that there is no enemy out there. What you need to conquer is here, within you." Laurin touched with his fingers Pasión's chest. "Your enemy is never another human, not even the pain you suffer, but it is your own fear, your own hatred, your own ignorance you may still be holding onto. But for now... if you cannot yet see those Athenian lads in there as other than your enemy, at least think, the best revenge you can have is to prove to be better than them."

"I'll do my best, Master," Pasión said, whose natural habitat certainly was not the gymnasium, even though he liked to move, climb, run, and swim out in nature. Laurin laughed at his answer.

"Once you get to know me," he said, "you will realize that I'm not expecting you to do your best. I'm expecting you to do the impossible."

Side by side, Laurin and Pasión stepped onto the training ground. It was a great open space, protected all around by sacred olive trees and a marble walkway bordered with columns. In its midst they found themselves in front of fresh Athenian cadets on their first day of training: a row of sparkling eighteen-year-olds, proud of their tensing muscles and oiled nude bodies, masking their fears very well, ready for action — ready for anything.

"Ephebes! Youths of Athens!" Laurin addressed them in his golden voice, which left little room for deviance. "I am your new trainer, Laurin, son of Talesander. You may have heard strange rumors about me in town — and if you did, they were probably all true." That made the youths laugh. "Yes, I did travel to the Far East when I was your age and yes, I have been to the realm of the dead. But I'll leave it up to your reason to believe or not whether I really was buried alive underground for three months." The youths laughed with him, again, but also began to think.

"And this is Pasión." He pointed at his attendant. "He is from Melos."

The trainees started to fidget and muttered some remarks to each other. The first man in their line, who stood there in a stance, with his bulky chest wide open, raised his voice.

"Are you bringing here the enemy?" It was Alcibiades, the younger son of Athen's larger-than-life statesman and general. Both he and his father were much talked about; some people praised their brilliant rhetoric, charming spirit of enterprise and grandeur of living, while others warned of their supreme arrogance and unscrupulous ways.

"The Melians are not our enemy. They are our victims," Laurin stated. "You seem happy about that. Have you been celebrating our conquest of Melos?"

"Of course, we have." Alcibiades and some of his friends nodded with self-conceited smiles. Laurin moved a step closer to them.

"Have you raised your cups over the victory?" he asked.

"Aya, we have."

Pasión looked at them straight: even though their sight burned his skin like acid, he decided to just stand there in modest grace, without motion. Beyond doubt, this was a time for him to observe, not to act.

"So, what do you think?" Laurin stepped to face them all and sharply whipped down on them with his voice. "What were the Spartans doing while you emptied your cups in celebration and fooled around with your fathers' flute girls?"

The smile of the youngsters faded a little.

"We are at war!" Laurin let out a yawp. "During every moment you spend in idleness, swapping juicy details of your sex lives, bragging about what great bullies you are, there is a Spartan wolf out there sharpening his teeth and claws, getting ready to kill you!"

Some of the young men began to exchange worried glances — the masks of fearlessness were falling off their pretty faces.

"While you eat your honey cakes," Laurin continued boldly, "the Spartans drink bull's blood. While you lay down on your pillows, they sleep in the swamps, and while you take massages, they take whippings from each other, until they feel pain no more. You entered the military today, they entered it at the age of seven. How long do you really think it will take them to overpower you when they decide to siege us?"

Now there was silence — fear, where previously was laughter and pride.

"Pasión." Laurin now turned to his new attendant. "Tell these folks: What happened to your father?"

"Killed in action," Pasión said in a simple, steady voice.

"And to your mother?"

"She died of starvation."

"And your brother?"

"Sold to the silver mines." Pasión conveyed it as a fact.

"Do you want this to be the tale of your family, too?" Laurin put the question to the cadets. "Because it surely will be if you do not change your thinking and make training your utmost priority."

"Aya, sir!" Alcibiades now straightened up his body, seemingly impressed by the brutality and violence in the words.

"Aya!" the entire row of ephebes echoed him.

"Very well then." Laurin gave him a nod. "Let us begin. Alcibiades, attack me!"

"Attack you?" the powerful young man asked back, with the incredulity of someone who believes he'll win.

"Yes. Attack!" Laurin stood by his word. "Try to kill me."

"What if I succeed?" asked Alcibiades, while his body already jumped to the side into a sparring stance, with arms high up and well extended.

"We can talk about that afterward. Now stop wasting our time. Attack!"

Thus, without further delay, Alcibiades attacked. He quite knew what he was doing: slithering forward swiftly, he launched a punch towards Laurin's face, but only to distract. He just needed a glimpse of time to bring his weight to his rear leg and deliver his signature front kick. He was quite a champion at bringing a force into his opponent's stomach more than enough to break a spear: aligning his core, legs, and ankle to strike perfectly never before failed him at debilitating any opponent.

This time, however, the kick never landed. How it happened seemed too fast for the eye to follow, but Laurin must have stepped to the side, and somehow swept the knee off balance, as Alcibiades found himself face down on the ground the very next moment. Laurin had twisted his right arm into a lock behind his shoulder blades, which was so painful that Alcibiades quickly raised his index finger in submission.

Laurin then demanded three others to attack him and for all three the fight ended in a similar fashion. Immediately, as they reached close to Laurin's body, they were brought out of balance, down to the ground. It was infuriating, like a circus magician's trick, for which there had to be an explanation, yet nobody could figure out what.

Laurin announced that he would teach them to fight but could not do so unless they reached sufficient levels of conditioning. Then he put them through a drill quite unlike anything any of them experienced before. Laurin's training was brutal in the extreme, yet he never demanded a task he didn't perform himself also. All the while, he moved along with seeming ease, shouting instructions, encouragements, and observing his trainees.

Pasión could feel his eyes on himself a lot and sensed he was watching him closer than anyone else in the group. Not wanting to shame Laurin, he told his body that it would be quite all right to die on this beautiful sunshiny day of early spring, rather than giving up. Amidst all the physical discomfort that training too hard too quickly brought upon him, Pasión was feeling good as he realized he wasn't doing this out of obedience, but because he had someone who believed in him. So it happened that the entire time, while many of the others fell out and took long minutes to stand up again, Pasión kept running, kept pushing, kept pulling way beyond the point he thought was possible.

Pasión did not disappoint, but Laurin did not fail to show him some magic, either. Towards the end of the training, when tiredness had already taken their best, Laurin grabbed an upright bar at two points and — with staggering ease — lifted his body into a horizontal position in mid-air. Then he jumped off, lined up all his cadets, and watched them one by one to try and fail at the same feat of strength. Pasión sidled to the end of the queue, winning some time to think. From there, he observed how everyone, even Alcibiades, lifted themselves up but fell back from the pole. Absorbed, he hardly noticed that suddenly, Laurin stood at his side.

"What is it," he asked him the most unexpected question, "that you love to do most in life?"

"Art," Pasión said, delighted that he had a chance to share this. "Making paintings, mosaics, and — mostly — sculptures."

Laurin took his answer with an endearing smile.

"If you wanted to make a statue of him," he then pointed at Alcibiades, who was still trying his luck at the pole, "could you do it, so that it stays in mid-air?"

"Yes." Pasión thought so. "But the statue wouldn't hold the way he is trying to do it."

"So, how would the statue hold?" Laurin asked while both of them gazed at Alcibiades, who was, again and again, swinging himself into mid-air but kept falling back, barely ever reaching the horizontal posture.

"The arms would have to go wider to create a large supporting triangle," Pasión collected his ideas. "And the hand… yes, the fingers of the lower hand would need to point downward for a better hold, not to the side like he's doing it. And those shoulders would have to open, I mean, come out more to the front. Depending on the material, a statue in mid-air would also need additional support."

"Where would you place that support? To the arms or legs?"

"No."

"Where?" Pasión looked at the moving, struggling human body with intense attention, and something shifted in him.

"To the center point of the body," he said, upon which Laurin nodded and left.

Yet, the moment lingered on, and in its depth, touched on eternity. In some wonderfully peculiar way, it seemed to Pasión as if he had been at this place and at this particular time before.

"Hold on to that bar," he heard the voice of Chairon, the centaur. "I will be with you and support the center point of your body."

As soon as Alcibiades gave up, Pasión stepped forward. It felt like a dream. He grabbed the bar with one hand pointing downward and the other forming a wide triangle with his chest. Then he pushed from below and pulled from above, utterly trusting that once in the air, Chairon would hold him at the center point of his body. Thus, before he knew it, and as if time itself came to a halt, he was up in the air, his figure forming a perfectly straight line.

Never before had Pasión felt so alive than on this day. As he brought himself back to the ground, he saw that all Athenians had gathered around him and were now clapping in acclamation. For Pasión, who had magically mixed senses, the cheering did not just create a great sound, but a whirling wind of rainbow colors in front of his eyes, which carried him away from things well-known and took him to hitherto unknown dimensions of joy.

For the rest of that day, Pasión felt like a Persian prince. At home, Laurin instructed Medea to feed him well and Diona, the slave girl with the hair of a golden river, to also give him a massage — to make his muscles limber. Laurin, who lived a healthy, disciplined, and rigorous yet fabulous life, had a home bathroom. Here, in this serene chamber, hallowed by the scents of a fragrant altar, Diona bathed Pasión with heavenly oils and god!... was it delightful to feel female fingers on his skin again, after those endless months since Pasión was last touched by a woman. He had to be very careful not to desire her. Instead, he let his mind escape into that sweet, colorful medley of scents Diona conjured up on the altar: cinnamon

blended in with rose petals, on top of piney frankincense. Her craft was pure alchemy: the spicy warmth she created filled the room with the power to dispel all
pain inherent in our existence.

"You are very skilled at your art," he said to her when Diona turned him on his
back and Pasión had a chance to look at her. "Where did you learn it?"

The girl, slowly and thoughtfully, smiled at him but did not say a word.

"What else do you do?" Pasión attempted another question. "Can you play
some music?"

Diona looked at him with her big, brown eyes, nodded slightly, but again did
not say anything. Instead, she sat Pasión up and began to gently comb and balm
his curly hair.

"But you are not mute, are you?" Pasión whispered and touched her arm in a
protective move.

Diona then brought her face close to his and whispered into his ear, like a
frightened deer, "I'm not allowed to talk to men other than Master without permission."

Hearing that, Pasión's relaxed mood tensed up a bit.

"What happens if you do?"

Diona said nothing but turned around and Pasión could see her bare shoulders
and the top of her velvety back. It was covered with fresh, red stripes left behind
by a whip.

"Laurin…," he asked, aghast, "does that to you?"

"No," Diona quickly whispered, "not him. Medea."

That old hag! The thought of her sent a ghastly shiver down Pasión's freshly
rubbed tissues and oiled skin.

"Don't worry," at last, he said to Diona. "I'll find a way to talk with you. And…
many thanks. You're divine."

Pasión's unease only dissolved in the evening when he was ordered into Laurin's study. His master received him like a celebrated friend.

"I was impressed by you today," he said to him, and that made Pasión melt. "I was impressed by your mind: it made your body do things that exceed your current athletic level. My intuition was correct: you are indeed made of stuff capable of impossible attempts."

"Thank you, Master," said Pasión carefully, not to allow his upcoming pride to rise to arrogance.

"Do you have any pains or strains?" Laurin wanted to know.

"Well, I feel a pull in the back of my thighs, and my ankle is a bit twisted."

"Which side?"

"The right."

"All right, lay down here." Laurin pointed to the bed, like a good doctor. Then he sat down in a cross-legged posture next to Pasión, took his leg, and began healing it.

"Master," Pasión said, while he couldn't help but immerse himself in Laurin's striking features. His hair was black, his skin darker than his, yet his face was like finely drawn, delicate. "May I ask you a question?"

"Please do."

"How did you do it?"

"Do what?" Laurin asked while he did not look up from Pasión's thigh he was engaged with.

"Fight them like that," Pasión asked like a little boy, hoping to find out about the magic trick. "Those lads were strong and skilled, yet you flicked them off like flies."

"In essence, I was doing the same as you did on that bar." Laurin eased the hold of Pasión's leg.

"But that was Chairon!" Pasión suddenly let him in on his secret.

"Chairon?"

"Yes, he's a centaur," Pasión said while he sat up and pulled in his legs, which felt fully restored. Hugging his knees, he looked at Laurin like one boy to another, ready to reveal something gripping. "I can meet him mostly in my dreams, the way my mother taught me to. He was the one who also told me last night to come and see you, else I would have never dared."

"Well, I am," Laurin smiled, 'truly grateful to Chairon. Today, he also seemed to have brought some really good energy for your use. As you have Chairon, people in the East talk about dragons and serpents rising up the spine, we in the West have our gods and demons: essentially, all these beings are manifestations of an invisible world, which surrounds us at any given moment but also springs from inside us. We all are citizens of two worlds simultaneously, even if not many are aware of that. For the initiate, the invisible landscapes become visible. Some, like yourself, already have a natural knowledge about them. It is magic — minor magic — to know how to manipulate these energies to effect changes in the visible world: to create, to heal, or to fight with seemingly superhuman strength."

Pasión also crossed his legs now, but he shuffled forward to be touching close to Laurin. He seemed transfixed.

"Minor magic?" he asked. "Is there also major?"

"Yes. Our path is about mastering great magic, which is much more interesting, much more mind-blowing, and much more miraculous than manipulating matter. It is the work of transmutation."

"Transmutation?" Pasión looked at him. The word sent chills of secret recognition over his body, but perhaps even more beautiful was the way Laurin said it. Meanwhile, night was falling.

Laurin continued, "Transmutation means that you do magic on yourself. You transform whatever is inside of you… your anger, your hatred, your fears… you take your love, your desires, all your conflicting desires… your shame and hopes… the ancient beast's instincts, your noblest thoughts, and your darkest horrors, your talents as well as your pitiful weaknesses … you take all that chaos inside you and turn it into life eternal. You take what you want and transform what you do not want; whatever you decide, you do it with your own intent. It matters not what others say, it matters not what I say, it matters not what the teachers, the philosophers, or even the gods say, it matters only what is your own experience. You are the artist, Pasión, the supreme artist of your own future, in this life and the ones to come; you chisel away inside of you what you do not want, and keep your essence of beauty, wisdom, and love, so you become what you want."

Upon these words, Pasión began to shiver. Laurin laid himself down and shared his blanket with him yet again. Pasión pulled himself close to his fiery, magic-infused body. Laurin turned the oil lamp off. Deep darkness and silence covered them in silk.

***

"Come close to me: you are shivering."

"I shiver because… I'm afraid of you."

"Why… would you be afraid of me?"

"I'm beginning to fall in love — with you."

"Then fear not, for I already love you."

***

Sofia woke up with a racing heart and her tears welling up. What evil dream was this that it allowed her to hold him and whisper words of love for the first time, but only to awaken her a cruel minute later! Now she found herself in a world frozen with a loneliness only those who had once known unity and were torn from it can feel. It felt unbearable.

She heard a knock on her bedroom door.

Leave me be, she thought. Leave me alone with my grief! What grief was this, anyway?

Still confused and shaken, Sofia slipped her feet out of bed. She took her cherry blossom robe, which was a precious gift from her Japanese father, flung it over her silky, sculpted shoulders, and opened the door.

Cynthia stood there with a merrily steaming cup of coffee and a wrapped present.

"Happy non-birthday, my dear," she said, smiling. "I know you don't fancy presents for special occasions, so I got you a special present for a non-special day."

"Thank you." Sofia curiously took the present and her coffee; sipping it, she headed to the kitchen. Cynthia followed her.

"Open it," she said as soon as Sofia laid the item on the kitchen counter.

"All right," Sofia said, letting her hands study the shape of the object first. It felt like a large, framed photo.

It turned out to be a painting rather than a photograph — and it took Sofia's breath away to see it!

"I thought this was lost!" Sofia exclaimed, taken aback as if she looked at a miracle.

"I know," Cynthia said proudly. "Can you believe it? I found it while clearing out the attic. Do you remember it?"

"Of course," Sofia said, staring at the painting. With great artistry, it showed a mysterious-looking little valley. It was tucked in between cliffs, reaching up to the sky. Juniper and pine trees were growing here and there, even out of the rocks, which then lay flat in the air at lofty heights. At the end of the valley, in surreal fashion, two figures were walking up on a vertical cliff, and even water was running backwards. There was a picturesque hermit cave, too... "I painted this when I was but a toddler. Everyone thought I was a child prodigy when I created it, but it turned out it was a once-in-a-lifetime stroke of genius."

"It was remembrance." Cynthia changed the tone of her voice. "This picture is very important, Sofia. You painted it to remind yourself. It shows you the place where you will find him."

"But where is this place?" Sofia cried out loud.

"I don't know," the old lady only said. "I don't know anything, really. It's just that sometimes I receive intuition from there," and she pointed her finger upward, "to tell you things you need to hear."

Sofia got herself lost in the picture. It was then that she discovered a detail so stunning she almost dropped the frame. On the painting, next to the little cave, she had painted it, at the age of three: the same statue she was now in love with, while in the making. And in the bottom right corner of the painting, in ageless, timeless letters a title was written:

Laurin's Grove

Where is this grove? And who is Laurin? Sofia's thoughts were racing wilder than ever before, but at the very same moment, her phone rang. The call brought her devastating news.

While Sofia listened in silence, Cynthia watched her in earnest. It is happening, she thought to herself, it is happening now.

Alarmed, Sofia hung up the phone.

"It is David," she said. "He was in an accident this morning. He's in the hospital, and his condition is critical. I need to go…"

As Sofia entered the hospital room, immediately, she was somewhere else. The gates of both worlds were open. The visible world and the world usually hidden from the naked senses were there simultaneously, overlapping and co-existing in one perceptual reality. This was the most curious sight, as if two motion pictures were filmed above each other. Sofia could see the hospital room: David lying motionless on a bed with tubes coming out of his body and beeping life sign monitors attached to him, but behind that opened another, spectacularly otherworldly sight. Amazingly, Sofia could make it out as clearly as she normally saw physical reality. There was the River Lethe, so shallow that David was standing in the middle of it. He smiled at Sofia as he noticed her coming.

"David," she said out loud, or so it seemed. Sofia noticed she was hovering, like in previous experiences when she was out of the body. Feeling light and ethereal, she was able to float as long as she believed she could, able to communicate with thoughts rather than language, able to make a statement without saying a word. "How are you?"

"I'm fine," David said cheerfully. "I just don't seem to be able to decide which way to go: shall I cross over, or do I still need to return to that wreck?" he said, pointing to his badly damaged body down there, which was now only transparently visible.

On the other side of the river, a quite different sight emerged: there was open sky, in the middle of which a cinnabar red, circular gate gave entry into a celestial landscape. There were the most beautiful, crystalline trees, pine forests in the distance, and lotus ponds with flowers of never-before-seen colors. Sofia recognized it: this was a Pure Land! She could see its inhabitants from a distance, blissful beings bathing in white light. Many of them came to see David and saw her as well.

And then — only for a fraction of a second — she saw him on the other side. More clearly than ever possible in physical reality she saw the Beloved whose statue she admired and painted as a little girl, whom she held last night in her dreams!

"Cross over!" Sofia shouted to David. "I will come with you."

But that very moment, the ground began to tremble.

Where previously the safe, little river was flowing, the crust of the Earth opened: with tremendous, thundering sounds, rocks split and crushed onto each other. The split became deeper and steeper every minute. The little river gained momentum: the brook became a stream, the stream became a river, the river became a waterfall passing by the gigantic rocks which had just formed. The ground crashed into a tremendous abyss.

"Stay," David warned her. "I'm staying too."

At that moment, a terrible demon appeared from the abyss with a distorted face and green glowing eyes.

It shouted at Sofia: "You shall not enter here! For you, the Cinnabar Gate remains closed."

Immediately, the vision — the cliff, the water, and the voice — all disappeared in an instant. Sofia found herself shaking, standing next to David's hospital bed.

The ECG alarmed. She quickly checked. David was waking up from unconsciousness.

He opened his eyes and said to Sofia with a kind, but painfully extorted smile, "I guess this just answered my question. I couldn't leave if you couldn't come."

While doctors streamed into the room, David felt his injuries again: he was back, trapped in a completely paralyzed body amidst an ocean of pain.

Chapter 5
The Dog Who Did Not Exist

All men are by nature equal,
made all of the same earth by the same Workman;
and however we deceive ourselves,
as dear onto God is the poor peasant as the mighty prince.

— Plato

Eros, the great demon, would not wait long, of course, to strike down on them. Were Laurin and Pasión not the most desirable victims, in which the demon could easily ignite that mad, passionate love that animals lack the patience, and gods lack the desire for, hence only humans can ever feel? How could the two resist the demon's attack; Pasión with such excited, youthful juices running through his body, and Laurin who had the most fiery life force circling in his veins? Can any of us ever resist the demon whose spear pierces our hearts with such sweet ache that we do not merely tolerate, but invite him into our bedrooms, into our poetry, even onto our training grounds? For isn't it that we happily lay awake in honey-dripping poses of torture all night, in overwhelming longing for the beloved, rather than let our desire go and enjoy the peace instead, as Eros had already spoiled that peace for us, making it seem a dull, terrible bore…

Many of the mystical adepts warned against the traps set by Eros and recommended avoiding his entire business — nonetheless, Laurin knew that was but another, even more elaborate trap. For he had seen many students of magic stay away from the company of women and pretty young boys altogether, sitting year after year in calm postures of contemplation, but Zeus almighty! What was brewing underneath? The more pressure they applied to their desires, the more momentum those desires gained, waiting to erupt at the slightest touch of Eros's spear — which sometimes happened in terrifying, but way more often in highly ridiculous ways.

No, Laurin knew Eros was not a demon to run away from, not an enemy to be destroyed. Instead, he aimed to tame Eros by using the powerful chemistry it provided towards an alchemy of inner transformation. Thus, one morning, when Pasión was still asleep and Laurin leaned up on one elbow to watch him, he observed his own right hand with fascination rather than distress as it touched over Pasión's strengthening body not much like a healer anymore, rather as a lover. Laurin decided to allow Eros to run its course, yet to remain careful not to rush before the boy was fully healed. He wanted to give that finer, more eternal love some time, which was, day by day and night by night, growing between them also.

"No training today." Laurin smiled at Pasión as he opened his eyes. "Tonight is the symposium. Kindly assist the servants with the preparations; I will need to go away for the day."

The symposium! Pasión had been nervous about it all along. Back home, he used to attend many such banquets, but this was the first time he had to rehearse how to serve wine to guests!

At least, the day went by quickly. He had to prepare the symposium with Kosmas, another slave of the household, who was strong but quiet and usually worked away in Laurin's vegetable garden and orchard, where most of the food for the kitchen came from. Together they carried a dozen couches into the banquet hall and laid them out all along the walls, around the pompous mosaic floor and the decorative columns. Afterwards, the two of them went to get the krater: a wine vessel quite impressive in its size. They were carrying it across the yard when they saw Diona running towards them.

"Quickly, boys! Please," she begged. "Hide him for me!"

With great urgency, Diona handed over an unexpected thing to Pasión. It was a puppy dog: as red as a fox and full of newborn delight.

"Please!" Diona urged him, distressed. "I'm not allowed to have him. She must not see!"

This was when Pasión sighted that Medea, the old hag from the kitchen, came chasing her — waving a wooden spoon like a vile caricature of herself.

"Where's that dog? Hand me over that dog!" she demanded, pointing with the spoon at Pasión.

Pasión had just slipped the little creature into the still empty krater, which they now carried over their shoulders.

"There is no dog here," he said.

"Where's the damned beast?" Medea shrieked. "I saw a dog!"

"There is no dog," Pasión repeated. "The dog you want to find… does… not… exist!" he said slowly like a snake-charmer, which eventually made Medea turn on her heel and leave. Yet, she disappeared like someone who had lost a battle but was not yet willing to give up on the war.

Conveniently, Medea was not allowed to enter the banquet hall, which allowed them to further pretend for her that the dog did not exist. Pasión placed the puppy among those cozy cushions waiting for the guests, like just another feature of the room.

By the evening, the room began to fill with venerable strangers. Pasión felt ever so grateful that Diona was also required to join the symposium as a musician, and he did not have to stand alone. He would have been even more nervous if he knew that the night was to be spent in the company of some of the most important artists and thinkers, not only of contemporary Athens but the entire human history. He didn't realize when Kallimachos entered who he was: his own hero sculptor, whom he had wanted to meet his whole life. He didn't notice when Socrates came, of whom the Oracle said was no man wiser and whose fame had reached Melos and Pasión's family long before this day. Even less did Pasión know that the young man who accompanied Socrates was Aristocles, who would be remembered by a nickname as one of the brightest minds who ever lived.

Initially, Pasión had his eyes only on Laurin, afraid that he would call him out — and he did!

"Come, Pasión," Laurin announced, once all the guests were seated. "Walk around the hearth with me three times to show my friends and the world that you now belong to me, that your life belongs to mine, and that my life belongs to yours."

Of course, Pasión knew about the ceremony to welcome a new slave into the house and was not surprised that he had to undergo it. He saw his own father conducting plenty of these rituals, but they were often more humiliating than welcoming — after all, this was the time when slaves regularly were stripped of their names and given a new identity as the property of their owner. Yet, Laurin did not change his name. Also, he did not welcome him into his household, he welcomed him into his life. The words he used were not the ones customarily used for slaves, the words he used rather resembled those used for marriage.

After the circumambulation of the hearth, many of the guests congratulated Laurin, and some cast appreciative looks at Pasión.

Laurin then stepped to a small table, on which various musical instruments were displayed: a flute, a lyre, and a cithara. He picked up the flute and gave it to Diona. "Now it is time for you to play," he said.

Diona took the flute. Her melody came slow and haunting... full of longing... as if she knew of a world beyond the stars... a world so beautiful that it could never be found here on Earth, knowing which turned day and night into grief... but it also made life worth living. As Diona played, all the men in the room felt bewitched.

Pasión too stood there like he was in a trance. Listening to her enchanted him to the core of his wonderful being. He took the melody to his heart as it came in circles, over and over again, each time spiraling higher. When the song was about to take flight, Pasión could no longer resist. He cast an imploring look at Laurin, and when he saw his master nodding, Pasión grabbed the lyre.

He too began to play.

Spellbound, none of the guests could move or speak while the two of them made music. Diona and Pasión were lifted up to heights where the rules of this world no longer applied. Up there, floating, there was no ban on speaking to each other. Instead, they were carried away on the wings of a language that could fly like birds and move much faster than words, which can only ever crawl on the ground like mice.

For a moment, the two of them had all the great men below their feet, sitting humbly and holding their breaths. Nobody, however, was listening more attentively than Aristocles, the young student of Socrates, who had a tear of fascination in his eyes upon Diona's melody.

When they stopped playing, all too sudden, the spell broke like a carelessly dropped cup. The guests began fidgeting and moving around in loud conversation. Diona was sent to serve food and Pasión to serve wine. Only Aristocles watched still and jumped up as he saw them leaving the room. He ran to Diona and grabbed the young woman's arm.

"I know that place you were singing about on your flute," he told her in a voice of quiet, but passionate excitement. "I know because I've been there," he added with great emphasis.

Diona looked at him, astonished.

"It is the world of ideas, where all things good, true, and beautiful originate from, isn't it?" he asked Diona, looking at her with inquisitive, penetrating eyes.

She nodded and dared to smile a little, but then rushed out of the room, as was her duty.

What an extraordinary young man, Pasión thought to himself, watching Aristocles as he mingled back with the crowd. He had never met anyone quite like him before. What piercing eyes! What passion! What curiosity! He couldn't quite get him out of his mind even after the next great surprise, which came when Laurin announced the elected master of ceremonies for mixing the wine with water and performing the ritual offerings. Pasión's knees began to tremble, as Laurin called out, "Kallimachos! You shall be for tonight the master of ceremonies."

Kallimachos was the sculptor Pasión wanted to meet his entire life. Kallimachos, who could make stone look like white linen, marble-like soft skin… Kallimachos, who could drill holes to make shadow and light appear like locks of hair. How amazing it was that Pasión got to see who he was! How frustrating that ritual prevented him from even saying a single word! Instead, all Pasión could do was watch him scatter drops of wine in honor of the gods and take jars of wine from him. As much as he searched for his eyes, Kallimachos did not even look at

Pasión: he hardly noticed him more than the krater for the wine or some chairs in the corner.

Hence, all that remained for Pasión was to carry wine around for the guests. No one spoke to him until he reached the last couch. Here was Aristocles, the fascinating youngster, talking to Laurin, the only one at the symposium who did not drink wine.

"You played magnificently!" Aristocles exclaimed as soon as Pasión arrived at them and set his piercing eyes on him. "You're so beautiful, it almost hurts my eyes. Laurin, what exquisite creatures you have found! Both, they played music like the gods."

"They certainly did," Laurin agreed. "Especially as they weren't merely playing music — they were making love."

The remark scared Pasión. Did he unwittingly ignite Laurin's anger or jealousy? Carefully, from the corner of his eyes, he observed him. Luckily, Laurin's eyes sparkled with joy as he looked at both young men with good-willed fascination, while Diona's puppy dog was sitting on his lap.

"Pasión, whose dog is this?" he asked and seemed in a light-hearted mood.

"Oh, it is Diona's," following an intuition, Pasión said the truth, "but we pretend he does not exist, as she must hide it from Medea."

"Medea," Laurin repeated the name with a dark hint. "That old hag poisons my house with her vile temper. She is the worst with Diona, jealous of her beauty and good heart."

"Why don't you dismiss her then?" Aristocles suggested.

"It was my parents' dying wish to keep her in the house," Laurin said. "Mind you, I'd rather have a dog who does not exist."

"Kanéna," Aristocles named the pup, "the Dog Who Did Not Exist. Keep him! Quite suitable for a man of the mysteries like yourself. The dog shall remind you of the dream-like nature of all reality."

"He shall," Laurin said and stood up. "Give me a moment. Indeed, I'll go and instruct Medea straight away not to dare and harm this animal."

As soon as Laurin left, Aristocles turned to Pasión.

"He is going to initiate you, isn't he…," he asked immediately, "into the mysteries?"

"Yes," Pasión said timidly — proud but hoping this wasn't breaching any confidentiality.

"That will be impressive if he does that," Aristocles said. "He'll find it very hard."

"Hard?" Pasión was surprised. "What do you mean?"

Aristocles smiled at him kindly and offered him a seat at his side on the couch.

"Come, I shall tell you," he said and poured Pasión a cup of wine. "But first, talk to me. You have not always been a slave, have you?"

"No," said Pasión. "I'm from Melos."

"You know, I was once a slave too," Aristocles said.

"Really? How come?" Pasión asked, intrigued, while he took a sip. He couldn't even remember when he last tasted wine: like a little gulp of fire, the red liquid rushed straight into his blood.

"In this perpetual war we have all over Hellas, such things happen all the time, don't they?" Aristocles lifted his shoulders. "I was caught up in a raid and captured while traveling with my family. Oh, boy! Once I'd been a slave, I never looked at things the same way again. I was really scared… but also came to realize what a nonsensical world we have created for ourselves, us humans. I thought: if I, Aristocles, a descendant of the great king Codrus and our great lawgiver Solon, can be declared a mere object from one minute to the next, something was not right. I refused to accept my new status, not only because it was inconvenient to me, but mainly because it defeated logic: I knew that I was the same person before and after the raid. Slavery, thus I concluded, could be nothing but a social fiction, lacking inherent legitimacy."

Stunned by such words, Pasión studied his new friend, who looked even younger than he himself. His skin was smooth: Aristocles was not even out of puberty. Yet, he seemed to produce wit and wisdom as if he had been observing the world for endless years.

"Luckily, my slavery didn't last very long," Aristocles concluded. "I was quickly ransomed back by my folks. Are you from a rich family?"

"Yes, I am."

"Do you think they will come for you?"

"No." Pasión quietly shook his head. "None of them survived."

"Oh, in that case, I say, if you must be a slave... to be Laurin's... is the best that can happen. Mind you, I would gladly be his slave, if he initiated me into the mysteries in return."

Pasión smiled but also used the chance to ask, "Why did you say that Laurin will find it hard to initiate me?"

Aristocles, upon hearing this question, moved closer to Pasión and said confidently, almost whispering, "He would have to free you. As a member of the Order, he cannot keep an initiate in bondage. But Laurin will find it hard to free you."

"Why?"

"Because he loves you. And Laurin likes to own what he loves."

"How do you know?" Pasión asked, a bit frightened. "Did he say — "

"No! I have eyes to see such things," his new friend replied. Pasión did not doubt his words: indeed, the gaze of Aristocles was so sharp, it seemed to penetrate into your soul and see through all things illusory.

It seemed Aristocles also saw Laurin coming. Pasión did not and flinched, as his master suddenly towered above them. Aristocles, however, looked at him with calm and ease.

"Laurin," he asked him, "are you ever going to initiate me?"

"No."

"Why not? Don't you think I'm worthy?"

"Quite the opposite," said Laurin. "You are among the rare ones who initiate themselves."

With that, Laurin left them and joined his other guests. Pasión went around with the wine jar a second time, as Kallimachos allowed for two rounds at this symposium. Afterward, however, he returned to Aristocles. The two of them sat together all night long and became increasingly oblivious to the world around them. As the night deepened, so did their conversation — they talked about many strange and wondrous things. Pasión opened his heart: he told his new friend about the colorful island he grew up on to become an artist and about his centaur guide, Chairon, whom his mother taught him to meet in dreams. They held a lengthy debate whether transcendental beings such as the centaur were really out there or simply part of the mind, and whether the distinction made sense in the first place. They talked about the true, the good, and the beautiful, and helped themselves to more wine than the protocol allowed for. Finally, Aristocles even promised Pasión that he'd find a way to arrange a private meeting for him with Kallimachos, the sculptor.

Time went by so quickly that they hardly noticed that most guests were gone, and some had fallen asleep on their couches. Aristocles raised his cup for the last time as he saw Laurin coming towards them and said to him, "I hope you don't resent me for having stolen your boy."

"Not at all," Laurin said with polite ease. "I'm happy to share him with you. He will, of course… receive his proper punishment tomorrow for drinking away the night instead of tending to our guests."

"Oh, come on, Laurin, don't be such a tyrant!" Aristocles said. "We burned down his house, starved out his family, killed his fellow countrymen… don't you think we owe him an apology by letting him drink at least a few cups of wine?"

"Sounds like a meager apology to me."

"Perhaps, but you want to whip him for having a little wine I poured him?"

"I didn't say that. But a severe session at the gymnasium, Spartan style, first thing tomorrow morning will do good by reminding him that he can't expect magic from his body if he poisons it with alcohol. That is something you, my promising young friend, may want to take into consideration also."

"Yes, Laurin." Aristocles nodded. "Yes, I hear you."

"Well, then, I shall go to bed now," Laurin declared. "Pasión, you stay here and clean up this room before anyone else wakes up. Make sure you serve the early morning cabbage soup as soon as Medea has brewed it for those with a hangover, including yourself. Good night!"

Pasión had curled up on the floor of the banquet hall, as if doing repentance, and found it hard to fall asleep. Mentally, he was preparing himself for hard training tomorrow and tried to get some rest, but the loud snoring from an old man in the corner kept him awake. He noticed previously how Laurin had been talking to this ragged fellow all evening, who was now sleeping on his back with his potbelly hanging out. How disgraceful... Pasión knew it wasn't his place, but he still wanted to ask Laurin why he invited a character so ugly and unkempt. Later, Pasión drifted off into a semi-sleep, during which he smelled Medea's stinky cabbage soup and wondered whether it really helped against headaches or was just another old wives' tale... Then, he was abruptly woken up by some strange sounds.

He heard labored, agonizing groans and cries. Pasión stood up, walked around softly, and soon noticed they came from — Aristocles. Pasión quietly walked over to his wonderful new friend, who appeared to be suffering a nightmare: his body went into spasms and made moves as if he wanted to get out of some confinement. Pasión put out his hands and laid them on his shoulders, unsure whether he should shake him.

Laurin, who always slept like a cat, peaceful and sound, yet with ears perceptive and eyes ready to open at any moment, must have heard him, too, as he came rushing in.

"Careful." He held Pasión's hand gently back. "We must not wake him up too suddenly."

But Aristocles had already opened his eyes: when he saw Pasión, he grabbed his hand, when he saw Laurin, he let out a gasp. Disturbed, agitated, yet excited he uttered, "Never in our whole lives do we see the truth. Never. Never! Never!! The entire world as we humans know it, is but a mirage of the mind."

Aristocles noticed that he was holding Pasión's hand so forcefully that he nearly broke his fingers, so eased his grip.

"I had the most extraordinary dream," he stated.

"What was it?" Laurin wanted to know — he had a serious look on his face. By now, the ragged old man had woken up too and came over to join the tale.

"In my dream," thus Aristocles began, "all of us were sitting not in your banquet hall, but in a cave. We were all slaves, all chained to a wall. Behind us was a fire. Free people were walking around and doing things, but we didn't see them. We only saw their shadows cast on the wall, dancing in the flames. It was all a black magical theater of illusions. Only you stood up, Laurin. You told us to break our chains and leave the cave. We were excited, Pasión and I, to follow you outside, but also scared of the flames and blinded by the light. Finally, we started to break our chains, to leave the cave… That is when I woke up."

On Aristocles' face, there was still a bit of shock and pain from the dream, yet also relief that he was now in the company of some who could understand the extraordinary.

"It is painful to wake up to the truth," Aristocles let his thoughts linger on, "but it also sets us free. If every form there ever was and will be, including every form we ourselves ever take, is but a puppet in the shadow theater of death, it also means that no form has inherent existence. Therefore matter, after all, cannot be what the world is made of. The mind is the creator and master over matter — and since each of us possesses a mind, we can withdraw from the sufferings of the world, if we find our way back into the world of ideas."

"I told you," at last, Laurin said, amazed. "You will need no initiation. You are initiating yourself. You have vast, natural wisdom — broad like the field of possibilities for every creation. Your name should be Plato."

"I like that." The ragged, old man giggled. "That name suits the boy."

He then, unexpectedly, turned to Pasión, "Your name I know because Laurin told me a lot about you, Pasión. But quite unfortunately, we did not get to speak to each other last night. Therefore, you do not know mine," he said. Pasión was surprised: the old man sounded awkward, just as he was ugly, but there was an earthy, quite unparalleled nobility in every word he uttered. And Pasión was even more surprised, even ashamed of himself for the prejudices he harbored when the old man introduced himself — as Socrates.

***

Sofia knew what others did not suspect: how great a tragedy it was for David to have survived. How unspeakably magnificent the realm was where he could have gone to if it wasn't for her sake! The realm into which she would have followed him if it hadn't been for some ancient curse or misfortune. How can anyone stay alive and stay sane knowing that such a place in the transcendental realm exists, while being cast back on a barren Earth?

To find a way to think about this all, Sofia kept Plato's classic allegory of the cave at the forefront of her mind. No one in twenty-five centuries has found a better way to describe the human condition than through that vision of a cave in which we are held prisoners, watching but shadows of the real things we never get to see whilst trapped inside. David and Sofia had briefly left the cave and now their misery derived from being forced back into it.

How tiresome it is to walk when you remember floating, how tiresome it is to speak when you remember sending out your thoughts freely, and how tiresome it is to breathe air when you remember breathing in love!

How unbearable it is to know that there are better worlds, but denied to you, how unbearable it is to feel homesick, trapped in a time and space alien to your being, how unbearable it is to hold a memory of something forgotten, once priceless and now lost, seemingly forever…

One night, however, Sofia was walking in a dream. She maundered through a lush, misty green forest. Her dream was magical, as she felt it was not created by her sleeping brain. Rather, she had found herself somewhere else, while her body was resting for the night. In the forest, she went down a path amidst gigantic old trees, glossy mushrooms, and moss, soft as velvet.

From the mist of the forest, Sofia saw someone coming towards her. At first, she thought it was a man, but then she discerned a body behind his body: a back leveling with the ground and another pair of legs. Even though he was wearing clothes and had a civic sort of look on his face, this man was also a horse.

A centaur! Sofia recognized with awe, as she had never seen a mythic creature face to face before.

When Chairon reached Sofia, he said to her, "I have known your friend."

"My friend?" Sofia wondered what she could hope for.

"Yes, the one you love. The one you are seeking. In olden times, when he still needed me, I was his teacher, and he was — I must confess — my favorite student. Even though I have taught all the great heroes: Achilles, Patroclus, Odysseus, and even some gods: Dionysus, the lustful, and Asclepius, the healer — to me, Pasión always remained my dearest student."

Pasión... just when Sofia heard this name, her forehead, her hands, her skin, her entire body began to tingle as if picking up on some invisible current. At first, it seemed it was coming from the centaur, but then no! It was coming from herself, from everywhere and from nowhere at the same time, in the same way as the centaur's voice now seemed to come from within, as much as from without.

"The two of you will meet again," he said. "Even though he is very far away from you now, you must, and you will find each other."

"How can I find him?" Sofia asked him, quietly and full of hope.

"By doing always the one next thing in your life which feels in accordance with your highest hopes and visions, leaving all fear and all doubt behind. What is your highest hope at the moment?"

Without any thought or hesitation, Sofia knew the answer.

"To heal David."

"Then go and do that!"

'Can you teach me how?"

"No, I cannot." The centaur laughed. "I cannot teach you, because you already know more than I do. But I can take away any doubt you may have in yourself. Let me give you this."

Chairon stepped closer to Sofia, took her hand, and placed a ring around her finger. It was a silver ring in the form of a lyre, surrounding a lapis lazuli stone.

"This is who you are," the centaur whispered to her. "The secret of your healing power is in your touch and in your voice. I'm giving you this ring, as it belongs to you, it always has. In the morning, it will be a powerful reminder to you that our meeting was real and that meeting him will be real too."

The next moment, gone was the forest, gone was the centaur: Sofia had suffered another sudden and cruel awakening. She dared not to move for long minutes after she opened her eyes, hoping the ring, which the centaur promised was proof that their meeting really happened, would still be with her. Finally, she put her hand into her other hand, but all she could feel were smooth fingers. There was no ring, not on her finger, not on her pillow, nowhere in her bed, nowhere in her room.

"Of course, there isn't," the tyrant known as rational thinking told her in its usual icy, sobering way. "This had only been a dream."

Sofia made herself a coffee with breakfast while she tried to hide her disappointment. But this only forced her to think what a drag, after all, life was. She had to rise morning by morning and feed a body, which did not know where to go. She felt confined thinking thoughts she had thought before and taking steps she had already taken, just because the magic she carried in her heart had no place to hatch in this world.

During these morning minutes, while she got dressed and left the apartment, all she could see was a world filled with bathrooms and toothbrushes, massive locks on entrance doors, graffiti on dark staircase walls, stinky rubbish bins and recycle containers, among which Sofia moved like a princess dropped by a twist of fate into a ghetto.

But just as she was losing all memory of the magical forest and all her hope in wonder and healing, walking out of the apartment building, Sofia stepped on something hard. It hurt her foot. She looked down. There was a dirty handkerchief somebody littered on the sidewalk, a puddle of oily rainwater, and unceremoniously lying on the ground, her very own silver ring in the form of a lyre!

The soul can go through centuries, from one futile, wretched life to the next futile, wretched life. Millions upon millions upon millions of moments may pass by without the slightest recognition. Millions upon millions of words can be spoken by the teachers, silently or aloud, without being heard. All the while, pleasure rises, pain falls, senselessly bringing forth foolishness upon foolishness. None of these moments, none of these words, none of the pain, and none of the pleasure matters until comes one special moment, like the last particle of air moving, which finally lifts those wings up into the air. After this one moment, consciousness, which aimlessly used to crawl on the dark ground, can suddenly lift up.

Illumination does not end suffering, as it is not yet awakening, but it allows for leaving behind the dusty dirt ground of doubt, instead, to fly with purpose.

Sofia picked up the ring, marveled at the dark blue lapis lazuli stone at its middle, put it on, and walked on — but walking now felt so full of joy, easy, and light as if she levitated feet above the ground and had the kindest winds of the universe carrying her forward.

She went straight to the hospital.

"David," she told him without any quibble. "I have news for you. We will heal you. I know now without a shadow of a doubt that you'll leave this hospital on your own two legs, and you will make a full recovery."

"Good," said David with an impish smile on top of a still completely immobile body. "Good that you have become aware of it. I knew it all along."

A little puzzled at the answer, Sofia sat down by his bed.

"How come?" she asked.

"You have that ability," David said, convinced. "It's an ancient heritage. I'm not in your life by chance. Some of us carry an ancient obligation towards each other and we do whatever it takes, consciously or unconsciously, in any pleasant or unpleasant way, to fulfill our obligations."

"Yes, I can feel that too," said Sofia, as the words *ancient obligation* sent a subtle, but salient recognition of truth through her mind. She was curious to learn more but knew how much pain it cost David to speak. There will be time to understand everything, now it was time to act. "By the way, they know me in this hospital as a doctor. I got permission to come and see you at any hour. I will come every day in the morning and every day in the evening, when times are quiet, so I can sit here with you and let the healing unfold….," Sofia said, while she laid her hands over David's chest. "Now, close your eyes and think of your highest hopes and visions…"

This was the first day since David's accident that Sofia went up the marble steps of the museum smiling. At the top, Sofia took a deep, fresh breath, grabbed the stone hanging around her neck, and went to her statue for quiet contemplation.

By now, Sofia got used to people coming and going in and out of the museum hall and learned to pay little attention to them. But today, she spotted an intruder. A woman, wearing linen khaki trousers and an earthy-colored shirt, stopped by her statue with a tape measure and a clipboard. She did not merely study the statue — she behaved as if she owned it! First, Sofia felt disturbed in her imaginary privacy with the statue. Then, she had a look at the woman and found she was to her liking. Yes, she had this athletic touch, and a lively, sparkling vibe, combined with inquisitive scholarship — there was even something familiar about her.

"Excuse me." Sofia stood up and went to her. "Do you know anything about this statue?"

The woman looked up from her clipboard with a sharp look. She looked again.

"Sofia?" she called her by her name! Why was she so familiar?

"Oh my god … Alana?!" Sofia cried her name out loud, as her mind finally put memories to the face. Before they knew it, the two of them gave each other a merry great hug; once, they went to school together and used to be good friends. Yes, why on earth had they lost touch since? "I hardly recognized you," Sofia said as she looked at her again, "even though you haven't changed!"

"Neither have you, Sofia… in what? Ten, no, twenty years — I don't even want to know how long it has been! What are you doing here?"

"I'm in love with the statue you are studying," Sofia said, disguising the truth as a witty remark.

"I don't blame you," her old friend said, charmed like every time someone shared her interest. She was all too happy to skip decades worth of small talk to get straight into the one and only passion she knew, which was archaeology. Even in school, Sofia remembered Alana hiding books of ancient languages under her desk, which she studied during every class. "We all love this statue," Alana said. "It alludes to such a great sense of mystery."

"Yes!" Sofia couldn't agree more. "What a shame that we don't know anything about it!"

"What makes you think that?"

Sofia looked at her rediscovered old friend. How attractive this woman was! She lived the life she always wanted to live, devoted to a work she adored: her sun-tanned face exuded joy and satisfaction, which kept her young forever.

"Well, the caption only says a Greek slave, nothing more, no name, nothing."

"That's all the public knows, yes," Alana said, but then flashed a proud smile. "But meanwhile, we know a lot. I am the curator of this statue."

Sofia listened with shock, as her friend, who just seemed to have dropped here from the sky a minute ago, pointed to the statue and said, "His name is Pasión." Incredibly, Alana told her the same as Chairon last night in the dream. Like then, so now, it gave Sofia the sacred shivers to hear it.

"And recently we have found incredible details about his life."

"What details?"

"Come," Alana said. "Come with me. There is something you definitely want to see..."

Chapter 6
Breaking the Seven Seals

"Follow me," Alana said. "Let's go to the basement."

Sofia hurried along with her friend down the marble stairs of the museum, into a part of the building which was prohibited to the public and housed the Archaeological Institute. Alana rushed her, as if something couldn't wait, into modern research facilities, which were sterile and humidity-controlled, yet felt to Sofia a bit like present-day alchemists' labs. Alana's own wonderful office was full of relics from the past: an antique Map of Ancient Athens on the wall, shelves covered with ancient papyrus rolls and fragments stored between protective layers of glass.

"These here are the ones interesting for you." Alana pointed at some scrolls on her desk. "They contain the tale about your statue. These scrolls were found on a funeral pyre from the 4th century BC."

Sofia, who had been marveling around the room like in the past's sacred shrine, came over to the desk, but the scrolls Alana showed her seemed like a cruel joke. Those things were so badly burned that they looked like charcoal, certainly not like anything that could ever be unrolled and deciphered.

"The tale of my statue?" Sofia shook her head. "But how? We cannot possibly read anything written on those."

"Oh, but we can." Alana beamed. "Watch this!"

On her desktop computer, Alana set into motion a quite incredible series of pictures.

"This is the newest technology. We can X-ray through a roll like this," she explained what Sofia was seeing on the screen. "An algorithm puts back together all the transverse sections to make the scroll look virtually unrolled."

"This is surreal," Sofia said, as on the screen she watched the papyrus roll unfolding. Still, it was one burned, black sheet.

"But then..." Alana announced, "Here we go! Now we send infrared light through the letters and voila, technology becomes indistinguishable from magic!"

"Oh my god," Sofia whispered as she saw slowly appearing out of the dark, obscure background, visible letters in ancient Greek. "Is this about him?"

Alana looked at Sofia happily, knowing what she had to say would make her heart jump.

"Yes... his entire life is documented on these scrolls! Written twenty-five centuries ago by the Athenian nobleman who owned him as a slave."

Sofia stood astounded. Touched by wonder, like a child who had just found a golden door opening into a magical theater, she wanted to reach into that monitor to grab what was inside, yet, she had to wait and rely on Alana's skills of interpreting it all.

"Tell me...," she entreated Alana. "Tell me about him!"

"Pasión was a young artist from Milos Island — captured and sold as a slave when Athens put his hometown under siege during the Peloponnesian war."

"A siege?" Sofia was caught up by the word.

"Yes. We remember those classical Athenians as bringers of democracy and high philosophy, but they did not hesitate to starve people who refused to pay them tribute. Civilized humans remain beasts underneath."

"Yes, I've seen that," Sofia said in a tone that sounded haunting to Alana. "I've been a UN medical personnel during the longest siege in post-world war Europe."

"Were you?" Alana sounded shocked.

"Yes," Sofia said quickly. She regretted having said even that much, as she wanted to quickly bring the conversation back to Pasión. "What else do you know about him? How much did you already read?"

"Almost all of it," Alana said. "By and large, I have reconstructed the text, even if at places the interpretation is not quite clear. Soon it will be ready for publication."

"Publication?" Sofia was caught up by the word.

"Yes, although part of me feels almost guilty publishing it." Alana understood her concern. "While I was deciphering the text, I felt like I was trespassing… reading hot, juicy details about the love life of this Athenian who was so deeply in love with his slave, like you are now with his statue! Essentially this is a private diary," Alana got into explaining. "Such a thing was unheard of in his time! Don't forget, this was the era of Socrates, who warned his contemporaries about the dangers of books and writing, as he considered such things detrimental to natural memory. He saw aghast how youngsters, like Plato, exteriorized their memory on paper, as we worry about our kids hanging out on the internet, instead of reading books! Yet, this Athenian wrote as if papyrus was his only friend. And what a story it was! Listen to this."

Alana began to shuffle through some of her notes from the table and read out loud what she found:

> *I am most reluctant to admit it, but I'm so glad he is my slave. I would be terrified if he was a free man, if he could leave me at a whim, anytime he pleases, without me having any right or means to bring him back. At the same time, I observe him, as he is not a born slave, neither do the higher powers mean him to be a slave: he drips sweet drops of nobility with every word he utters and with every move he makes. He eludes heavenly humility, yet without any need for explanation, he silently demands to be treated like an equal and most importantly, to be treated well.*

> *Soon I will initiate him into my sacred mysteries, as I can feel he is ready to know the deeper truths about life and death. On that day, it will be my duty to free him, as we cannot keep our fellow initiates in bondage. That will be hard for me to do, perhaps the hardest thing I will have ever done, but I truly and utterly love him. And love must not be selfish.*

In the meanwhile, I observe him, and he does not seem to suffer (from his captivity), as he — how sweet it is to write this — loves me as much as I love him. At night he cradles himself into my arms like a newborn god and confesses to me that he dreads even the idea of having to sleep without me.

Damn it! I'll order these notes to be burned at my funeral pyre along with my own dead body. I hate the idea that anyone would read such confessions of mine...

"I don't mind!" Sofia called out fast and forward. "I need to know more! What happened to Pasión?"

Fired up by Sofia's lack of reserve, Alana told her the truth.

"Eventually, he gave his life to save his master's."

Stunned. Startled. Petrified and becoming light-headed, Sofia asked, "How... How did it happen?"

"Pasión jumped in front of a Spartan spear that came flying towards his master. It was during those days when the Athenians got caught up by the Melian curse: twelve years after overthrowing Melos, the Spartans sieged their city and starved the Athenians out just as systematically as they'd done with the islanders. Athens eventually surrendered, which ended the Great War. Pasión died in his master's arms."

"Another siege." Sofia sighed, with her thoughts gone far, far away. "What was the master's name?"

"He signed every scroll with the name Laurin."

Suddenly for Sofia, there came darkness.

Deep darkness.

Upon hearing the name Laurin, she fell into a colorless, shapeless emptiness, in which the entire world as she previously sensed it, disappeared. There were no more colors to see, and no more shapes to perceive, no more sounds to hear, and no more textures to feel. There was only emptiness all around her, but it wasn't an empty sort of emptiness, but rather an emptiness pregnant with all possibilities of creation. And from that emptiness, came the voice of Chairon, the centaur and told her:

> *Don't dwell in the sorrow of the six scrolls.*
> *The lover you thought was dead,*
> *Has since become immortal.*
> *To see him, you must dream.*
> *To touch him, you must die.*
> *And to be with him forever,*
> *You must let the Rains of Sankhara,*
> *Wash away all things of time and space.*
>
> *The gates of forever closed on you, as sacrificed,*
> *But be blessed to find your own hidden portal.*
> *Seek out the seventh scroll you had,*
> *Which always was and always shall be thine.*

Sofia had no recollection of anything else and came back to her senses as she felt Alana touching her shoulders.

"Are you all right?" her friend asked with a dutifully worried look on her face. "For a moment it seemed you passed out."

"Yes, it was very strange," Sofia admitted that much. "I'm all right. Alana, how many scrolls did you find?"

"Six." Alana questioningly looked at her.

Strangely, without hesitation, Sofia retorted, "There is also a seventh scroll."

"Good gracious!" Alana stared at her. "For a moment you pass out and become another proponent of the seventh scroll theory! My students will certainly love you. They are convinced that a seventh scroll exists and contains some great metaphysical truth. Would you like some coffee?"

"Sure," Sofia said and followed Alana to the coffee machine, where she put fresh ground coffee into a new filter. Sofia decided to push her luck with a friend whose mind was much more academic than inclined toward the transcendental. "What great metaphysical truth?" she echoed.

"These people were Orphic mystery students," Alana explained while organizing two coffee mugs from the creative mess that surrounded her. "They weren't interested in philosophical discourse, rather wanted to find practical applications for all secrets of life and death. Some of them claimed to have found the key to…"

"The key to what?"

"Immortality. Sugar or milk?"

"No, thank you," Sofia said slowly, her mind being fully caught up in the word immortality. Whatever it really meant, it appeared to Sofia like a scent to a dog. It had to be followed, like hunting after prey which has never been caught before. "Do you think Laurin was involved with pursuing immortality?" she asked.

"Well, according to his own writing, after Pasión's death, Laurin was inconsolable," Alana replied while she handed over a cup of black coffee to Sofia. It smelled promising. "He survived his much younger lover by fifty years! Being an initiate into the secret mysteries, so my students speculate, he must have spent half a century finding an occult way to be reunited with his lost love — and whatever he found, he described in the seventh scroll."

"But you don't believe in this seventh scroll?" Sofia asked, hoping it would prompt Alana into talking more about things she might know.

"I would consider it a fairy tale… if there wasn't some evidence suggesting it may exist."

"Is there?" Sofia looked at her old friend as if she wanted to invite her for friendly sparring.

"Well, there is," Alana agreed, "because Laurin himself attested that he wanted to write a seventh scroll."

That's it, Alana, Sofia thought, keep talking! Give me more.

"Unlike the other scrolls, Laurin planned this one not to be burned, but to be preserved with utmost care. He wrote that the seventh scroll was locked up in an air-tight container and kept underground. Essentially, he wanted to create a time capsule and make sure the scroll would be found. Ironically, the six scrolls he ordered to be burned, to make sure they would never be read, we could read. However, the seventh scroll, which he intended for the future to read," Alana looked up from a sip of her coffee, "we could never find."

"I will find it," Sofia said, with a conviction she herself did not quite understand.

Alana looked at her in earnest. She was struck by how crazily alive Sofia looked: yes, there was pain and trauma in her past, still, she exuded undying ardor and such healthy zest for life, as if her whole body was soaked in the very essence of existence. At this moment, the souls of these two friends found each other. Somewhere between the academic fields and the murky waters of transcendental speculations, there was a place where they could meet: it was the sacred ground of passion they both had plenty of.

"If you think so, why don't you come with us?" Alana suddenly smiled. "In a couple of weeks, we are starting new excavations at the site where the scrolls were found."

"Come with you?" Sofia was just as surprised at Alana's offer as she was amazed by her own confidence! "You would want me to join your team? The only experience I have with excavations is digging out corpses in a war."

Alana became serious as she spoke.

"Yes, I would, and I'll tell you why. None of us became archaeologists because we thought listing up museum catalogs was important. We all became archaeologists because, at one point in our lives, we had a genuine encounter with the past like you did when you fell in love with an ancient statue. Yet, most of us forgot this original passion, sitting for too many years in dusty university libraries, studying to impress old professors, who looked like artifacts themselves, rather than teachers... I saw the passion in you just a minute ago. I would love for you to come with us and bring your passion to our endeavor!"

Sofia felt so touched by the thought that she was being invited to discover the past she had fallen in love with that she stepped forward and gave Alana a heartfelt embrace.

"Thank you, Alana," she softly said. "There is nothing more I would like to do! But I cannot…" She stepped away from her.

"Why not?"

"I have a friend who lies paralyzed after an accident. I want to help him and need to be near — well, I'll need a miracle, but I want to heal him."

"I understand," Alana said with a compassionate, heart-warming smile. "Don't worry, I do want to find the seventh scroll too and if we do, you'll be the first to receive notice. It would be quite a sensation actually. Can you believe this: if we did find it, Laurin's seventh scroll would constitute the oldest paper-based book ever found intact!"

Sofia took a deep breath. She felt touched, surprised, elevated, and inspired. Even though she had to walk out of Alana's office, her steps were at ease, as if she was levitating above the ground. Before she left, Alana said one last thing to her.

"It would also be interesting to find this scroll, as Laurin said it contains detailed instructions about a portal between the lovers."

***

Every night, Pasión slept in Laurin's bed. Every night, Laurin flooded his body with healing flow, and as they slept, he gathered him into his arms to keep all evil away from him — humiliation and disgrace, loss of soul and spirit — which could have been his lot as a slave. Even Eros he first kept at bay — until one night Laurin noticed that the healing stream was no longer flowing from his hands into the boy's chest: a sign that it was no longer needed.

That very moment, another current took over: it was the dragon-blood fire of lust. Pasión immediately noticed the change: instead of the soft, healing glow he was used to, Laurin's touch now ran over his body like volcanic lava rushing through twists and corners, melting everything with its heat. Pasión seized the moment and responded by allowing his hands to glide over Laurin's body, which was to the touch like iron covered in thick velvet. Finally! They both felt momentous pleasure neither of them had known before. Like in a trance, Pasión found himself lifted up and turned around. Laurin had such strength and control in his movements that he could throw him and catch him gently, with such ease as if Pasión was feather-light. It felt intoxicating, yet, as Pasión lay on his stomach, he began to think and he began to tremble.

"You're shaking," Laurin whispered to him while he blanketed him with his own body.

Pasión hated his own confusion: everything Laurin did to him felt like exhilarating bliss; he wanted to become his lover, even his plaything, whatever he desired. Yet, he only got so far as faltering out that he was afraid. Deep within his body, Pasión was still haunted by memories. He said he remembered his friend's cries when his father raped him night after night.

"I am not your father," Laurin breathed the words into Pasión's ears, so close as if they shared one mind. "I had a father like that. You and I, we both are children of the shadows. But I certainly do not rape. Sleeping with me, my dearest, is not your duty, it is your privilege. You must not be afraid; if you want me to stop, just tell me so and it is my promise that I will…"

While speaking this way, Laurin touched Pasión, stronger and deeper, slowly becoming irresistible. "Relax…," he whispered to him. "This is like life: if you resist, you feel pain, if you allow, you feel bliss."

Laurin's words worked their magic: the more Pasión listened to them, the less he grasped their meaning, but the more his body gave in.

Ice is impenetrable, but warm it up, and you may glide through the water, warm it hotter still, and the vapor will offer no resistance at all. Such was Laurin's alchemy of love. He took Pasión's body, frozen by many evils he'd seen and delicately but steadily heated it, touch by touch, heartbeat to heartbeat.

Whisper by whisper, he told Pasión to open up for him: it was a spell, but also came as a serene command. Laurin's touch felt gentle, but also a lot like that of a predator who had to hold back not to bite down. "I do you no harm," he promised yet again. "Only I want to penetrate you as to meet you at places where you thought you'd forever remain alone."

Laurin knew what he was doing: he loved to seduce, and soon let the gentle touch flare up into mad passion between them. Yet, some profound care remained even in his wildest touch, to let Pasión know he'd always catch him should he ever fall. Together, they leapt to heights neither of them previously knew existed, heights at which you forget your name, your gender, your race, and you exist for the sole reason why the entire manifested universe came into being: to experience the absolute loving presence of the Other.

"I want to tell you something," Laurin said after they fell back into each other's arms, and Pasión was ever so grateful that his words kept coming at him. "The whole of Athens thinks that you are my pet slave. This is no surprise, as you are so very pretty, and they believe that you are some sort of fondling, like a rich woman's Persian cat."

Laurin nestled Pasión's face into his hands and traveled his gaze to his eyes.

"But I need you to know that you are not a pet slave to me. Neither simply my future initiate. For reasons still unknown, you feel the closest to me among all human beings, free or slave, man or woman, among anyone I have ever met."

Pasión pulled himself so close to Laurin, as only he could, and placed his hand on his heart. He wanted to signal that he listened and reciprocated, but was unable to speak: infused with bliss, he couldn't say a single word. His mind, however, was racing, in search of a way to express his feelings.

"Laurin?" finally, he asked. "Why do we never sleep in your bedroom? You always sleep just here, in the corner of your study…"

"I suppose," Laurin said, a tad surprised, "for the same reason why you were afraid of me earlier tonight. The bedroom was my parents' bedroom. It is full of shadows."

"Yes," Pasión remembered, "it is also very bleak."

"Have you been in there?"

"I sneaked in, once," Pasión admitted. "I was thinking… Laurin, if you permit… can I paint it? I cannot say things as beautifully with words, as you can, but I can show my love through art. If you let me paint on the walls of your bedroom,

I promise you, once I've finished, all the ghosts will be gone from that room forever."

"You never fail to intrigue me," Laurin said. "Where would you get the paint you need from?"

"I don't know." Pasión thought for a moment. "Back on Melos, I used to make my paint from the volcanic minerals of the island. Here, in the city, I'm not sure."

"Why don't you come to the market with me tomorrow?" Laurin concluded. "We shall see whether there's a vendor with such supplies."

"Thank you," Pasión uttered, heartfelt.

"Anything," said Laurin. "I would do anything for you and I will. I already know that I will love you until my last breath — and beyond. I will love you in this life and the next, and if the gates of liberation will ever open to me, I will not enter them, unless I can enter them with you."

Pasión loved to hear these words, but he could not yet fully grasp their meaning. There was no way for him to know that Laurin not only meant them with utmost sincerity, but would in the future remain faithful to them, regardless of the unspeakable price he would have to pay to do so.

***

What had just happened? While Sofia was walking to the hospital, she felt a power rising within herself, as if merely having heard the name Laurin gave her far greater strength than she ever had by herself. What these ancient fellows were really doing in the realms beyond life and death, she could not yet tell from what she learned in Alana's office, but one day she'd find out. Until that day, she knew it was magic. Magic, she saw in action and witnessed many times. Magic, Sofia had always known, was real.

It had very little to do with pulling rabbits out of a hat, laying tarot cards, or turning lead into gold.

It had more to do with making changes in the invisible world of thoughts, sentiments, and energies to create tangible effects and shifts in the visible world.

Ultimately, magic had to do with choice — one powerful choice any human can make, but few of us ever do.

Magic comes with the courageous realization that there is another way to look at the world. The widely favored perspective is to see the universe as a collection of atoms, organizing themselves into molecules, molecules organizing themselves into cells, cells organizing themselves into life: life inventing life, life moving life, life eating life, life falling apart again into protein, protein falling apart into molecules, molecules falling apart into atoms. It is assumed that there is no purpose to any of it, nothing but randomness and chaos governs a cold, meaningless, and indifferent universe. In the large scheme of things, it doesn't make a difference what any of us humans ever do: the mind, after all, is nothing but a strange product of the brain and will cease to exist upon death. According to this view, we are ultimately powerless, but also devoid of any responsibility.

Those courageous to take responsibility, however, may change the assumption: think of mind, not as a product of matter, but the other way around: matter derivative of the mind. In this view, the mind is regarded as fundamental, as the original source of all creation. This is magic: the mind has the ultimate power to create all there is and all there could be, as it also has the ultimate responsibility. Every moment, under every circumstance, in which a sentient being thinks a thought, the universe is being shaped. Our lives are not only important but decisive for the form and future the world takes. Every time we have to make a choice towards the good, the true, and the beautiful or away from it, the entire creation is affected by the outcome.

What if consciousness — the very essence that allows us to feel, think, love, and evolve — was really the fundamental creative power in the universe? What if it really was the mind which brought the world into being after all? What if it really was true and the world of ideas was primary to the world of forms and the muses existed before temples were erected?

Sofia came to the same conclusion as the mystics of all times: the only way to know whether magic is real is to live as if it was. If it isn't, in a few decades it won't matter anymore. If it is, having lived that way would be the only thing that mattered.

On this day, with the silver ring on her finger, Laurin's name echoing in her ears, and Pasión's beautiful features in her memory, Sofia decided to live life again entirely in alignment with magic.

When she arrived at the hospital, Sofia no longer even felt human. Some ancient, fearsome power overtook her body and mind that compelled her to disregard her surroundings, as well as people's feelings and thoughts that habitually would reach her awareness. Straight away, she sat down next to David's hospital bed, placed her hand at the bottom of his spine, and told him, "I am going to dismantle your reality so that your mind can create a new one."

For seven days and seven nights, she sat at David's bedside, and each day she moved her hand a bit higher. Every day she spoke a verse that had risen from the depths of her cosmic memory:

I am breaking the first seal,
she said on the first day.
The ground we walk
is an illusion,
The Earth we live on
is an illusion,
Our tribes, our nations
are but illusions.
So are
the trees,
the mountains,
the clouds and
the rain.
Wake up from the dream!

I am breaking the second seal,
she said on the second day.
The Other you talk to
is an illusion,

Anyone else out there
is an illusion,
Our lovers, our families
are but illusions.
   So are
   the kisses,
   the hugs,
   the cuddles and
   the tears.
   Wake up from the dream!

I am breaking the third seal,
   she said on the third day.
The empire you are building
is an illusion,
Your own importance
is an illusion,
   Your house, your castle
are but illusions.
   So are
   your work,
   your money,
   your name and
   your fame.
   Wake up from the dream!

I am breaking the fourth seal,
   she said on the fourth day.
Your emotions
are but illusions,
Your attachments
are but illusions,
Your heartaches, your desires
are but illusions.

So are
the letters,
the messages,
the love songs and
the bombs.
Wake up from the dream!

I am breaking the fifth seal,
    she said on the fifth day.
Your words
are illusions,
Your opinions
are illusions,
Our news and our stories
are but illusions.
    So are
    the books,
    the poems,
    the spells and
    the curses.
    Wake up from the dream!

I am breaking the sixth seal,
    she said on the sixth day.
Every life you live
is an illusion,
Every death you die
is an illusion,
Your guides, your teachers
are but illusions.
    So are
    the scents,
    the colors,
    the melodies and

other sensations.
Wake up from the dream!

I am breaking the seventh seal,
    she said on the seventh day.
Hell below
is an illusion,
Heaven above
is an illusion,
Angels, devils, and the demons
are all but illusions.
    So are
    the gods.
    You are consciousness.
    You are eternal.
    You create it all.
    Live up to your dream!

On the seventh day, David moved his body and sat up on the hospital bed without aid. He had his hands closed over his chest in a fist. Slowly, first with pain, but then with greater and greater ease, he opened up his fingers. Nestled in his palm was a silver pendulum in the form of a lyre with a tiger eye stone in it.

"I must tell why you brought me back to life," he said.

"Why?" Sofia asked, feeling endlessly tired and endlessly grateful.

"I came back to take you to the Hierophant."

"Who is the Hierophant?" Sofia asked. The word sounded ominously promising to her.

"The Hierophant is the immortal member of the Order to which I also belong. He will let you drink from the Water of Memory so that you can finally remember who you are, what happened to you in the past and in the future, where you are going."

Chapter 7
The River of Dreams

"G o with me," said Laurin.

Pasión loved these morning walks. Time and again, at rosy sunrise, his master liked to take him into the hills surrounding Athens. On such occasions, Laurin taught him many things useful for living in both worlds. He practiced combat moves with him. He showed him how to draw in the invisible energies from the environment to move faster and run farther. He revealed ways to focus his intent toward any goal he may envision. Through exercises Laurin gave him, Pasión became stronger, more serene, and powerful.

Today was a mild, early dawn: heralding a hot Greek summer day, yet still fresh and invigorating. A breeze coming from the Mediterranean brought in the scents of the sea and wild herbs which blended in with Pasión's favorite fragrances: cedarwood and rose petals. The cedar scent came from Laurin's skin, the rose fragrance from the black curls of his hair.

"I must confess," Pasión had to say, "I'm finding it increasingly difficult to be in your presence when not permitted to touch you."

Laurin took his hand and pulled Pasión close to himself.

"At the very least in my thoughts, I'm always holding you," he said. "I am always with you."

He let them wrap their arms around each other, as they went on walking at a dreamy, leisurely pace.

"Today I shall tell you a bit about the nature of our Order," Laurin said, and Pasión listened, ever so grateful to be held in love, surrounded by nature and the mysterious.

"We are not sophists, and we do not entertain philosophical theories. We do not debate. We do not lead processions through the streets to holy temples. We do not consult the priestesses at the oracles, and we do not ingest mushrooms or magical herbs — although those experiences can be useful, as our goal is to break through the illusion of matter."

"The illusion of matter?" Pasión repeated, while his expectations were building.

"Yes — you don't think that the world which surrounds you, the stars above and the thousand things on earth, are real in a sense that they have innate, inherent existence, do you?"

"No, not at all," Pasión was quick to say. "After my mother showed me how to meet Chairon in my dreams, I really had to re-think what was real. As my dreams became more like reality, ordinary reality became more like a dream."

"Exactly." Laurin nodded. "The ice began to melt."

"The ice…" Pasión sounded surprised. "What do you mean?"

"Have you ever seen ice?"

Pasión thought for a while, and then burst out, "Hermes, yes… that's when water turns solid, isn't it? We had that once, a long time ago, when I was a child. One winter night, it was so cold the water outside on our porch turned hard. When we touched it, our fingers got stuck to that strange surface! We were all scared, thinking some curse of the gods was upon us." Pasión laughed. "But then people from the island who had been traveling explained what it was. Truly, this ice was the most bizarre thing I'd ever seen!"

"In other parts of the world, ice and snow are quite common. Very high up North, people build tent-like houses of that stuff."

Pasión looked amazed — but then Laurin revealed why he was telling him all of this.

"The mind behaves similarly to water," he said. "Water can turn into solid, into liquid, or into vapor, depending on the temperature. The mind can also produce solid, liquid, as well as ethereal worlds. Our ordinary reality appears very solid. For thousands upon thousands of years, habit has solidified it into what most people now call reality. But your mind becomes more fluid when you dream: in a dream, you can fly, talk to centaurs, and visit otherworldly realms. In death, your mind becomes so delicate and air-like that it can easily disappear or rearrange itself to create brand new worlds."

The fluttering little psyche — a bright blue, yet almost translucent butterfly — which was flying around them for a while, briefly touched Pasión's shoulders, then disappeared into invisible heights. Pasión looked after her for a short while before bringing his attention back to Laurin.

"When I was your age," he told Pasión next, "I had to leave my father and my mother, for I could no longer stand the darkness they brought upon the house. Seeking to leave the world of shadows behind, I put one foot in front of the other and kept walking — for days, for weeks, for months, and finally, for years. I always kept going East, but only when I arrived did I realize what I was searching for. Alive today with us is the greatest teacher, the Siddhartha Gautama. With great fortune, I met him for a moment and for a moment only, but that moment changed me forever."

"What happened at that moment?" Pasión halted his step and looked at Laurin. He wanted to hear precisely every word he was now saying.

"He told me this: It is your mind which creates the world."

"Nothing else?"

"Nothing else."

"But…" Pasión tried to think. "How can my mind create the world as it started long before I was born?"

"The mind which creates the universe is the same as the mind which operates in your individual consciousness — like water in your cup is of the same essence as water making up an entire ocean. It is the mind — neither the gods nor the atoms — which is the fundamental stuff everything else derives from. This may sound like a mere theory but think of its implications: you as a human being can, by changing, developing, and evolving your mind, change, develop, and evolve the entire universe."

"Yes, that indeed is quite an implication," Pasión said. "But can you prove this at all?"

"Well, well, well…" This was the kind of challenge Laurin enjoyed. "Could you think of a world without colors?"

"Sure," Pasión replied. "I wouldn't particularly want to, but... it's certainly possible."

"And a world without shapes and forms?"

"Yes, there still could be textures."

"And if there was no matter to attribute any textures to?"

"There could still be sounds and waves, like heat."

"And if there were no sounds and waves?"

Pasión had to think.

"There still could be thoughts."

"All right — and could you think of a world without thoughts?"

Pasión suddenly felt trapped.

"Well, no," he concluded. "I need a thought to imagine a world without a thought. I may be able to imagine some sort of empty thought, without any particular content, but there still would be the mind."

"That's the point. Mind is the thing we cannot think away. It is for this reason that we treat it as our fundamental reality."

Saying this, Laurin looked at Pasión and studied his face. He saw him doing exactly what he did not want him to do: Pasión was intellectually battling the concept, his mind working through arguments and contra-arguments about its own status in the universe.

"All right, you're not quite convinced," Laurin concluded. "Close your eyes!"

This made Pasión nervous. He sensed something fearsome was about to happen, but Laurin insisted. "Close them!"

Finally, Pasión obeyed. Inside the darkness of his eyelids, he soon felt a cool kiss from Laurin. It came, not as usual, to his lips or neck, but to his forehead — a bolt of joy traveled through the center of his body. Then, he was no longer standing! No longer was there ground under his feet, no longer could he smell the raw, sea-infused air of the countryside. Instead, he was traveling at the speed of light through his own inner universe. At the end of the rapid journey, he found himself lying on silky sheets and felt something sniffing around his face.

"Good morning." Laurin's voice came from the dark and sounded cheerful.

Pasión jumped like a wild animal hit by an arrow! He opened his eyes to see Laurin smiling at him, while Kanéna, the Dog Who Did Not Exist, was rubbing his nose at his face. They were in Laurin's house, back in bed as if they had never left at dawn.

"What sort of wicked sorcery is this?" Feeling gulled, Pasión's beautiful eyes sparkled with anger. "How did you get me here?" he demanded.

"In truth, we never left," Laurin said. "I apologize if I scared you. This was to illustrate that your mind is certainly capable of creating the world for you. You were dreaming, but your dream was indistinguishable from one of our regular walks into the mountains."

"Yes, I see — but how can you get into my dreams?" Pasión asked, his anger slowly turning into awe.

"It is something we learn after our initiation," Laurin replied. "Within the Order, we hold keywords — which have certain vibrational qualities to give members access to non-ordinary realms."

"What realms?"

"With the small keyword, you can access at will the realms of dream," Laurin said as naturally as he would be talking about a training regime at the gymnasium. "And with a great keyword, you have full conscious access to the realms of death."

The tension, which previously held his body and mind in a suffocating grip of distrust, began to ease. Yes, why would he be scared of the miraculous? Was there anything more miraculous than the love he was allowed to feel towards Laurin? If Laurin had found a way to open the well-guarded chambers of his heart, why wouldn't he find ways to open realms of the unknown?

"Who gives us the keywords?" Pasión asked.

"A keyword," Laurin explained, "is not something merely given. Think of it more as accumulated. Energy is needed to access the dream worlds and a lot more energy to access the realms of death. Every member collects that energy over time through focused intent, accumulated merits, and practiced acts of compassion. The keyword holds that energy in place, ready to be activated when the initiate requires it. Usually, initiates set their passwords themselves — if they are lucky, a Hierophant or a senior member of the Order will help them."

Hearing the word Hierophant lifted Pasión into a moment of sacred silence. He remembered his mother sometimes talked about such once-human gods, but at the time, he wasn't sure whether they really existed.

"Hierophants," Laurin revealed to him, "are enlightened members of our Order, who have attained immortality — not of the body, as we do not aim for such thing — but of the mind. They can manifest their consciousness into any shape or form they want, to any country, at any time in history. They may even bring entire universes newly into being, should they decide to do so."

"Have you ever met a Hierophant?" Pasión wanted to know.

Laurin shook his head.

"Currently, there is no Hierophant alive and walking among us. Although I have intuition, there will be one soon."

"And how does one attain immortality?" Pasión asked further while the Dog Who Did Not Exist settled into Laurin's lap.

"First, the initiate must purify their mind," Laurin said, "and fulfill their original intent — for each and every one of us is born out of a dream of the mind, which seeks to live itself through us. It is a form of beauty, a fountain of joy, a source of happiness."

"How long does it take?" Pasión could not cease to ask questions. "To purify…"

Laurin took into his hand the pendant Pasión was wearing and showed him also the ring he had on his finger.

"These stones," he said, "are not ordinary jewel stones. In the beginning, when the apprentice begins the journey on this mystical path, the stone is a black obsidian. But it changes its color and chemical compound as the mind of its owner changes. You know that you have purified your mind when the stone you are wearing has become clear — when it has turned into a diamond. And that is a process, which is not measured in weeks, months, or years. It is measured in centuries — that is if you are an initiate. If you were a common mortal man, it would be measured in eons."

Pasión would dearly have listened more, but there was no time. They had to go to the gymnasium, where Laurin put Pasión and the cadets through a training session which made him forget about anything more subtle than sweat.

***

The director of the emergency department respected the transcendental, even if he wasn't overly interested in the details. He gave a moving little farewell speech, as David, who could now move and walk freely, was leaving the hospital. The doctor publicly and openly admitted that he could not account for the recovery that they witnessed in this case. He called it a miracle of God and said it was a humbling experience to see a power in action that was greater than science.

"Isn't it strange," Sofia said afterward to David, "that a learned doctor like him was willing to attribute unexplained healing to some invisible god rather than opening his mind to a science of the unknown?"

It was a rhetorical question, of course. Sofia knew that in order to study the unexpected — instead of belittling the most promising effect ever observed in the history of medicine as "only placebo" — the people involved would themselves need to change. All those aged and bearded professors, doctors, and scientists, who have fallen asleep inside the centennial castle of materialism, would need to wake up, only to find their whole edifice covered with cobwebs of outdated thoughts, overgrown by the foliage of outdated methods, blocking the light of anything new.

David and Sofia, however, were more than willing to cut through the thorny bushes of limiting beliefs, intruding deeper on the path of curiosity to kiss awake the miraculous. They talked about magic… magic which originates from the point of singularity in the innermost depth of one's being then spirals outward and brings forth for ever more ten thousand things… magic through which mind impacts matter, the I impacts all there is, and the now impacts eternity. Such magic — which can heal the sick, resurrect the dead, and make a man walk on water — is of such an unfathomable nature that the hardened and the fearful will deny it, the kind and curious will celebrate when it unfolds, but only the bravest will ever attempt to penetrate into its staggering essence.

"Go to Greece," David said to Sofia, with a powerful conviction in his voice. "Find that scroll. Find out what Laurin bequeathed on us."

"Yes, I shall." Sofia nodded. "What will you do? Are you coming with me?"

"No," said David. "I must go and find the Hierophant."

And so, the very hour when Sofia took a flight to Athens, David began to walk. He heard no inner message and saw no outer clues, yet he trusted the journey to unfold.

David walked out of the city, into the countryside, through fields and forests. He went farther and farther away from all and everyone. At night, he found a river the stars shined their light upon.

He just followed that river. That river of dreams.

***

When Laurin and Pasión returned from their day of training, they heard heart-piercing screams and cries through the courtyard. They hurried up their steps to the kitchen, where the shouts came from.

A ghastly spectacle awaited them. On command, Kosmas had been holding down Diona, while the tyrant old woman Media devastated her with a pair of rusty scissors. Diona's long river hair lay cut on the floor.

"What, in the gods' name, is going on here?" Laurin demanded.

"This girl," Medea was eager to report in a nasty, self-righteous tone, "is entirely out of control. I'm coming home from the well this morning, yes... and here she stands, chatting again to yet another man. But this will fix it, sir, this will fix it! No man will look at her again once I shave off the rest of her hair."

Laurin stood there, not quite believing the scene he was witnessing.

"Who was she talking to?" he asked.

"That young friend of yours, sir... What's his name..."

"Aristocles," Diona said through tears, while she got away from her attackers. "Aristocles asked me where you were, and I told him you would be back late in the afternoon. Only that. I haven't talked to him any more than that."

Diona ran over to Pasión and Laurin and began to quietly cry sad and desperate tears.

"You are still beautiful, Diona." Pasión felt compelled to step closer and tell her, whatever punishment may come for it.

"My mother told me never to cut my hair, for it is a river of dreams," Diona brought through her lips. She looked out of her large, chestnut brown, water-veiled eyes and drove her fingers in sorrow through all that remained of her disheveled hair. She appeared so soft and vulnerable, so fragile and lovely that Pasión couldn't help but wrap his arms around her. Laurin didn't stop him.

He himself looked shocked at this entire appalling scene, but in a minute collected himself and said to Medea, "Now, since you seem to have thought this over so well, have you also considered the appropriate punishment?"

With a satisfied grin on her face, Medea began saying, "The punishment for talking to men is usually — " but Laurin interrupted her.

"I mean your punishment."

"My punishment?" the old hag cried out, aghast.

"Yes, your punishment for damaging my property."

"Damaging your property?" The old woman now seemed alarmed.

"Yes, this girl had the most stunning hair in the whole of Athens, which you mutilated, making her look like a soldier. Certainly, this constitutes serious damage done to my property."

Laurin remained frowning and unmoved even when the old woman changed her look from stern to scared and her expression from boasting to begging.

"Sir, I only had your best interest in mind," she tried, but again Laurin interrupted her.

"Your privilege to manage the household is hereby withdrawn," he said, and his words came down like a curse. "Your privilege to punish other slaves is withdrawn."

Medea wanted to open her mouth to object.

"And your privilege to speak when not asked is withdrawn also."

Laurin said nothing else to the old woman but waved her out and tended to Diona instead.

"What did your mother mean," he asked her, "when she said your hair was a river of dreams?" Laurin, who had magic in his veins, paid close attention to those words.

Diona looked up from her tears to the man who was her owner, but who never before paid any personal attention to her. The look in his eyes was of such genuine interest that Diona opened up and told him the fantastic truth.

"Every night I close my eyes… I'm no longer a slave girl… but live as a warrior princess in the land of gold… where people are strong and kind… who treat me as their equal. Now, my hair cut… I cannot go there… for it was my dream river of hair which took me there."

Saying these words, words upon words, brought tears and more tears into Diona's eyes. She seemed to have forgotten where she was and whom she was talking to. She just cried and cried.

"Diona, Diona," Laurin tried to get through to her, first in vain, but then raised his voice: "Warrior Princess!"

The girl looked up. Laurin could tell that her tears covered a grief so grand it was impossible to express. The story she shared was not some childish dream, but an authentic account of a gateway into another world that she held and lost.

"Diona," he told her with honest compassion. "Don't cry. We'll grow back your hair."

"But that will take ages!" Pasión said, feeling with her.

"No, not ages," Laurin countered. "Only seven days and seven nights."

On the first night, Laurin ordered Pasión and Diona to come to bed: not into his study, where the two men slept every night, but into the previously abandoned master bedroom. By now, Pasión had decorated its walls with wondrous paintings and mosaics depicting fabulous scenes of mystic seduction: satyrs chasing young girls in olive groves, fauns sleeping in flashy poses, exhibiting their irresistible sensuality, watched by nymphs and sirens. In the middle of the room stood a cedar-wood four-poster bed, richly stacked with pillows and velvety duvets, beautifully framed with curtains bound by thick ropes.

Diona entered, a little timid, as she never shared a bed with any man before and did not quite know what awaited her. Yet, she found herself drawn to the enchanted room flickering in the cozy glow of oil lamps. She was delighted to see that Pasión was already there, who was familiar to her touch and whose soul felt kindred to hers. It was such a fine thing that Pasión smiled and told her it would be all right because when Laurin entered the room, she felt overwhelmed by his powerful presence.

Their master walked slowly around the walls and marveled at the new artwork. He didn't say a word, but Pasión detected that his silence was not indifference, but a loss for words. Slow and easy, with a single, kind smile he laid himself down on the bed with Pasión and invited Diona to join them in their midst.

"Just hold on to me," he said to her. "There is nothing you have to do, just lay here with me and hold on tight. I shall transfer you some of my magic… to bring you back the river of dreams."

Diona took it in with fascination as Laurin pulled her to his heart. With coy caution, she snuggled up to his source of power. When Laurin closed his eyes to sleep, she at once dared to turn her head back to Pasión, who laid his hand over her and carefully, gently moved in close to her too. Diona felt safe for the very first time since she had been forcefully taken from her home as a little girl. The three of them remained nestled together for the rest of the night, neither saying nor doing anything else to each other. Yet, while they slept, their heartbeats began to mate, and their invisible spirits spoke to each other in the ancient, inaudible language of oneness.

By the second night, Diona's hair had grown back to shoulder length. The girl was enchanted, while Pasión began to be afraid of Laurin. There was something uncanny about seeing one man's ability to grow hair at will, even more so than witnessing him healing injuries or walking into your dreams. Suddenly, a glimpse of the thought came to Pasión how dreadful it could be if Laurin ever became angry. How dangerous it would be to displease him… to turn against him. And if he desired you, was there any way to escape him?

Pasión saw what he was doing with Diona. It all looked beautiful: Laurin held her night after night in his arms, so she felt increasingly comfortable with him. He allowed Pasión to snuggle up to her also and showed no signs of jealousy. He looked into Diona's eyes for long, long minutes and caressed her soul with words of wisdom.

Diona was beautiful and buoyant, fragrant, and full like a ripe fruit. Pasión knew that Laurin would have her — but he wouldn't be satisfied by simply taking her body, which he already owned. Instead, he seduced her masterly, step by step finding his way forward into every recess of her heart and soul as well.

"What if," he gently whispered to her, "life wasn't really what they told you it was? What if the purpose of your life wasn't to peel vegetables in the kitchen and play the flute for rickety old men? What if the purpose of my life wasn't to sweat all day long in the gymnasium to turn my body into a killing machine and young men into weapons of war?"

Diona looked at him, intrigued, her eyes opening larger still.

"What else, Master?" she whispered back to him. "What else?"

"Feel for yourself, maybe your body knows the answer," Laurin said. "Take mine, do with my body whatever you want, and see what it reveals."

"Whatever I want?" Diona was incredulous. "With your body?"

"Yes. Hold me, kiss me, bite me, hit me, kill me, love me, whatever you want. My body is yours."

Laurin laid back and closed his eyes. Startled, Diona looked at Pasión, who gave her a nod of encouragement, and then looked at the man who exposed himself fully to her. Certainly, she was curious to touch him, even though at first, she didn't know how: her hands dutifully executed the massage movements she was drilled to perform. Then, however, curiosity slowed her down and she took the time to feel this sweet strangeness, which comes from touching the skin of the Other. She sensed a strength in Laurin which surely would be frightening if turned against her, but now felt most reassuring. At the same time, she sensed the enigmatic vulnerability of those who always must be strong, yet long for some velvety kindness, of which she had plenty to give. As she thought about this, the quality of her touch instinctively changed: it was no longer just the touch of a slave girl, it became the touch of a lover.

"What if," Laurin opened his eyes, turned Diona on her back, and returned the touch, "the purpose of our lives was to love each other?" he whispered.

A fire started burning inside her, which Laurin noticed and carefully avoided to satisfy.

That night and the next, Laurin showed Diona ways in which her body was capable of feeling pleasure. He continued to grow the river of dreams and he touched her but didn't let Diona fully touch him until she could not hold back. That way, Laurin made Diona forget the grim tales told by Medea and other slave women featuring how dreadful it was to be laid by men. Laurin waited until she desired him and took her only then. He whispered "warrior princess" to Diona to remind her of the celestine connections to divine lovers in her dreams. So, by the seventh night, Laurin had raised a woman who did not merely tolerate men but lived to love. By the seventh night, Diona's hair had grown back to its full length.

Yet, more than by that miraculous feat, Pasión was astounded by Laurin's question the next day.

"Do you desire her?" he asked.

Pasión tried to find some words.

"She is a gorgeous young woman… she is divine," he hesitated, 'I'm a healthy ma — "

"I take that as a yes," Laurin said. "She will remain in the enchanted bedroom you so wonderfully transformed. She is a good lover now, and she is all yours. You may go in with her as much as you like and love her as much as you both want to love each other. Protect her. She is one of us. Make sure the hag never touches or harms her in any way again. I shall sleep in my study again and expect you to come and sleep with me every night as we did before."

Pasión found himself speechless.

"Master," Pasión began slowly, "you don't…"

"No, I don't need anyone else, as long as I have you."

"Why… why do you think I need anyone else?"

Laurin smiled.

"You are so young, female attention will do you good. Your body will be more content with the continuous presence of a woman. Moreover, she is a young woman too, who needs the loving attention of a man. I think she'd hate me if I sent in the gardener to her, wouldn't she? You are perfect for her. Love her, and she will reward you richly."

"Yes, Master," Pasión said, and with that the matter was considered closed.

Shortly, Pasión had a life that many of the free and wealthy in the greatest cities of the Hellenic world would have admired. He was loved by two of the greatest lovers, gained spectacular muscles through Laurin's great training at the gymnasium, and conversed with the greatest minds not only of his time but perhaps of all times, Socrates and Aristocles. Of course, he was not free, but he started to see his lack of freedom as a tribute to his love for Laurin, thus it bothered him little — he would have stayed and continued life with him, even if he was free.

There was only one thing which he missed: he was still dreaming of that other teacher too, who could teach him about art. He wanted to learn more about making statues. And for that, he soon jeopardized everything.

Chapter 8
Crossing the Gates

"How are you, my friend?" Aristocles asked as he came into Laurin's yard.

"I'm all right, Plato," Pasión said, using his friend's new nickname. "It's really good to see you," he added, as he was feeling lonely.

Laurin had been gone for days. Sometimes he left like this: without telling anyone in the house where or why. On these occasions, Pasión would get some much-needed rest from training yet felt despondent without him. Even loving luscious and succulent Diona could not keep him away from loneliness: his mind, his heart, his skin were all aching for Laurin's stern, yet loving and invigorating presence. On days like this, he had to fight with a strange sort of angst, as if abandoned.

"I came to keep my promise," Aristocles said to him. "My promise to take you to the sculptor Kallimachos!"

"You don't say!" Pasión jumped with joy and sweet surprise. "When?"

"Today… well, now… There was a little symposium at Kallimachos' house last night. I mentioned you. Imagine, he remembered you serving the wine and playing music with Diona. He said it was divine and wanted to see you this morning."

"Oh no." Pasión's heart sank. "This morning, I can't leave. Laurin isn't at home!"

"When is he coming back?"

"Usually, late afternoon, sometimes late at night — but he may not even come back tonight. He's been away for days."

"We'll be back before him, then. Come, I brought two horses," Aristocles said hastily and grabbed Pasión's hand. "You don't think Laurin would mind you meeting the sculptor, do you?"

"No, I don't think he would," Pasión said hesitantly, as it still felt wrong to leave without his permission.

Yet, urged by Aristocles, Pasión soon found himself on the back of an impressive ebony stallion, riding across the city like one of Athens' golden youths.

The ride was fast and furious, scary even, as Pasión realized they were heading straight to the gates, where they had to pass the guards. But for Aristocles, leaving Athens was a most natural thing to do: the guards cheerfully bowed to him and did not ask who that other young man with him was, his slave or his lover. What did such a thing matter to them — as long as he was not a fugitive, whom they would have to capture and crucify...

Outside Athens, the air smelled of freedom: how exhilarating it was, this invitation for adventure!

How fast could I ride? Pasión thought to himself. Could I ride faster than Plato?

Pasión gained ecstatic momentum as he galloped ahead with full force. He left his friend far behind, so much so that if he wanted to run away now, Aristocles had little chance to catch up. Then, Pasión turned back, beaming.

"Did you think of running away from me as soon as we left the gates?" Aristocles asked, as their horses met again.

"Of course I did," Pasión said with mighty honesty. "I wouldn't be human if I hadn't. But look, here I am."

"Refreshing that someone dares to tell the truth." Aristocles nodded. "You need to know that in case you wanted to run away, I wouldn't hold you back. In fact, I would give you all the time and money you needed to get away. But you also need to know that I know you would not want to do that."

"No," Pasión agreed earnestly. "I love Laurin too much."

"More than your freedom?" Even though Aristocles sensed the answer, he wanted to hear it.

"Freedom is what I'm yearning for most." Pasión stepped with his horse closer to his friend, while he admitted this. "But I know I won't be free just because I'm declared a free man again by society or because I run away into my freedom. That would only be freedom of my body — but in my mind, I am only free when I live my own, authentic life. I live when I create my art, which lifts me out of this world of shadowy forms and allows me to connect with the world of ideas, and when I am in Laurin's arms. Only then. Laurin is my freedom."

"Zeus almighty!" Aristocles exclaimed. "Kallimachos will love you — although he won't understand such subtleties. He's not nearly as deep an artist as you are. He may be a technically superior craftsman who can make statues that will impress people in a thousand years to come with their execution of shape and precision of form. You, however, my friend, are capable of creating a statue that will make someone in a thousand years fall in love with you — because your statue will carry your essence."

"How would you know?" Pasión asked, amazed. "You've never seen any of my statues!"

Aristocles aligned his horse side to side with Pasión's.

"No," he said, looking at him. "But I have seen your soul."

Kallimachos' house was surrounded by a peaceful orchard, watered by a small stream that gave enough water for various kinds of fruit trees to grow. At times, luscious figs and juicy pomegranates, at others, sweet growing pears and red glowing apples ripened. Grapes wined everywhere, even around those sculptures the artist scattered in the garden.

Kallimachos may not have been the greatest artist of Athens but was perhaps the cleverest who invented the best new techniques. Pasión walked around in awe, scrutinizing from up close those tiny holes he drilled into the statues to make stone hair look soft and stone clothes as delicate as if you could easily wrap them around your shoulders. By no mistake was Kallimachos called the perfectionist and Pasión memorized his ideas to try them one day for himself.

Then they saw Kallimachos coming. He was a sturdy, thickly bearded man with large, cow-like eyes.

"This is my friend, Pasión," Aristocles introduced him graciously. "You met him at Laurin's symposium. He's a sculptor whose greatest wish back home in Melos was to meet you, the master of the craft."

"Laurin's slave," Kallimachos mustered Pasión as if he were a new tool. Then he just picked up a piece of wood from the ground and threw it at him. "Let's see what statue you can make of this, boy."

To Pasión it felt as if the sculptor had thrown a weapon at him: aiming straight against his dignity. Aristocles looked back at him apologetically as Kallimachos took him into the house for conversation, leaving Pasión outside like a stray dog.

Pasión stood dazed. Hatefully, he held this crooked, useless stick in his hands. What a ridiculous idea to make a statue out of this: it had so many tortured twists and turns, so it would only break if someone tried to carve it. Nevertheless, he called after the leaving master.

"Could I get a chisel, please?"

"In the shed," Kallimachos countered without turning back. "All you need is in the shed."

For the first time since being in the belly of that horrible ship, Pasión now truly felt like a slave. Never before had he been abandoned with a stupid, impossible task while the free men went away to talk. What horrible fate Laurin had been sheltering him from! How different it was to be at his house, where his thoughts, his soul, his feelings were honored! He must tell Laurin how deeply grateful he was as soon as he was back with him. It was laughable: now that he found his hero sculptor, he loathed him and wanted to go home, where he was loved. For long minutes, Pasión got lost in longing for Laurin, so he hardly heard as Chairon's voice came into his head and said that the task he was assigned to wasn't impossible after all.

"I'm not in the mood for this, Chairon," Pasión protested. "I want to go home to the only true master I will ever acknowledge from now on. This is just a piece of stick, an awkwardly crooked, god-damned piece of stick. Almost no wood on it, not enough to carve legs, not enough to carve arms…"

Then he laughed, and Chairon laughed with him.

In the afternoon, when Kallimachos and Aristocles came out of the house again, they found Pasión lying on his back in the grass. He wasn't working, he just bathed his magnificent face in the golden sun filtered by the green leaves.

"So, you didn't find a way to make a statue of that stick," the sculptor said. "Well, I wasn't expecting you to. That stick was useless."

"Yes, it was, sir." Pasión sat up. "So much so that the stick itself got agitated about its own futile existence. Eventually, it escaped from me and turned into a snake. It is now stealing apples from your tree, I'm afraid."

Bewildered, Kallimachos glimpsed in turns at the mad boy and the apple tree. Then he saw it.

The sculptor let out a gasp. Around the tree, the perfect illusion appeared. A snake was crawling up the trunk: the stone white eyes it had glittered in the light, and its scary liana tongue twisted around the ripest of all apples.

"To Zeus." Kallimachos stood there in awe. How little the original branch was altered: only a few cuts made, a patterned skin painted, and sparkling stones given as eyes, yet the entire composition was so ingenuously placed around the tree that it made the perfect impression of a crawling serpent.

"This is remarkable," Kallimachos said to Aristocles. "I haven't seen quite anything like this before. You see, everything is wrong with this. The boy used fewer carvings than would be necessary to make the statue proper, yet you see the snake standing out and looking alive in the eyes of the beholder even though halfway it still is a branch. Imagine what this boy could do if he ever learned any proper techniques."

"I would assume he has learned proper techniques already — " Aristocles remarked, but the sculptor interrupted him.

"Kindly ask Laurin for his price. I want to buy him. He surely would be of greater service to me than to him."

Fortunately, before these words could send Pasión into realms of horror, Aristocles let out a hearty little laugh.

"Ask, I could," he replied. "But I can already tell you that Laurin will not sell Pasión, as he is deeply in love with him. He'd rather die than part with him."

"Shame." The sculptor shrugged his shoulders. "I could utilize his talent, not only his body."

"Laurin may agree for Pasión to come and take some art lessons from you," Aristocles suggested.

"Nah." Kallimachos waved dismissingly. "If I don't have him work for me, it's a wasted investment."

On the way back to Athens, Aristocles expressed his regrets for the way the sculptor treated Pasión, unable to see his soul, unable to look beyond social conventions.

"Never mind, my dear Plato," Pasión said, riding the black stallion at his side. "I've learned more this one afternoon than I could have ever hoped for."

"Really? How come?"

"I learned that I don't need a teacher of art other than Chairon. I learned that I shall never accept any master other than Laurin. I know this now."

What Pasión did not know while they happily rode back to Athens was that something significant was happening at another time, in another space. He did not know that a woman, who will not be born for twenty-five more centuries, is now — in her own present moment — also embarking on a journey to Athens. She is not coming on horseback, but boarding an impressive machine that can fly. Even less did Pasión know that the sole purpose of her journey was to find… him. He simply knew he was heading home to Laurin and would be glad to see him — or so he thought.

Pasión was expecting Laurin not to be home yet, but there he stood in the hallway, as the two youngsters, happy and laughing, sweaty and rushed, entered the house. They looked at Laurin, hoping for him to catch their elevated mood, but he remained motionless, wrapped in hard silence. Aristocles began to speak, explaining his promise about going to Kallimachos, but Pasión wished his friend would stop talking, as he sensed something harrowing. Unheard of before, Laurin was, in fact, angry.

"So, you dare," Laurin reproached Aristocles in an icy voice, "to remove my slave from my house and get him out of the city? Are you mad?"

Pasión, anxious about the rising anger, stepped in front of Laurin to request kindness for his friend, but he was only met with fury. With his long fingers, Laurin grabbed his throat and pushed him against the wall. Pasión's heart jumped with fear. He sensed how all too human and fallible Laurin was at this moment: a man in this state of mind was capable of anything. How dreadful this was: never before had Pasión seen Laurin out of control!

"I warned you, didn't I," he hissed at him, "that you'll have my goodwill as long as you show me due respect and do not turn against me!"

"Master, I never turned against you…," Pasión pleaded, and Laurin released the hold on his throat, but only to grab his neck and push him along the corridor.

"No? Haven't you left my house and crossed the city gates without my permission?!" Laurin raised his voice dangerously. "The guards could have killed you. The guards of the city could have killed you! You made yourself a fugitive slave, for fuck's sake!" Laurin's voice, commanding, pleading, threatening, was full of insane love and crazy care. "Do you have any idea of the anguish I suffered thinking that perhaps I had to find you crucified at the wall?! I cannot stand the thought of losing you. Do not ever make me think that I might!"

With that, Laurin cast Aristocles out of the house, drove Pasión farther down the corridor, pushed a petrified Diona out of the door, and threw his slave on the cedarwood bed. With a speed that should have belonged to the devil only, he took the ropes off the curtains, tied him stretched out between the four posters, and thundered down on him.

"I'll do what I promised to do when you show me no respect," Laurin said. Pasión turned around, and that's when he saw that Laurin was holding a whip. He lifted the boy's clothes and brought down the leather on his naked skin.

"Laurin!" Pasión cried out, in shock and anguish more than in pain. "Please stop this insanity! I only wanted to learn about sculpting… thought this was a once-in-a-lifetime chance… not in my wildest dreams… rather nightmare… would I ever think of going away from you. I desperately love you! Please, please, please stop this madness. You don't want to… harm me or disfigure me, do you? Please."

Getting out of breath, Pasión fell silent, and so he heard Laurin behind him letting out a deep sigh.

"You are right," he was surprised to hear Laurin say. "I am full of anger and fear right now, and I must not strike you in a fury. Wait for me here. I will go out now and come back when I have sufficiently calmed myself down that I won't whip you out of anger or frustration, but as a useful disciplinary measure."

Thus, he left Pasión suspended between the posts, between the worry for their love and the fear of some crazy, unexpected pain, between all that had been and whatever there was to come. Pasión tried to think back to the first night in Laurin's study, where his new master said that he would punish him if appropriate, but never damage him. He also reminded himself of their eternal connection on the soul level — and that helped Pasión to escape despair in this whimsical moment. Deep within, he even wanted to hope that there would be some higher outcome to this.

By the time Laurin came back, he had regained his calm.

"I thought about this," he said in his usual stern, but warm voice. "You have made a fool out of me and endangered your own life by riding out of town, for which I must punish you as your master. But I am also your friend, therefore I'm giving you a choice."

Pasión turned and looked up as much as he could. He held his breath.

"If you want, I shall untie you and set you free to leave my house, never to see me again. Or you stay and take this punishment on you to make things right. Once I start the whipping, you cannot change your mind. Now it is your choice."

"This is not a choice, Laurin," Pasión responded, hissing. "This is cruelty. You know I'd rather take an obsidian knife and cut out my own heart for you to take it than leave you. Why do you think only you have the privilege to love madly? I love you madly too! You do whatever you want with me, for I cannot leave you."

"All right," said Laurin, who seemed to have fully regained his posture. "Remember, I will not harm you, I will not injure you, I will only cause you pain. Temporary pain. Don't resist it: let its waves wash over you and move with it. In the end, it all will be right."

Pasión felt safer now, sensing that Laurin's hand holding the whip was at least not led by vengeance, but in some strange and mysterious way by the force that guided his life path. At the same time, this made it all harder on Pasión, as he so wanted to touch Laurin now, to feel him skin-close and make up for whatever angst he had caused him by disappearing. Instead, he felt the first blow.

Laurin remained true to his word: his motions were controlled, but when he said pain, he meant pain. Pasión wanted to follow his advice and take the blows like waves passing through him, but it was an infuriating, intense torment, which made the animal in him want to jump up and escape. Stroke after stroke, his body ran furiously with offense. Soon, Pasión felt a rhythm to the pain. Not unlike drumbeats for rowers on a ship, it allowed him to imagine fiery waves going through him, instead of receiving angry cuts. It was all coming and going, coming and going…

It was still unbearable. No matter how much Pasión tried to breathe into it and let the waves of pain wash over him, his agony reached an intensity that sent his body into a strange and immensely powerful state of vibration. His ears were throbbing with a sound like a mob of horses running past, and his entire body started to shake uncontrollably.

And then, suddenly, everything changed forever.

Pasión found himself floating in the darkness of eternal emptiness: with all the pain he still carried, he fell to a groundless ground.

He wasn't alone. Pasión felt someone very close to him, whose presence he perceived as comforting beyond measure.

"I am sorry," he heard a voice out of the dark, "for the pain you had to endure."

The face, that belonged to the author of these words, leaned into his, touching ever so slightly his cheeks with soft, black locks of wavy hair.

But it was not Laurin.

It was a woman.

"Who are you?"

"I am the Other," she said. "The Other who has loved you at the beginning of time, who loves you now, and who will love you forever. Let go of the pain. We are in eternity now."

She extended her hand to Pasión, lifted him from the groundless ground, and pulled him into a cosmic embrace. In a whirl of limitless dance, they moved freely like fish in water: up to heights, back to lows, floating in space they traveled to the stars. The music of the spheres erupted for them, and again they felt like at the beginning of time, when the mind was free to become anything. Stardust. Rain. Thunderstorm. Lizard. Bird. Wild wolf. The sweet frankincense essence of ancient mysteries. The Alpha and the Omega of any new creation. Instead, they've chosen to become two humans, who entangled their particles so they would spin together, for all time, no matter how far space-time dispersed them from each other — always seeking the Other's love. For, as it was pronounced at the beginning of it all, to the source — where the mind could take back its undivided power — neither of them could ever return without the Other.

For now, Sofia and Pasión happily floated around together. After a while — perhaps habit had them — they looked out for a place where they could land and rest a little. They noticed underneath them a picturesque little town. It was a warm summer evening down there: people happily walked in cobblestone alleys or sat for dinners and drinks at lantern-lit outdoor cafés, with oil-painted, whirling clouds above them. Sofia and Pasión looked at each other, smiling over the enchanting scene and so, in an instant, they found themselves sitting at one of the tables.

"You look even more beautiful than I thought you were," Sofia told Pasión. "So far, I have only seen your statue. Are you happy in the life you're living?"

"Yes," Pasión said, amazed. No one had ever asked him that. "Yes, I think I am. The good thing about being on earth is that you can create lasting things. I can make a statue and put it somewhere, and it will be there tomorrow. Here, in the realms outside of time and space, it only costs me a thought to make a statue, but will it be here tomorrow?"

While he spoke those words, Pasión created in an instant a statue of her just by thinking. Here it was, a magnificent classic Greek statue of Sofia, in the little garden of lanterns, where they sat together so content.

"Where will you be tomorrow?" Pasión asked her. "Where can I see you? Where do you live?"

"Right now," she said slowly, searching for something her thoughts could anchor to, "I don't remember much. My only reality is sitting here in love with you. But... London comes to my mind. Have you heard of London?"

Pasión shook his head.

"No, I don't think so. Is it far from Athens?"

"Yes, quite far."

"What is your name? Do you remember your name?"

"Yes. My name is Sofia."

Pasión had only one moment in this timeless time to enjoy the sound of her name.

"Pasión," she whispered to him in distress. "Something is wrong."

"What?" Pasión asked with concern. "What is wrong, my love?"

"I think I'm dreaming," Sofia suddenly realized. "This is a dream, and I'm about to wake up!"

"No! I'm not a dream," Pasión tried to reassure her. "I'm real."

"I'm being pulled away from you," Sofia said in a voice of growing panic. "Something forces me to go back!"

At first, Pasión thought she was teasing him, but then he noticed she was indeed becoming more and more distant.

"No!" he cried out, trying to reach out and hold on to Sofia.

"No...," Sofia echoed him. "No... No... No..."

They both screamed now with all their might into the endless distances of space and reached for each other's hands, but there was nothing either of them could do. By now, Pasión felt the same cosmic pull. Even while he still held out his arms, even while he could still see Sofia as she was becoming smaller and smaller. Her picture appeared more and more distant, while Pasión himself began to fall backward through the dust of time, and he surely would have fallen to the bottom of despair, if someone had not caught him.

But someone caught him, and it was Laurin.

Pasión noticed that he was back in his earthy realm as he tasted tears and blood in his mouth. He found he was no longer shackled, but his body was shaking. Laurin lay next to him on the bed, observing him with some level of worry. Yet again, he remained true to his word: as the punishment was over, so was all his anger gone and he seemed as caring as ever before. Pasión grabbed his arm like a falling man would a branch on the side of the cliff and pulled himself to him. Never before had he been so shocked in his life.

"Please," he somehow uttered. "Hold me."

"Of course," Laurin said and urgently took his body, making sure he touched and protected its every inch. He let him rest, and only after Pasión felt calm again, he asked, "What happened?"

Pasión did not wait: as all the shaking of his body had ceased, he began his wondrous tale. He told Laurin how he left his body and went somewhere else. Pasión hoped with his life that Laurin would understand the significance of all he was telling him. And he did. Immediately.

"What did this woman look like?" Laurin asked.

"She was dressed in the most unusual fashion," Pasión hurried to answer, "wearing clothes such as I have never seen before. All her garments followed tightly the shape of her body. She had hair like you. And her body was slim, yet muscular, much more muscular than Diona's or the other girls' around here. Somehow, she was awe-inspiring, intelligent, and powerful, like you or Aristocles, unlike any of the women we have around here."

"Do you think she might be from Sparta?" Laurin took a guess.

"No, she said..." Pasión got lost in his powerful memory. "Laurin, do you know of a place called London?"

"I have traveled a lot," Laurin said, "and spoken to others who traveled — but no, never have I been to or heard of a place called that."

"She certainly was from another country, or even from another world," Pasión summed up his impressions, "yet, she felt so wickedly familiar."

"What language did you speak?"

"No language…," Pasión pondered. "We simply exchanged thoughts."

Laurin, to Pasión's surprised delight, smiled and gently stroked along Pasión's hair on his forehead.

"I am sorry it had to be through pain," he said kindly, "but now you have been out of your body, talked in a wordless language to a being from another space or time… Do you know what this all means?"

Pasión looked at him with eyes wide open.

"It means that you are ready, Pasión."

"Ready for…"

"Yes! Ready to be initiated."

Chapter 9
Laurin's Grove

"I'm coming," Sofia whispered into the silence of her mind.

She was sitting on an aircraft to Athens. It very much felt to her that she was in the right place, at the right time. Since she had decided to join Alana's team in Greece, her soul was rejoicing. For the soul cannot be fooled: when one is fulfilling life's highest purpose call, it is rejoicing; when not, no amount of tranquilizers, therapy, or mantra chanting can take away the unease.

Even if she did not quite know what she was doing or exactly where she was going, her heart jumped with joy as they flew over little lamb-wool clouds, underneath which she recognized the coastline of the Aegean Sea. The waves from up there did not look more than tiny, off-white strokes of a careless painter's brush, but the view suggested to Sofia something extraordinary: life richer and larger than she had so far known. This was more than the promise of a season in the sun any tourist would delight over: what Sofia felt was the vitalizing force of the miraculous breaking into her life. The shadow cast by a wing of the airplane looked like a fast-swimming sea monster, which followed Sofia until they landed. At that moment, her eyes watered. She felt this inexplicable hope to meet the impossible and find her way back into an ancient home of her heart, but this hope was infused with a lingering sense of great loss and the reminiscence of a tragedy she could not remember.

Sofia remained in this ambivalent mood throughout the afternoon. She decided to take a stroll across the city before calling Alana. As she walked across the world-famous site of the Agora, a part of her felt she was walking on a ground that belonged to her and to which she belonged, yet at the same time, the buildings seemed alien to her. Mostly, she looked at the archaeological ruins with noted indifference, even resentment — only a few buildings sparked her interest. Taking a glimpse at the Temple of Hephaestos sent her shivers of magnificent pride: it was still standing, after twenty-five centuries, virtually unscathed! Of course, it was built when the gods still walked Athens, it was built when Pasión was still alive...

In the evening, Sofia first called David, instead of Alana.

"I had a dream with him." She had to tell David about her otherworldly experience with Pasión. "It was not an ordinary dream: I lifted out of my body and perceived his presence so clearly and distinctly as I would anyone in physical reality. However, in the end, we were torn apart by a creepy, invisible force — neither of us could do anything about it. My god, it was so devastating."

"Yes, it would be," David agreed. "I know you won't find peace until somehow you find him again. Where are you now?"

"I'm in a shabby little hotel room in downtown Athens."

"Do you have any idea where to go to find out more about him?"

"No..." Sofia sighed. "Only a hunch."

"A hunch may be all you need in the world of ideas... Like a scent that the wolf can follow. What is your hunch?"

"Do you remember...," Sofia began, "when I told you about this painting Cynthia found in the attic? The one I made when I was a toddler... it depicts something my soul remembers. I know I have to go there, but how can I find a place based on nothing more than a picture of some landscape?"

"What does it feature?" David wanted to know.

"It's quite magical," Sofia said, as she grabbed the painting, which she always had with her. "It shows a small canyon, with cliffs on both sides. It looks like an open cave — high up in the air, trees grow out horizontally from the rock walls. And here's the curious thing: I also drew two figures walking up the near-vertical rock wall, standing tall, seemingly defying gravity and — even water flowing backward! The statue is also in my painting, in the making..."

While Sofia was speaking, she heard David typing something on his end.

"Go to the Davelis cave!" he suddenly said.

"What's that?"

"I don't know," David admitted. "But I searched *water flowing backward —
cave — Athens* on the internet, and this is what I got. Listen: 'The Davelis cave is
today a site for many supernatural speculations and rumors, such as water flowing
backward, time and gravity behaving anomalously. According to some sources, it
has been used for sacral purposes as early as the 5th century BC in Ancient
Greece.'"

"Oh my god…," Sofia whispered. Suddenly she knew they had caught the right
scent, as a sacred shiver ran through her arms.

"'And listen to this." The excitement in David's voice grew. "In antiquity, the
area was used as a marble quarry, which supplied the building of the Parthenon
and provided marble for some of the most distinguished and beautiful classic
Greek statues.'"

"I have to go there," Sofia said, without thinking twice. "How far is this cave?"

David typed again and said, "About an hour's drive or less, from where you are
now. Then you'll have to hike into the Penteli mountains north of Athens."

"I am on my way then," concluded Sofia. "I'll go there first thing tomorrow
morning, at sunrise."

"So shall it be! And I'm back on my mission too," David, contentedly, concluded. "I don't want to speak too soon, but it feels I'm very close to finding the
Hierophant."

***

The next morning, a repentant Aristocles was standing at Laurin's doorstep, who
wanted to make it right for causing worry and earning Pasión a punishment. When
his friend explained that all was right in the end, as the events were now leading
to his initiation, Aristocles' bad conscience turned a bit into envy, but he still insisted that Pasión take the black stallion as a gift to compensate for the pain. Laurin
let him have it; furthermore, he ordered it, along with his own snow-white filly, to
be tucked up straight away. They were going on a journey.

So it happened that a little while later, Laurin and Pasión, master and slave,
riding on a black and a white horse, left two admiring friends behind: Aristocles

and yes… Diona, who also looked towards the two men disappearing at the end of their street with molten crystal tears in her eyes.

Once again, Pasión rode through the gates of Athens, this time fully legitimized, in the company of his master.

"I also have a present for you," Laurin said as they left the city. "When we arrive, I will give you what you always wanted — what you want most in this world."

He didn't say more, neither about the present nor where they were going, but rode ahead, leading Pasión into the rocky, sparingly pine-covered mountains of the North. After a while, they came up to the beginning of a path, which grabbed Pasión's fantasy at once. There, they dismounted the horses. Laurin whispered a strange, other-worldly tune upon which the two animals disappeared into the landscape. The two men began to hike up that path, which sparkled in the autumn sun, mostly in white, sometimes in green, red, or violet hues. What an amazing thing! Pasión now noticed what was so beautiful about this track: they were walking on natural marble stones, indigenous to these mountains.

Pasión kept looking down at the ground, marveling at the rocks, and so he could hardly keep up with Laurin, who walked rapidly up the trail amidst thorny bushes and scattered little groves of evergreen trees. But his master did not seem to mind, no, he even enjoyed Pasión's fascination with the stones and kept looking back at him, smiling. Pasión loved the fresh air, which sounded spicy to him, infused with thyme and rosemary. Higher up the mountain, Pasión noticed a large cave entrance, which looked like a yawning mouth of the earth, waiting to swallow up whoever dared to come close. Even though it caught his attention, Laurin signaled him to keep going. Little did the student foresee that soon he would have more than his comfortable share of caves…

Higher up, past the cave entrance, their path took a sharp left turn: here, the marble path turned pure white and the foliage lush and green.

"We have arrived," Laurin suddenly announced. He pointed to a dense row of thriving pine trees and said, "This is the border. Hidden beyond here is my home: the secret place of refuge for my soul in this life. On days when you wondered where I went, I came here. Once you enter, this place will also be yours."

Laurin sounded solemn, kind and loving, but — almost imperceptibly — also filled with some sorrow.

"Pasión," he continued, "the laws of my world are different from the laws of Hellas and the rules of men. In the world of my soul, there is no such thing as slavery. Once you step through this border, we will no longer be master and slave, only teacher and student, free man to free man, soul to soul. In here, you will receive your initiation, upon which you will be free in the human world also, as it is against the ethics of our Order to keep a member in bondage. I'm saying this so that you are aware: as soon as you step through this wall of pine trees, you will be a free man. These are the last moments in your life when you are still a slave, and you never again will be.'

So powerful and unexpected came these almighty words of liberation swooping down on the eagle wings of joy that Pasión's lips could hardly say a word. In his body, he sensed not only his joy, but the hardship Laurin was going through these very moments. He knew that Laurin found it difficult to let go of ownership over him.

"Can I then say something," Pasión therefore whispered to him, "while I am still your slave?"

"Yes, please do."

"I wanted to say this ever since I've been at Kallimachos' house," Pasión began. "I deeply regret going there without your permission, but I do not regret going there. He showed me something invaluable. He showed me how it could have been — if someone else had bought me on that fateful day. He treated me like a tool and made me really feel — horribly — like a slave. I want to thank you, Laurin. You saved my life, my soul, my dignity: without you, I would be dead by now, inside or out. I love you. I'm in love with you as much as a man can be in love, infinitely, absolutely, without restraints. And I'm only hoping that I will have the chance to repay your kindness — in this life or the next. Worry not: even if I'm no longer your slave, I will always be yours. I will never leave you."

"Be careful," Laurin said severely. "An initiate does not promise something he may not keep."

Luckily, before Pasión could ponder upon these ominous words, Laurin pulled aside the branches of a pine tree and pushed him into freedom.

The shock of what waited for them on the other side was so great that Pasión quickly forgot what Laurin had just said. Over here, it was pouring down with torrential rain! Apocalyptic clouds darkened the sky, and it thundered so loud that Pasión could hardly hear his own voice.

"Where are we?" he tried to shout over to Laurin, but he had gone ahead and could not hear him. Gone was the sunlight and in the sinister twilight Pasión could only roughly make out that they were standing at the end of some kind of canyon. With wide movements of his arm, Laurin signaled him to follow, as he climbed over large, scattered rocks blocking the mouth of the valley. Pasión followed the climb: it was neither too steep nor too high, yet frantic fear grabbed him with every step he took.

I cannot breathe, came the thought to his mind. I must turn around. I must turn around now!

"Ignore that fear!" Laurin shouted back at him against the wind and thunder. "There is no real danger here. It's merely an illusion!"

Only his deep trust and affection for Laurin helped Pasión to climb over those rocks into the valley: every step leading there was scary, even repulsive to make. Amazingly, the creepy sentiment ceased as soon as they were over the rocks.

Down there in the valley, narrowly tucked in between cliffs stood a little cabin. Laurin ushered him in and let him sit by the fire he kindled. He brewed an infusion from dried herbs that were hanging from a beam on the ceiling: Pasión's body thawed, and his soul softened in the warmth.

"Is it always raining here?" he asked.

"No," said Laurin, "sometimes it rains, sometimes it shines, like everywhere else, but this is a different world and the weather is different here from the rest of the region. It won't rain forever — as soon as the sun comes out, we'll go out and I'll show you my Grove."

Inside the cabin, in stark contrast to being out there on the rocks, Pasión felt shielded and protected from all the harm in the world. In here, he had a wonderful sense of arrival. He was at a base of safety, like in Laurin's arms: from here, he was willing to take anything upon him, whatever his initiation may require.

When the rain stopped, they went out to inspect the little landscape around the cabin Laurin called his Grove. Now, in the sunlight, the canyon looked delightfully and wildly romantic. Pasión marveled at the cliffs and pine trees, which heroically grew from the rocks and lay flat high up in the air. Underneath these soaring trees and rocks, at lofty heights, delicate little flowers were growing in fertile ground. A gentle stream flowing from a pristine spring watered bushes, olive, and fruit trees Laurin had planted when he first came here.

"What is up there?" Pasión asked, pointing at the end of the valley, which had a steep incline without any visible path leading up there.

"There is nothing," Laurin said. "Up there, the world comes to an end. Welcome to Laurin's Grove, in the Valley at the End of the World!"

Pasión thought of these words as poetry — perhaps as a greeting for him, who arrived at the end of his search. But no! Soon, he would learn that Laurin literally meant the end of the World. In a few weeks, the two of them would take a walk up there and Pasión would learn that it is possible to walk up that vertical wall as gravity will come to an end there and so will everything else. Water will flow backward and so will time. Up there... were no more mountains, no more trees, no more rocks. No more clouds. Gone will be all the ten thousand things of creation. Up there is nothing but Emptiness — but it is not an empty Emptiness, but rather an Emptiness pregnant with all the possibilities of creation. Laurin called it the mist of time, that mystical substance that holds the Mind, therefore the potential for everything that ever was, ever could, and ever will be.

That mist comes down into the mountains at night and permeates the many tunnels and potholes that are everywhere in the region. When the mist enters the caves, it eases up the laws of physics. It brings the mind of the initiate closer to its original state, in which it is free to create and not so much bound by its own previous creations. The mist makes it possible for the initiate to get into the right frame of mind to overcome time itself and step out into a space without time.

As yet, Pasión knew nothing about any of this. For now, he lovingly took Laurin's hand and walked, free and enchanted, around with him in his Grove.

"Your ring…," Pasión noticed as he touched Laurin's long fingers, "is different. It changed its color. It is now emerald green!"

Pasión looked at it, amazed.

"It's transmuting," Laurin whispered, looking at the ring, his face bathing in wonder. He, too, only noticed it now. "The first time it happened to me in this life."

"What is that?" Pasión asked. "What is happening?"

Pasión was curious like never before, but Laurin said very little.

"As the mind becomes more pure, these stones change," he only said, almost as if to himself. Pasión wanted to learn more, but he saw on his face that Laurin was contemplating for himself. Such was the nature of these magic stones: they changed — from black obsidian they turned into amber, from amber they turned into a tiger eye, from a tiger eye they turned into emerald, from emerald they turned into lapis lazuli, from lapis lazuli they turned into sapphire, and from sapphire — when the mind of the initiate was fully purified — into diamond. Members of the Order observed these transmutations through centuries — for each one to occur it usually took many lifetimes. No one, however, could ever foretell when and how a shift in consciousness would cause a stone to transmute. That was a special and miraculous event each time.

Laurin speculated that his stone turning into the emerald green of the heart had to do with his willingness to give up ownership of his love. Else, it remained a cosmic riddle and he chose to speak about something else instead.

"Look." He pointed to a little cave that was towards the front of the valley where they had to climb over the fearsome rocks in the storm. "I like to sit in this little cave and contemplate. Now you are welcome to use it too to retreat if you like, during your initiation."

With these words, he showed Pasión the entrance to the picturesque little hermit cave, which was a long step above ground level. It had a round window looking out into the valley.

"And over there, behind that tree," Laurin now pointed to a conifer that grew at the cave entrance, "is my present I promised to give you."

Pasión's heart jumped in excitement, but also with a little fright. Laurin had told him he would give him what he wanted the most in the world. This could prove but also smash Pasión's treasured belief that Laurin could see into the depth of his soul.

Yet again, Laurin did not fail to amaze him. As Pasión looked behind the conifer tree, he learned that Laurin did not only see him fully but indeed knew what his soul most wanted to do on this earth.

Behind the tree, Pasión saw the most magnificent piece of man-sized, superb quality, crystalline marble. Gleaming in the sun, it was standing there, waiting to be chiseled.

Chapter 10
The Tunnels of Destiny

J oyously, sensing that she was moving towards a higher purpose, Sofia began her hike up into the Penteli Mountains north of Athens. She was wondering how the ancients found their way, as she had to hold on to her phone for that modern magic of satellite navigation. While she was walking, David called.

"Sofia, I found him!" he said in a great, inspired voice. "I really found him — or better to say, he found me."

"What's that, David?" Sofia held her phone away, wondering what was wrong: she found the line breaking up.

"The Hierophant," David said, but Sofia hardly could hear him. "I found him! He said he'll come to you and speak…"

Sofia moved the phone around, trying to get a reception, but it went silent and finally stopped working altogether.

She looked up, and right in front of her stood a monstrous utility pole holding the power lines that stretched all across the mountain. Sofia could hear electricity sizzling in the air. "What ancient connections we must have lost," she wondered, feeling alienated, "that we so painfully rely on all these electronic connections instead?"

Yet, she had no time to ponder for too long, as something else grabbed her attention. Something astonishing. Her eyes saw someone from the cloud-covered distance coming down her path. Her heart felt… oh, her heart… lord almighty! — that was indescribable! With every step the figure took towards her, and with every step she took towards it, Sofia felt better and better. She began to sense a subtle, yet profound happiness all around, which became more and more tangible with each of these steps. The crisp autumn air filled with a gentle, life-affirming light and a wordless promise of eternal renewal. As it touched Sofia, all her doubts, all her loneliness, all her pain began to melt away as if the one who was walking towards her was in some unexplainable way the living proof that all would be good in the end.

As they neared each other, Sofia glimpsed the face of a kind-looking old man with silver hair and a shortly trimmed silver beard. Or not? No! When he moved closer — perhaps as he turned his face in the rays of the sun — Sofia made out that his long hair was black and his face much younger than it first appeared. But wait again! How is such a thing possible? Now she did not see a face at all, but a skull, as if death itself was moving towards her. Yet, the skeleton soon gained back flesh and blood and assumed the form of a sparkling, seductive woman.

"Don't be afraid," the apparition said while it shifted again, this time into the shape of a little boy. "Your brain doesn't know how to interpret the experience — how to see the one who is from everywhere. I am all these men, all these women, all these children, because I remember being them all."

"How is this possible? Who are you?" Sofia asked, amazed. At this moment she also noticed that a small, foxlike dog had been around them too.

"I am the Hierophant," the figure said, and now his outward body shape settled into that of a young man: so beautiful, innocent, and pure, he could have been a Greek god coming to life. Yes, he resembled Pasión, and even though it wasn't him, Sofia felt thrilled by the likeness.

"You are so familiar to me," Sofia whispered. "Have we met before?"

"Oh, yes," came the answer. "We have not only met but we are intrinsically connected."

"How? My heart and my soul can remember you," Sofia spoke softly, "as I feel great, overwhelming love for you. Still, my brain does not remember anything. I know there is more to my existence, but goodness... I don't even remember myself. Do you know who I am?"

"Yes, I do," the Hierophant said gently.

"Can you tell me?" Sofia urged him, but the Hierophant shook his head.

"No, I cannot, simply because with your present conditioning, you are not likely to believe me — in which case, you'd have to reject me: your brain would filter out and forget our meeting. However, we cannot afford that! That would be an unforgivable waste of this most precious, present incarnation of yours, Sofia. Therefore, instead of telling you directly who you have been and who you are, I shall show you the path to find out for yourself. I trust you will believe your own memories, once you learn to remember. You have a powerful past, and it is your destiny to find Pasión — as it is his to find you. Go straight ahead on this path: you are going in the right direction; the answers are all up there."

"What is… up there?" Sofia asked.

"There are places in this world," the Hierophant stepped closer to her and slowed down his voice, "where reality is less dense. Places where the icy rigidity of reality may become more fluid and may even begin to flow. Normally, the mind, although it is the creator, is bound by its own creation: everything that it ever thought, now exists and holds the mind in the grip of its own forms, habits, and laws by its own inventions and creations. Once the mind has thought of gravity, for instance, the whole universe started behaving accordingly — how can that be unthought? Once the mind has thought of civic life, laws, courts, and warfare came to exist, how can all that be unthought? The mind is bound, Sofia, not just by the thoughts it thinks today, but by the thoughts it has been thinking for millions of years. You need to learn how the mind can return to the original dream state, where it is still free to create. Some places on earth are closer to this original state, and at those places, some restrictions of our physical reality can be overcome — such as time. You are walking towards one of these places," said the Hierophant, while he pointed up to the rocky, sparingly pine-covered mountain behind him. "Go there to find Pasión."

"Can I really meet him up there?" Sofia asked as if ready to enter a dream and never come back. The words of the Hierophant sounded hauntingly familiar to her.

"Yes," the Hierophant said.

"Do you mean his soul?"

"No, the soul, or eternal essence of a person, you can meet anywhere, anytime, if you know what you are doing. In these mountains you can meet the historic person Pasión, as still alive."

How thrilling was that to hear! Love desires to meet not merely in the soul, but desires to meet in the body. Even though right now Sofia found it hard to believe, a part of her knew the Hierophant was telling things that were natural to him, and therefore possible.

"How do I do it?" she asked. "How can I meet him?"

"Like everything else you do in the world of the mind: you grab your intent. It is important — by all means, Sofia! — that you do not give in to doubt or any shade of fear. Walk this place as if you owned it, because you do. Live as if you were in charge, because you are. Allow your intent to be the driver of the world, because it is. Everything out there is a manifestation of your thoughts, maybe a thought from a minute ago, maybe a thought from the beginning of time. It is up to you now to think your way towards him. Follow this path," said the Hierophant, and pointed to a track leading up the mountain. It looked alluring to Sofia, but still, she could not yet leave.

"Did you know him?" from deep inner wondering, she had to ask the Hierophant.

"Pasión?" The Hierophant smiled. "Yes, I know Pasión very well. But I think you're asking me whether I knew him at the time he was alive in Ancient Greece…"

"Yes."

"This is a complicated question," the Hierophant said. "To put it simply… he was my father. But he died before I was born, so I never got to meet him."

Tears, hundreds and thousands of year-old tears, sprung from Sofia's eyes, full of emotion.

"Can I hold you before I go?" she asked, knowing without understanding that it was someone from her true family — even closer than family — she was now departing from.

The Hierophant nodded, with powerful joy in his eyes, and embraced her.

God… surely, my pen isn't sharp enough to do the experience justice, how it felt to be touched by the Hierophant. Truthfully, I can only say, the Hierophant

— instead of some boring sainthood — radiated a sweetly erotic, comforting assurance that all will be well. Love permeated all, and the universe had already begun to move irrevocably towards the good and nothing but the good, the true, and the beautiful. The presence of the Hierophant was like a safe place among the stars, and it was hard to leave him. Sofia quickly felt abandoned, thrown out into the cosmic storm again, as she walked away from him. Luckily, the small, foxlike dog was sent with her to show the path. Kanéna, the Hierophant said, was the name of the Dog Who Did Not Exist.

***

At night, Pasión liked to lie on a large, flat stone in the canyon grove and watch the strip of sky visible between the cliffs. He liked it most when Laurin joined him. When he could feel his body close, a curious sort of magic always occurred: the stars appeared brighter and seemed to move faster — so fast that it created the illusion as if the whole canyon was flying with them in outer space like some ancient spaceship made of rocks. On these occasions, they felt like forefront explorers of the cosmos, connecting with the entire, unbridled glory of this terrible-terrific existence called life.

"Laurin," Pasión whispered to him on one such night, "how is it possible that amidst these fearful rocks, you created such a safe place of peace?"

"It's a metaphysical trick, you see," Laurin said. "Everything in creation is balanced, as it must be. We always live in the tension of opposites. You felt my whip, now my love tastes sweeter. You felt slavery, now your freedom feels greater. There is no joy without pain, no value without loss, no love without fear — and I'm using that to our advantage. I surrounded the valley with a dark, fearful flow of energy: that's what you felt when you climbed over those stones. I use fear as a shield: that negative flow always keeps intruders out. At the same time, it allows for the inside of the valley to remain positively charged — for us to stay content and loving at all times. That way, the statue you are making is also going to be infused with the flow of love and nothing but the flow of love."

Pasión smiled up to the night sky. He knew Laurin mentioned the statue because curiosity was killing him. Pasión told him that he was working on a statue but erected a screen around it to keep it a surprise. He had decided to create a gift: Laurin gave him what he wanted the most, he wanted to give him back what he loved the most.

"No surprise without a secret," he said to Laurin, but then — worrying he might have been too impertinent — he quickly brought the conversation back from the statue to the previous theme. "Yes, those rocks at the entrance of the valley were genuinely frightening."

"Still, you were good at restraining your fear," Laurin acknowledged. "Fear," he added, "is only an unpleasant reaction to danger. You master fear as soon as you accept death at any moment of your life. The only way you can do that is to always be where you need to be and always do what you must do, following the most authentic path of your heart. Then, and only then, you need not be afraid. Then you can tell yourself when you are very, very scared that it is all right to die right here, right now. That thought takes you to the safest spot — like climbing beyond those rocks. That is where you want to be, at any given time: at that one spot beyond fear."

These words came as great value to Pasión because soon he had to put them into practice.

His initiation had begun.

Every day at dawn and at sunset, when the gates of the two worlds were open, sometimes even at night, Laurin sent him into one of the cave tunnels that were everywhere in these mountains. Pasión discovered that there was a substantial subterranean cave system here, effectively a labyrinth of hidden passages, potholes, and chambers.

"These tunnels," Laurin said, before he expected Pasión to enter them, "are infused with magic. They reflect your mind and bring what is inside you to the outside. By the way, the entire world is like that, you just may not notice it always, because the reality humans are used to is pretty solid, frozen to ice by countless years of previous creation, habits of thought, and collective reinforcement. Here, however, magic warms up reality, so it slowly becomes more liquid, more dream-like. That allows you to experience what truly is inside you: the good as well as the bad, the beautiful as well as the nasty. You have to accept it all: learn that inside of you there is evil as well as there is virtue. It's a paradox because, at the same time of accepting that, the only way to get out of some tunnels is to hold onto the most positive thought, sentiment, or energy available to you at the moment and walk away from the rest without turning back. Do not fight evil. Do not pretend that bad things don't exist — that is a common, fatal mistake. Rather, keep all evil as a well-guarded and regularly observed potentiality nearby and never allow it to turn into actuality."

This became Pasión's main guidance in the days to come, during which Laurin sent him into the caves. He soon learned that any tunnel could turn into a tunnel of delights or into a tunnel of terrors. The place really was a theater of the mind, which brought into being any thought or sentiment the initiate held at any moment, regardless of whether or not he was aware of it. For instance, the student could go into a tunnel believing he was holding the intention of love, only to see beautiful naked girls everywhere, turning away from him in disgust, signifying what he felt was lust, not love, and he had to realize that he never even knew what love was. Another time, he may have gone in by holding the intention of wisdom, only to find rows of mocking faces laughing at him for believing he was already more sapient than a Hierophant. Pasión suspected that it was only a question of time when any of the cavities would turn into a personal tunnel of terrors, where he had to face his greatest fear — but then nothing happened as he expected.

He must have gotten lost, venturing too far out in one direction, because suddenly he was somewhere else.

"This is no longer the labyrinth," Pasión noted for himself. "None of my thoughts manifest any more in any way."

He could think of whatever he wanted, from something as shallow as feeling hungry for Diona's stuffed vine leaves to something as profound as Laurin's teachings about duality, the cave walls just remained cave walls and revealed nothing. This brought him more unease than any frightful thing he might have encountered. Being out of the labyrinth meant being out of Laurin's reach, away from his beloved master's tutelage. He tried to calm his nerves and master his rising fear, making it a priority to find his way back to him. Walking and crawling through wet, slippery tunnels, he kept his thoughts focused on that hot, cinnamon-scented mushroom soup Laurin liked to cook in the cabin on the cool, autumn nights. How delightfully relieved he would feel when this was over, and he'd be in his arms again!

Eventually, the passageway through which he was moving came to a crossroads. Lo! Suddenly… a roaring fire lit up in the shaft to his right! First, the warmth gave him a cozy feeling, but the temperature rapidly grew to crazy heights: the heat and the fumes caused Pasión to recoil. However, there must have been others, as the fire was soon doused with water, and the rock cooled down fast. Pasión crawled back carefully to give himself a vista about what was happening. In the shaft on his right, he saw a row of naked men coming forward. With their pickaxes, they began hitting the rock that had gotten brittle from the fire. These were miners! Pasión had reached a mine! The workers were obviously slaves: branded and chained to each other, they carried lights mounted on their heads in small terra-cotta dishes filled with oil and wick. Their misery was difficult to watch and became unbearable as one of them turned his head and looked Pasión straight in the eyes.

"Pasión," a ghastly-looking miner called out his name! "Pasión…"

Oh, what a shock it was to realize the voice was familiar! What a shock when Pasión realized whom it belonged to…

"Moris," he whispered, filled with terror, the name of his brother.

"Help me." The brother reached out with his cracked hand full of scabs and grabbed onto Pasión's silky skin. His voice was rasping as he demanded: "Take me out of here."

"Yes," Pasión brought out from his lips, squeamish with pity. "I will tell Laurin that you — "

"Tell Laurin…," the brother angrily interrupted. He looked at Pasión with disgust. "Yes, go, tell your lover that you left your brother rotting in the mines. Tell him that flies are colonizing his wounds, and the poisonous fumes are slowly, but surely, destroying his lungs. You know what? I won't be alive by the time he finds me. Why don't you let me out now? Why don't you take my place for a change?

Then I could also go and try out those velvety pillows you've been sleeping on, tasting that wine you so elegantly learned to serve, and talk to your philosopher friends about my thoughts on life. Take my place!" the brother demanded and — going crazy any moment — he rolled his bloodshot eyes and danced his tongue madly around his lips while he began to pull Pasión forcefully into the mine shaft.

Pasión, as if defending himself against a snake that would surely poison him if he didn't defeat him in one quick move, sharply hit his wrathful brother with a knife-hand strike, slipped out from his grip, and backed away.

He quickly retreated into the dark passageway he came from. It was beyond doubt that he had to escape: his dark brother was furious and vicious enough to chain him into that gang if he only could. Yet, Pasión moved, loaded with guilt: he sank his head, not only to pass through the low rock ceiling but also in shame. He felt deeply and metaphysically scared — as if the whole cave was watching him. Someone else knew he was there.

Someone was watching him… Pasión, used to seeing forms and shapes in rocks, couldn't help but notice a pair of eyes and a nose bulging out from the cave wall. On scrutiny, it wasn't human; it looked more like a helmet. Yes, it was a war helmet! Yet soon it began to shake and wobble, detaching itself from the rock wall. The figure wearing it began striding towards Pasión.

Even if he couldn't see the face behind the mask, it was such a familiar, yet frightening presence that Pasión immediately recognized it.

It was his father.

The father looked at him and let out a mocking laugh:

"Here is my son, the slave! Crawling in the dark, with his back bent, soiled water running down his face. A slave trying to become immortal, by digging underground, like a mole."

Pasión wanted to interrupt him, tell him how wrong he was, but his heart, his lips, his soul felt paralyzed.

"Are you aware, my son," the father now made his voice friendly, which only came across even more sinister, "what kind of immortality these people are offering you? An immortality which requires your personality to morph, your body to die, an immortality which requires giving up yourself, to become a no-body and a no-thing at a no-time, in a no-space. What kind of immortality is that? It can only be an immortality for the fools and the slaves! Oh, what a pitiful branch you joined, you moron! Don't you know that there is an immortality other than this wretched Order has to offer?"

"Is there?" Pasión asked, provoked by his curiosity.

"Another immortality — yes! — which doesn't require your person to change, which doesn't require your body to die. That is the immortality of power! We all have just a limited amount of life force, and when that is spent, we either die or we take the next portion before it is over."

"And where do you take these portions from?" Pasión wanted to ask again but disciplined himself this time not to say a word. Yet, the father seemed to read his thoughts and answered the question never asked with a smile previously never smiled.

"These tunnels do not just lead to the rituals of the Order. They also lead to the silver mines of Laurion — and the silver deposits. Don't be fooled: it is not silver which is the real treasure in there. It is the elixir of life, bottled to keep your body alive for as long as you drink it, once every hundred years or so. Make sure you get initiated, my son. Make sure Laurin gives you all the passwords. And at the end, make sure you kill him, so that we have the access."

"What?" Pasión cried out in rage! "Kill Laurin? Father, are you mad? He is the only one who really ever loved me — he and my mother."

"Your mother," the man behind the mask hissed out, "was a meager woman. I only married her in order to get access to who the members of the Order are, so that I can kill them."

"You killed members of the Order?" Pasión asked, feeling faint — but the truly ghastly thing was, this didn't really surprise him.

"Yes, that was my profession."

"Why? Why would you do such nasty deeds?"

"The Order is harmful to us."

"Why would it be?"

"It teaches people not to be afraid of death," the father said. "Those who are unafraid of death are invincible, impossible to rule. We, who have higher ambitions and aim for real power, cannot have that. We want the masses under our control."

"That is your ambition?" Pasión felt he had enough. "How boringly obvious… I am disappointed. Wouldn't it be more riveting if you had something new in your plans? Now get out of my way," Pasión raised his voice up high, "you are just a ghost. I am going through!"

With that, he just pushed his body through his father's apparition, which felt like sticky dust, yet harder to get rid of than he thought. It was still there, behind him, as if waiting for him to turn back.

"Kill Laurin! Now you think that Laurin is such a great love of yours but watch what he is capable of doing against you, if he ever gets jealous," his father said last. Pasión tried not to let such a thought penetrate his mind, but with these words, his father already planted doubt — like seeds of bad weed — into his mind. "If you don't kill Laurin," the father said at last, "I will do it. And then I will kill you."

Determined not to listen, Pasión kept going ahead. But as soon as he left the father, another apparition blocked his way. It was his horrible aunt Suha, who used to rub ginger into her slave girl's eyes every night until she went insane.

"Don't you have a heart?" she blackmailed Pasión in a bitter-sweet voice. "Leaving your poor brother…"

Pasión thought if he ignored her, she'd vanish; instead, the apparition sent thousands of tiny thunder bolts into his skin as soon as he went closer. Thus, Pasión found himself caught in a crossroad tunnel blocked by his brother, father, and aunt, trapping him in the evil ways inherent in his family. It was his dark, endless underground moment frozen in time. He sat down and decided to search for an idea that could come to his rescue.

By now, he knew that he was still in the labyrinth: his father had been long dead, the mines of Laurion were a day's walk away from here, and everyone and everything he saw was an apparition. Yet, Pasión was strangely disturbed by one particular remark. Would Laurin really get jealous, and would he ever turn against him? And does the Order really demand his person to morph into a no-body…

Then Pasión laughed a hearty, liberating laugh. Wasn't it crazy that he had to be caught up in darkness to receive an illumination? Why would he not want his person to morph into a no-body? How small does one have to be to hold on to the tiny identity of one human being? How ignorant, how scared must people be, like his father, who try to preserve their present form at all costs, turning it into an eternal prison. The mind is not limited to the human form! The mind is free to become anything. His mind, Pasión pondered, could right now become a seed of a tree and grow his way out of these caves. He could right now become the ocean… The mind is greater than the human form. Letting go of the small identity opens gateways and closes none.

As if the caves wanted to reward Pasión for the wisdom of his thought, the mists of time slowly began to whirl around him like invisible, cosmic dervishes, enveloping him in an upward-moving, expanding spiral of warm light which began to defrost Pasión's various habits through which he believed himself to be human, until his body felt softer, lighter, more fluid and it began to flow.

He was now water.

Human consciousness is grand. It is of the same essence as the cosmic mind, the stuff dreams and nightmares and all the worlds are made of. Once Pasión turned his consciousness into water, it began to flow, inside those dark caves, it filled out every subterranean corridor and every gap it could find, and it found them all. Pasión became greater than human, and no longer needed to find his way out of the labyrinth as he himself became the way.

***

Sofia was contemplating what strange, reality-bending things may occur once she was up on that mountain: would she — perhaps — witness an ancient statue of her beloved coming to life… But events unfolded differently from what she could have ever imagined.

While she was walking, her body began to morph. As if something was pulling her upward, she grew taller, her breasts went flat, but her groin filled up. She looked at her hands: they were strong, but the skin was young her body… no, it was his body… very slim. The same thing was happening to her that she had witnessed in the Hierophant. Suddenly, she was walking in another body: it was the body of an adolescent male. Seeing through his eyes, how different the world looked! The eyesight of the young man was exceptionally good and Sofia — or whoever she was at the moment — could see further than she was used to…

He gazed into the distance, now marching in a sun shining brighter and stronger, searching for his friend whose name was Jesus of Nazareth. All night long he had been pleading with his father, the powerful governor, not to harm him. He told the father he wouldn't just be executing another innocent man, something which the empire has done all too many times, no! He would be depriving humanity of its greatest teacher. But he wasn't able to explain to his father that this man had taught him how to lighten up into a mode of healing and even how to walk on water. "If he is such a great magician," his father only replied, "surely, my soldiers won't be able to catch him anyway." But they did. Looking out of the sharp eyes of the Roman youngster, Sofia saw the Hill. It was a strange sight: she could neither see the buildings nor the people, trees, or rocks, but only the crucifixion: only Jesus and his tormentors. What shock! What pain! What a ghastly surprise! The event wasn't some religious scene, as millions of paintings, statues, and writings yet to come would depict it. It was murder of the worst kind. And no painter later would ever approximate the profound, out-of-this-world beauty of Jesus. He radiated such great divine loving attraction that it was inconceivable how anyone could even think of harming him. Yet, this is exactly what humanity did: it took the most divine beauty and dragged it through the filthiest of dirt, the lowest of blood, and the greatest of suffering. The Roman youngster could not bear the sight for long; soon he turned his head around. He walked away, burdened by guilt and grief. He began to think that maybe the One of Nazareth wasn't such a great magician after all, if he let this horror happen to him — he thought this not because he believed it, but to ease the unspeakable terror he felt over not having been able to prevent his death.

Sofia remained stunned after witnessing the tragedy of tragedies: the destruction of heavenly beauty on earth.

Soon, however, she noticed turning into a woman again: not her present self, but someone with a bonier and weaker constitution, more prone to illness. She was furiously running around, which made this body gasp for air, still, she was trying to be as fast as possible and carry as many scrolls as she could. The Library of Alexandria was burning! Sofia saw the flames, and she saw the hatred on the faces of those who set the knowledge of the ancients on fire. Sofia could also see the horror of horrors: not only the visible, physical books were burning, but also the eternal ideas embedded in those scrolls were leaving earth, flying back to the Eternal Library where they had come from, perhaps waiting for a better time and a better place, where they could come back to be appreciated and acted upon in grace. Meanwhile, all these ideas were lost for humanity, which did not only kill the divine beauty, it also killed the truth carried by the wisdom of the ages.

After running, Sofia suddenly found it much easier to move. She no longer had to use her legs, because whoever she was transforming into this time was riding a horse. This body, female again, felt much healthier and stronger. She also looked majestic, with long, blue-black hair flying in the wind behind her, proud breasts, and muscular shoulders. Yet, inside her, panic rose to unbearable intensity: she turned around and saw the reason. White settlers were destroying her village, raping and killing whoever wasn't fast enough to escape. Gone was not only the native tribe, murdered were not only the people, gone was the good life, which once upon a time was connected to the web of all-there-is.

Finally, however, all these ghastly events from the deep, forgotten past were gone also. She was no longer the Roman youth who saw the crucifixion, no longer the lady philosopher trying to save the library, no longer the indigenous woman escaping from the white settlers' attack — Sofia's consciousness had returned to the present moment, in which she was hiking up the Penteli Mountains.

She sped up her steps, almost as if she was hoping the faster she got up there, the sooner she would be away, away, away from all the horrors of humanity.

There must be something good left after all, Sofia again thought to herself — and there it was.

She saw the little foxlike dog, which the Hierophant called Kanéna, The Dog Who Did Not Exist, run ahead, showing her the way to a small, hand-carved sign that said:

To the Water of Memory

Kanéna wagged her tail and ran back into the misty distance where the Hierophant came from. Sofia was alone again and even had to get used to being back in her own body. She had to touch thyme and rosemary, marble rocks, and pine trees to find her sense back to reality, but she no longer knew what kind of reality she was accessing. She'd arrived at the entrance of a picturesque little grotto.

She stepped inside and found a pond.

The pristine water reminded her how thirsty she was, so she bent down to drink. As she took the third deep sip, that's when she saw it! The water was very deep, and someone in there was struggling to come out to the surface: someone beautiful and in need of help. Sofia wished she still had the excellent eyesight of the Roman youth, but soon she saw him anyway. She recognized immediately who the man in the water was.

"Pasión!" she cried out to him. "Pasión!"

She dived her arm into the water and Pasión — not an apparition, but a flesh-and-blood human being with a real hand — grabbed it. Sofia pulled him, and with a powerful jump, Pasión, whose statue she fell in love with, stood in front of her, as fully alive and tangible as a man can be, coughing up water and laughing with delight.

Chapter 11
With You in Eternity

Knowing that Pasión would come out of the caves any time soon, Laurin stepped out of his cabin and let his eyes skim over the valley. He bathed himself in the savage tranquility of his place and contemplated a little about the screen in front of the statue in-the-making.

Suddenly, like a newborn brook, water came escaping from the little cave where Pasión used to practice these days. Very quickly, water levels were rising everywhere, and streams made their way out of every crack and cleft. Laurin sensed the extraordinary. He knew this flooding had to do with Pasión and his consciousness rising. It was common in the first stage of the initiation process that students learned to transcend the human form and experience being something else. Once they accepted that being human was a transitory form, they could embrace transformation as a way of life and evolution as its meaning.

When Pasión assumed his human form again and arrived back at the cottage, Laurin happily invited him in to sit at the hearth. With a dry blanket over his shoulders, Pasión gulped down his cinnamon-spiced mushroom soup, by now convinced that Laurin must have been stirring into it some of the liquid fire of life every time he cooked it.

"Could it really be true," was the first thing Pasión asked, "that my father was killing members of the Order?"

"Quite likely," Laurin said. "Our enemies have been killing us for centuries, and they will go on killing us for many more centuries to come. Indeed, they often marry kind and inexperienced members to get close to us. There's a spiritual war going on, Pasión, and they have an easy time killing us because we are committed not to kill them."

"But why?" Pasión cried out with youthful indignation. "Why should we be their victims? Why don't we turn into flooding waters or volcanic fires to destroy them in revenge?!"

"In revenge…," Laurin slowly echoed the words. "You already know the answer. Revenge, my friend, creates the very same vicious circle that keeps humanity trapped in its current pitiful state. Think about it: if we kill them, they come back anyway, reborn even more frustrated and full of even more hatred. Thus, the hostility only deepens and escalates further. On the other hand, if they kill us, as inconvenient as that may be, we come back stronger, more compassionate, and more resilient. They don't know that it's impossible to destroy us. They don't know that it is impossible to destroy magic because it directly derives from the primordial mind." Laurin looked at the boy, not sure whether he was still listening. Something seemed to cloud Pasión's mind.

"Laurin…," he asked, "could you ever become jealous?"

Laurin looked surprised.

"I am human," he said, after brief contemplation, "so yes, but I doubt I would ever give in to such nonsensical emotion. If you love me, then any interest you may have in others is curiosity. It's part of human nature, and it's wise to just let it be. However, if you are interested in someone else because you no longer love me, then I shall let you go. Love is about allowing and setting free: I have learned that, and I must not unlearn it."

"I do love you and always will," Pasión was quick to say. "Forgive me. Some dark things my father said in the cave linger on."

"Now, that is," Laurin pointed out sharply, "how they can really harm us! By planting seeds of doubt and fear into your mind and into your heart. The mystical path allows for no hesitation! It is like walking a hazardous terrain: if you stumble and fall on ice, you freeze forever, if you stumble and fall on fire, you never get away from the spot alive. Keep your faith, Pasión — in the path, and in the ones who walk the path with you."

"Of course." Pasión regretted having said anything.

"But for now," Laurin added, "your task is just to rest. You will need it. Tomorrow it is time for me to take you into your Tunnel of Destiny."

On the next day, Laurin took a tiny torch and the longest rope he had with him.

He led them to the cave Pasión saw the first time they hiked up to the Grove. Inside, Laurin pointed out a cavity at the bottom of the rock wall. As tiny and narrow as it was, it looked impossible for a human body to ever squeeze through it. Yet — without mercy! — that was their entrance. Laurin crawled ahead, and Pasión followed him faithfully, albeit he found himself almost consumed by some ancient fear of getting jammed forever. He had to recall his master's previous teachings and remind himself that it would be all right to die here: the mind cannot get stuck and would simply leave the place in case the body perished. So, he followed his master's every clever move as he made his way through the narrow and deep, sometimes near-vertical shaft down into the mountain. Pasión mimicked him as he himself didn't know what to do: how to rotate his shoulders, where to put one leg, where to cross the other, how to let himself down safely with the rope to the next foothold, before pausing and sinking a layer deeper — and again, a layer deeper into the womb of the earth. Once he hit his head, and once he hurt his elbow which remained painful afterwards as he put his body weight on his arm at every descent. Yet, as he had fully let go of his fear, the descent became a fantastic adventure. By the flickering of Laurin's torch, he saw tiny hibernating bats — wrapped up in their wings they looked like Diona's stuffed vine leaves — clinging with their minuscule feet and fingers onto the rough walls.

"Don't disturb them," Laurin said. "If you wake them up, they'll lose their temperature control and die. And watch out for the steps!"

This is how Pasión noticed they no longer needed the ropes. No longer was it an effort to descend farther, as there were stairs carved into the ground! Man-made stairs that led somewhere.

They led into the sanctum.

The sanctum was a roughly carved little, round space tucked in the midst of natural rocks; it only had an altar stone in the middle and a triangular tunnel at its end. Invisible to the eye, but tangible for those with a perceptive heart and soul: the place was surrounded with strong will and good intent.

"I will leave you here," Laurin announced with no further comments.

"Yes, Master," Pasión replied obediently, by now used to being left alone underground. "When are you coming back?"

"Never," Laurin said. "This is the Tunnel of Destiny. It is your work to find your way out."

Without any further delay, Laurin truly began his ascent! He pulled the rope up behind himself and also took with him the small torch, their only source of light.

Perhaps this was to become terrifying after all, Pasión thought to himself. There he was, left behind, plunged into utter darkness...

For days, he attempted in vain to find his way out. Regardless of how hard he tried to pull himself up or where he placed his feet and his hands, without a light, without Laurin, and — mostly — without a rope, it proved impossible to climb back. During countless painful attempts, he fell back on the ground and hurt himself, time and time again...

The cozy little chamber, which was peaceful and inviting at the beginning, now became threatening. What felt like the womb of the earth, now seemed to have turned into a tomb.

Essentially, Pasión found himself buried alive.

There was one thing, however, which rendered the place different from a grave. Feeling his way through, Pasión found at the end of the triangular corridor a sacred little pond. This, in one way, made the place much kinder, yet in another, even more horrifying, as the sacred pond was filled with the Water of Memory. So, when Pasión drank from it, this water did not only quench his thirst, it also satiated his hunger and fed his mind. Pasión could no longer comfort himself with the idea that his body could die in here and his consciousness would then leave. No, the Water of Memory strangely held his body, as well as his mind, captive. Every drop he swallowed gave him another vision of life — and every such vision felt like a real experience. One moment, he saw himself as a gymnast winning the Olympic Games, the other moment, he felt himself being touched by beautiful women. Every such moment led to suffering because every vision was very soon over and to ease the horror of that, Pasión needed another sip... Thus the powerful play went on and on and on... until he'd had enough of it.

Pasión began to understand where he had come from was not his way out; neither could he stay here and keep drinking from the illusions of existence forever. These labyrinths had been planned in a way — by whatever visible or invisible forces constructed them — that once you were inside, you could never go back or stagnate, you could only advance.

In an attempt to put an end to all the illusions, Pasión lay down on his stomach, so that his mouth was right at the water, and he did not have to move at all. This time, however, with every drop of water that reached his lips, he refused to look at the illusion it brought. Instead, he hushed the illusion away like a passing cloud in the sky and aimed to look behind it. What was behind all the illusions? What was behind all of his hopes and fears, dreams and aspirations? Pasión gazed at the water of the pond, disregarding anything that came and went by. Eventually, the surface became clear, and so did his mind.

After a while, out of the darkness came a light. At first, it was only a dot, which looked like a far-away star from an endless sky reaching across time. The little star called Pasión like the night calls wild predators. Pasión submerged his face into the water to see closer. He saw that the water led through a tunnel, so he began to dive through it. At first, he was thankful he had spent so much time underwater whilst growing up, but soon he had to wonder how long the tunnel was, and whether he would ever make it out alive... But then he saw... the same face that was so painfully and violently pulled away the last time he saw her in his vision!

Immediately, Pasión recognized Sofia! Immediately, he knew, even if he had to do it without breath, he would swim to be with her! The tunnel underneath the sacred pond turned out to be deep... deeper still... and deeper still... Yet, Pasión swam and swam, thinking of the fish who turned amphibian... an amphibian waiting to breathe. The movements of the arms became harder, the lungs begged for air, the last minute felt spent, but then the tunnel mercifully began taking him up... He swallowed water... On the verge of passing out, however, Pasión felt a hand pulling him, and finally, he could jump and take a life-saving gasp of air. He coughed and laughed with all his heart.

Perhaps it was the sunshine pouring in from behind her, but Pasión saw Sofia in such an other-worldly glow that her beauty touched him in a way he could sense, but not understand.

"You are not human, are you?" He looked at her with awe and wonder.

"I assure you," she replied, "that I am."

"Or perhaps you are not from this earth?"

"I am."

"Then why is it that you are unlike any woman I have ever met? I can't help but ponder: what is so different about you?"

Sofia looked at him, and for the first time, saw the magical luminosity of his eyes, which she could not see on the statue: eyes with a rim dark as rocks, surrounding blackness, like the night sky.

"I am from a different time," she spoke, as simply and truthfully as she could. "I am from a time that is 2500 years into your future."

She studied Pasión's face — which exuded intelligence — and wondered how a young man of ancient times could take such news. She wondered how she would react if someone claimed they were twenty-five centuries ahead of time.

"My mind is trying to grasp that," Pasión said after some thought, "but I'm afraid, it is failing miserably. How can the human mind contemplate time as vast as that?"

"I don't understand either," Sofia spread his hands, "how this happened to us. I'm only glad it did."

As they stood together, the magnetic tension between them became nearly unbearable. Yet, Sofia was afraid to touch Pasión, the man of two thousand and five hundred bygone years: his beauty was so magical, like that of a rare and fragile bird whose wings could break in human hands. Also, Pasión was afraid to touch Sofia, as he couldn't decide whether she was a goddess or a siren, a mirage or a dream. Only slowly, step by step, did they move towards each other, but then nature quickly did the rest.

Their bodies met with an explosion of delight. One touch of each other, one breath from each other, one look into each other's eyes, and gone was all pain, gone was all sadness, gone was all loneliness from the face of the Earth.

"You do feel human," Pasión whispered to her, as he touched her arms and her back, "only better than human. Your skin tastes like nectar, your hair feels like the ambrosia of the gods."

Pasión forgot to think: he only obeyed his heart and his body and squeezed Sofia so tight it would have hurt if done by anyone else.

This place where they were was Little Eternity: every moment they spent lasted forever, and their meeting rendered them inseparable from the beginning of time and would keep them inseparable until the end — and beyond.

"I do not ever again want to let you go," Pasión whispered.

"Please, never do," Sofia whispered back. "Stay with me. Walk with me."

Together, they stepped out of the cave: around them in Little Eternity, the trees, which in an ordinary Greek landscape would grow olives, here grew precious jewel fruits of wisdom. They were kept strong and vibrant by streams filled with the Water of Memory. Crystals of truth sparkled in the air as the wind carried the most wonder-filled teachings, which transform everyone they surround and do not even need to be heard…

"How did you find me?" Pasión asked during their next eternal moment. Sofia was delighted to see that his curiosity was stronger than the strangeness of their case. Through it, Pasión was already bridging the ravine of time between their cultures.

"I fell in love with your statue," she said truthfully.

"My statue?" Pasión's curiosity lit up like fire.

"Yes, that amazingly perfect one you made for Laurin as a present," Sofia said simply, but then she saw the shock in his eyes!

"I am only roughing it out!" Pasión's eyes looked at her incredulously while he made this incredible realization: "You saw a statue I made, which I myself have not completed and not seen yet."

Then he exclaimed, "And Laurin! How would you know about Laurin?"

Sofia understood that she should have been more careful and revealed things step by step, but it was too late, now everything fell on Pasión at once.

"Laurin wrote about you and his life with you on a series of scrolls," she explained.

"He wrote...," Pasión repeated the words, thinking. "He wrote about us on a series of scrolls... What a brilliantly strange idea! That's him: Laurin is always full of unusual ideas. And those scrolls survived 2500 years?"

"Yes," Sofia said. "I found that incredible, also. They were found on..." She wanted to say "on Laurin's funeral pyre," but she paused, careful not to say something that must be ghastly for him to hear. Strangely though, Pasión repeated the words.

"Laurin's funeral pyre. What a ghastly thought... but how can you read the scrolls if they were burned on the funeral pyre?"

This was when Sofia noticed: all the while they were talking, their lips did not move! They did not speak to each other at all. How could they, anyway, as they did not have a common language? Here, in this little nook of eternity, thoughts found their way into each other's minds without the need for either sound waves or vocabulary and grammar. (It is for this reason that human beings can very rarely meet here: that is only possible if their souls hold no secrets from each other.)

As Pasión thought of a question, Sofia found herself merely formulating an answer in her mind and he already heard it.

"Technology?" Pasión picked up on Sofia's thought. "What is technology?"

"It's a type of magic." Sofia organized her thinking in a way she hoped a man from the fifth century BC would understand. "Not the type of magic that works with thoughts and sentiments, but the kind that manipulates matter."

"Black magic, as my mother would call that kind."

"Your mother would be quite right," Sofia agreed. "This type of magic produced a lot of harm all over the world around us, but it can achieve quite some feats too. We have flying machines, which can transport us to the other side of the Earth within a day, while others can fly all the way to the moon. We can send messages anywhere in the world as fast as you can blink your eye, and we can see each other, hear each other from any long distance."

"How extraordinary!" Pasión opened his mind wide. He wanted to know more, more, and more… Suddenly, he had an ingenious idea.

"When you think about these things," he suggested, "can you try to remember using them?"

Sofia understood immediately what Pasión wanted: if she went back into her memories of everyday life, that would let him witness the twenty-first century! He would learn what she knew without having to explain anything.

So she began to remember for him… She remembered talking on the phone with David about the Hierophant… switching the lights on in the hotel room… flying the airplane… driving to the airport… going online… watching a film — and as she remembered, Pasión saw everything she saw as if seeing through her eyes, heard everything she heard as if listening with her ears, felt everything she felt as if touching through her skin. There was no limit to the thoughts, the knowledge, and the emotions they could exchange… They had eternity wrapped up in every single moment.

"This is most extraordinary," Pasión exclaimed again in awe. "More wondrous than anything I have seen any time in my life…" he — who had seen more in his young life than most mortals do in many lifetimes — said. Now he had seen more than Laurin and his philosopher friends, perhaps even more than the gods of his time… Pasión was feeling a vast, deep, and boundless connection with this woman of the future.

He wanted to know more, he wanted to know everything! Thus, he began to ask question upon question.

"Is Athens still standing in 2500 years?"

"Yes!" Sofia gave him a happy smile. "Thriving and growing, now it is the capitol of the whole of Hellas. Look." She recalled her memory of the Temple of Hephaestos. "After all these centuries, it is still standing!"

"Incredible! And Sparta?"

"We only remember it from history," Sofia thought. "Today, I don't even think there is a village left of it."

Sofia could sense great Athenian pride rising in Pasión upon learning this. She tried her best not to think of Sparta and Pasión's death through a Spartan spear, but failed, as a thought about trying not to think of something is a thought itself of the very same thing.

"I suppose," Pasión said thereupon, "it doesn't matter how I die and when I die. Here I am, with you in eternity, where I can see the future of thousands of years to come. What difference does a single of our human lives make, which is but a single step in the eternal journey of our consciousness?" As he said that, Pasión's mind lit up with a fabulous idea.

"Do you think I could live with you in the future?" he asked excitedly. "As a member of the Order, I will be learning occult knowledge about dreams and dying: I shall be able to direct my rebirth! Yes! I want to live in your time! I want to fly an airplane with you, Sofia, all the way to the moon. We shall find a hotel where we can switch the electric lights on and off at night."

"How would we find each other?" Sofia asked, taming her joy.

"I shall come somewhere great and famous… at some event, which cannot be missed or overlooked." Pasión was weaving his ideas further. "Are there still Olympic Games in your time?"

"Oh, yes…"

"For the whole of Hellas?"

"For the whole of the world!"

"How amazing! How wonderful! And the victor of a competition is still awarded a laurel wreath?"

"Actually, in my time, the winner is awarded a gold medal."

"A gold medal! I like that. And all the athletes fly there on airplanes?"

"Yes, all the athletes fly there on airplanes." Sofia laughed. "Even women athletes," she added meaningfully.

"Women are no longer confined to their kitchens?"

"No, women are no longer confined to their kitchens."

"Sofia!" Pasión grabbed her hands, trying to channel his excitement into a serious plan. "Let me try this! I know I have to die in my time first — eventually, everyone has to — but as consciousness continues, I shall…" Pasión held a dramatic pause. "I shall aim to be reborn in your time."

Sofia was only beginning to grasp the glory of what he just said, while he already went on.

"Tell me: when is the next Olympics?" he sounded practical and straightforward.

"It will be next year," Sofia said. "It will be held in Japan. In Tokyo, Japan," she said, and Pasión saw the proud memory of her Japanese father.

"And what will that be: next year?" he then asked.

"That will be the year 2020 after Christ," Sofia said, and upon these words, eternity almost felt as if it came to a standstill.

It became so quiet as if everything ever created held its breath. The moment became an eternal silence within eternity — and as such, it became impossible to forget.

At that special moment, Pasión made a pledge.

"I will be reborn in your time. I will come and meet you at the Olympic Games in the year 2020 after Christ." Pasión was looking forward to finding out who Christ was and where Tokyo, Japan was, but now it was not the right time to ask. "I will train for the competition, and I will become a champion so that you can see me. That way we will find each other — in your time — and we can be together in a physical life. Sofia, do you think that would be possible?" Pasión asked with great hope permeating his thoughts.

"I believe it would," Sofia said, as by this time, she had convinced herself. "If I can walk here in love with you, born 2500 years before me, how could I say that anything was impossible? If you have teachers who can navigate the higher dimensions and teach you how to navigate your rebirth, it will be possible for us to meet in my time. Next year, at the Olympics," Sofia said, with glorious hope… but also a sadness that she did not quite know where it was coming from.

Pasión noticed it and thought maybe she was tired from incessantly transmitting to him all this knowledge about the twenty-first century. Maybe she needed a rest…

"Please, come," Pasión said tenderly, "let me show you something also. Let me show you the tranquility of the ancients."

They were walking by a grove of precious jewel trees, under which Pasión found a bed of velvety moss. They lay down, wrapping themselves in each other's arms, with their backs against a wide tree, and looked into the horizon. The eternal day was coming to an eternal end: darkness fell on the sky behind the diamond trees.

"I have a good memory for any shape and color I have ever seen or heard. So, this will be like a film," Pasión announced, proud to use his newly gained knowledge about the future.

Lo and behold! As he said that, a wonderful image of an ancient theater appeared looming against the night sky. "This is one of my favorite memories. Laurin doesn't even know I was there. As a slave, I wasn't supposed to be let into the theater, but I wanted to see him act. He is a member of the chorus! My friend Plato sneaked me in, like into so many other places."

"Plato!" Sofia exclaimed.

"Yes, my friend Aristocles, but we nicknamed him Plato. Do you also know about him from Laurin's scrolls?"

"Not from Laurin's, but his own writings. He documented all his philosophy and the teachings of his elder, Socrates. Everybody knows Plato — he is remembered as the greatest philosopher of the ancient world: his wisdom is as fresh today as it was in your time."

"Excellent!" Pasión let out a pleased outburst. "I will tell him that, he shall love to hear it."

But then, Pasión brought his attention back to the theater. Pasión's memory and powers of perception were so sharp, that Sofia felt she was with him in that ancient outdoor theater… She could even feel the breeze of the place against her skin. How much quieter the world was back then, how much brighter the stars, how much mightier the darkness! Sofia felt her body relax deeply against Pasión's chest while she watched actors in masks and the chorus coming on stage. As the play went on, they gave voice to haunting words:

> *Worse, worse still will come!*
> *Dragged to the bed of a Greek!*
> *A curse upon such a night!*
> *A curse upon such a Fate!*

"This is when I began to forgive the Athenians," Pasión whispered to Sofia while they were watching his memory of the play together. "After they conquered my island town of Melos and enslaved whoever they did not kill, they staged this play. They did a horrible thing, but their conscience did not let them sleep at night. The best of them began to think about what they did. This is all about the horrors of war and the wrongs of conquest, killings, and rape."

> *Still, there is some good in this,*
> *because if the gods did not turn everything upside down,*
> *if they had not buried below the earth everything that was above it,*
> *the world would not have heard of us.*

"This voice," Sofia gasped as she heard something majestic. "There is this one voice coming out of the chorus, so much more powerful than all the rest combined."

"Yes, that is the voice of Laurin!" Pasión said. "His is a voice magically trained, it draws you in like nothing else in the world does."

The whole while, Sofia felt enchanted by this one voice, by the voice of Laurin. Even though she could have not possibly heard it before, it sounded so familiar. Even the words that concluded the end of the play, did not sound unknown to her:

> *The world would not be singing of us.*
> *The Muses would have no cause to sing about us*
> *to the coming generations of mortals...*

"Who was Laurin really?" Sofia pondered after she saw the memory of the play. "I want to know! Where can I read his seventh scroll?"

Pasión said that he didn't know about any scrolls in the writing.

"But there is a place, where I sometimes see Laurin going, when he is carrying secret writings of the Order with him. If he wanted to hide something, maybe he would take it there. On the left of the entrance to the great cave at the marble mines, there is a cleft between the rocks. A path spirals down from there. But I never dared to follow him more…"

"Left of the entrance to the great cave," Sofia repeated the words and thought of Davelis. Even though it had a bigger entrance in the future, Pasión thought it was the one he meant. As if her mind just waited for this essential information, now that she had it, she asked no more. She was no longer thinking of the past and the future, only of the blissful present moment. She let herself fall into the silky seduction of Pasión's embrace and eventually, fall asleep in his arms.

Pasión and Sofia were as content as only the lover and the beloved together can be. They no longer felt ancient or modern, Greek or English, man or woman, instead, they came together as one, sharing body and mind. They had seen the two worlds: the world of time — past, present, and future — and the world of no-time — the eternal moment of now in which the inner and outer world meet. They had learned that — in essence — they belonged to no place, and they were no-bodies: they only belonged to each other.

What they did not know was that eternity belongs to those who stay awake. As soon as they fell asleep, neither of them was any longer in eternity, and they were no longer together.

Chapter 12
The Barricade

Loneliness was overwhelming her. It had caught Sofia like an anaconda rising from a sunken jungle. At first, it even felt right: she was more familiar with this suffocating feeling in her heart than lying in eternity with her beloved. Soon, however, the snake wrapped her up into an invisible clasp which felt unbearable, yet it would not ease until she found Pasión again or Pasión found her.

After she had woken up by the trunk of an olive tree and found neither Pasión nor the precious jewel trees of eternity in sight, Sofia went back to the lake in the cave. There, she watched the surface of the water for three days and three nights. It was in vain: she did not see Pasión emerging again.

Then she drank from the Water of Memory and remained for another seven days and seven nights at the lake. Watching the surface of the water was still in vain: she never again saw Pasión emerging.

In futile despair, she returned to civilization, charged her gadgets, and finally called Alana.

"I am in Greece," Sofia told her on the phone. "Tomorrow, I can come and support your excavation."

Alana was overjoyed to hear from her, even though Sofia didn't tell her that she may now be hot on the trail to the seventh scroll. For now, Sofia kept that as her secret, as it was the only trace she had left from Pasión: she intended to follow it up and return to the mountains — alone.

The entrance to the cave at the ancient mine is abandoned today but easy to find. Over and over again through the centuries, the site had been defiled and damaged. The mouth of the cave is now torn wide open, so it is impossible to miss. Rumor has it that during the Cold War, overseas secret forces bulldozed down the stalagmite formations, which once guarded the entrance, as they wanted to extract marble dust from the cavity for building spaceships. This was perhaps true, perhaps just one of the many urban legends concerning the region. For uninitiated folks, the magic inherent in this place was ever so inextricable that it gave rise to many wild theories and strange tales of the supernatural.

Sofia kept away from the lore and began her own search in quiet contemplation. She turned left at the entrance of the cave, just as Pasión had told her, and there she found gigantic, sharp-edged rocks. She felt invited to climb them and took a seat on the largest and highest one. Up there, her eyes caught a tiny purple flower that made her way of life in an impossibly small rift in the rock. How resilient is life, she thought. The cave entrance, once destroyed, remains destroyed forever, but life — it can be killed a million times, a million times it comes back, transmitting its mighty secret, wrapped up invisibly into the smallest double helix. Life knows what matter does not: how to bring forth the knowledge of the past all the way into the future.

While Sofia was thinking along these lines, her eyes closed, and out of the darkness behind her lids, the memory of a voice emerged. Interestingly, it was not Pasión's, but Laurin's voice.

She noticed it had a certain frequency that somehow could reach beyond the human realm. It was magical and enigmatic, yet when Sofia tried to hum along, it came surprisingly easy for her. The same sound Laurin used effortlessly arose also from her own depths. Its majestic power filled her with such joy that she almost forgot about all her grief.

The frequency was most curious in its workings. Nothing changed in Sofia's surroundings except a certain quality of reality itself. The difference could be likened to a dream, in which the dreamer becomes aware that she is dreaming and learns to use the wonderful scope of the soft, malleable, liquid-like dream state to change anything or everything within the experience. Something similar happened to Sofia now, only in the reverse. While humming Laurin's tune, she knew she was awake, but the more she stayed with it, the more the world around her became like a dream. Reality began to liquify like ice in the springtime.

Sofia's mind opened as she began to walk: space expanded, matter lost its density, and the air blossomed with wondrous prospects. Holding the tune made her steps floaty. She walked into a cleft between the rocks and indeed, discovered something there! She found an inward-spiraling, narrow path that led her inside a hidden space among the rocks. But it was not too deep, and soon it seemed to come to an end, where nothing but rock walls surrounded her.

Ordinarily, Sofia would have simply turned around like a child disappointed that her fairytale adventure ended too early, shattered at the rocks of reality. However, walking in the dream, the narrower the path became, the wider Sofia's mind opened up, and the more convinced she became that there was a way in. She touched and tested the walls everywhere, almost hoping that in this dream-like state, she would be able to glide her hands through it. Instead, she found a carving. It looked hauntingly familiar. Sofia was sure she had seen it before — but how was that possible? She studied it for a little while: the image was hollowing inward, like an inverted relief. It gave her the impression of a keyhole.

However, it was bigger and had the form of a lyre.

Now she knew it. Reflectively, she took the ring off her finger.

With care, she placed it into the carving of the rock: the ring — like a key — fit perfectly, like into its own mold. Sofia turned it slightly, and that little turn began to move everything else with it. Slowly, ever so slowly, like in a story from the Arabian Nights, the rock, like an ancient door, began to slide: the mountain opened up and let Sofia step in. As soon as she took her ring back, the door closed behind her immediately. Still, she feared nothing: intuitively, she knew that the rocks didn't close to capture her: she had the ring, but the cave had to be protected from strangers.

Sofia was no stranger in here. Yet, she was the first person whose feet had touched this sacred hideout since 372 BC, the year Laurin died.

***

For now, in Pasión's life, that year was still in the future. It was not yet past, and the past was not yet legend. Twelve years had passed since Pasión, amidst his greatest fears at the slave market, saw Laurin and put all his trust and hope into him. Now, the year was 404 BC, and Pasión was about to receive his initiation.

"Ours is the oldest mystical Order in the world," Laurin said with kindly chiming pride. "It existed in times before the great flood, and it will exist until the last human walks the Earth. Yet, it has no name, no institutions, and no processions. Currently, some call us the inner circle of the Orphic Mysteries, and there is some truth in that, but we have learned that names change as fast as the wind blows, and Truth must never be put into a creed. We found that churches, sects, and organized mysteries sooner or later become corrupt and fall into the mire, as all human institutions are bound to. What is essential about our Order neither can be named nor needs to be invented: it arises from our innate call to eventually overcome the human condition. Even if all of us died and all our words would be forgotten, new members would rise in generations to come who naturally carry and continue our aspirations. Pasión, are you listening?"

Indeed, Pasión was just staring into the fire as if he wanted to see behind the flames like he had looked behind the water surface, from where Sofia's voice emerged.

"I'm sorry, Laurin," he said truthfully. "I cannot concentrate or think of anything else."

Yes, Pasión could hardly handle the existential despair that came over him after he had lost connection to Sofia and her world. It made his torment even harder that Laurin ordered him not to talk about his experience. He said whatever happened in Little Eternity was a concern for the Assembly: until it was convoked, Pasión had to wait with the powerful first telling of his narrative. Laurin tried to distract him by talking about the Order until he noticed that Pasión was in serious distress.

"Are you grieving," he then asked him, "because the experience you had filled you with so much love that you cannot bear having lost it?"

Almost invisibly, Pasión nodded. It freed up his emotions that Laurin seemed to know what he was going through. The hot drop of a tear fell on his cheek, which felt cold against the crazy dancing flames of the fire. Laurin caressed away the tear on Pasión's face with his long, silver-covered fingers and said, "If so, it'll be all right. You can go back to Little Eternity as many times as you like. Each time, you can only remain for as long as you can stay awake, but the portal will remain open for you. I'm only asking you: don't go back before the Assembly has heard your narrative. That way, we can all help you."

"Really?" Pasión lifted his face, relieved. "This is great news, thank you."

Laurin pulled him up from the chair and wrapped him in his arms and all Pasión's angst and loneliness melted away in an instant.

"Let us go and call the Assembly," Laurin decided, "so that we don't lose any further time."

This was elevating. Pasión quickly regained his curious enthusiasm, wondering where they would go to call the Assembly, but Laurin only went as far as the threshold of his cabin. There he took a deep breath and began to vibrate his voice. He created a tune that resembled the sound he used to call the horses, but this one was deeper and more intricate, blended with melody and words. It had the power to pass through mineral, plant, and animal life to reach the human minds it was intended to reach.

"Could they hear that?" Pasión asked, disbelieving, as Laurin returned to the hearth, like after a job well done.

"They received it, yes," Laurin said. "All the initiated can feel this vibration, which will prompt them to come."

"When will they be here?"

"It may take days, even weeks," Laurin said. "Most of the initiates are traveling and may have to come from far away. Let's hope they are not on the other side of the world, and it won't take months."

It didn't take months, but it certainly felt like it. Waiting during all this time, there wouldn't have been much more for Pasión to do but watch the sky, day-dreaming that an airplane might fly by and take him to be with Sofia. As he knew, however, that this wouldn't happen for now, he returned to his statue in the making.

Behind the screen where he worked, he had an obsidian mirror Diona gave him before they had to part. It was Melian, which Laurin bought for her once, at the market in Athens. Now Pasión used it to ensure that the statue had precisely his features.

While working, he thought of Sofia, but he also thought of Laurin — he thought of Laurin, but he also thought of Sofia. He knew, in the present, he would gift the statue to Laurin, but in the future, Sofia would find it.

While working, some poor artists have their hands guided by the knowledge of their craft. Others are luckier and are guided by the Muses. But Pasión's hand was neither moved by skill nor inspiration alone; he was the truly blessed one, as his hands were moved by Eros, the Demon. He was no longer simply chiseling the marble, he made love to it. Before every touch, he took a deep breath in, and with every touch, he exhaled that breath into the statue. When it became more complete and beautiful, he placed his body so close that the life force of his heart beating reverberated in ecstatic reverence into the cold stone.

Without being aware of it, Pasión was applying an ancient technique of magic that was not without danger, because by doing this, he infused the artwork a little bit with life. His own life. With every touch he applied, he left a little grain of his soul in the statue, binding himself to it for a very long time to come.

For now, he was working, day in and day out. He forgot about himself, and he forgot about time… until he chiseled the last touch and gave the marble one last kiss.

He stepped back and he marveled: Pasión had surprised himself. His master-piece was completed.

"We are ready," miraculously, he heard Laurin's musical voice calling him at the very same minute. "The Assembly has arrived. We are ready to commence your initiation."

How glorious it will be, Pasión thought to himself, when the initiation ceremony is over, I can present Laurin with my gift.

The initiation! Pasión followed Laurin with awesome expectations of perhaps some grand ceremony or solemn meeting. Quite to the contrary, the Order was beyond anything theatrical, and certainly beyond applying tricks for the mind. It staged no mystical dances, brewed no magic mushrooms, and burned no sacred fumes. Still, meeting the Assembly was the most other-worldly, hallowed experience Pasión had ever lived through.

A small group had gathered in one of the larger caves. They were sitting in a circle of seven little fires, without any robes or masks to impress. Yet, as Pasión entered with Laurin, the small Assembly of Seven began to hum a delicate, ethereal tune. At first, it was barely audible, but in a short while, the sound resonated throughout the entire cave. The vibration it set off hit Pasión as hard as a spear piercing through his heart, but the pain was not caused by the humming, but rather by some hidden recognition that he had been missing this for his entire life: this community of pure love. The pain softened, as a deep remembrance allowed this love to spread across his whole being. He felt the mystical presence of Chairon, his mother, and all his invisible helping friends, as well as Laurin's love, seven-fold, enveloping him everywhere around.

Pasión looked at the others. They understood him. Their eyes twinkled at him by the peaceful fires. Once upon a time, at their own initiations, they had also awakened to the same truth which now hit Pasión so hard: that genuine love was virtually unknown in our current human realm, people mistaking longing and lust, controlling, and clinging to it. Only the initiates were ever fortunate enough to have love in their lives and love in their fellowship.

The group was hauntingly interesting, like an occult family to Pasión which he hadn't known before yet always missed. Some of them, it seemed, were foreigners: yes, there was a man from the land of the Himalayas and a priestess from the distant North who had ice-crystal blue eyes and long, white hair. A little girl, not older than nine years of age, ran to Pasión as soon as he sat down. With the unspoiled innocence of a child, she flung her arms around him and stayed sitting in his lap. Pasión could not explain it, but he too felt unparalleled affection towards this little one.

His attention was grasped by a tall man whose skin was so black he must have come from Africa — a rare sight indeed in the Greece of his time. Pasión marveled at him in the flickering of the fires, as it amazed him how old he appeared: not his face, not his body, but his being felt immeasurably old. In the group, he seemed to be the first among equals... but as Pasión kept observing him, he realized, this man wasn't quite their equal. He recalled his mother and Laurin telling him about higher members of the Order who have transcended the human realm and came back to help others. Could this man be one...

"Are you the Hierophant?" Pasión asked him in awe.

The old man modestly shook his head.

"I'm an elder of the Order," he said. "I've been around for a long time, my stone is now of Sapphire, but it is not yet Diamond. I am not yet a Hierophant. The only enlightened one we currently know of on Earth is the Buddha in the East, but we are anticipating a birth soon in the West, too. My name is Nákash."

Pasión bowed to the wise man.

"Now, sit with us," Nákash told him, "and tell us whom you have met in your Tunnel of Destiny."

"It was Sofia," Pasión began to talk: it came like a flow. How relieved he was that he no longer had to hold in the unspeakable! He hoped these members of the Order would somehow be able to illuminate Sofia's mystery for him.

So, he told them about his wondrous tale with the woman from the future, and they listened with such great curiosity that it lifted Pasión's words up like wings. As well as he could, he told them about the terrific technologies of her time, and they listened like children enchanted by stars and galaxies. He told them about the Olympics still to be held in two and a half thousand years, and finally, he told them about his promise to meet her there.

"Yours is a great story," Nákash said at the end. "The best of all. Here on Earth, minds live through various stories: there are stories of warriors who are either barbaric or brave, artists who go mad or become gods, kings who may be tyrants or wise rulers, priests who torture, and priests who enlighten. There are wonder-filled stories of healers and saints, but yours, Pasión, the story of the lover, is the primordial reason for the universal mind to create anything: its ultimate glory and consolation is to gain the capacity for love and to experience being loved by the Other."

Everyone in the Assembly listened attentively, some nodded: undisputedly, they understood the utmost importance of it all.

"Your story is your destiny," Nákash continued. "And the sole purpose of our Order is to help you, like all our initiates, to fulfill your destiny."

"But… what is my destiny?" Pasión asked out loud. He had heard so much: his mother taught him that we are here to overcome the human condition. Chairon taught him to follow his dreams. Laurin taught him that the way of overcoming evil in ourselves is not by suppressing it but by knowing it. Still, "I don't know what my personal destiny is," he said.

Behind the fourth fire, the Nordic priestess moved her beautiful head.

"Was there nothing while you were with Sofia in Eternity," she asked, "which made your heart laugh and your whole being shiver with child-like excitement?"

"Yes!" Pasión exclaimed. "When I thought that I wanted to be reborn in Sofia's time and find her."

"Then that is your destiny," Nákash said in his deep, powerful voice. "Do it. Do what you want!"

"Can it be that simple?" Pasión asked, stunned.

"There is nothing simple about it," Nákash replied. "You said yourself how many false desires you had to push aside in the Tunnel of Destiny before you saw Sofia in the Water of Memory. But when you find your true desire, you need not worry about anything else, as it matches the desire of god."

"Your words sound so wonderful and make my soul sing!" Pasión said. "Yet, I always thought that our higher destiny was more like being in the service of others."

"Yes, that's right, in the service of the Other. And do you think you can be of any better service to Sofia than by finding her?"

The question swayed across the room like a wave of liberty and brought about a festive frame of mind. The members began to rise to stand around the fires.

"It is time," Nákash announced, "that you become a member of the Order. Seven of us are ready to vow to help you fulfill your destiny. Are you ready to vow that you will help seven others to fulfill theirs?"

"Yes, I am," Pasión said, and his knees began to shake.

And so Nákash began:

> *Seven to help Pasión*
> > *say after me*
>
> *I vow*
> > *…I vow*
>
> *that I'll do everything in my power*
> > *…everything in my power*
>
> *in this life and all the next*
> > *…and all the next*
>
> *to help you find Sofia*
> > *…find Sofia.*
>
> *Put your hand into the fire,*
> *if your vow is sincere,*
> *your skin shall not be harmed.*

One by one, the seven members of the Order who were present put their hands into the blue flaming fires in front of them: at first came the little girl, who showed no fear, and as the seventh, came Laurin. Last, Pasión vowed that he would help seven members of the Order when the time was right to fulfill their destinies. He, too, put his hand into the fire: it was hot and fearsome as he was moving towards it, but his skin felt enveloped into powerful icy coldness while inside.

After the vows were taken, the members — one by one — left the cave, like after a simple work well done, although none of them departed without giving Pasión a heart-felt embrace and words of welcome into the Order. Only the little girl, still clinging to Pasión, lingered on and Nákash, the wise old man, waited to take her home.

"Do you remember each other?" he asked with a kind smile, as he watched the little one still clinging to Pasión.

"Remember?" Pasión looked stunned.

"Everybody," Nákash said, "who was here today, has known you before, in some other place, at some other time, in another life. Aliana," he turned to the little girl, "do you remember anything about Pasión?"

"Yes, he is quite a man now." These words came out of her mouth so unexpectedly, that they surprised even the little girl, Aliana, herself. She then started to ponder and said, "Although I don't remember him, I'm very happy with him. He must be someone I very, very much loved."

"Yes, you loved him very, very much," Nákash repeated her words. "And you will remember him. Your destiny is to remember the past, the present, and the future and how it is all connected."

The little girl looked again at Pasión. Suddenly, her face grew dark.

Her eyes looked as if they had seen something sinister behind the veils of this world.

"He gave us human flesh to eat, didn't he?" she whispered.

"Human flesh to eat," Pasión repeated, while chills went down his spine and goosebumps exploded on his arms. "You knew it? Are you talking about Moris, my brother... you remember Moris?"

"Be careful with him, he is full of darkness," the little girl said, but it seemed someone else from inside her spoke those words. Aliana carried the past in her. The words became distressed. "I haven't eaten for so long," she mumbled. "I feel weak... concerned that I won't be alive for long enough to bring you into the Order."

The realization came to Pasión as a miracle, a most daunting miracle.

"You were my mother," he said out loud and pulled little Aliana close to his heart while he saw Nákash quietly nodding. Their reunion was a transcendent joy. It was also a tremendous, heavy-weight perception that life, after all, was much greater than the skin capsule of the body or the daily thoughts running through the brain.

"You have brought me into the Order," Pasión said to her softly, still holding her. "You have given me your pendant, which saved my life by bringing me to Laurin, and Laurin brought me into the Order."

Aliana gave him a wholehearted but fading smile, which showed that she understood but had become fatigued.

"She is only learning now to remember her cosmic past," Nákash explained to Pasión, "and it is a tiring task. I shall take her home now. Come, we'll walk you back, too."

So, it happened that Pasión arrived back at Laurin's Grove hand in hand with the little girl, Aliana, and together with Nákash, the wise one. Laurin, however, was not there.

"What a pity," Pasión said. "I wanted to ask him whether I could go back to the Tunnel of Destiny. I can't wait to tell Sofia the good news that you will all be helping me to find her in her own time."

"No more do you need to ask Laurin," Nákash told him. "You are now an initiate of our Order, which means you are a free man in society as well as in spirit: nobody else can ever tell you what you shall or shall not do. Climb the tunnel yourself, if you can, and tell her. Do what you want!"

How strange does freedom sound, when for so long we have been used to bondage? How unheard of to do what we want! Still, Pasión did not need to be told twice: with endless gratitude to Nákash and overflowing adoration to Aliana, he said goodbye.

He then went and got himself some ropes. He fixed a tiny oil lamp onto his forehead like he saw the mining slaves wearing in his vision. He felt guided by a call from the future as he began to descend into the cave. Without thinking, only following the memories, hopes, and dreams of his body, he knew where to place his legs, and where to position his arms to let himself down safely into the sanctum. He was absolutely sure that once he got to the Water of Memory, it would not take him too long to push aside any distracting desires: the erotic tension spanning over twenty-five centuries was almost unbearable; all he could think of was touching Sofia, all his intent was single-mindedly focused on getting back to her.

Even so, he could not. When he reached the end of the triangle-shaped corridor, something was blocking his way. At first, he thought it was a large stone, then he saw it was the back of a man who lay there motionless, seemingly asleep. Pasión touched his shoulders lightly, upon which the man roared like an animal as if such a small move had caused him great pain.

"Do you think," he let out an angry outcry, "I will just let you abandon me for some… woman? I am your real family!" the man said and turned around.

"Laurin!" Pasión called out, shocked as he saw his face! "Are you blocking my way to Sofia?! You took a vow to help me. You took a vow to help me!" he shouted.

Determined not to let anyone or anything obstruct his way, Pasión pushed him angrily into the water and tried to jump in after him.

Yet, as he dived in, he hit his head hard. There was no water. It had all been turned into stone, which barricaded his way from getting back into Little Eternity.

Chapter 13
The Lesser of Two Evils

"**M**elos? Anyone else for Melos?"

The captain of the ship shouted his last call, roaring deep into the twilight wind. Most of his passengers had already boarded, but he knew there was always somebody late — somebody distracted on their journey. Lo and behold! A lone rider came galloping towards his ship.

"Melos, yes," the rider said as he arrived in front of him. "I want to go to Melos."

"Of course." The captain smiled broadly. "Who wouldn't want to go to Melos — the most beautiful island in the whole of the Mediterranean? Ever been there, sir?"

The rider ignored the question but declared to pay a good price if he could travel in style and receive good service and meals on board.

"Of course, sir." The captain nodded as he swept his eyes across the newcomer. No, he didn't mind when this kind of traveler was aloof and rude: the captain only saw his stunning stallion and his fine linen clothes; he only saw his expensive jewelry and money bag. He knew this one alone would pay more than all the other folks on board combined, and money was badly needed these days. More and more seaways got blocked by the war, and a lot of merchandise ended up at the bottom of the sea instead of its designated destination.

So, when the new traveler asked to be seated on deck, the captain and his crew laid out silken pillows and woolen blankets for him, as well as ordered a slave girl to serve him honeyed wine, cheese, and olives, or anything else this fine young man with the silver coins wanted.

But damn it! Pasión alone knew the truth.

He may have fooled the captain and the crew into believing that his journey was in pursuit of pleasure but lying to himself turned out to be much harder. As the ship gracefully left the harbor, Pasión may have been on his way home, had his cup filled with wine, and this tasty girl seated at his feet, nonetheless the sea felt to him like a deadly abyss — a hideout of sinister forces that conspired to haul him away from everything he knew, loved, and valued. Worse still! Even though he was returning to Melos not only as a free man but as a man with money, as an initiate, and as an artist who just completed a historic masterpiece, he couldn't help but feel that his journey to Athens — yes, when he was brought as a miserable, frightened slave in pain — had still been the better one. Back then, like a spider using his own silk, he succeeded in weaving a web out of his dreams, attracting love and magic for himself. Now, this web was torn, and Pasión was falling, falling, falling into a dark abyss hitherto unknown.

His world had changed overnight, and it changed without mercy. Yesterday, Pasión was beloved and surrounded by sparkling mysteries. His life was full of adventure, holding the promise of an unspeakably hopeful future... Today, he was finding himself alone on this alienated planet where he could touch no one and no one could touch him.

Few of us could ever imagine how devastated Pasión became by losing Laurin. Those who feel like established members of the regular human race — those who are part of a family, a village, or a tribe — will never fully understand his misery. Only those of us with a certain magic in our veins, who are homesick for the stars, and sometimes sense our souls belonging to a better world, can understand how rare it was to find someone of our kind. If you find them but afterward lose the One, you lose everything: your whole world.

In the life and the love Pasión had with Laurin, every moment was an immersion into a better world: grander, more beautiful, and yet to come on Earth. Every moment with him brought upon the unshakeable conclusion that the essence of the universe was magic. There was this ongoing revelation that life was worth living. Laurin understood how to transform suffering into awesome hard training, sadness into reaching for beauty, and all hardship into some lesson for strength. Despite his toughness and affinity for discipline, Laurin loved like silk and never let stern philosophy or civic ideas of righteousness get in the way of humanity and passion. So why, why, why? Why did he have to destroy all of this out of petty jealousy? Why wasn't Laurin wise enough to know that Pasión wouldn't love him less because of Sofia, even if she had something Laurin could never give him: the future. "And why?" Pasión also asked himself. "Why did I leave him on such a whim?"

But, of course, it wasn't on a whim, was it? He could no longer allow Laurin to treat him like his property, tell him where to go, and what to do. Pasión needed to grow out of such dependency and — as painful as it was — take ownership of his life. Therefore, even if it felt strange that he was using his freedom to go back to hell, where his town was beleaguered, his people destroyed, and his house burnt, he decided to go home.

The journey on sea lasted long, which gave Pasión some wanted and a lot of unwanted time to reflect. Like in a film, which kept playing on his mind, he saw the tragic events of the past day, over and over again...

Over and over, he saw himself climbing out of that cave again... he was so full of fear and fury that he just ran around for hours like a madman incapable of comprehending the calamity that had happened to him. He saw himself, again and again, wandering amidst the thorny bushes all night long, treading on many little marble paths, lost and disoriented. When the sun rose — and that was stranger still — he heard Laurin's voice calling him, as if forth from the night and out of this dark loneliness.

But then how casual Laurin was about the tragedy he caused! In a most bizarre way, he suddenly just stood there in front of Pasión, in the company of Nákash and with the two horses set up with provisions for a journey. Laurin told Pasión that he must come with him. He said that he must come with him!

"We can talk about it later," Laurin dared to push aside Pasión's objections. "We must go immediately to Athens. There is a lot of political upheaval, and I'm worried, especially for Diona's safety."

"Diona is your slave, not mine," Pasión threw at him angrily. "She's not my problem. But that horse is mine. Plato gave it to me."

"Yes, that horse is yours," Laurin said in a soft, sad voice. It disturbed Pasión to think back that neither Laurin nor Nákash said anything else or tried to stop him as he jumped on his horse and rode away in a frenzy.

No, Pasión did not understand anything anymore. On the way to the ship, Pasión bathed himself in a stream and cleansed his clothes — why then did he feel so filthy still? Everyone knew Diona and Pasión were sweet lovers, brought together by Laurin — why then did he pretend he didn't care for her? On the ship, he touched the hair of the slave girl which was silken soft and smelled of almond blossom – why then did he send her away in anger?

In hindsight, how awful he felt about everything! He had ridden away like a thief in the night: only after he was far on his way did he notice that his horse was not only carrying food but a bag of Laurin's silver. Now he was rich and free, miserable, and unloved.

As the ship arrived at Melos, the island looked nothing like that devastated ghost town Pasión remembered from the time he was taken away from there. The streets were vibrant with the yellow, purple chitter-chatter of merchants and citizens enjoying a winter season in the sun. All these men, selling and buying, taking boat rides in the bay, and gossiping about the latest battles, were Athenians, and Pasión felt quite at home among them. They had cleared away the corpses, restored the bungalows, fed the cats, and put geraniums into the windows. Like many generations in history, people were quite happy to live on in oblivion and walk on the buried dead, letting children roll their balls where not long-ago blood was flowing.

The topography of the old streets hadn't changed: Pasión's legs took him on the best-known path back to his old house. Here he was, walking again, as a free man who lost the freedom of his heart, as a mystical initiate who lost his magic, as a son who lost his mother yet again, but also as an artist who had not lost anything, only gained experiences through his extraordinary life.

The house did not fail to shock him. The bitterness was in the contrasts. On the street, Pasión found — instead of a burned ruin — a beautifully rebuilt facade. Someone was putting generous piles of money into the building, yet — remarkably — the renewed house did not look Athenian. It appeared not only through and through Melian, but exactly like Pasión's family home brought back to life! The entrance waited, unlocked, so Pasión, with a natural sense of ownership, simply walked through.

What a strange sort of hell he discovered inside! Parts of the house were rebuilt and refurbished: overabundant with Persian rugs and carved, silver-inlaid furniture, it seemed as if some profiteer tradesman had moved in. Other parts, however, which were smutted but not destroyed by the fire, were left untouched: blackened by soot and ashes, it all looked like a spooky, nightmarish version of Pasión's once beloved home. Even the pillow on which his mother's head rested in her final moments was still on the sofa, sticky from fire, littered by mice.

This is disgraceful, Pasión thought to himself. Perhaps I had to come to finish the work of the fire.

Inside, he could no longer linger on; his legs took him to the yard. Eerily, everything was there as he left it: the life-size alabaster statue of Aphrodite he was working on last still stood, untouched. Pasión looked at it like an old man would look at the gawky drawings of a child. The old man knows the value of a child's drawing, which is not, of course, in its artistic excellence, it is in the trying: without the efforts of the child and the mistakes of the youngster, great art of that ripe age would never come into being.

The striking difference between this unfinished alabaster statue from the past and his current artwork left Pasión quite amazed. Here was a piece of alabaster shaped like a human. There, in Laurin's valley stood his soul, wrapped in a timeless coat of marble, infused with eternal love and magic, ready to come off the pedestal, whenever his lover would be lonely...

"Do you need a chisel?" he suddenly heard a voice asking from the entrance gate of the garden.

No, I need a pick-axe, Pasión thought to himself, but then turned around to see who it was...

And there he stood — not as a dark vision from some underground tunnel, but in his life-sized, sun-tanned, flesh-and-blood reality: Moris, his brother. With a broad, welcoming smile, as he saw Pasión, he opened up his arms to a wide embrace.

***

Laurin returned to Athens and immediately wanted to see Socrates. Perhaps he was hoping for some calm thoughts from his old philosopher friend, but instead, Socrates arrived more agitated than Laurin ever was. It was no surprise: after he'd seen Athens rising like a Phoenix from the fire of the Persian war, he now had to watch his city plunge back into chaos and even darker times. Day by day, he watched citizens limping back from battles no one remembered any more. Night by night, he heard neighbors' screams, as men were slaughtered on the streets for having the wrong friends and women were dragged away for having false friends.

"I'm training my mind to accept being killed by a Spartan spear," Socrates pondered out loud, as he took the cup of that potent red wine Laurin handed over to him. The two of them had gathered for a friendly, private conversation in Laurin's study.

"Are you mad?" Laurin raised his eyebrows at such an idea of nonsense. "Why would you train your mind towards such a poor outcome?"

"It wouldn't be such a poor outcome," Socrates countered. "I'd rather die by a noble enemy than in the crossfires of our own idiotic domestic disputes."

"Are the Spartans such a noble enemy?" Laurin asked, while he poured a little bit of wine into his own water too — for him to do so was the exception of all exceptions. But, of course, Socrates noticed the reason, as the boy was missing.

"Oh yes, they are," Socrates said regarding the Spartans. "We are killing each other: they need do nothing else than wait until we bleed ourselves out. The Spartans are loyal to themselves and harmonious in their ways. And they know how to embrace the good in life!" the old man said with a sigh as if recalling some long-gone memory of beauty. "Watched as their naked women danced on the foamy banks of the Eurotas, chanting their way into the night under the starry sky. Oh, Spartan women — good heavens, they are strong, muscular, and smart — I could love them like I love the boys. No, I'm telling you, my friend, it would be no shame to die of a Spartan spear."

"Why are you talking like this, Socrates?"

"I don't know. It's some strange presentiment," Socrates said, with some darkness in his voice. Then suddenly, he asked, "Where is he?"

"Who?"

"He, of course."

"Well, I gave him his freedom," Laurin admitted. "And he took it."

"Never mind." The old philosopher shrugged his shoulders. "He'll come back soon."

"Yes, he will," Laurin said to convince himself.

He looked around, and he almost felt as if Pasión was there in the room with them. They were certainly not alone. Yes, he had a sense of being stared at, and as he turned, a pair of moist, deer-brown eyes were watching from the corridor.

They belonged to Diona.

She waited patiently for the two men to finish, but when Socrates left, the same sacred second, she ran up to Laurin, and in defiance of all manners and etiquette, nestled herself to his chest.

Surprised, Laurin began to feel his way into her current being. She was frightened and delightful. He drew her closer in and laid a protective arm around her bare shoulder.

"Master, thank you for being back," Diona quietly said, in a voice shaking. "I've been so afraid."

Laurin let his hand slide down her long river hair, letting her be tight in his embrace. He always knew Diona was charming and essentially one of their kind, but tonight her aura held something ever so magnificent, it actually entranced him. Despite her fear, somehow the girl was filled with celestial harmony and joy.

"What are you afraid of?" Laurin kindly asked her.

Diona looked at him with those large, deer-like eyes, but only shook her head.

"I cannot tell you," she said timidly. "I shall not provoke your anger."

"Diona." Laurin took her head between his two hands. "Have you done something wrong?"

"No!" Diona was quick to say. "No... just Medea said some owners get really mad about this kind of thing. Alcibiades killed one of his girls..."

"That old hag again!" Laurin exclaimed. "And you don't think I'm such as monster as Alcibiades, do you?!" He felt offended by the name alone: wasn't it enough that this megalomaniac father and his son split and pushed Athens to the brink of war with Sparta, now he was bringing fear into Laurin's home.

"No, of course not!" Diona urgently said. "You're a good man, Master, a very good man. Perhaps that's why I'm so scared to anger you."

Laurin noticed that Diona was not only scared but deeply confused, so he invited her to lie down with him.

"It's all right," he soothed her. "Just breathe with me. Sleep here with me tonight, until you relax to tell me what is causing you fear."

Laurin felt his strongest protective instinct rising even before he noticed why. He felt Diona's body turning more serene in his arms as she took over his slow and calm breathing rate. As it was in his nature, Laurin allowed his hand to glide over her body, dispensing his healing life force. It felt good to touch her, not only because her skin was silky soft and smelled of almond blossom but... sweet Muses! What was this extraordinary beauty and power she carried? As he slowed down his movements, Laurin noticed with astonishment that Diona's physique somehow or other contained even more magic than his own life force-infused body.

Could this be? When Laurin finally felt what this was, he still couldn't quite believe his senses. Could this really be? He pushed himself up on his elbow and kept his hand over Diona's belly.

"Diona," he said to her in awe. "You're not alone. You are carrying a child."

"Yes," Diona said, surprised how he would know. "Are you not angry, Master?"

Laurin silently shook his head, disbelieving the question.

"I feel most delighted," he assured her. "I'm not quite sure what is happening," he whispered to Diona as much as to himself, "but the child you are carrying is not an ordinary human."

Resting his hand over Diona's womb, Laurin detected the finest vibration of life emanating from it.

"He feels pure like only those can be who have transcended the human realm," Laurin spoke. His voice sounded amazed; his eyes sparkled with zest. "I don't know how we have possibly deserved and attracted this bliss to us."

What an unexpected, most welcome miracle this was! Amidst all the darkness into which Laurin's world was threatened to sink, with Pasión gone and the Spartan enemy lurking around like packs of wolves, a Hierophant was about to be born!

"Is Pasión the father?"

"Yes, of course," Diona said, startled. "Master, I would never… without your permission…"

Laurin nodded and smiled.

"He will come back," he said, caressing Diona's hair. "Pasión will come back."

"Will he?"

"Yes. He left because he thought I did something against him. Something dreadful. But it wasn't me. When he finds that out, he will return. And now he will definitely return when he finds out that he will be a father. I hope that it will be sooner, rather than later."

The night — as Pasión would say — wrapped them in sonorous star shine. Diona snuggled up to Laurin and began to let go of the terror… Now that he was here and approved of the child, Diona knew, her baby was safe.

"Laurin," she whispered to him, sharing at last her fear, "I'm so relieved you are not angry… You've arrived just in time."

"Just in time… for what?" Laurin asked with a dark presentiment on his mind.

"Medea said that masters get angry for unwanted children in the house. She wanted to take care of it — as she put it — this morning, so it's gone before you knew about it."

Upon these words, it was as if the gloomy gates of Hades had all opened. It broke into Laurin's consciousness with full realization of what great evil he was harboring throughout the years!

"Medea…" Laurin repeated the name one last time. "She will never cause harm again to you or the baby. Don't worry. I'm your owner, therefore your child is also mine, and I promise you, Diona, that I will keep both of you safe and out of harm's way. There is only one task for you to do now. Raise the quality of your thoughts and feelings as high as possible. We shall sleep side by side, every night, and we shall use the master bedroom, for your best comfort. You will spend your days exclusively playing uplifting music and talking to my sophist friends, Socrates and Plato, who will be invited every day. Your child is divine, Diona. Nothing but the best preparation for his arrival shall suffice."

Very early in the morning, while Diona was still asleep, Laurin went straight to the kitchen. There they were: Kosmas, the garden slave, and the hag, Medea.

"You must leave my house," he said to her without evasion. "Take all your belongings and the money I allowed you to collect and never come back!"

"You cannot send me away," Medea said in a voice that sounded disgustingly confident. "You have vowed to your parents that you will keep me forever. As an initiate of the Order, you must keep your vows!"

"As an initiate of the Order," Laurin repeated the words, repulsed that she dared to speak them, "I must keep the Hierophant safe. I am choosing the lesser of two evils. Go!"

Laurin ordered Kosmas to ensure that the old hag was removed from the house and never again could try to harm Diona again. Kosmas, who ever so often had to execute Medea's mad and cruel orders, was only too happy to comply.

Laurin, himself, rushed to the market. He wanted to get there during these hours of dawn when all the women and slave girls were at the wells and exchanged news. He told as many of them as he could that Diona was pregnant, and the father was Pasión. Quickly, he made it sound like he was giving out a great secret, ensuring that the message spread across the land as fast as wildfire. Laurin gave silver coins to every beggar, to all the waifs and stray kids who agreed to tell every-one that Pasión was to become a father. Laurin wanted the news to reach his love soon. He didn't know that Pasión was long gone from Attica, and he also did not know what great peril lay in hoping to rush his return.

When Laurin returned to his home, he saw something was terribly wrong. Someone had forced the entrance gate open. It was a horrible déjà vu — similar to the time when Medea forcefully cut off Diona's magical hair. He rushed into the kitchen: it was empty, Kosmas must have already gone to work. As he hurried down the corridor, the worst fear of his life grabbed Laurin: what if Diona and her divine child were in peril? In his house! Under his watch!

He reached the master bedroom, where he saw his worst presentiment realized. Medea had broken her way back into the house! And it was not just her, an evil greater than her was working through her body, holding a knife in her hands.

The whole murderous scene unfolded with cruel precision and in slow motion in front of his very eyes. Diona had just risen from the bed and stood with her back to the door, unaware of any peril. Unsuspectingly, with one casual move, she turned around, making her pregnant belly a perfect target. Medea, on the other hand, moved with a precision that looked impossible from a rickety old woman like that. It seemed as if her motions were directed by a grander, darker force — the kind that can jeopardize the very existence of the Order itself. Medea's half-blind eyes were suddenly sharp with vision; she threw the knife with the perfect use of force and focused straight at the abdomen.

Laurin's combat-trained eyes knew that the knife would be right on target even before it hit Diona.

He jumped.

He allowed everything he knew, he had, he valued to jump with him.

The past he didn't want to lose, the present he did not want to die, and the future he so desperately wanted to believe in, all jumped with him. Not only did his muscles move, but the life force that circulated in his veins activated fully and so did the universal mind that allows creation to unfold as a delicate balance between good and bad, but always interferes to halt ultimate evil.

Laurin jumped and caught the knife in mid-air.

He then turned and stabbed the old hag right in the heart. Medea fell dead on the spot.

Chapter 14
The Last Symposium

Never before did Pasión find his brother Moris to be so kind and considerate as he was now. Moris seemed possessed by a jolly good mood as he saw Pasión again: he flung his big, pudgy arms around him and patted his back merrily.

"We will be family again," he said over and over again. "I was hoping you'd be back one day. Look, I even bought you arty stuff."

With these words, Moris proudly presented him with items he kept locked in the garden shed.

"Here, I got you chisels and drills — these are of various sizes; I got marble and ivory for you to work with, and sheets of gold leaf to decorate."

Pasión looked amazed. Still, the moment seemed coerced. Like olive paste under pressure, he felt emotions being pressed out of him: he couldn't help but remember how he wished he had all these things once upon a time in this garden. What would he have given if his father permitted him marble? What would he have given if his brother stood at his side instead of laughing art off? However, once these sentiments were extracted, all that remained in him was the hard mark of suspicion.

"Interesting," Pasión said. "Previously, all your life, you made fun of art, like it was the greatest lunacy."

"Why would I have done that?" Moris opened his eyes wide. "I think you remember I was teasing you a lot, but all older brothers do that."

Moris seemed to be thinking while he continued, "I'm not as stupid as I used to be, you know. I've changed. Those mines have changed me."

Moris sat down under the young fig tree as he said that.

"I can imagine," Pasión said while he thought how oblivious his brother was about sitting on their mother's grave. "I am sorry that you had to endure that."

"Yes, I hated you," Moris suddenly admitted. "Every minute in the mines I hated you. Like I hated you when we were kids, and you were Mamma's little miracle boy: so beautiful and brainy. You were the talented one with those fine fingers and eyes that changed color in the freakin' moonlight. And I was just this ugly thug of a kid who only had his fist. Yes, I always wanted to beat you up because you got on my nerves! While in the mines, I pictured you day in, and day out as the silky lover of some posh Athenian. I called you a traitor in my thoughts! But then came the flood…"

"Wait!" Pasión picked up on that word. "What flood…?"

"One day," Moris began like telling a tale, and the anger disappeared from his voice, "we were working down the mines, as always, when there was an explosion. First, we thought this is it, we'll all die, and our corpses will rot in here, like that of the last forsaken brutes of the earth, but then the mountain shook, and water sprang from the ground. I nearly drowned, but at last, most of us escaped. Twenty thousand slaves! In the chaos, 20,000 slaves — so I've heard — ran away. Of course, only after we killed the supervisors and stole from the silver deposits of Athens."

Pasión listened in silence: he was thinking deeply about the flood he caused in the cave and also about the bag of silver he had — unknowingly — taken from Athens.

"Here comes the thing," Moris said in an unusually congenial voice, "when I was hit by a wave of water and nearly died, I started floating above my body. It was the strangest thing. But man! I suddenly understood what our mother was talking about all these years. All this babbling about the invisible world and the soul suddenly made sense to me. My soul traveled far into those shafts and underground tunnels, feeling weightless and at ease, until I saw…"

"Saw what?"

"You!" Moris most unexpectedly said. "I saw you, or your soul maybe, riding the waves. At that moment, I had this feeling that it was you who raised the waters that saved me. There and then I thought that we, brothers, must not be foes in the future. In fact, I stayed underground and learned about magic, like you did. I came out of the caves determined to bring you back into my life so we can be one family again."

The words of the brother were so handsome, that Pasión was struggling to understand why his stomach tightened into one painful knot while he listened to them. It was not until he went to sleep that this suspicion rose from his guts to full awareness.

At night, after years and years of silence, Chairon, the centaur, appeared in his dreams. Pasión could sense the graveness of this unforeseen visit. The centaur made no bones about his coming.

"Go back to Laurin," he commanded, "to Laurin and the Order — the people you belong with. You have a child waiting to be born."

"A child?" Pasión asked, stunned. "But… how can I trust Laurin ever again?"

"The question is," the centaur retorted, "how can he ever trust you again — you who have trusted your bodily senses, like an ignorant fool, instead of listening to the invisible heartbeat of the world, like an initiate!"

Chairon let out a puckish laugh, which soon turned into something more sinister: he lifted his front left leg and with his front right hand took it off! He swung the severed leg all across the space, then held it in front of Pasión's eyes. While it blocked his vision, strangely, Pasión could see through it at the same time. Behind the leg, the centaur's face became blurry.

"Beware," his voice sounded as if it came echoing from outer space, "in the realms of death and dreams, many entities can manipulate your perception. If you trust what you see, so easily can you be led astray."

This is when Pasión saw that the blurry face of the centaur assumed the features of Laurin. With quite a shock, he got the message.

"It wasn't Laurin! But…," he still wondered, "who would do such a thing: assuming the form of Laurin to deceive me and block my way to eternity? Who would want me to stay behind…"

The centaur didn't say a word, which made Pasión feel dumb and perplexed.

"My brother?" he finally tried to answer his own question that a part of him was not quite ready to know.

"Your brother," the centaur said, "has the same magical blood flowing in his veins as you do. Even though he was never meant to use it, he has received an accidental, dark initiation in the mine."

Having said that, Chairon put his leg back on and assumed his regular form.

"Listen, Pasión, my all-time dearest student," he said with loving solemnity. "I've taught you much when you were younger and needed my teachings a lot more than you need them now. Yet, there is something else I need to tell. It will be my most important piece of teaching, which you should always keep in mind as you proceed on your path. This teaching is not cozy and comforting like those things I told you when you were a youngster — but it is the truth."

Pasión listened most attentively.

"Whenever you are moving towards your destiny and to the extent you are moving towards it," the centaur said, "you mobilize forces in the universe that will try to stop you. Regardless of the helpers at your side, the counter-forces will hit you. They will move to hinder you, even kill you. And there always will be humans to aid these forces of darkness."

"Why?" Pasión asked, stunned. "Why would humans do that?"

"I do not know the answer to that question," the centaur replied. "I do not even know anyone who might. This seems to be one of the great riddles of the world. We understand that the mind can only create a manifest world by contrast: light only exists because of darkness and heat only because of cold. Creation moves towards the good, the true, and the beautiful by transcending the bad, the wicked, and the ugly. The Order you are a member of, Pasión, exists for the purpose of aiding that sacred process. But every time the Order brings forth a Hierophant, somewhere else in the world a dark commander will rise. This is the grand enigma: why some humans would work towards the bad, the false, and the ugly, when they have a choice."

"My father said when I met his vision in the cave," Pasión recalled, "that their aim was power and manipulation."

"Yet, that explains nothing," the centaur said. "Power and manipulation are tools, not aims. The great riddle remains: why would anyone want power and manipulation when it ultimately leads to unhappiness? Why would anyone choose unhappiness over happiness? Understand this, Pasión: the choice of evil, not the existence of evil is the great riddle: it remains the great unknown, perhaps even the great unknowable. It defies all reason and sentiment. Yet, those who choose evil always exist; while you and the Order advance towards your highest destiny and help each other, they work to hinder you and will become increasingly more organized, controlling, and effective as time progresses. Beware."

"Laurin is a great teacher regarding the dark forces," the centaur continued. "He is an advanced soul, close to becoming a Hierophant himself. In this life he has overcome some of his last petty weaknesses: he used to be possessive and domineering but setting you free has advanced him. Go back to him, and that will advance you!"

"What shall I do with my brother?" Pasión felt unsure.

"Your brother is serving the forces of darkness. Yet I am telling you, do not hate him, and do not fight him. Usually, the greatest mistake regarding evil is to fight it, as in most cases, the act of violence only increases it. In a strange and mysterious way, we need to respect evil, as we do not understand it and hence cannot know how it may serve the world. Does the sun have the right to hate the shadow it casts? Do not hate your brother. Once you have seen what he has done, do not fight him, but leave him and go back to Laurin and the Order. Turn yourself towards the light; that way the shadow will always remain behind you and won't block your sight."

"But what is my brother doing?" Pasión wanted to know.

"You shall see for yourself," the centaur said. "Come with me!"

Free and floating out of his body, Pasión followed the centaur. Chairon took the road to the harbor that Pasión had walked before a thousand times but now saw it with different eyes. Some things, which were always there, faded out of his view, while new things appeared, sparkling and surreal, as if the whole neighborhood got covered in some fairytale dream dust. What a wild, whimsical adventure it was to follow a centaur in a dream body no one else could see, walking unnoticed into the crowd that was still rather lively despite the late hour: merchants negotiated, seeking benefits and various pleasures for the night. Pasión had to think of the cinematic films Sofia shared with him. This experience felt as if two movies were playing at once: the film of Pasión's dream overlapped the reality of the people at the port.

This is how Pasión spotted a sight so strange that very few people ever get to see anything like it. He saw his brother talking to a merchant, but he too consisted of two overlapping pictures! In one picture, Moris looked like always, but in the other, he looked like an important Athenian strategus... and that is how the merchant perceived him, as someone with high-ranking military powers.

"Yes, sir," Pasión heard the trader addressing his brother with utmost respect. "We'll deliver the marble and the terracotta as agreed, two amphorae of wine, three amphorae of olive oil. The cost of the work is on us, sir, tribute as agreed upon. Naturally, yes. Have a wonderful evening, sir. It's been a pleasure."

Just watching the blurry scene confused Pasión's mind. He couldn't quite understand how Moris succeeded in sharing his own dream reality in which he was an important Athenian military strategist with the mind of the merchant who — as a result — perceived him as such!

This was due to his brother's dark initiation.

"Deception," the centaur softly commented, "manipulations, hypnosis, treachery, and lies — those are the hallmarks of dark magic. It's seldom used so blatantly; usually, it is wrapped up in a greater conspiracy to fool the masses."

"I have to go home," Pasión quietly concluded. "Home to Laurin."

"Yes," said the centaur. "Make sure you take a Spartan ship."

"A Spartan ship?"

"Yes, no other ship will reach Athens from now on."

With this ominous sentence, the centaur left, and Pasión woke up from his dream.

At once, he felt alert. There were noises around the house: soon he picked up that it was his brother talking to the traders who had delivered the merchandise. Amphorae of wine and olive oil were handed over and loudly clashed against the stone floor. When Pasión heard the traders leaving and Moris mixing wine with water, he rose and went to confront him.

"Would you like to try some?" Moris held a cup of wine towards Pasión as soon as he saw him appear in the doorway.

"It was you, wasn't it?" Pasión pushed away the wine and did not wait to ask.

"Was me, what?"

"You were the one who blocked my way in that cave!"

"Yes," Moris said without even blinking.

"How dare you?!" Pasión expelled his anger. "How repulsive, how treacherous. And here you stand, offering me wine as if nothing happened!"

"But brother-heart," Moris said in a voice sweet and soothing. "What else should I have done? You were still under the spell of your Athenian slaveholder. Wasn't it my duty as a brother to do everything in my power — especially in my newly gained power — to free you and bring you back home?"

Pasión felt a frustration that was hard to keep inside; to save himself from exploding, he headed for the door, wanting to leave and never to return. But Moris jumped in front of him and blocked his way yet again.

"I was already a free man," Pasión said into his face. "And because I am, I'm choosing to go now. Let me go through."

Moris, fully back in his old spirit of the bully, put his arms across the entrance.

"You are not going anywhere, little brother," he said, mockingly sweet. "In a shrunken family like ours, the younger brother is like a wife. You will stay here and work around the house. If you could be his slave and his slut, you can also be mine."

While he spoke, the face of Moris distorted into an appalling smirk. It was so terrifying, Pasión had never seen anything like it. Later, he tried to imitate the grimace in a mirror, to remember it in case he ever wanted to depict some mythological evil on a statue, but regardless of how much he tried, he never even came close to it. It was as if something utterly alien and non-human had taken over his brother's face, and Pasión was forced to look Evil straight in the eye.

"Moris," he tried to sound as calming as he could, "I wish you the best, I really do. But I cannot stay here with you. Let me through that door, please, let me through."

By now, Pasión felt truly trapped and uncomfortable, like in his childhood, so many times afraid of his brother. He felt the nervous currents rising within his body as Moris demonstratively picked up the sledgehammer that the construction workers had left at the door. It was a menace.

"You stay here, you little sonofabitch." Moris became openly hostile now. "You do what I say."

Pasión backed up a few steps. With his foot stepping backward, he felt one of the large amphorae filled with the newly ordered olive oil blocking his way.

"Let me out," he repeated to Moris. "I do not want to cause you harm, but you must let me go."

Moris let out an ugly, hysteric laugh.

"How can you possibly harm me?"

Pasión didn't say a word, only gave the amphora behind him a forceful kick like a donkey.

Then he stepped to the second amphora and repeated the action. Oil ran everywhere across the room, amidst broken pottery.

"You are so scared, brother-heart," Moris laughed at him, "that you need to destroy our resources?"

Pasión still didn't say a word, instead, he moved across the room. That was when Moris saw what he was about to do. Pasión wanted to grab the lamp! In panic, and to stop him, Moris threw the hammer at him, but Pasión caught it and used it to destroy the third amphora.

The entire room floor had turned into a pool of oil.

"Damn your eyes!" Moris yelled and ran against Pasión! He wanted to grab him by his neck, but Pasión pulled away as fast as fury. A smaller, more vulnerable opponent in a fight always has the advantage of bringing an element of surprise into every strike he makes. Pasión had this advantage doubly: Moris had learned, year after year, that fighting his brother was as easy as tossing a bird around in the wind, but little did he know that the bird had grown claws over the years, and the wind he could move had gained the strength of a tornado. Moris could simply not comprehend the speed and strength that came out of Pasión's still-young but no longer so tender body. Instead, Pasión grabbed his throat. Not only so but Pasión lifted his big brother with merely one hand while he picked up the oil lamp with the other.

Of course, it was not only muscle that worked inside Pasión's body but also two of the most powerful forces within the human realm: the power of vision and the power of intent. His was a vision very few mortals ever fully grasped: the vision of eternity. His was the powerful intent to show up for a woman who would not be born for another twenty-five hundred years and to return to a lover who could show him how to get there. He was determined not to let anyone, or any obstacle, block his way.

"Get yourself out of here," Pasión whispered to Moris, who surprisingly found himself trapped in this powerful grip. "This house shall be no more. I erase it from the past, I erase its memory from the future. You have never fed us human flesh, and my mother has never died in here. You were never a bully, and I was never that scared little kid who thought he had to be afraid of you. Those sentiments never existed, and there is no memory of them in any record anywhere in the universe. Go now, Moris, go and find yourself a reputable profession to pursue."

Moris, frightened by these words more than he ever was in his life before, ran out as soon as Pasión let him go.

But Pasión… he walked out of the room very slowly. He said a final goodbye to his mother's memory. Now he was looking forward to seeing the little girl, Aliana, again, hopefully soon.

When he was at the door, he dropped the oil lamp. First, the floor, then the house went up in flames and this time, completely burned down to ashes. Pasión walked away and never looked back.

***

During these days, Diona spent as much time with Laurin as he would allow her, which was almost always. Every night and all night long, Laurin held her in the proximity of his hot and healing body, and so he became for Diona a source of safety she had never before known. Yet, even with the great menace of Medea gone, Laurin warned her that his house was not as safe as it felt: war was drawing in closer and closer, and it could become dangerous to stay here, behind the world's best-protected city walls.

"We may have to leave Athens before your baby is due," Laurin predicted. "Don't worry, though, I have a secret retreat, which is truly invisible to the world."

"Who will be there," Diona asked him that night, "to help me when my baby is born?"

"I," Laurin said simply. "I will be there."

"You, Master?" Diona asked, surprised. "You're not a woman, how would you know of such things?"

"I'm not a woman... now... but I've been a woman many times. I remember childbirth, I remember many female things."

Diona opened her eyes wide in the dark. They had already switched the lamp off for the night, but in the small starlight filtering into the bedroom, she tried to see the face of Laurin who spoke of such wondrous-curious prospects.

"Everything will be fine," Laurin told her. "You must not be afraid of anything. The birth will be easy and will come without pain, as your child is a purified, enlightened being who is no longer causing pain to anyone, lest his own mother. He will never be ill, never misbehave, never say anything that is not an expression of the highest truth, as he is someone who has already completed the cycles of human birth and rebirth."

"How do you know of all this?" Diona asked, looking to get a glimpse into such secrets.

"I've been a member of the Order for many lifetimes now."

"Oh! Whenever you talk about the Order," Diona said, rapt, "I sense such wonderful awe: a sacred sentiment is running down my spine and goosebumps erupt on my skin. How I wish I could learn about the Order!"

"Certainly," Laurin surprised her by saying. "As the mother of a Hierophant, you shall receive your initiation."

Diona began to express her excitement, but Laurin called for silence.

"Hush!" he said. "I'm sensing something…"

"What, Master?" Diona whispered. "What is it?"

"Pasión," Laurin replied, with a quiet and most relieved smile. "I can sense him approaching us. Pasión is on his way home!"

***

"Where are you from?" the captain of the Spartan ship asked but didn't seem to believe when Pasión said he was Melian. "You sound like you have an Athenian accent," he suggested with suspicion.

"Yes, because I have been a slave to the Athenians for ten years," Pasión explained.

"Then why, for Poseidon's sake, would you want to sail back there?" the captain asked, with growing impatience in his voice. The Spartans were docking for water and provisions only: he wanted to move on quickly.

"Now I have family there… to protect," Pasión said. (Chairon's remark about a child had remained strongly on his mind.)

"You might be too late for that." The captain seemed more cheerful saying that and shared a smirk with his crew. The Spartans all looked now like well-pleased little devils. "You've been warned," the captain added, but when Pasión offered to pay ten times whatever fee he thought was appropriate, he gestured for him to come on board, and blissfully paid him no more attention.

Sailing on the sea again… this time the wind seemed to have carried away all of Pasión's thoughts but one. Gone were his thoughts about Melos and the Spartans, or about that danger the captain suggested; gone was politics, war, and peace. Pasión fretted only about whether Laurin would ever forgive him for running away like this. He drove himself near mad panic upon the possibility that Laurin could reject him — he would have much rather jumped off the ship and become food for fish than face that. But the sea was calm and appeared friendly, covered with a silver-grey fog… It gave Pasión hope that all may be well in the end.

Yet, the illusion of peace did not last for long. Out of the mist, the first images that emerged from the shore were images of doom. In the beginning, there were only silhouettes on the horizon, but they gained movement and color in the twilight winter sun. First, Pasión saw only one or two of them rising, then they came by the dozen… Spartan warships! Before Pasión knew it, he was surrounded by hundreds of them! Here and now he understood why Chairon had told him to take a Spartan ship: they ensured that no others would make it to the harbor of Pireaus any longer.

Thus stood Pasión on deck and watched an almighty danger unfolding. The greatest strength of the Hellenic world's most famed city was becoming its ultimate weakness. For too long had the Athenians remained behind their superior walls and fortifications, for too long had they relied on their fleet to bring them supplies from overseas. They held out during plague and upheaval. They held out watching from their hideout how the Spartans burned down all their crops and fields in Attica, but in their latest battle they had now lost too many of their ships, and that left their harbor open to attack. Pasión thought immediately: the Spartans were surely not seeking to wage a battle at sea, as they were only great warriors on land, not so on water, no… they had come to barricade the port.

The Spartans came to put Athens under siege!

This insight put Pasión into a sad, yet strangely solemn mood as he watched this glamorous tragedy commencing. He thought of Melos: his memory of the Melians putting a curse on the effigy of the Goddess Athena now overlapped the reality of it happening. He remembered the wise words of his mother warning that curses backfire. Could he have suspected back then that one day when the curse hits, the Athenians would neither be enemies nor strangers to him but friends he belonged to...

What meaning do these words hold anyway: friend, enemy, or stranger? They change as fast as the wind turns! The Athenians, now his friends, used to be his enemy. The Spartans, now the enemy, used to be friends with Athens against the Persians. The Persians, once their enemy, are now best friends of Sparta against Athens. Everybody is to everybody: sometimes enemy, sometimes friend, sometimes stranger. What folly to kill or die for something that only lasts for a blink of an eye!

Pasión now understood the maxim he learned in the Order: Do what you want! Would enemies even exist, he thought, would the necessity of war arise, if everyone did what they truly wanted? Sure, wine may taste sweeter after a battle, and all the women and pretty boys tend to rush into the arms of the victor, but would anyone's first choice really be to go to war?

How long will humanity take to learn about the futility of warfare?

Meanwhile, empires will keep rising, empires will keep falling... Those who seek liberation can use the powerful play to express what is within. Pasión welcomed the calamity as he hoped Laurin would believe his sincerity if he dared to enter this cauldron of war for his sake... He must!

To Pasión's surprise, by the time he reached Laurin's house, the threat of warfare seemed to have vanished. Perhaps the Athenians were so accustomed to the permanent, sinister menace of war that they could continue to live fully even if the world around them was coming to an end. On the street, children and dogs came to greet him. From inside Laurin's house, Pasión heard music: Diona was playing her favorite song on the lyre. Kosmas, who was still Laurin's slave, opened the door and let him in with a friendly, yet measured smile. Guests were talking, wine was flowing... Full of heart and full of mind, life continued without constraint: in the midst of this full catastrophe, Laurin was giving a symposium!

However, chatter and music stopped as soon as someone noticed that Pasión was standing at the doorway. A quiet murmur made its wave across the room.

Every pair of eyes peered to see him, and the air became deadly quiet. Laurin was sitting at the farthest wall and remained absolutely motionless as he saw Pasión.

"The Spartans…" Pasión began to say, as he felt was his duty, but more words refused to leave his mouth. His knees were trembling. First, he felt like a little boy, then like a naughty lover, and finally, like a dead man who was awaiting judgment over his soul.

"We know," Socrates stood up and rushed to his aid. How glad Pasión was to see again the ugliest and wisest man he ever knew! This time, the wild philosopher — so unlike him — was bathed and smelled nice. He put his arms around Pasión and helped him inside. "We know," he repeated. "We are not in denial. We know we are on the verge of a Spartan siege, but since we cannot do anything about it this very moment, we decided before we go and meet this new danger, we shall empty our cups and remember who our friends are. C'mon, my boy, join us, let's embrace the good and the pleasant while we can."

"Pasión." Plato was immediately at his side too. "You must tell me all about your initiation. I'm so jealous, in the best sense of the word: give me sparkly metaphysical details, please."

Pasión so wished to join his friends' conversation, still, he signaled the philosophers to wait. He couldn't help but stare in one direction, frightened, as Laurin still hadn't spoken, still hadn't moved.

Plato respectfully stepped aside and let Pasión, like a prodigal son, approach his master and lover, his abandoned friend. Laurin just sat there, like a crownless king on a heartless throne whose thoughts and feelings his subjects cannot guess. To Pasión, he now felt like some fateful Egyptian judge in the afterlife who would soon put his heart on a scale to weigh whether he was worthy of eternity or shall be devoured by the gatekeeper.

"Am I invited?" Pasión carefully approached him, risking a faint smile.

"No, you are not invited," Laurin said. He didn't sound angry, rather deeply serious.

"Laurin, I…" Pasión began, knowing that he owed him more than a few pretty words, yet even those did not come to his mind.

"You are not invited." Laurin spoke instead of him, "because you are at home, and a man does not need to be invited to come home. And I don't care where you've been, what you have done, and why you left, I only care that you came back to me."

He rose to his feet and extended his arms to Pasión.

"You still don't understand, do you?" he said, seeking his eyes. "I really love you: I am the one who loves you, forever and without restraint. There is nothing you can do, there is nothing that can happen, and there is nothing I can do either which would ever change it because while you've seen Sofia in eternity, when I was there, I saw you."

Holding Pasión by his hand, he stepped forward with him and addressed his guests.

"My dear friends," he spoke, "please welcome home Pasión. He used to be my slave, but now he is a free man. You shall witness, according to the laws of our city-state that I have freed him. Pasión is my love, my fellow member of the Order, and he is the father of Diona's soon-to-be-born divine child."

All of the Athenians made loud noises of joy, some even had tears in their eyes upon these words. Several of them stepped forward and embraced Laurin, Pasión, and Diona, who was called to put down her lyre and join. Pasión gave her a heart-warming smile and laid his hand on her belly, acknowledging his child.

Plato watched them from a polite distance, as he could tell the three were sharing emotions of a lifetime, but as soon as the crowd started to move again, he wanted to ask Pasión all about his experiences.

"If not tonight," he said, "but soon come to me and tell me everything you experienced. I shall write it down. I'm making it into a habit now to write down everything interesting I'm learning. One day, I shall save the best and make it available for future generations to read."

"Oh, for goodness sake!" Socrates exclaimed. "Can anyone stop this madness?!"

"Which madness?" Laurin joined in. He sat down close to Pasión, so their bodies touched: it was priceless pleasure to feel each other again close by.

"This young generation," Socrates complained, "wants to write things down!"

"And what is wrong with that?" Laurin asked.

"Well, everything's wrong with that! Eventually, it will make their memory so weak that they won't even remember any of the great epic poems unless they have it scribbled on some scroll. But worse still: writing will produce dead knowledge. For what is the use of an opinion if the man to whom it is addressed cannot reply to it? Shall he just drink it up? Take it for granted? Without asserting in healthy debate that the opinion of the other is good wine or fresh water and not poison — "

"But, Master," Plato interrupted him, "wouldn't you think that there was value if future generations could read about our ideas so they can debate them among themselves? That way, our thoughts could spark debates of the future and knowledge can evolve, not only over one lifetime, but over centuries to come."

Socrates did listen tentatively to his words.

"I'm dreaming of a proper institution," Plato continued, "where knowledge can be debated, spread, and preserved: a training ground for the mind, as we have the gymnasium as a training ground for the muscles and skills. One day, when all of the upheavals are over, I shall build my academia!" Plato announced this like a magic word.

"You may build your academia, my child." Socrates shrugged his shoulders. "I still think knowledge written on paper is soulless. Like a statue an artist made to raise desire in the viewer. And then I'm standing there in front of it with my desire hardened, but the damn thing has no ass and cock of flesh to satisfy with. That's wrong! That's cruelty."

The guests were rolling with laughter, only Pasión watched them with silent joy. He wanted to save this scene in his memory forever, to remind himself why he learned to love the Athenians so dearly. Here they were, having lifted their city in less than a generation from being a war and plague-infected shithole to becoming the most stunning democracy the world would ever remember. In claws of danger, they still had no time for lamenting anything. They remained sanguine even in the face of new and real peril, filling the future with fresh hopes even if they may never come. They were forever curious, like Pasión, addicted to innovation, which made them adventurous perhaps even beyond their power and daring beyond good judgment. Yet, their conduct birthed the best of humanity: the ability to keep treasuring the dream, whatever terror surrounded them, or was there yet to come.

Later in the evening, Laurin took Pasión away from the guests to be with him alone for a moment. Pasión couldn't quite believe how it felt to be with him again: Laurin's love was as passionate as ever, he felt erotic heatwaves emanating from his body towards his. But this time, there was something more too. This time, Laurin's love felt so purified and deepened that it reminded Pasión of something out of this world. It reminded him of the other-worldly, immense love he felt at Little Eternity.

"Pasión," Laurin said to him in earnest. "As a citizen of Athens, it is my duty to remain in the city and help protect it. As a member of the Order, it is my duty to honor my vow to help you fulfill your destiny. The two duties cannot be fulfilled at once: they are, under the present circumstances, mutually exclusive. A sacred vow has a prevalence over social obligations. Therefore, we have to make arrangements for the two of us and Diona to leave the city. We must not stay here and fall martyr to the Spartans; you must come with me so I can train you how to influence your own rebirth. In fact, come to my study as soon as the guests have left or fallen asleep: I shall start instructing you how you will find Sofia."

"Sofia," Pasión repeated the name Laurin uttered. "Laurin, are you not jealous of Sofia?"

"No," Laurin said sincerely, "I am not; I never was. You are here with me now, and that is all I care about. I'm here in the present, Sofia is in the future. How can I compete with someone in the future? Even if I could, why would I want to? If there is one thing I believe in, it is evolution — that the past is always giving way to a better tomorrow…"

Chapter 15
The Spartan Spear

"**O**ur Order," Laurin said and stepped closer to Pasión, "can help you to set keywords that grant you secret access to transcendental terrains. With time, every one of us obtains a small keyword to access the dream realms and a great keyword to access the realms of death. In the other-worldly realms of death, our Order has set up the Pure Land of Elysium: it is a mystical place of endless joy and peace, dedicated to reaching enlightenment. From there, you can choose your own rebirth, if you wish, and join Sofia in your next incarnation. Therefore, you will need to get there and to get there, you will need to attain the great keyword."

It was nearly dawn; Laurin and Pasión were back in the study where they first connected once upon a time. Standing close, Pasión could breathe in the scent of Laurin's cedar skin and rose-scented hair. Freely, he let his hand glide over Laurin's smooth, skin-covered iron muscles and thought how he never ever wanted to be another minute without him.

"Laurin," he whispered to him, "I cannot listen to your explanations if you are standing so close to me. Then I only want to touch you."

Laurin looked at him. Oh, mighty Gods of the Olympus! Pasión's beauty almost hurt his eyes: it felt an impossible miracle for such perfection to be alive. Yet, here he was, coming into his arms... Yes, they both hoped that they would never have to be without each other again. Never, not even for one moment.

"That's all right. I don't want to explain further, either," Laurin whispered while he drove his fingers deep into Pasión's curly hair. "I want to show. To begin with, today I shall show you how I am using the small keyword. I will take you to the realm of dreams with me. Keywords only work in the right field of vibration — this you won't understand unless you experience it with me." Laurin's whisper became almost inaudible. "Come close. You have to feel my body... to feel the vibration I'm talking about."

What followed was the most extraordinary experience Pasión ever experienced with his master. Laurin sat down in a cross-legged posture and invited Pasión onto his lap: belly to belly, heart to heart, throat to throat, forehead to forehead they were facing and embracing each other. Then Laurin started to make love to Pasión but not with his body as he usually would but by merging their life force energies. Still, Pasión's pleasure started to rise as it usually would. Laurin told him not to waste it but to use it to bring the energy upward.

More words and explanations were not needed because Laurin was leading like he always used to guide their bodies. Now he was guiding the life force within, awakened by their desire for each other. It started crawling higher and higher along their spines, like a serpent along a tree, giving them spiraling, growing waves of rapture.

Pasión suddenly thought all lovemaking in the past was spent, as Laurin was now opening new dimensions of bliss for him. If in the past he felt pleasure in one body part, he now felt it in his whole body. If in the past, he felt pleasure only in his own body, now he felt it in Laurin, also. The two of them merged into one being, feeling each other's feelings, hearing each other's thoughts, beating with each other's hearts. Their unity made their awareness so grand that they started to fill up the room, which soon became small like a coffin, so they began to expand beyond the limits of time and space. Like water in a cauldron above their fire, their consciousness started to lift and expand.

Now, Laurin was ready to utter the small keyword to cross over into the realm of dreams with his beloved.

But it never happened. They were brought back into the cruel reality of their time. Screaming was coming from all around the house. From their dreamy flight, they crash-landed back in the room. Back on the bed, they could hear that the remaining guests had woken up and ran around in a frenzy.

"The Spartans!" Pasión and Laurin heard them shouting. "All men to the weapons! The Spartans are invading our city!"

***

Coming back from the Penteli Mountains, Sofia thought it most agreeable that her hotel room had this quaint and over-sized bathtub. It was rose-pink and — like the whole establishment — had seen better days, but it carried a certain charm of bygone days she liked. There was a vintage poster of Parisian perfumes on the wall, which reminded her that the senses needed soothing, and her exhausted body needed rest.

Sofia immersed herself in the warm, scented water. She was longing for comfort — not because she had been up alone in the mountains for many days and nights, nor because she had to return through some of Athens' roughest alleyways and crime-infested corners. No, danger and discomfort she was well-trained to face, but something unthinkable had happened to her while inside the mountain!

Sitting in the bathtub, she kept pondering how such a thing was possible. She remembered the poet who once asked a question similar to her current concern: What if in your sleep you went to heaven, dreaming that you picked up a strange and beautiful flower, and when you awoke, you had that flower in your hand?

Ah, what then? asked the poet.

Ah, what now? asked Sofia.

The events she just came back from gave her a puzzle greater than her mind could solve!

Earlier in the day, Sofia had been inside the mountain, where she went down the spiral path intoning Laurin's mystic tune. Her consciousness had gradually shifted away from ordinary perception. Things that ordinarily belonged in the realm of dreams became possible. Inside the mountain, she moved in a dream-like fashion: without thinking and without limitations, she simply began to do what her intuition told her to do. She began to dig at a spot which — somehow — felt familiar to her. She kept digging until — from deep within the mountain, from deep within her heart — something emerged.

It was an ancient amphora.

Sofia held the amphora with great interest and joy. She felt like Coleridge, the poet, must have felt when he found that rare heavenly flower in his dream and hoped to bring it back into waking reality.

It gave Sofia the most disconcerting, yet exhilarating and promising surprise, when walking down from the mountain, she noticed that the amphora was still with her. She had brought something back from what seemed to have been a dream! She pondered how this could have happened: it seemed that her concept about the different levels of reality was becoming outdated in understanding the mystery unfolding in her life. She was hoping this all would be a revelation regarding her connection with Pasión and the ancient world, not some harbinger of madness.

There was only one way to find out.

Coming out of the bathtub, Sofia went to sit in the lounge chair in her hotel room and stared at the coffee table where she carefully had placed the amphora.

"Hello, Alana," she called her friend.

"Sofia, where are you?" Alana sounded worried.

"I have some potentially mind-blowing news," Sofia said. "I believe I have found the seventh scroll."

"Where? How?" Alana was not quite trusting her ears.

"I followed my intuition."

"Well… Where is the scroll?"

"Here in front of me, on the coffee table. In an amphora."

"Do not open it!" Alana cried out incredulously. "You should not even have removed the artifact from the site. It's a criminal offense in this country to do so."

"I'm aware of that," Sofia said, while her voice gained an almost threatening level of strength. "I'm even planning to take the criminal offense to the next level."

"What do you mean?"

"Alana…" Sofia said, "I may not yet understand it fully, but we are involved in a sacred-mystical matter. For this reason, I'm not willing to give this artifact to any authorities. I'd rather burn it in front of their eyes before they get to it. However, if you are willing to help me, date it, and translate its content for me — and if the scroll permits — afterward, I will give it to you, and you can place it into any museum you wish."

"It will not be my decision," Alana said, "but all right. I guess no harm will be done if I look at it first. To be honest, I think you may be mad! Still, I'm your friend, and it feels right to help you. But tell me: if you haven't opened the amphora yet, how can you be so sure that it is the seventh scroll it hides?"

"You are right, I cannot be sure," said Sofia. "Only my intuition tells me so. You will need to look at it and carbon test it to determine its authenticity. I can bring it over in the nightly hours when everyone is gone from the labs," Sofia suggested.

Alana laughed.

"We are all nerds, there are always some of us in the lab. Half of us sleep in there in sleeping bags, the other half without. But yes, just bring it in in the evening. I will lock the door when we work on it. Sofia," Alana asked last, "are you sure you are not going mad?"

"If going mad means to move my usual point of perception," Sofia paused for a moment, "in order to perceive worlds hidden for most then yes, I am going mad. And it feels just right."

***

By the time Laurin and Pasión crashed from their other-worldly journey on the rock bottom of their contemporary reality, the remaining guests had made their way through the house, growling and howling. They went to search for Laurin's armor and weapon cabinet. Apparently, the Spartans had broken through the fortification nearby, launching a street battle hitherto unheard of. It remained unclear whether this was a planned attack or just war-time mischief, but from moment to moment it escalated into something unexpectedly big. As they both arrived and joined the guests in the armory, Pasión could feel the people's blood boiling all around, regardless of how much wine was still mixed in with it. In Laurin's eyes, however, he detected something he'd never seen there before. It was confusion —
as if the man was experiencing something he believed shouldn't be happening.

"What do you have for us, Laurin?" Socrates asked, sober only as a priestess of Delphi. "Enough weapons for all? The battle's raging in front of the house; we can't be expected to go and get our own!"

"Should be enough, yes," Laurin said, almost dreamily, as he opened his cabinet of weaponry. "Mostly historic weapons I collected as art, but they'll do."

Saying these words softly, Laurin started to hand out a piece of armor and a weapon to each man who lined up. He himself noticed as he took the first spear out that his hands were shaking. A terrible, dark fear came rising from his guts, so powerful that it surprised him. However, it was not a feeling he could afford to attend to right now. Some of the men standing behind him were youngsters he had personally trained to fight, who were now looking to him as a source of strength. Therefore, Laurin commanded his fear to subside, even though he knew there must have been a very good reason for it to arise.

Instead, he turned around and said to the young Athenians, "Whatever happens, today we will defend our city. We have built it from the dumpster it had become after the Persian invasion, and in less than a generation, it became the most famed democracy the world will ever know. Today, we will not give it to a few street hooligans from Sparta."

The words came from his mouth flat and aloof, still, they did not fail to inspire. The young friends, Plato and Pasión, took some noisy jumps up into the air: they both felt their muscles tensing and the red beast awakening within — at this moment, Pasión could better understand mankind's addiction to war. Danger makes a brave man come alive, it gives his strength a stupendous burst and a wonderful sharpening to his senses. What a glorious illusion war was: a chance to fool the mind that we can escape death, as long as our weapons succeed in killing the enemy.

"Let the enemy be fed to Death, let us be the immortals!"

"Yes! We will not give up the city," Plato echoed the words of Laurin. "Let us rise! There is no better cure to such mighty hang-over headache as slaying some Spartans for breakfast."

"Very well then," Laurin tossed a weapon at him, "take this spear."

While he was handing out all his various equipment, Laurin noticed it wasn't going to be quite enough for everyone.

"I have only one piece of armor left. Who should get it?"

As Laurin asked that question, he noticed someone lined up with the men, seeing who reawakened his fearful feeling of foreboding. Diona was standing in there! Why wasn't she hiding?

"Diona, darling," Laurin said with a kind but urgent strength, "don't stay out so long! Be quick to hide!"

"I came for a weapon, not to hide," Diona asserted, in a powerful manner unusual for her. "I'm coming with you."

"Are you mad?" Laurin snapped. "With a baby in your belly, you certainly do not belong to a battlefield!"

"But do I belong to be left behind," strangely, Diona raised her voice, "to sit and wait unarmed, for any Spartan to come and rape me, destroy my baby, and sell me as a slave again?! Let me fight, Laurin, you know I can! Since you grew back my hair, I am again a warrior princess every night in my dreams. I have been your docile slave and haven't rebelled my whole life, but now I refuse," and she repeated the word *refuse* most boldly. "I refuse to face the horrors of war without a weapon and a fighting chance."

Laurin looked her in the eye.

"What do you want?" he asked.

"Bow and arrows."

Laurin threw his last set of lightweight bow and arrows at Diona and gave her the last piece of armor. He gave Pasión his last spear and ordered him and Diona to take the two horses. The old war-hammer, which he once got as a keepsake from a barbaric tribe he befriended during his travels, he handed over to Kosmas and wished him good luck.

There were no armors left for Laurin and Pasión, and for Laurin, not even a weapon. Thus, Laurin himself went naked: unarmed, and without a horse into what was to become Athens' deadliest battle in the city.

The enemy had been slowly filtering in throughout the night. By the morning, it had become an organization of a few dozen cavalries and many hundreds of infantry. The Athenians, sons of the sea and the wind had so far cleverly avoided any ground battle with these fiery Spartans, who drowned easy on water but made the scariest opponent on land.

They were now all lined up on the streets of Athens: in their war-helmets designed to terrify, the Spartans did not even look human. They appeared like dark angels of revenge, sent by the gods to execute a fateful punishment for grandeur, resistance to which was meant to be futile.

The knees of the Athenians, despite their brave hearts, trembled as they saw them nearing. The Spartans had a leader in the middle of their front row, who halted his horse and his troops, confident that as soon as they moved again, they'd bring bad news for the young democracy here.

In truth, this deadlock could have ended catastrophically for the locals, but miracles sometimes do happen.

Unexpectedly, it was not the Spartans who made the first move: out of the improvised Athenian crowd, the first arrow came flying. It was shot with such mythic precision that it hit the Spartan leader straight in the throat, on that one tiny spot unprotected by his armor. The rider, who carried the bow, broke out of the multitude and revealed herself as a stunning goddess on a shiny black stallion with hair long like a river, flowing behind her in the wind.

"I am Pallas Athena!" she shouted, louder than thunder. "Lacedaemonians, leave our land!"

The Spartans, shaken by superstition, hesitated for a moment, which turned the valor around. Now it was the Athenians who, bathing in the power field of their goddess, found utmost confidence and began to slay the Spartan wolves as if they were only sheep.

The only Athenian still frozen was Laurin: transfixed, he watched the warrior princess who had emerged from dreams. Laurin knew that the reality of the soul was stronger than a single present life, still, witnessing an eternal form coming alive took his breath away.

The heroic goddess, sitting on a horse he owned, was Diona.

Her sight amazed, as well as terrified Laurin. He knew she was moving other-worldly forces stemming from her dreams, but he also knew how difficult it was to wield such powerful magic. Right now, Diona had grabbed the long spear of the Spartan she killed and used it in close combat to pierce through one soldier after the other, while she herself appeared invincible. However, one-second break in concentration — one thought of doubt — would be enough to snap her out of this heightened state, leaving her vulnerable to instant attack.

Yet, the powerful play was already raging, and there was nothing Laurin could do to stop it. Rather, he jumped on the horse of the fallen Spartan leader and grabbed a lost spear. Since he had taken a vow against violence, instead of killing, he made himself useful by saving as many of his fellow Athenians from getting hit by spears and arrows as he could. He saved the lives of dozens that day, even though many of them would never know it was him.

The battle boiled with fury, which the Athenians loved, and the Spartans regretted. As bravely as they fought, it turned out the Spartans could not counter the immense faith of the Athenians, who believed their patron goddess was with them. So it happened that one more time, Athens succeeded in saving her legendary fortification. The fights lasted from sunset to sunrise: by that time, the Athenians had killed or chased out all Spartans and closed the gap in the wall.

The doom, however, happened before that.

It happened between the fourth and the fifth hour of the battle, or was it between the sixth and the seventh — would that even matter? Laurin, committed to saving lives without killing, became a bodyguard to all who needed him, especially those from his household. Diona, in heightened enchantment, held out without a single mistake and never required his help. Pasión fought, strong and competent as well. Kosmas, however, needed intervention twice: both times, Laurin deflected spears flying unnoticed toward him. The greatest difficulty he had was with Plato, who once got stuck in dreadfully close combat: Laurin could hardly pull the attacker away from him without causing fatal damage. All in all, hellish, full-burning combat was taking place everywhere around: in order to live and let live, Laurin had to rely more and more on his ability to slow down perception.

That was what he did too when that particular Spartan spear came straight at him. It looked dangerous and strong, like a mythic flying serpent sent by the Lord of Death himself. Yet, when Laurin slowed down his senses to gauge its trajectory, he saw it was to hit his right shoulder, so just by leaning a bit to the side, he could easily avoid it. Laurin looked over behind him to see whether there was any Athenian in danger, but there was not.

He concluded the spear represented no danger.

This was an error in judgment Laurin could never forgive himself during the many years of his long life to come, even though he pondered it over, and realized over and over again that he could not have foreseen what was coming.

In a splinter of that unfortunate moment, when Laurin turned back on the horse, someone else saw that spear flying towards him and moved. It was Pasión! He thought Laurin was in mortal danger and jumped his horse to hit the spear off its course. Laurin saw his lover successfully bringing the weapon to the ground. Then Pasión looked at him also: their eyes met as they smiled at each other in this last unharmed moment together.

It was interrupted by the convulsion of Pasión's body. This is how the unthinkable happened: invisible to them, another spear, from another soldier, hit Pasión from the back and went straight through his chest.

In a frenzy, Laurin jumped off the horse. He prayed in silence to have enough time. When he reached and lifted the fallen Pasión into his arms, blood was already pouring out of his wound like a fountain of pain. Diona appeared, and Laurin let her know with a single move of his head that she shall be the sentinel and keep their spot protected. Then he inspected the wound and saw that the spear had found the heart: any amount of life force energy he could give Pasión would only delay the inevitable. Laurin wanted to wail, cry out in immeasurable sorrow, but he had no time for that.

He had an overriding personal choice to make that would change the course of everything. Thus, he gathered all his calm and spoke to the beloved.

"Pasión, my love!" Laurin whispered like to a child just being born. "Does your pain allow you to listen to me?"

"Y… yes," Pasión labored to say, still, Laurin was glad he was fully with his senses.

"Good, good," he kept telling him. "Hold on to me, my beloved, hold on to me and everything will be fine. Listen," he said again while he sent enough life force energy over into Pasión's dying body so that he could pay attention. "The spear hit your heart. At this point, you will inevitably die, there is nothing I can do to save your life. I am going to give you now the Great Keyword: it will take you, after you die, straight into the Pure Realm of Elysium. Are you with me?"

"Yes," said Pasión and tried to show that he was smiling within.

"Good, my love, good." Laurin held him, caressed him, cradled him. "There is nothing you have to do, just take over the vibration I will bring forth now — like we were doing earlier at dawn. This one will be greater, and feel even better. When both our bodies feel it, I'll give you the word. You only must say it, nothing else. Once you are leaving, don't look back!"

After he said that, Laurin began to open the gates for lifting a consciousness into the Pure Realm. This was a most extraordinary endeavor, which required a psychic energy field so powerful that it took an adept centuries to accumulate. Laurin had been collecting his merits over many lifetimes by accruing all his dedicated good thoughts, words, and deeds for becoming able to perform this feat once.

If the soldiers on the battlefield had been aware of what was occurring in their midst, they would've dropped their weapons to witness the miraculous. But it all was, of course, not visible to the ordinary eye. It could only be felt, like an invisible shield, the vortex of energy kept all the fighting away from them and soon began to lift Laurin and Pasión to magically blissful levels of consciousness.

"The keyword is," Laurin then said, "magnificent."

"Mag… ni… fi…," the dying Pasión stammered each syllable, struggling to finish the word.

"Say it, say it fully," Laurin strongly and most anxiously urged him, as only a fully uttered word would take him off.

"…cent." Pasión finished the word. "Magnificent," he said it again.

Uttering the keyword accelerated the movement of energy, which united the two of them as no lovemaking on earth could ever do. For a moment, they found themselves in the state of ultimate, in common life unimaginable, happiness. The very next moment, however, the same vortex that created their unity began to lift Pasión's consciousness upward. But it dropped Laurin, who was still bound to the body, back to the stone-hard ground of the battlefield, next to Pasión's lifeless body.

Thus, it happened.

Pasión had died.

The shock from the fall and from the loss was so inhumane that it broke even a man mentally as strong as Laurin. When Pasión was gone, he let out a disconsolate cry so loud that all the warriors, Athenians, and Spartans, froze in their battle for a minute, forced to stand silent with his grief. When the battle recommenced, Laurin sprang on a high hill and put out his arms wide, like on a cross. So, he exposed his chest to wait for the next Spartan spear to pierce him.

But it never came. It was not his fate to die on that day. It was his fate to live another half of a century in excellent health until his last breath, never to lose his vigor and stamina, never to have sickness or dementia ever dull his pain. It was his fate to remain strong and suffer the full impact of his grief, which never weakened, never ceased.

There on the battlefield, standing alone, Laurin wasn't lying to himself: he was frightened — yes, terrified! — of all the horror that he had brought upon himself. He knew something no one else did: this day, he didn't only lose his true love, he lost his own chance to enter the Pure Realms after he died.

Understand, Pasión was a novice: he hadn't even begun to accumulate the necessary merits to gather good energy for a great keyword. He was too young and new to the Order. If he had simply died, his consciousness would have traveled to

Hades, that somber, shadowy terrain where most of his Greek contemporaries went after death. But Laurin loved him so much that he could not stand the thought of that. Therefore, while Pasión was dying, Laurin decided to get him into a Pure Land at any price.

But what a price it was! Since Pasión had no dedicated, meritorious energy himself to fuel a journey into the Pure Realm, Laurin had used his own. Now, like a rocket launched, it was all used up. For himself, Laurin had neither any energy left nor enough time in this single life to gain it back.

In order to send Pasión to the Pure Land, Laurin had effectively given up his own entry to Elysium.

At once, he was no longer in a better position than any mere mortal. In fact, his lot became worse since he was fully aware of the future awaiting him. He knew, that when his day came, he would die like any other. He would go to Hades, drink water from the river Lethe, and forget everything: he would forget Pasión, forget the Order, forget that he ever was an initiate who had access to higher worlds. He would be born again, suffer, and die — over and over again. His lot would be worse than that of others because he would retain a longing that he would never be able to satisfy. This longing would make him try, over and over again, to fall in love, but all his affairs would end up in disappointment because Pasión, his true cosmic partner, would not be here on Earth. He would always carry a mystical hunch with himself that there must be more than meets the eye, and that would incline him to experiment with outstanding, even outrageous ideas. Lifetime after lifetime, he would be persecuted for that, branded as a heretic, like all seekers who haven't found good refuge yet: he would be ridiculed, tortured, excommunicated, crucified, and burnt at the stake over and over again. Until the day when he could acquire a body capable, and an intellect sophisticated enough, to set aside the social norms as well as the resistance to finding the way back to the Order, he would have to wander, from one vague, dark life to the next, not for mere centuries, but eons. Laurin — as he was still alive and had not yet lost his memory of initiation — saw the immense suffering he would be subjected to in all these ignorant lives to come, and in facing that, he allowed himself to weep.

After the battle, he sought solitude and exile away from the company of his fellow men. Somewhere, he picked up the blade of a fallen soldier and cut his own majestic long black hair with it. He sprinkled his rose-scented black curls over Pasión's dead body and set it all on fire. No one should see Pasión dead, no one should mourn him; that right Laurin retained solely for himself. Long after the Spartans had withdrawn and were pushed outside the city walls again, long after the Athenians cried over their dead and celebrated their victory, Laurin was still out there, roaming the streets, aimlessly. He let tears flow from his eyes, more and more tears and cared nothing whether anyone might see him like that. Strangely, no one saw him, and he met no one. For countless hours, he just walked on blood and corpses, always alone, like in a ghost town, as if he was in Hades already.

Perhaps, his tears would have spread into an endless ocean, ultimately drowning him, if at last someone had not come rushing towards him whose sight he could not entirely ignore.

It was the Dog Who Did Not Exist, wagging his tale. He reminded Laurin that life would go on despite the greatest cruelty which may occur. Laurin didn't have it in him to impose his own personal hell on this innocent creature and searched his mind to say something good. To his own surprise, it didn't take long to find it on his mind. He squatted down and whispered into the dog's ears, "I have some good news, my friend. Pasión is rescued from the grim grip of death forever."

With this thought, he stood up again, and his tears turned into a profound inner smile.

Why mourning, he thought to himself, like a fool? Nothing was in vain, quite the contrary... Pasión is in the Pure Land!

Pasión is in the Pure Land! his soul echoed in ecstatic reverie. His love would never ever have to be reborn in any lower realm. He will never ever have to endure suffering, neither physical nor mental. By now he must have passed the Cinnabar Gate and was protected and guided by Al'Om, the Order's oldest and most accomplished Hierophant.

Was there anything more to wish for in life? The blissful truth of what he had accomplished finally dawned on Laurin: he had set his Beloved free and rescued him from all present or future suffering.

Is there anything more and anything better a man can do?

No, and no prize, Laurin concluded, was too high to pay for that.

Suddenly, it felt a waste to wander around aimlessly. After all, he still had a purpose in the here and now. He had to go home to Diona. A divine child, the Hierophant the Order has been waiting for, was about to be born and needed a father.

Pasión's child was about to be born!

Chapter 16
The Past and the Present

P asión is dead!

"Pasión is dead," Diona repeated, training herself to survive the thought. "The father of my baby!" she cried out.

Laurin was unable to utter a word but caught her before she would collapse and held her tight.

"Yesterday, I was a warrior princess like in my dreams," Diona lamented. "How could I not have seen it? How could I have not prevented it?"

Both their hearts broke by this same evil thought, their tortured hearts: every moment broken by grief, every moment restored to beat again by the cruel will to live. Broken, yet beating, their hearts went on working and pumping, destroyed but restored, again and again, like the liver of Prometheus, punished for a crime which was no sin.

"I am torturing myself with the same question, my love," Laurin said. "But this question we must silence, else it will trap us in furious madness forever!"

Kosmas entered the room, as he had been ordered by his master. Laurin went to his tidy desk where he had prepared two parchments and a sizeable bag of silver.

"This is a legal document," Laurin said to Kosmas while he handed to him one of the parchments, "attesting that from today on, you are a free man. Furthermore, it's transferring ownership of this house over to you, for I shall never again return to Athens. Take this silver as a sign of my gratitude for your loyal services and as a foundation for your future. Make no mistake about it: the Spartans didn't give up. They will besiege the city, and your freedom will seem like a burden at first. But if you survive, and so I wish for you, the skills you learned working for me will allow you to live a good life and start your own family, if you like."

One of Kosmas' eyes shed tears over his good master leaving while the other laughed in joy for winning this unexpected fortune and freedom. Diona, however, looked beside herself, as Laurin wanted to reach for the second parchment.

"No, no, no, no, no," she objected franticly. "Master, please don't free me!"

Laurin looked baffled.

"Yesterday, the Spartans were more afraid of you alone than all the Athenian men combined, yet today, you'd be afraid of your own freedom?"

"No, you don't understand," Diona insisted. "I want to be yours. Yesterday I was fighting the Spartans like an Amazon because that was required. On other days, I'm tame and docile because that is required. At any time, I'll do whatever lifts you up, for that is why I live. That is my purpose."

Laurin looked at her with all his sincerity: he could sense she was voicing a deep truth of her soul, which intrigued him, but this was not the right time for contemplating it further.

"Of course," he told her. "I always meant that you shall come with me. We'll raise the child together but join me as a free woman."

Laurin spoke, soft and inviting, but Diona only shook her head.

"All right," he agreed. "We can postpone this. Sooner or later though, I will need to free you, as only then can I officially adopt the divine child who must not grow up as a slave or a bastard. And you will comply because that will be required," Laurin said and closed the issue for now.

"There are more things in heaven and on earth than meets the eye," at last he told Kosmas, as they departed. "Watch out for the unusual, and pay attention to the miraculous, for if you do, you'll step on your path of final freedom."

Laurin and Diona could no longer leave Athens following the regular roads. The Spartan hold on the polis got stronger by the hour. Therefore, they had to enter the subterranean tunnel system of the Order through a hidden entrance at a member's house. Once underground, Laurin promptly found his way through the labyrinth, but even the shortest path to his secret Grove was a long one. For half a night, they hiked in the dark. Laurin had to force himself not to think of yesterday when they still meant to take this journey together with Pasión. Instead, to keep their minds off fear and grief, he spent the hours underground narrating to Diona wondrous, mystery-filled tales of human beings who bravely faced the adventure of escaping the cycles of life and death for an ultimate rebirth in a higher existence. Oh, what a relief it would have been if he could only speak about his misfortune, as he doomed himself while sending Pasión to Elysium! Yet, he had decided not to burden any living soul with his tragedy. Instead, he carried the burden of his dark future alone.

Diona did not need to climb the scary stones that protected Laurin's Grove. As they emerged from under the Earth, they found themselves in the small cave, which used to be Pasión's place of contemplation… only such a short time ago!

In the morning, they stepped out into a glorious sunrise, and the most amazing, yet unnerving surprise waited for Laurin. Of course, he knew that it was there, but had forgotten about it in the midst of all the recent upheavals and tragedies: he was staring at the screen Pasión had erected.

"What are you looking at, Master?"

"There's a statue behind this cover," Laurin revealed to Diona. "Pasión made it as a present but never got the chance to give it to me."

Diona felt the gravity of the moment and nodded solemnly, encouraging Laurin to unveil it.

He pulled away the cloth.

When Laurin saw it, he forcefully grabbed Diona's shoulder. Like a climber of a cliff holding on to a bundle of grass to keep him from crashing into the abyss, he wanted refuge. Diona understood he might break down in tears — she herself was close to that — but Laurin only stood there, frozen, calm, and quiescent as if time itself had come to a standstill. The miracle he was looking at was not merely a masterpiece of art but an embodiment of Pasión's life — his essence as ennobled beauty and eternal love.

"On the one hand, this is right," Laurin said, as he finally could speak. "Pasión's beauty is worthy of eternity and demands to be among the gods. It is right that he is in Elysium now," he declared. "On the other hand, this is so wrong, as the only true place for him is to be with me. His soul belongs to my soul. We eternally belong together."

"You won't give up on Pasión, will you, Master?"

Laurin smiled — for the first time since the tragedy — like a teacher hearing a question only a greenhorn may ask.

"Of course not. I will find him: if no longer in this life, so in another to come, if not on this earth, so in any other realm. I only wish some of the gods would indeed come and help me in my quest."

"Oh, but so it will happen," Diona said with conviction. "Whether you still believe it or not, the gods will come." And with these words, she took Laurin's hand and laid it over her pregnant womb.

***

Sofia felt unnerved. She took the elevator as she felt some irrational fear that she might stumble on the stairs and drop the amphora. It was at the reception, though, that she nearly let the artifact fall. She only wanted to deposit her room key, but looking at the receptionist was like seeing a ghost!

"Am I so scary?" the young man seemed provoked.

"Excuse me?" Sofia asked, confused. In her momentary perception, this young, bearded Greek had a hostile spark in his eyes and was wearing a war helmet, like an ancient warrior.

"Do I look so scary?" he asked again. "The look on your face…"

"Oh, I'm sorry," Sofia said hastily. "I just forgot something in the room."

She ran up the stairs and slammed the door as if escaping a resurrected enemy. Quickly, she rang David.

"What's wrong?" Her friend anticipated trouble before she even said anything.

"David," Sofia began, "you have brought to me the Hierophant, and I've been to the cave. Something extraordinary is certainly happening, as I even got an artifact, which could be the scroll, but right now, it feels like I'm going mad! A minute ago, the hotel receptionist looked to me like a gory Spartan soldier."

"Did you drink from the water of remembrance?" David wanted to know straight away. "From the water inside the cave?"

"Yes, many times. I've stayed in the cave for three days and three nights, and then for another seven days and seven nights, waiting for Pasión — and if that doesn't make me sound crazy, I don't know what does," Sofia interrupted herself.

"Well..." David began to apply his thoughts, "in a conventional sense, you probably are going crazy right now. Some of your ancient soul memories are seeping through, but we live in dark new ages — those of us who glimpse into greater dimensions of existence easily wind up confused or worse. You know it more than anyone that our lunatic asylums are full of potential shamans, healers, and mystics: people who peered behind the veil, just — through lack of support — never learned what to do with the greater reality they saw. But you, Sofia, are destined to riddle it out. Remember, when you healed me from the paralysis, and I returned from the realm of death? I was bringing a message for you: that you will finally remember who you are, where you are from, and where you are going."

"But that's the trouble, David: I know less than ever who I am! All I wanted was to leave the battlefields, leave those besieged Balkan cities, leave the UN convoys, and get a job to help the dying. Instead, here I am, worrying about my sanity. Instead of clarity, I'm gaining confusion."

"Those waters in the caves are much more contaminated than they would have been in ancient times," David speculated. "They still have the power to boost your eternal memory but only bring you flashbacks and scenes, which are random at first. You may have to painstakingly put them together, like pieces of a puzzle."

"Yes," Sofia agreed, "like pieces of a jigsaw puzzle." She was thinking back on the peculiar images that came to her in the mountains, most memorably when she witnessed the crucifixion, for which she felt strangely responsible. How many other stray images would come to her mind before it would all begin to make sense? "It's all rather confusing."

"Yes." David understood. "It is bound to be, though: like a snake shedding old skin, you are growing out of your little, skin-encapsulated ego — and the process may be unpleasant, yet it can no longer be reversed. Your only chance is to find your greater identity instead of plunging back into madness."

These words resonated with Sofia and made her feel strong.

"My memory of eternal things is only awakening, like yours," David said at last. "Yet, I know beyond the shadow of a doubt, that I am here on a sacred mission to assist you. I'm here for you, and I sense, so is Alana. Go to her and read the scroll. I can feel that something good is about to happen."

Encouraged by the conversation, Sofia got the amphora into her hands and, without giving the receptionist a second look, took it to Alana. Her scholarly friend awaited with an impish sort of excitement.

"Girl, girl," she scolded, but with a tiny little smile at the corner of her lips, "if your mystical intuition is correct, we may be hiding the world's oldest book from the authorities."

Alana took over the amphora with utmost professional care, but Sofia, to her delight, detected a rebellious streak in her ways. Alana proceeded like a university graduate who applied all the skills from business and law school while working for the mafia. This air of anarchy felt right, for Sofia despised the idea that the amphora and its content may be treated as some historic artifact, officially the property of the Hellenic Republic. It was bad enough that Pasión's statue was still in a public museum and not in her own sheltered possession, where it — ineffably — belonged.

Now she watched in awe how Alana prepared the amphora — the age of which was still uncertain — to be opened. Like an alchemist who puts the philosopher's stone into a cauldron, Alana placed it into an insulated glass enclosure, which looked like an incubator for babies. What will come to life in there? Sofia wondered. What if there really was a scroll? What then?

Alana slowly began to remove the lid, working painstakingly in rubber gloves fitted through portholes in the glass. Meanwhile, Sofia noticed her heart beating faster. Certainly, it would fundamentally shift her understanding of reality if her intuition proved right and what she had found was indeed Laurin's seventh scroll. It would mean that her inner voice was to be trusted more than all the outside influences and opinions. It would mean that she could trust the miraculous more than the profane. It would be a first sign of stepping into that enlarged reality David was speaking about. Although Sofia didn't know what the new reality would be like, she felt drawn to it, like a tadpole is drawn to exploring the unknown life on land.

She needed to know more and break out into new dimensions... Her hopes were wonderfully strengthened as Alana slowly but surely pulled out a rolled-up scroll from inside the amphora.

Neither of them dared to say a word. In sacred silence, Alana removed a tiny sample of the scroll. Sofia watched, mesmerized, as she subjected the sample to a reverse sort of alchemy: she placed it in a test-tube, mixed it with silver, and sealed it with a blue flame. Then Sofia received a first impression of what a game of patience this was going to be: they had to wait all night long for the mixture to combust in a muffle furnace, for it to turn into graphite.

During that process, they tried to sleep, but Sofia kept waking up every hour. At night, she had strange dreams in which her body morphed from one body to all the bodies in which she lived throughout lives upon lives, centuries upon centuries. She went from child to adult, from senior back to baby, from man to woman, and back to man again. In the morning, she could not remember any of it but felt foggy and tired as her brain worked hard, and she could only keep herself awake with a cup of strong coffee. She waited long, in front of another lab, where the graphite was sent through an accelerator to isolate and measure its radioactive C14 content, giving out its age.

Sofia felt like those friends and relatives of her patients who were forced to wait in the hospital corridor — or in front of a military hospital tent — while their loved one was undergoing a critical operation. How many times had she seen them jump to their feet, preceding the pronouncement of life or death? Impatient to even wait for the words, they tried to read from the tiniest smile on her lips, which could mean that their loved one had survived.

Sofia felt similar when Alana finally came out of the lab with the results of the carbon dating. Mercifully, her lips did move into that tiny smile!

"We have an error margin ranging between 100 and 200 years, which I may be able to narrow down after conducting some paleographic studies. Overall, for now, I can say that the scroll you found is from the late sixth to the fourth century BC."

"Twenty-five centuries," Sofia said in awe.

"Yes," Alana nodded, "something like that. In any case, the scroll is authentically from Laurin and Pasión's time period."

"Can we read it now?" Sofia asked with utter excitement and hope. "See whether it was really written by Laurin?"

Instead, she received another lesson in patience.

"It will take three weeks just to safely unroll it. But hey," Alana said, "you will need a month to celebrate! Carbon dating proved the scroll to be authentic. I must congratulate on your mystic inner voice: it was telling the truth."

***

Laurin was telling the truth when he predicted that the baby would be born without any pain or complications. The divine child came into this world like a gentle breeze, which set into motion wind chimes and prayer wheels, diffusing all across the land, astonishing, nameless teachings most humans were not even ready to hear. Laurin, however, listened from the first moment on. In a strange and inexplicable way, he felt that through the baby, he was holding his salvation. In his eyes, he saw the future, consciousness in its most expanded form. The newborn was exuding such exuberant joy that it was forever impossible to feel unhappy or disheartened in his presence.

Immediately after he cut the cord, Laurin laid down next to Diona, face to face, looking at her, and placed the baby into the sacred space between their hearts. There, the little one went and suckled milk from Diona's breasts but later reached for Laurin and slept on his chest, drinking the spiritual milk of the life force energy that flowed in his veins.

Laurin found it most soothing to hold the child at his heart: it was the only ointment for his wound of grief. There was something of Pasión in this child, more than merely his genes: with his birth, he brought their eternal love back to life.

"Look," Laurin whispered to Diona, "the baby knows everything that's happening around him. His consciousness is very old — older than us — and fully developed. He understands every word we say, he just cannot reply yet because the vocal cords of his body are not developed yet. Watch him," he said while he held the baby up.

"Little one, please nod, if you understand what I'm saying."

To Diona's amazement, the baby nodded and let out a delightful little laugh. She, as his mother, had a question straight away.

"Is your name Dion?"

Again, the baby nodded and let out a delightful little laugh.

"I heard this name last night in my dreams," she whispered to Laurin.

Laurin, silently, like a sacred word, repeated the name Dion, while he laid the baby back between them. There, he slept night after night, every night, nestled in Laurin's magic, covered by Diona's river-long hair of dreams: they gave him safety, he gave them solace. Oftentimes, Laurin liked to put baby Dion on a pillow next to his own face and look him in the eyes. If they say eyes were portals to the soul, Dion's eyes were portals to eternity. Every time Laurin looked through them, a million years of his own past and future were looking back at him: past stars and galaxies, future waves and potentialities, bringing closer a secret message that in the end, it would be worthwhile to hold on to the cosmic dream, whatever terror meanwhile may arise.

When Dion was a year and a day old, he said his first words.

Diona came rushing to Laurin, who was tending the garden he now spent most of his days with. There he was growing impossibly large and vital vegetables, heavenly fruits on paradisiacal trees, mushrooms amidst green-green moss... Diona thought it was pure sorcery. With great concentration and focused intent, Laurin even created sunlit hot spots in the middle of the deepest winter, to grow good food all year around, even when their war-stricken country was starving.

"Come, come," Diona called him with the excitement of a mother. "Dion is trying to say his first words." Laurin followed Diona, rushing back into the cottage. "I think he is trying to say ma-ma," she said, going back to observe Dion closely.

"No… No…" The baby was babbling on a blanket near the fireplace. Laurin listened with eagerness; it didn't sound like he was trying to say ma-ma, it sounded more like na-na.

"No… Nothing," the child said, and scared for a moment his baffled mother.

"Nothing… Nothing…," he repeated.

"Nothing is lost," he finally said and crowned his conviction with a delightful round of a golden little laugh.

On many occasions, Laurin tried to ask the child more; he wanted to know who he was, but Dion spoke very little. He preferred to be quiet and play with animals in the sacred groves rather than seeking the company of humans. He did acknowledge that he was a Hierophant but said very little when Laurin asked how he achieved liberation.

"You will understand who I am," he only said, "the day you find your own liberation from the wheel of life and death. Until then, the best way for you to understand me is to think that I am your future."

Despite all his curiosity, Laurin was wise enough not to push for more: a Hierophant only ever withholds information if giving it would be detrimental, cause harm, or misunderstanding. In general, Laurin showed high and extraordinary levels of discernment by never forcing anything on him and not interfering in the child's development. Instead, he allowed the innate wisdom of the divine child to unfold naturally. Humanity has an unfortunate tendency to kill the messiah, in whatever form it arrives: the murder often begins by attacking the soul of the child, forcing it through various exercises into submission and conformity. Laurin, quite on the contrary, permitted Dion to do what he truly wanted and stepped out of the way when it was necessary. Even when Dion expressed his wish to be taken to the elder of the Order and began to spend more and more time with him, Laurin let him. He understood that a god needed the company of a highly developed being, not to lose his brilliance in the midst of our polluted world, even though he greatly missed Dion whenever they weren't together.

Despite his usual quietness, however, one late summer evening, sometime in his seventh year, Dion came to Laurin in the garden and initiated the conversation. He went straight to the point.

"Father," Dion said to him. "I don't like the thought that you'll have to wander aimlessly for eons just because you have donated all your meritorious energy to my other father."

Laurin nearly dropped the trimming knife he was using, so astounding was what this child said. Extraordinary it was, even in magical terms! Laurin never told anyone what happened in that hour when Pasión died, not a word.

Did this mean that even his most private burden someone, somewhere, somehow in the universe had been witnessing?

"I have a plan," the child said before Laurin could think or say anything else and broke out in his heavenly golden laughter.

And before Laurin could ask what that plan was, he noticed that Dion did not come by himself. Suddenly Nákash, the wise elder of the Order and a familiar-looking young girl stepped forward from behind the trees.

"We have discussed your son's plan in great length," Nákash said earnestly to Laurin. "I believe it has substance and can work well. I am here to endorse it."

"What is the plan?" Laurin asked, incredulous at such a kind-hearted conspiracy.

Dion, the divine child answered.

"You have given your energy selflessly. Now members of the Order shall give you their energy selflessly."

"No," Laurin quickly said, alarmed even by the thought. "I can't take that kind of sacrifice from anyone! Slow their progress down for my — "

"Of course, we knew you'd say that," Nákash interfered, "but it won't. The genius of Dion's idea is to allow a large number of members to make small contributions over a long period of time. That way, they have a chance to practice an act of unconditional loving-kindness, which will add to their merits. It means, what they give will come back to them. It also means that it'll be a slow process, which won't be completed in this lifetime of yours. Instead, it may take centuries, even if the number of our members grows over time. But! It won't take eons like it would if you were left alone."

Laurin's heart fluttered like a caged bird seeing the keys that could open the lock, but his brain remained suspicious.

"Could this really be a success?" he asked. "We know from our early experimentations with keywords that they are sensitive to any small change in vibration. If they are pronounced differently, say with a foreign accent, they would lose their power. Country borders, cultures, accents, and dialects all change over time…"

"Yes," Nákash nodded, "we have thought of such complications also. We came to the conclusion that in this particular case, we must avoid the use of a keyword. Instead, we shall take a physical object to become the carrier of all the collected energy, even with all the risks that this entails."

"We need an object in your possession, which shall survive centuries," Dion added.

Laurin looked up from his deep thoughts. He saw a leaf slowly gliding to the ground in the still warm, summer breeze. The leaf, in its simplicity, happily heralded the autumn, and had no reason to rebel; it was quite all right for leaves to die, to give space for renewal in the spring. No, there was nothing wrong with mortals having to die, Laurin thought to himself. In this great, never-ending experiment called life, many passing stories and forgettable episodes have to be eliminated to extract what the mind wants to keep for eternity, to find what must never become food for fugacity, futile decline, and destruction. What was in Laurin's possession that would survive centuries? What was worth eternity if not his love for Pasión?

At once, Laurin, Dion, and their visitors all turned their heads in the same direction. Behind the falling leaf, in the last rays of the evening sunshine, they glimpsed Pasión's marble statue…

The little fellowship smiled in unison.

"Yes, father, that is my plan," Dion said. "We will slowly, but surely turn Pasión's statue for you into a future portal into the Pure Realm of Elysium. When the work is completed, the statue shall be the greatest object of magic the world has ever seen," he added, with a golden little laugh at the end.

***

"Is there any way to speed up this process?" Sofia asked Alana while she watched her friend laying the scroll into a rehydration chamber to be unrolled day after day but only inch by inch.

"Yes, digital scanning would be a lot faster," Alana reminded her, "but that would involve other scientists. You said that you didn't want that."

"No," Sofia reassured her. "All right then. I'll practice patience."

"Good." Alana smiled. "It's a good thing. Remember: time is a wild beast that needs to be tamed. It's better to reawaken the past gently."

***

The young girl that had accompanied the elder Nákash now stepped towards Laurin and spoke to him in an elegant, considerate voice.

"My name is Aliana," she said. "You may remember me; I was there at Pasión's initiation. I am also the reincarnation of Anisa, Pasión's mother from Melos."

Their eyes met and became teary. Laurin opened his arms into his most congenial embrace.

"You freed my son from slavery, you freed him from ignorance, and you freed him from the claws of a dark death," Aliana said sincerely. "My gratitude towards you is endless like the ocean and endless like the starry sky. Please, give me the honor to be the first who puts energy into your portal. May you be reunited with him as soon as we can work it."

Laurin nodded gently, however, neither of them could say anything else more. It was too much for one day! "We shall come back tomorrow to commence the ritual," Nákash announced. "But for tonight, we all must rest."

"Laurin," the elder had one more important thing to say before they left, "time is a curious beast. It likes to devour memories, and even the ones it cannot swallow it tears into pieces, warps, or distorts. There are epochs in history when almost all of truth is forgotten, and such epochs are about to come. To bridge into the future, I advise you to make written notes about our mystical project. Ensure you hide your scrolls well, at a place where you or future members of the Order can find it, in case the oral transmissions may be forgotten."

"I will," Laurin agreed. "Like my friend Plato, I too shall write."

That night, long after everyone went to sleep, Laurin lit the oil lamp. He used the best quality Egyptian papyrus and the best quality of black carbon ink, as his notes on this particular scroll were meant to last.

With his silver-covered, beautiful hand, he began to form in calligraphy his very own letters of hope:

> *I, Laurin, son of Talesander, am writing these words, in the first year of the 94th Olympiad. I am writing this to remind future members of a mystical enterprise our Orphic Order has initiated on my behalf. I am writing this to remind ourselves that the statue of Pasión — the young man who was enlisted as my slave in the last twelve years in Athens — is not an ordinary object of art.*
>
> *Therefore, if you, in any future century, are deciphering this document but do not know anything about the Order or Pasión, I appeal to you most sincerely. I request you to respect the past and burn this scroll.*
>
> *However, if you are a member of the Order, please read carefully...*

***

The day had come. Weeks of meticulous and maddeningly slow work was behind them. Alana had been sleeping on the sofa in her office, Sofia mostly under her desk in a Swiss army sleeping bag that had been her traveling charm ever since her service days as a military doctor. Again, she had strange dreams, none of which she could remember but it felt as if her brain, like a computer, had begun to download data from some cosmic cloud. Sometimes, in the morning, she was even surprised that she had woken in a modern, sterile laboratory, as if her soul was expecting rocks and pine trees instead.

By now, Alana had laid out the scroll safely between glass sheets while its content had been scanned in. On Alana's desktop screen was a computer-enhanced and corrected version of the first paragraph, quite clearly legible.

Usually, Alana liked to be alone when reading an ancient text for the first time, but Sofia wouldn't move from her side. She understood that Sofia, as the founder of the scroll, had every moral right to be present. Sofia somehow belonged to the scroll, or rather the scroll belonged to her, although neither of them yet knew just how much!

"Oh my… God," Alana whispered as her eyes scanned the first line. She held her hand up for Sofia to see that her hand was shaking with excitement.

"What is it?" Sofia whispered as well: neither of them even dared to fully breathe.

"This truly is Laurin's missing scroll!"

"How do you know?" Sofia urged her to continue.

"The first word is Laurin! It says here: *I, Laurin, son of…* this name is not clear… it has an l here and ends with *sander*."

Sofia placed herself behind Alana's left shoulder and looked at the screen.

"Talesander," Sofia suggested. "Could it be Talesander?"

Alana looked at her, puzzled.

"Could be, yes. *I Laurin, son of Talesander, am writing these words…*" Alana read on and at once knew this was her one moment in time as an archaeologist. She had never, and will never see anything more exciting than this.

"We have a dating here!" she exclaimed. "Our brilliant Laurin did not fail to date his document," she celebrated. "*The first year of the 94th Olympiad…*"

"Which year does that correspond to?" Sofia asked eagerly, hoping that Alana wouldn't take too long to look up the conversion, but she didn't need to. Alana knew such things by heart.

"It is 404 BC," she said. Then she added with great, slow emphasis, "Sofia, with this, you have really found the world's oldest book on paper."

Sofia couldn't say anything for a minute. It was like in her dreams, except now she was awake, but memories from the cosmic cloud came again flooding — so fast, her head began to spin.

She looked up and saw that her own reflection mirroring back from the computer appeared above the papyrus text. Sofia never loved her own mirage as she loved it now. Never before had she been more grateful to herself for every breath she had taken in this precious human life. It was in this life that she finally acquired a body capable, and a mind sophisticated enough, that she could acquire ancient memories. As she remembered, her body became stronger, felt taller, and her mind was overflowing with gratitude towards herself, as it was in this life that she finally had the courage to follow her inner voice against all odds and remember who she was, and who she had been a long time ago.

"This is not a book," Sofia began to tell what she now knew.

"Not a book?"

"No, it is a private instruction, only for future members of the Order. Read on." Sofia pointed to the text on the screen.

"You are right," Alana said, shocked by the surprise. "It says: *I am writing this to remind future members of a mystical enterprise our Orphic Order has initiated on my behalf.*"

"It's about the statue of Pasión, isn't it," Sofia declared. "It says that the statue was not an ordinary object of art."

Alana checked the text and had to agree with Sofia yet again.

"Yes. Yes! Here it says: *not an ordinary object of art*," Alana echoed, sitting straight in disbelief. "Sofia, since when have you learned to read Ancient Greek?"

"I haven't," Sofia said. "I can't read this text, but I remember its content."

"You remember?!"

"Yes. For some while now, my consciousness has been tapping into memories from previous lives. It has all been rather fragmented and random at first, but now everything is becoming clear. Now I can remember it all."

"You mean." Alana asked urgently, "that you remember having lived a life in Ancient Greece?"

"Yes," Sofa nodded. "I do."

"And you were a member of this mystical Order?"

Sofia gave herself a pause. This was her great moment of archaeology — her excavation into the soul that had finally delivered her proof that consciousness lasted more than one lifetime between cradle and grave but wandered century upon century towards its own perfection.

"Yes, Alana," Sofia finally said. "I was a member of the Order. I still am."

"So, let me get this straight: you're saying… that you know the content of this scroll because you remember reading it in that past life?"

"No, Alana. I don't remember reading it…"

Sofia took a deep breath before she said it.

"I remember… writing it."

END OF BOOK ONE

PART TWO

Chapter 17
Elysium

Quick, so quick as only thoughts can travel, Pasión was shooting through milky ways and galaxies: it felt as if he was heading straight to the end of the universe.

There, at the endless end of everything, he reached the void: it was utter and complete emptiness, which felt so primordial that Pasión sensed it existed before everything else in creation ever existed. It was not an empty emptiness but pregnant with all the possibilities of creation — the past, the present, and the future.

As Pasión's mind observed the vast darkness, a pinpoint of light began to arise in the distance, which steadily opened into a red ring as he moved closer. Finally, he could see a gate of cinnabar red color in the middle of nothing. Pasión didn't know that the Cinnabar Gate was an entrance to the Pure Land of Elysium, but as intrigued and invited as he felt, he went through it. He was seeking to put his feet somewhere (like he was used to while walking the Earth): immediately, a first stepping stone came into being and so did the next and the next, as he stepped further and further.

Around his walking path, a spacious garden began to unfold. Some things seemed carefully crafted: there were statues featuring not people, but cryptic shapes and symbols. Other spots looked wild. At the horizon, pine forests covered misty mountains, and high rocks scraped starry-starry skies.

It was a mindscape so real yet so fantastic that here everything seemed possible. Pasión felt seduced by novelty: in a lotus pond, which presented itself to his right, he found flowers in colors he'd never seen before — they were not merely new hues, but entirely new colors he could see, hear, taste, and touch! Here existed a color for grief; here existed a color for glory! Here existed a color for Laurin's scent of rose and sandalwood; here existed a color for that gentle breeze of spring that used to sweep across the shores of Melos Island.

Pasión wanted to swim, to join some handsome ducks in the pond. He jumped in, but in the moment of his impact, those birds with the marble feathers and emerald green heads took flight. Their ability to fly away from the top of the water amazed Pasión; he wished he could do that too, and as he wished, he became one of them. Before he knew it, he was paddling industriously with his little duck feet in the pond, then opened his wings, and — although it was quite an effort to start with — he took flight.

Almighty soul of the world! This was a feeling Pasión owned right away and never again wanted to lose: flying! It was amazing, albeit quite laborious on duck wings. He saw an eagle, and wishing for the eagle's majestic flight, it merged into his body. No more laborious flapping with the wings; the eagle was soaring in the wind!

With superb eyesight, he could scan the landscape while focusing on the tiniest movement. Scan, focus, target, defocus, that was the order; scan, focus, target... He found a target: a mouse moving under an umbrella leaf! Suddenly, he could think of nothing else, and his sight and attention remained highly focused on the mouse. Mouse, mouse, mouse, juicy, juicy mouse. He, the mighty hunter, came power-diving down from vertiginous heights, grabbed the mouse with three golden claws, and bit with his beak into the delicious little flesh. Oh, that warm, life-giving blood!

But now! That pain... as the mouse was dying, Pasión had become the mouse!

Only it was his luck, a hand reached down and pulled him up, rescuing him in the last minute from the terrible claws of the predator bird that had pierced his chest.

The same hand now touched the heart of Pasión, who was now back in human form. The touch healed the wound pierced by the Spartan spear with the same healing force Pasión knew from Laurin but magnified a thousandfold in this celestial space.

Pasión looked up and saw a very old, very beautiful face. It exuded the old age beauty only those possess who have seen the deep and looked death in the eye, have walked its realms, and came back standing tall.

"Welcome," the elder said, with kindness coming from an infinite source. Pasión found it impossible to tell whether he was a man, or she was a woman: it seemed at this high level, no such distinction any longer existed. "Welcome to the Pure Land of Elysium. My name is Al'Om — it comes from Alpha and Omega. Alpha, as I am the first Hierophant who brought our sacred Order into being. Omega, as I also will be the last to remain. I am committed to staying until the very end when everyone returns to the source with all their experiences."

Pasión bowed respectfully. It was unnecessary to introduce himself, and he knew that.

"Is this all your creation?" He opened his arms all around the incredible landscape.

"Yes," Al'Om said and smiled. "This is the creation of my mind. Now it is the creation of your mind, also. Our Mind."

As the sage sensed Pasión's curiosity, he went on and said things that sounded like the teachings of Laurin on a greater scale.

"You see, consciousness in the universe is a singularity. The miracle of the mind is such that it is only one but quite a genius: it can restrict itself to only see parts at a time, which brings forth the opportunity of separation. So perfect is the illusion that humans live from life to life, most of them not even suspecting that they are talking to themselves and the events they are witnessing are but projections of their mind."

"So is all life but an illusion?" Pasión, in his forever inquisitive nature, challenged the sage. "Nothing but a cosmic trick of the mind?"

"Oh… but it's much more than that," the sage said, talking like a brilliant scientist presenting his invention. "It all has a meaning, a wonderful meaning!"

"What is that meaning?" Pasión asked, now that he had a chance.

"You are about to find out for yourself," Al'Om said mysteriously. "This Pure Land has some remarkable features, as you may have noticed: it follows your thoughts, but most importantly, it causes shifts between various points of experience. Here, in Elysium, you can live life from the perspective of all parts. You've just suffered that yourself: if you want to kill a mouse, so be it, but you are the mouse also. This is the only place where you can get a taste of both separation and unity of the mind. Now go, Pasión, you will re-experience the life you just lived. Examine it: find the one thing that was significant about it — for that will be the meaning of it all."

Pasión wanted to ask how he could do that, but Al'Om implied with a smile that it would all reveal itself: laughing, he only pointed up to the sky.

"Fly!" he said gloriously. "Fly, my friend, fly!"

That word, Pasión did not need to be told twice: he catapulted himself to soar again, this time on his own wings of intent.

Before he knew it, Pasión was in the air over the wild coasts of Melos Inland, harboring the desire to be born there, as he longed for sunshine, the salty water of the sea, and the warm body of the mother he knew and trusted. Almighty creation: what yearning, longing, and heartache a human life was made of! Pasión saw his birth and his life as a panorama of interrelated feelings, thoughts, and frequencies: all happened in an instant, yet this instant was eternal, in which every detail could be examined, how it affected Pasión, and how he affected others.

Soon into this experience, Pasión discovered something rather disconcerting. In life, whenever something happened that he perceived as good, it triggered some pain or caused someone else's suffering. Life mercilessly seemed to keep its accounts of good and bad in balance. Pasión saw that the fondness of his mother caused the bullying by his brother, his talent for art brought on his father's rejection, and even the beauty of his island was spoiled by the violence it suffered from the enemy. It seemed in this business of life there were no positive accounts: no bargain, no profit, no win.

Yet his mind, his greater Mind, did not give up: like a universal calculator, it went on... tirelessly seeking something in life that wouldn't level out at the end

— something that would make life worthwhile. Seeking, searching, scanning, it finally found an episode of an utterly different quality.

Oh, what bliss it was to live through it again! It was that night when dreaming with the centaur gave him the courage to go into Laurin's study. It was that night when his new master first took him into his arms.

How frightened, how utterly vulnerable he was that night! Having been sold as a slave, Pasión was forced to reach down to his deepest fear: that his soul could be invalidated, and his inner creative magic extinguished. What relief it was to arrive in Laurin's arms instead! How he wanted to merge into him ever since, to become one with him, never again having to leave that haven, that home, that love he found with him.

Here in Elysium, he felt he was there with him: he felt again how he was nestled in Laurin's embrace while drifting off to sleep. He had asked him whether he could stay for the night. *I was waiting for you my whole life,* Laurin said, *of course, you can stay.*

This time, however, Pasión didn't hear these words being spoken — this time, he experienced *saying* them!

He had slipped into Laurin's awareness. Pasión could hear his thoughts as his own like a hymn, coming from the depth of his being:

> *you came to me like a young cat lost in the night…*
> *not yet you know that you are the night*
> *and all the stars belong to you…*
>
> *you came in, shivering in fear of me!*
> *how lovely that you are afraid of me*
> *how lovely that I can take away that fear*
>
> *how lovely that you are my captive*
> *what a privilege it is to own you*
> *now I can keep you in my embrace*
> *now I can heal you and not let evil reach you*

> *your life could be over in a fortnight*
> *ruined and destroyed by the wrong master*
> *with me, your life will last forever*

How enchanted Laurin was by him! He held Pasión knowing he was the only treasure more important even than his mystical quest. Laurin had known something back then that Pasión saw only now, in Elysium.

Their love was not just mutual and absolute but held another most remarkable quality: no evil could ever level it. The time they shared added only to the joy and richness of creation, never to its suffering. For them, their love was that one thing of indisputable beauty and value to rise above all the terror and hardships of life and transmute all struggles into the most worthwhile adventure of existence.

Laurin always knew he was willing to do anything for it. The thoughts he had while looking into young Pasión's sleeping face gave it away:

> *I will take you into the stars*
> *through whatever hardship may come*
> *as you are invaluable to me*
> *as it is my purpose to do so*
>
> *no price shall be too high to pay*

Witnessing these words, Pasión felt not only beautifully touched but became frightened as he was grabbed by a sinister thought: How far would Laurin's love and safeguarding go? A dark presentiment urged him to search all his other memories with Laurin — he so would have loved to linger on amidst them — but he raced, raced ahead to the very end, where he suspected something unspeakable had occurred.

Pasión went to the moment of his own death. After his pain dissolved under Laurin's healing touch, he remembered his death as the most magical event: the two of them... embedded in a vortex of higher love, he felt rising... beautifully... into eternity.

But for Laurin! Now Pasión could hear what Laurin had spoken inside his own mind on that fatal day of the battle, which gave him the chills:

I have collected my merits
   Laurin cried silently into the void.
Now I'm summoning up my merits.
Now I intend to use my merits:
   my true thoughts,
   my true words,
   my true deeds.
Al'Om — hear me once:
   Drive up the cosmic vortex!

Al'Om — hear me twice:
   Open up the Cinnabar Gate!
Al'Om — hear me thrice:
   Free the Passage to Elysium!

And Al'Om had heard these unspoken words. He replied in thoughts that Laurin could perceive in his mind as Pasión was perceiving them now:

You are not dying.

I am not dying, Pasión is, Laurin had sent his thought to him.

If I open the gates now — the thought of Al'Om had come back to him — *you would use up your merits for someone else. You would not have enough energy left to activate the upward-moving vortex when your time comes.*

It doesn't matter. Open the Gate now, Laurin had demanded in his thoughts.

Are you aware of what you are doing to yourself? — the thoughts of Al'Om now thundered. *Are you aware of what is awaiting you? Look around you!*

As Al'Om sent this thought, the battle scene that was all around them that day went dark. Instead, panoramic images opened up from the void: they showed Laurin's soul cast adrift in the future, having lost what he had collected, forgotten who he had been, forgotten where he wanted to go, wandering through the centuries, wandering through all lands. Sometimes rich, sometimes poor, sometimes crippled, sometimes abled, sometimes man, sometimes woman but always carrying the invisible sign of a seeker but only to exasperate the demagogues and the fanatics, the lazy and the ordinary. There were the visions of the stakes ready to burn, instruments ready for torture, scaffolds, and dungeons, all the horrors that the lost seeker cannot escape.

Worst of all: centuries of loneliness were to come for Laurin.

Do you really want to plunge back into such darkness, Al'Om had gently asked Laurin after he had shown him the future awaiting him if he gave up his collected energies for Pasión. *Take all this suffering on you?*

Do not send fear on me, Laurin's thoughts retorted. *I am in a weak moment, already grieving. Just open the Gates!*

I am warning you exactly because you are vulnerable now, Al'Om warned him one last time. *You are supposed to come to Elysium next. There's a natural order to things.*

The natural order to things is Love, the thoughts of Laurin hit back without hesitation. *Open the gates for Pasión!*

And so, the vortex began to move...

Pasión had to break away from this terrible vision! He shook it off so that he could stand again on the grounds of Elysium and find some balance. The profuse tranquility and goodness of this place sheltered him from having to fully suffer Laurin's grief and misery. Still, it touched and disturbed him to his very core.

Then he noticed that Al'Om was standing next to him.

"Send me back," Pasión told him at once. "Send me back, I beg you. You know this was a mistake! I'm not supposed to be here. Laurin was meant to come here, not me. He worked for it, lifetime after lifetime, I'm only here because…"

"…he gave you his ticket to heaven, yes," Al'Om finished the sentence. "And yes, you are not quite ready to be here. Look how easily you are still drawn into despair and indignation. But you must not worry! I'm happy to have you here because I like you very much: your heart is in the right place, and you are a fully inspired, ingenious soul. Laurin did not make his sacrifice in vain. Your experience and your exposure here to higher existence will purify in you whatever still needs to be purified. You'll do well with the others in the Valley of Ideas."

"Do well?" Pasión echoed, disbelieving, while he felt perhaps some of his un-purified anger rising up. "How can I do well, here in Elysium, while Laurin — and whoever he becomes — is suffering and lonely down there? Al'Om, I'm plead-ing with you: send me back to him."

"That I cannot do," he insisted. "No one can go back into a life they just died from."

"Send me into the future then!" Pasión said, with excited hope in his voice.

"I'm afraid I cannot do that either," Al'Om said, full of regret, but firmly. "I took a vow that if you or anyone reaches this place, I won't let you slip back into the sufferings of lower-realm existence. Rather, I will help you to reach enlighten-ment in the fastest possible way. I must never break my sacred oath! However, to ease your pain and give you peace while you are here, let me tell you something you do not yet know."

Pasión was listening sharply: he really wanted to hear something that could disperse the horror of what he'd just seen.

"As it is currently unfolding, it is not taking Laurin eons to find his way back to the sacred path. He has help — which he never asked for — from the Order and even from you, through your son. In a joint effort, they are building a new portal for him. They are turning your statue into that portal! Your beloved will join you here; it's already happening."

"The statue," Pasión said dreamily and smiled as he undeniably adored the idea that his masterpiece would serve such a superb goal. "So, will Laurin be able to use the statue to come here and join me?"

"Not Laurin himself," Al'Om said. "Even with the help of many, it will take lifetimes before one of Laurin's future incarnations acquires a body capable, a brain sophisticated, and a heart purified enough to remember. It won't take eons, but it will take centuries. In twenty-five centuries, a woman will be born whose destiny will be to find the statue and discover its power."

"She?" Pasión asked, surprised for a moment, but his thoughts ran fast. The sage did not have to say anything else, as Pasión already knew. There was only one other human being he ever felt the same way towards as he felt for Laurin, and she was from the future.

The rebirth of Laurin must be...

"Sofia" he whispered in reverence: how majestically the pieces of the puzzle were coming together in this mystery of time! Pasión smiled and regained all his hope. He put his arms around the sage in joy.

"This is marvelous, thank you, marvelous news," he hurriedly said and ran off like a child from his parent.

Sofia was Laurin's future! That was all he needed to know. Pasión remembered every word he spoke with Sofia in Little Eternity: the time, the place, and his promise to appear and win at the Olympic Games. That was a promise he now had a chance to keep.

All he needed was to learn how to die from Elysium. This should not require the sage to break his vows. Al'Om said there were others: Pasión would find them, and someone would be able to help.

Soon, Pasión found himself hiking through the heavenly realm in search of the others. His heart felt contented, as his purpose was clear.

From this realm, he could really see life for what it was: a creative experiment of the mind to bring forth higher and higher worlds, with increasing levels of happiness. Human life was an alchemical process, during which emotions, events, hopes and dreams, satisfactions and frustrations, pain, pleasure, suffering, are all boiling together in that gigantic cauldron of time. Everything burns away, everything vaporizes, everything explodes, until something crystallizes and proves indestructible, worthy to be taken onto the next levels of existence. And Pasión's mind knew that this love he shared with Laurin-Sofia, he wanted to save and take into eternity.

So Pasión pondered while walking on a mountain ridge when he suddenly heard music coming from the valley below. His heart jumped with sweeping joy as he recognized the melody. And he thought he would never hear it again! It was Diona's song: the one they played together at the first symposium.

It was the same tune, but the interpretation was worthy of heaven: played in celestial harmony by thousands of new instruments the earth had not yet heard. Strongest of all sounds, Pasión could hear Diona's flute. How he wished he had carried a cithara with him… and as he wished, so he did.

The music wrapped him in happiness, which grew stronger as he began to descend from the mountain. The valley was filled with beautiful souls of all ages, colors, and genders. Some were playing the instruments, others — as Pasión delightfully observed — were engaged in creations of all kinds, even in his all-time favorite passion: sculpting!

Pasión hurried towards them, floating above the ground, but at some height, he sat down on a large, sun-warmed stone to play his cithara, joining in the music.

And the diamond souls in the valley heard him and took their melody to even greater, even more zestful and exuberant heights.

Now that you are here, we are even more complete, what invaluable happiness it is to us that you have come and found us, they were saying with every tone they played.

And when the music was over and Pasión drifted down to the valley, all came rushing, flying towards him.

"You are here," they called out in joy all around Pasión. "You are here!" The cosmic tribe came rushing to welcome Pasión as their own: one by one they joined in to hug him all around. They surrounded him like a hundred layers of petals in a rose flower of love. Their message was clear as morning dew: here you will never be alone, here you matter to us, here you will be loved, and we truly know the purest ways of love.

Pasión's heart was overflowing by the time the rose ball of hugs slowly dissolved. The embraces had eased one by one as everyone gently stepped back or flew away. In the space that opened up around Pasión, a young, divine beauty wearing a floating dress of red and white approached him. Oh, such a sweet familiarity! Pasión jumped with unexpected joy as well as doubt. Could she really be...

"Diona?" Pasión called her incredulously. "Is it you?"

The heavenly figure gently laid her arms around Pasión, embraced and caressed him, just as Diona used to do in life.

"I am the idea of Diona," she said. "This is my purest form, which lives here in Elysium. I am a being who can emanate concurrently into different worlds. In one world, I am a warrior princess, in another, I am Laurin's slave..."

"Oh," Pasión's knees went soft in a wave of bittersweet nostalgia. "I wish to be Laurin's slave again! Who would have thought that I would be here in the heavens but curiously would rather be back, as someone's slave."

"Of course, not anyone's, but Laurin's." Diona nodded. "I can understand that."

"Diona." Pasión seized the moment. "I want to be reborn to meet him again, whoever he has become throughout the centuries. Please help me! Do you know how one can be reborn from here?"

"No." Diona lifted her round shoulders. "No one before ever wanted to die from Elysium. But... I shall do some research for you," she finally said with a smile.

Diona then disappeared from his sight, but with her promise to help, Pasión now felt free to take his time and roam around this extraordinary realm. He let himself be drawn to the sculptors and noticed something astonishing. Here, the artists were sorcerers. Through their work, they brought new things into being — new shapes, new colors, even new forms of life. New, truly new things.

On Earth, nothing was ever truly new. While he lived and worked there as an artist, Pasión was achingly aware of that. Regardless of how creative, how ingenious he had been with shapes and colors to give them new meaning, he always had to remain within the boundaries of things that already existed. Nobody could ever break through this limitation of physical reality. A storyteller could think of something he believed was new, like a flying centaur, yet was that not merely an amalgam of things... a horse, a man, a bird... which already existed. As long as bound by physical reality, no one can think of anything truly new, but how different that was in Elysium! Here, the souls in their unfettered artistic splendor were able to create things that were entirely new: things I cannot name, as we have no words for them yet, things I cannot show, as we have no shapes for them yet, things I cannot explain, as we have no ideas for them yet. Still, I assure you: the diamond souls of Elysium are already creating shapes beyond squares and circles, colors beyond the rainbow, places to get together beyond the gymnasium and the academia... new ideas worthwhile to pursue are being created as we tell this tale.

Pasión dived into this prolific, visionary work with all his might, and there was even more! During the day, they worked in the Valley of Ideas, but at night, they flew — to send out dreams. Together, the tribe crossed the heavens but then dispersed in the starry sky in search of sentient, sensitive beings. Each of them went to find those sleeping humans who could pierce the veil of worlds and receive their inspiration.

Night after night, Pasión found sleepers behind moon-lit windows and built bridges of light to reach them. He whispered melodies and stories into their ears, stroked their skin as if with a paintbrush, and held them gently in various positions, forms, and shapes. Like a lover impregnating the beloved, he left seeds within artists for them to turn it all into music, books, paintings, sculptures, and new ways of life, which in turn would give inspiration to millions to make life pleasing and worthwhile. Especially, he sent out inspiration and guidance to those seven members of the Order he vowed to help fulfill their destinies. Nothing Pasión had ever done before felt more rewarding.

Yet, he never let a night pass by without searching for Sofia also. On many nights, he could find her, and on those nights, she saw him in her dreams. Sofia was a healer: not particularly receptive to creative ideas, but all the more receptive to Pasión's lovemaking. She could feel his silky-smooth kisses and caresses reassuring her of their eternal love while engaging the etheric senses. Still, only too often, did they also set Sofia's flesh-and-blood human body on fire: kindling her longing. After meeting in dreams, they both felt transfigured, but an ache carried over into their days for their reunion never could last beyond the morning.

Pasión began to wonder why the worlds were so separate from each other. Now that he had experienced for himself that it truly was the mind that created everything there was, he could not understand what the purpose of physical life would be. If the mind can bring forth realms so full of beauty and joy as Elysium, why would it want to create a world of physical forms so full of suffering and sadness, imperfection and evil? Pasión began to understand that the mind puts ideas to a test by letting them manifest in physical reality. Otherwise, an idea would remain but an idea: beautiful and perfect, yet static and thus incapable of change. Only by introducing impermanence, inviting death to come where life was once upon, and allowing the opposite of any idea to emerge too can creation be set into motion. Every soul examines an idea and decides whether it is worthy of eternity. Would the idea of Pasión and Sofia, the idea of being loved by the Other, survive the test of time?

One night, Pasión lay awake in his hammock on a golden apple tree and did not follow the tribe into the stars. He watched one last time, Elysium bathing in the gentle silver light of a thousand moons. He saw a beam of light coming towards him and on it, like a Moon goddess, was Diona.

"I have found what you asked me to find," she said to him in thoughts.

Knowing it was time to go, Pasión followed her on a long, nocturnal hike through the Elysian Fields. They went through meadows and woodlands illuminated by fireflies of good thoughts and luminescent mushrooms of ecstatic feelings. Movement was easy, even walking up high into the mountains, they could glide above the ground. For a long time, they spoke no words, neither in thoughts nor on the lips.

Finally, they reached a river in the highlands. Pasión watched Diona's splendid, slender figure against its silver shine.

"Diona," he wanted to ask her something he was always curious about. "On earth, were you ever jealous of the intense love between me and our master, Laurin?"

"No," she said and began to walk the path along the river. "Diona on earth was never jealous. Your love felt right, and you both loved me: I felt very good amid your warmth and exciting love."

"Don't you ever want to find your own cosmic partner though?" Pasión asked.

"No," she said decisively and kept on walking. "I don't have one. Most souls do not. We all are searching for that one thing we want to take into eternity with us, but it is different for everyone. The love I am manifesting is a different kind. I love to help when someone is bringing something. That is for me the most satisfying pleasure. You will be happy to know that in your last life we shared, Diona is staying with Laurin until the very end, never to leave his side."

Before Pasión could express his gratitude, Diona said they had arrived.

They were at the delta of the silver river, which opened in front of Pasión's eyes as a scenery of severe beauty — so unusual for Elysium, it was even sinister. The enormous body of mirroring water did not flow into an ocean but disappeared on the horizon between two mountain peak twins.

"What is this place?" Pasión whispered.

"This is the delta of the River of Tears," Diona told him. "The river consists of all the tears ever cried on Earth because of dreams unfulfilled."

"Why are you showing it to me?" Pasión felt an eerie shiver in fear of something Diona might say next.

"This is the river you have to dive into if you want to be reborn on Earth."

"Where will it take me?"

"Come, see for yourself," Diona replied and took Pasión by the hand. She lifted him, and together they floated above the scene, behind the twin peaks.

What he saw there made Pasión gasp in awe and surprise: the river came crashing down in the greatest, loudest waterfall in the cosmos, falling into Emptiness.

"If I went down this waterfall," Pasión said, alarmed "it… would surely knock me out."

"Yes, it would kill you," Diona nodded. "Your tender, etheric body from Elysium would be crushed by it. That's why this is the only place you can use to leave the Pure Realm."

Pasión remained silent. What an insane task this seemed to be!

"Are you changing your mind?" Diona looked at him.

"No. Never. But I am afraid. I need to collect all my bravery to do this."

"Come." Diona took his hand again and took him back to the delta where the River of Tears looked a bit friendlier. There, she took Pasión into her arms.

"I can emanate into multiple lives," she reminded him. "If you want me, I can come and support you in the life you are now birthing into."

"I will need a good Olympic trainer," Pasión said and laughed a little… but Diona took him seriously.

"An Olympic trainer," she contemplated the words. "All right, I shall be there for you."

Surprised, relieved, and touched, Pasión could speak no more. He went to the river.

Carefully, he stepped in. The water felt friendly at first, and it was deep only to his hips. When he took a few steps and his stomach and his chest quickly went underwater, he began to feel the power of the current. Only with the greatest difficulty could he keep his feet on the riverbed ground. He knew, with the next step, even if he tried to swim, he would be carried away.

One last time, he turned around and looked at Diona, whose long hair flew like a river in the silver wind.

Then he had to do it.

He focused his intent and said into the river:

> *I intend to be born again in the year 2000 after Christ,*
> *on Earth, in the city of London,*
> *by parents who understand who I am and support my goal:*
> *thus, I will attend and win gymnastics gold medal*
> *at the Olympics 2020 after Christ. So be it!*

With these words, he gave up all control. He took one more step and allowed the stream to take away his balance, to take away his mind, for the giant waterfall to suck him in. Immediately, he was reminded of the pain that was inherent in physical existence. Even if he had thought that the etheric body couldn't suffer, the water hit down on it like a thousand whips and destroyed it.

Nothing was left of Pasión in Elysium.

Yet again, he was floating as pure consciousness in the midst of the void. To his relief, however, he noticed that all of his memories and aspirations were intact. Thus, he felt happiness and joy while he was falling into the below.

"Sofia, my love," he smiled into a universe full of stars, "enough is enough. I am coming."

Chapter 18
Twenty-Five Centuries

R umor has it you can drive a blind man insane by healing his vision, if since birth he has never seen. He, who has been used to navigating the world solely by the other senses, never learned to interpret visual impressions. What is he suddenly to do with all those bright colors overloading his optical nerves? With all the shapes he cannot assign to any known object? How is he to distinguish between small, nearby, and small, afar? Step by step, such a man would have to learn to connect the idea of an object to the sight of an object, and also not to mistake a photograph for the real thing. Such learning needs time and patience, to allow the brain to adjust to a new, augmented reality.

Similar was the challenge and confusion Sofia had to endure, as countless memories from the past flooded into her brain. Once the gate of cosmic memory was open for her, Sofia began to remember not only the life she lived as Laurin in Ancient Greece but other lives, too — during twenty-five centuries.

"Alana," she said to her friend after they had studied the beginning of the scroll. "I need to leave now, but we'll be back in touch soon."

"You look tired." Alana stared at her, a tad worried.

"Tired would be all right," Sofia said. "It's worse, however: my head is bursting with information it was never meant to process, and my whole body is fighting nausea."

Alana offered to call a taxi, but Sofia insisted on walking. Instead of returning to the hotel, she hiked up into the Penteli Mountains. This time, she was going home. Her legs took Sofia, without a single step in the wrong direction, to Laurin's Grove.

Walking around the Grove in her enhanced state of consciousness resembled traveling in time. While Sofia looked around, centuries overlapped. One moment, she was Sofia and she saw an airplane flying above the cliffs. The next moment, he was Laurin and saw Plato coming. Plato had remained his last connection to Athens and used to visit him more and more as he got older. Plato told him terrible things: how the Spartans won the war, and how Socrates was poisoned by his own government. But he also told him things filled with hope: how the Spartans proved to be more noble victors than the Athenians had been at Melos and refrained from killing or selling the Athenians as slaves. Finally, Plato told him the most wonderful thing: how he founded the academia, which would forever remain a venerated place to train and develop the mind. There was greatness in those times! Sofia thought. Laurin himself would have lived a truly worthy life if not overshadowed by his loss and his immense grief over Pasión. Blissfully, he also received a lot of comfort: Dion was the happiest human the world had ever seen… a true Hierophant who remained joyful every moment of his life… Everywhere he went, flowers opened their petals and humans fell in love… Every day, the Dog Who Did Not Exist was running around in the Grove… and there was Diona…

Delightful Diona, with hair long as a river, remained at Laurin's side until his very late, last breath! She became an initiate: the most industrious student of the mysteries. Along with Aliana, the girl reborn who was once Pasión's mother, she was the one who donated most of her meritorious energy to the statue. And Diona's words were the last Laurin heard before he died.

"I vow," she had been whispering into his ears, "that I will stay at your side. I will follow you through centuries to come. I vow, when the time is right, I will lead you to find the statue. I vow I will bring you to the Hierophant to give you the Water of Memory. I vow I will stay at your side until you find Pasión, or until you want me to."

Sofia remembered the moment of Laurin's death as if it happened yesterday. The last thing he felt while alive was Diona's dreamy hair brushing against his face, and the first thought he held while leaving his body was his eternal commitment to finding Pasión again.

By now, the memories were hitting Sofia with such force that she had to find a place to lie down. Laurin's small cabin was long gone, of course, but Sofia found the large stone on which Laurin and Pasión loved to bathe in starlight at night.

She lay down on the stone and closed her eyes. Being here alone was heart-wrenching. Still, having found this place lifted her to heights where being lonely and heart-broken no longer mattered. Sofia now knew that all her yearning for a higher life and love was not in vain, now she could find Pasión again. Now was not a time to be sad and bereft. This was a time for great hope, a time for learning, a time to let memories flood in with full power.

First, it felt like an attack. As Sofia lay on her back, making herself fully receptive, thousands upon thousands of impressions rushed to her: shrill sounds and blurry pictures, fast turning into movies, with overlapping, mad storylines as if shot by a director on a wild trip. But Sofia took some deep breaths and directed the life flow energy inside her accordingly, the command of which she again fully owned. She succeeded in slowing down the flow and taking one memory at a time.

He was reborn many times; she was reborn many times.

He forgot everything — as he knew he would. Yet, at the core of his being, buried deep in the unconscious mind, he still carried the spirit of his old vows and aspirations. His mind no longer knew the name of Pasión, but his heart went on and on searching for him. Yet, to the horror of horrors, he was nowhere in time to be found.

He was reborn in the violent time of Rome, where he became a negotiator for peace. The enemy, Carthago, captured him and only let him go to negotiate after he had promised he would return. He kept his word, even though he knew he would be tortured to death. His eyelids were cut off and his body was left, tied on his back, to burn out in the desert sun. But during all this time, the horror of horrors was that Pasión was nowhere around.

He was reborn in a monastery, away from all that war and violence, in the Land of the Rising Sun. Lots of wonderful wisdom teachings and martial arts practices were available. There was also a lot of misguided intimacy: as boys, they were taken under the duvets of the elders, for warmth and satisfaction — and when he became an elder, he did the same with the boys. Little did he know that he would never find fulfillment with them since his heart was, in vain, seeking Pasión, who was nowhere around.

He was reborn, addicted to pleasures, to a mother and two fathers in a French bordello. There she became a celebrated courtesan, someone who practiced her art more for joy, and less for profit. Later, she was expecting a child, but the baby was stillborn. To overcome her immense grief, she became a nun, feeding the hungry and healing the sick. Little did she know that her loss was embedded in a more ancient loss, as her heart still unconsciously longed for Pasión, who was still nowhere around.

She was reborn, to become a blind priest, in a sleepy Celtic fishermen's village. Here he had all the time in the world and would find Truth again — surrounded by a loving family, perhaps even happiness. Yet, the one deep yearning was never soothed, as Pasión was again nowhere to be found.

Life after life he lived, death after death she died: suffered many great evils... mostly from the false religions: atrocities, torture, murder — committed shamelessly in the name of the prophets. Yet, the more lives Sofia recalled, the more hopeful she became. In twenty-five centuries, the consciousness that now became her, had never killed anyone, never harmed a living being intentionally, and had only increased her compassion for healing. He and she may have been lost for a long time and certainly committed a lot of errors but mercifully never fell into the traps of harmful teachings. Laurin's training still unfolded its protection throughout all these lives at a very deep level.

Then came Sofia! After seeing so many lives, Sofia finally saw herself! She discovered that she was indeed Laurin's finest and luckiest rebirth, who had brought the attention back to the transcendental. Being modern, educated, free-roaming, free-spirited, and brave, she could observe the nature of reality without much prejudice or unchecked social restrictions. She was the first in the lineage since Laurin who began to break out of various historical and physical limitations. She listened to the tiny voice inside more than to all the industrial, commercial, and rational voices of our world. And she dared to fall in love with a statue.

Sofia opened her eyes again and made an astonishing discovery: the eyes she now opened were not the same eyes she had closed. Or rather, it wasn't Sofia who looked out of those eyes, it was all those men and women she had ever been. The visions of the past transformed her being. She no longer identified with one gender, one name, or one life history. She could shift from Sofia's thoughts and feelings to the inner world of Laurin, or anyone else she ever was. She could even exist as pure consciousness, experiencing the present, remembering the past, hoping for many futures. Being Sofia had become an option. She could even choose not to be a person — rather, merge with the surroundings and travel on a cosmic web to the trees, the rocks, the sounds, or the distant sea, becoming the Universal Lover, seeking and reaching out to the Beloved all across time and space.

Approaching footsteps brought Sofia's consciousness from the universal back into the separate moment of the here and now. She was surprised that a stranger could penetrate the valley: Laurin's invisible boundaries were still working, and she was holding a powerful intent for solitude.

But it wasn't a stranger who was approaching. As Sofia turned around, she saw a woman in khaki shorts and a safari helmet. It was Alana. She looked fit and fetching, and Sofia smiled at her with delight. Soon, however, she noticed that her friend was distressed.

"Alana," Sofia asked, surprised. "How did you find me?"

"I was here before," Alana said. She sounded enigmatic but also confused and lost. "May I sit with you?"

Sofia offered her a place on the large stone, curious to hear what her friend had to say.

"Sofia," like a confession, Alana began, "there are things I haven't told you."

Sofia remained quiet and unmoving like a stone. She listened, waiting for Alana to continue.

"I haven't told you some things because I was not ready to face them myself. For instance, how Pasión's statue was found to begin with."

"In the museum brochure you gave to me, it said a team of archaeologists found it."

"The team came afterward." Alana was now telling something she had never mentioned before, neither at any conference nor in any publication, not even to her closest friends. "I was alone. I alone found Pasión's statue."

"Where?" broke out of Sofia. "Where was it when you found it?"

"Over there." Alana pointed to the little cave in which Laurin and, later, Pasión used to sit in contemplation.

Sofia remembered it well: Laurin indeed had hidden the statue away in that cave before he died. It was not merely hidden, but protected: Dion, as the Hierophant, was there, too, and sealed it energetically, so that no one could find it but a member of the Order. This could only mean that either the seal was not strong enough or Alana was a…

"How did you find it?" Sofia asked her before she would conclude her thought.

"This is why I never dared to speak about it," Alana said. "At that time, I hated to admit but like you, I was guided by intuition, even though my brain simply did not believe in such things. I saw dreams and visions that — as a serious academic — I tried to dismiss. Yet, this place drew me in like a magnet. I was searching for something, even though I had no idea what it was. When the statue emerged, you would think I must have been thrilled, having found a twenty-five-centuries-old classic statue in pristine condition and of prodigious artistic excellence… but no. The discovery almost made me angry! I called in a team of archaeologists to deal with the artifact, and I went to take a shower to wash off my shock."

Sofia tried to feel her way into Alana's reasoning.

"Why wouldn't you take credit for the find?" she asked.

"Because the very fact that I'd found the statue destroyed my image of who I was at the time. Worse still, it destroyed my entire understanding of the nature of reality. Intuition… cryptic messages from dreams… how could a learned scholar fit that into her paradigm?" Alana sounded like a defendant in some cosmic court. "If I validated such things, it would imply that everything I have ever learned and taught was wrong, or at least incomplete — that I have been a fool all along who built her life and career on wrong assumptions. For me, this was difficult… I couldn't handle any of it, until… you came along. At first, that was strange, too. My brain asked what on earth I was doing, inviting a mass grave digger into my sophisticated team, but my heart knew that I had to help you. In the end, when you found the scroll and remembered its content… that was like a revelation to me. You became the living proof to me that the soul was real, that transcendent worlds existed, and the deepest hopes of humanity for meaning were more valid than anything in this demystified, over-sanitized world we grew up in."

Alana noticed that she got carried away, so she brought her focus back. She looked at Sofia. It stunned her how beautiful she was — like a newly-born immortal! There was a new strength in Sofia's face, sparkling color in her eyes, and a divine shine to her long black curls.

"Sofia, forgive me. I did not remember who I was, therefore, I acted like a simple archaeologist. But now I can sense that it was not right to take Pasión's statue to the museum, and I don't want to make the same mistake with the scroll. I still don't remember who I am, but I must!"

Upon these words, Sofia silently handed over to Alana the bottle of water she was carrying around.

"Drink," she said.

"Is this…?" Alana looked at the water with awe.

"Yes," Sofia nodded, "it is the Water of Memory. Freshly refilled from the cave this morning. Drink. It is time."

Alana took a careful sip from the water. Like others before her, it came as a little shock that it looked like, but did not taste like, water at all: more like some sort of milk, which contains nourishment for the soul. Drinking it changes everything for good.

"It will take a while…," Sofia said. "In the meantime, please tell me what is bothering you. I can sense something else is not right."

Alana nodded and let it suddenly out.

"Before I came here, I noticed that my computer had been hacked."

Sofia paused her breath: this could be catastrophic news.

"Alana! The content of the scroll must not…"

"I had deleted all my computer files before it happened."

"Oh! Was it your premonition?" Sofia let her breath out.

"No, a man had called me, who said his name was David, a member of the Order, and as he said, also your friend."

"Yes, David!" Sofia exclaimed.

"He wanted to talk to you, but you were gone. So, he advised me to delete all my computer files and burn the scroll."

"Did you?"

"I deleted the computer files, yes," Alana said. "I made a safety copy of the scroll, which I carry with me." She pointed at the small memory stick hanging around her neck like a jewel.

Sofia nodded in appreciation but asked, "Did you burn the scroll?"

"How could I?" Alana said, aghast at the idea of such sacrilege. "The world's oldest book... I'm an archaeologist, Sofia. You can't possibly ask me to destroy such an invaluable artifact, can you?"

"Come, we must go." Sofia tapped her arm. "Without delay."

Alana stood up but — like a scholar who needed time to think — did not move at first. Yet, Sofia knew the bridge was already burning; there was no time for calculating its bearing capacity. She grabbed her friend by the shoulder.

"I have an idea about you," she said to Alana, "and if I'm right, you soon may remember that you too are a member of our Order. But in that moment when your memories flood in, you will also know that it is not just us. There is also a Dark Order. If they know about the scroll, the stance is worse than you think."

"What is the stance?" Alana asked, and a wave of acidic fear went through her body. Like Sofia, she also began to sense things: suddenly, she became aware of an unknown, unseen, but still existing threat. Like wild grazing animals, not seeing, not hearing, not smelling, yet sensing the predator approaching, the two of them sensed menace.

"I will tell you when you begin to remember," Sofia said, but she had to take a deep breath to settle her own nerves. She could no longer avail herself of the bliss of ignorance. She knew that if the Dark Order had taken interest in the scroll, something sinister was in the making. It was one of the oldest ambitions of the dark powers to find a ready-made portal to enter Elysium — and reach the Pure Realm, not in order to find peace or enlightenment, but to destroy it.

The gravity of thinking the unthinkable weighed on Sofia's mind. Still, she began to scuttle like a gazelle down the large stones and the marble lane that led toward Davelis Cave. Although they were in a hurry, Sofia wanted to show Alana the place where she found the scroll. However, instead of the spiral path leading into the mountain, she found something gloomy, which strengthened her suspicion that the Dark Order knew about the discovery. The entrance was now a garbage dumpster filled with empty, broken bottles, plastic cups, and rusty metal.

"This was the entrance to the place where I found the scroll," Sofia said to Alana. "It was down there."

"All this rubbish!" Alana shook her head at the sad sight. "How did you pass through all this rubbish?"

"It wasn't here. Someone has done this since."

With a shadowed expression, Sofia urged her friend that they should go.

On the way, Alana asked to soothe her lingering angst by talking.

"What is this Dark Order you mentioned?"

"Well," Sofia said, "not necessarily some organized, dark world power, although its adherents can gain highly impressive levels of organization. In essence, however, the Dark Order is a counterforce: acting against our aim to bring consciousness to higher and higher realities of evolution. Whenever we have lucidity, creativity, and more freedom, the Dark Order brings in lies, measures of brainwashing, and control to suppress all individuality and control us. Often, they infiltrate the police and government; more often than not, they are the police and government. They bring about wars, dictatorships, genocides... I'm concerned that during all these centuries they may have learned to think more ambitiously."

"More ambitiously?" Alana echoed, incredulous about what could possibly be worse than orchestrating genocide.

"Yes," Sofia said. "Throughout the centuries, they never could quite succeed with their evil endeavors, as our Order is under the protection of the higher realms.

In lack of the necessary merits and intentions, the Dark Order could never reach these Pure Realms. But now, they are hoping to find one ready-made portal..."

"The statue," Alana grasped. "Do you think they want to get Pasión's statue?"

"I'm sure, yes," Sofia said. "They first need the scroll, which contains instructions on how to use it. Through the portal of the statue, they could enter Elysium."

"Why?" Alana asked.

"To destroy it," Sofia answered and looked at Alana. She looked into her eyes and then looked deeper still.

Who are you? Sofia asked in the silence of her mind. *Reveal yourself to me.*

Slowly, Alana's face began to blur and looked like someone else, and again someone else, changing from moment to moment, until the vision clarified, and a long-known, friendly face looked back at Sofia.

It was the face of Aliana, Pasión's reincarnated mother from Melos.

This can't be, she thought to herself. This was perplexing: if Alana was really her, such an ancient member of the Order, why would she not remember anything?

Sofia decided to wait; she set the inquiry aside.

Soon, they arrived at the bottom of the mountains where the city began. They caught a taxi and hoped it would take them faster than walking through the rush-hour traffic.

During the drive, neither of them said a word. Privately, both of them collected some thoughts, some ideas, some strength. Sofia stared out of the car window, watching the city go by while their driver, honking and pushing, tried to rush his way through it — past tourists pouring through red lights, vendors of snacks and fruits, streams of cars and bicycles. Sofia thought of all these people still caught up in this system that takes away the magic of life. How easy it was to live without any clue about the ultimate nature of reality. How easy it was to avoid any sense of responsibility. How easy it was to avoid mind and meaning. Yet, the world filled itself with magic for those who dared to pursue the good, approach the truth, and look out for beauty — and that very attitude gave Sofia hope for whatever would happen next.

It was at the very last minute that they arrived at the archaeological institute! The scene looked menacing: a small caravan of police cars was driving straight to the front of the building. Neither Sofia nor Alana wasted time fooling themselves into believing that this might have nothing to do with them or the scroll in their possession.

"Stop at the back of the building," Alana instructed the driver. Sofia was struck by the audacity and determination in her voice, which was new. As soon as they got out of the car, Alana quickly headed towards a small back door, which only the archaeological staff and visiting scholars had a key to.

And in an inconspicuous moment, before she reached the door, Alana tore the memory stick off her neck and threw it into a thick bush by the building.

Once inside, they took the only elevator in the wing to Alana's office. To win some time, Alana locked the elevator door out, so that it could not be called from downstairs.

Yet, as soon as they arrived in Alana's office, the phone on her desk started to ring.

"Alana Melozar," she said and put the phone on loudspeaker.

"This is Warrant Officer Kaplanidis from the Hellenic Police. Dr. Melozar…" He held a dramatic pause, during which Alana quietly walked over to the wall that featured the Map of Ancient Athens. "We received intelligence that you are in the illegal possession of an ancient scroll that you found but failed to report."

The officer spoke very loudly, which Alana found lucky because while he talked, she could take the map off the wall and open the safe hidden behind it.

"Oh!" Alana said while taking the scroll out of the safe. "I assure you, Officer, I am in the possession of many ancient scrolls… none of them, however, are un-reported."

"We are talking about a scroll dating back to the fourth century BC," the officer shocked both Alana and Sofia by saying, "written by an Athenian nobleman of this time named Laurin, son of Talesander. The content: Orphic philosophy and mystery teaching. Does that not sound familiar, doctor?"

Sofia felt an invisible punch in her stomach: hearing her old name spoken with such bullying authority felt like trespassing the mundane into the sacred world. What a threat! How did they get to all this secret information? Who were they? Sofia observed that Alana trembled too, but outwardly she remained calm, as if by magic. By now, Alana knew something, she remembered something, she was more than she had been hours ago in the mountains.

"Oh that," she said in a confident voice and even let out a casual little laugh. While she laughed, Alana went to the incinerator and set its capacity to the maximum. "With all due respect, sir, you may be victim to an urban legend. All my students are dreaming of finding Laurin's mystical seventh scroll like the crusaders were searching for the holy grail." She slowed down her voice as she said the last words. "I'm afraid, both the holy grail and the mystical scroll containing some recipe for immortality are — "

"I have a warrant to search your office and for your arrest," the policeman interrupted Alana and announced that he was sending his troop up.

He may have interrupted her sentence, but Alana continued what she was doing. Sofia watched her, mesmerized and overflown with gratitude: Alana was no longer acting as an archaeologist. She was acting as a member of the Order, protecting hidden knowledge. She placed Laurin's ancient scroll inside the incinerator. It was the same machine she used some while ago to prepare a sample for carbon dating.

They began to hear the heavy steps from police boots coming closer.

Alana turned the switch on the incinerator. They could not see behind its heavy metal door, but inside a flame erupted so hot it consumed everything in seconds.

The police came in and searched the office for hours. They left no cupboard, no drawer, and no paper unturned, creating a huge, violent mess. Still, they never found what they were looking for.

As for Laurin's seventh scroll, nothing remained but a handful of ashes.

Unrecognizable ashes.

Chapter 19
The Dark Order

Sofia was sitting on one of the last remaining stones. She came here to connect with the spirit of the place, even though there was not much to see: only these few stones, left to ruin amidst some rubbish of the city. Behind a fence, a few refugee lads were playing cricket, perhaps oblivious that they were at ground zero of Plato's Academy. No one seemed to care about the building, which had since been destroyed by the followers of a distorted religion — no one, except Sofia.

At first, she let the sadness wash over her. What sort of barbarians were her contemporaries? How could they abandon a site of such enormous historic importance to neglect? Soon, however, she found a new frame of mind: the building may be gone, but the idea behind it had survived! Wasn't it the greatest testimony to Plato's true teaching: that ideas were stronger and primary to matter? Isn't there an academia in every major city in the world today? Isn't the very word not part of virtually every language now? Isn't it taken for granted that there is an institution for advancing the mind, as there is a gymnasium for training the body?

It didn't matter that the building collapsed, as the idea had survived. It didn't matter that Laurin's scroll burned, either, as Sofia remembered it, Alana copied it, and they would now be able to act upon the ideas it contained.

As Sofia pondered, Alana came, smiling. Last night, they had found it wise to leave the archaeological institute separately and agreed to meet at Plato's forgotten academy the day after. The charges were dropped, as the police could find no evidence, but both women felt the dark forces lingering on.

Alana embraced Sofia and whispered into her ear, "I got it." She fiddled with the memory stick, which was again hanging around her neck. In the hours of dawn, she had found it in the bush, exactly where she had dropped it.

They started walking to gather themselves and make an action plan in accordance with the spirit of the scroll.

They were not alone.

As soon as David learned that the police were harassing them, he took a flight to Athens. Since the morning, he had been preparing a suite in one of the expensive — therefore well-guarded — downtown hotels, creating a secret, safe place for them to talk, which he sealed hermetically from any dark intrusion or spying. When Sofia and Alana arrived, David didn't meet them in the lobby, either. Instead, he instructed the concierge to take the two guests to the suite and only opened the door after the bellboy was gone.

Inside, David had conjured up a different world using powerful energies and intent. Aromas of almond blossom and soft candle-lights suggested he had opened the gates of both worlds. The scent was strikingly familiar and comforting to Sofia... She wondered where she knew it from, yet at first, she could not remember.

"Take your clothes off," was, surprisingly, the first thing David said. "Just in case the police installed some bugs — here are two bathrobes to put on instead..."

Alana, who had never met David before, grabbed a bathrobe without questioning him.

"Wait!" Sofia, however, said before David could walk out to give them some privacy to change.

She wanted to find out about him before they were to do anything else.

She went up to David, and a little distance away from him, she looked deeply into his eyes. She asked in her mind: "Who are you? Who are you really?"

Straight away, Sofia noticed that the bond between them was strong and ancient — not as flaky and pliant as most human-to-human relationships tend to be. She had been missing him, as they hadn't met since he found the Hierophant, but now she sensed something even deeper, something more profound than their friendship in this life.

As Sofia looked into David's eyes, twenty-five centuries were staring back at her!

The shine of these eyes she remembered, from all of these centuries. These deer-like, hazel eyes had been looking at her during all the lives she lived since Laurin...

These eyes belonged to his wife when he was the peace negotiator in Rome. She was the one begging him not to go back to the enemy's camp, as they would torture him to death...

These eyes belonged to the peaceful gardener at the Monastery in the Land of the Rising Sun. He was the one who always listened to him with compassion and gave him console, ever without judgment, without dogma, without prejudice...

These eyes looked back at the French prostitute, as she sought refuge with the good nuns. She was the elder sister who took her in when she lost her baby and searched for a new way of life...

These eyes looked back lovingly at the blind priest, wrapping him up always in a blanket of love. She was his wife, who allowed him time and space to find his way back to the wisdom path of truth...

Sofia let out a silent, grasping cry of joy when she finally realized who David was! Most reverently, like never before, she took him into her arms. Behind his current, masculine features, she could smell the scent of almond blossoms and feel the eternal comfort of that river-long, silky hair.

"Diona," her whisper traveled centuries. "You truly have fulfilled your vows. You've stayed at my side, you led me to the statue when the time came, and you have brought me to the Hierophant as you said you would."

"Yes," David nodded, and when Sofia slowly released their embrace, he took a small bow. "Still and forever, now and always at your service. Now it is the time for me to fulfill yet another vow: to help you find Pasión again and reunite with him. Now is perhaps the last chance."

Alana looked at them with fascination.

"Did you always know?" she asked David incredulously. "You knew all along who you were and who we were?"

"Yes," David said. "Even before I saw Sofia and heard about you, I was aware that we were connected, and as a member of the Order, was searching for you."

"I don't understand," Alana wanted to know. "I too am an ancient member of the Order, even trained in previous lives to remember my cosmic past. Why did I forget everything and only remember after Sofia gave me a drink from the Water of Memory... only when I needed to burn the scroll?"

"You needed to forget," David said as a matter of fact. "You planned yourself to forget before you were born into this life. How else could you have engaged yourself so strongly with academic science and archaeology to put yourself into exactly the position in which you could help us?"

Alana looked at him in her serene, inquisitive way: she seemed to understand. David did not speak any more, only turned away to let them remove their clothes.

"What is that?" he asked when they had changed into the bathrobes, but he saw that Alana was still wearing something around her neck.

"This is my memory stick," Alana said, proud that she had it, "to which I saved the content of the scroll."

"Is it?" David said softly, but Sofia could detect a little turbulence in his voice. "Can I have a look?"

Alana handed the memory stick to David who looked at it with suspicious eyes. Like all their clothes, he subjected it to a series of odd treatments after he signaled for all to remain silent. He copied its contents to a laptop and then inspected it under a magnifying glass. Next, he went into the other room, where the hotel safe was, locked the memory stick into it, amidst a few pillows.

"This memory stick had a built-in microphone and camera, Alana," he said. "It has been broadcasting everything you have done, seen, said, and heard, ever since you've been wearing it."

Alana stood stunned, staring into the distance, which became her staring into the past. She recalled how one day, years ago, she took the memory stick off her neck and put it on her kitchen table before stepping into the shower. Afterward, it wasn't there. She went frantic with worry, rage, fear, and spent half the night turning her apartment upside down until she fell asleep from exhaustion. The next morning, the stick was back on the kitchen table, which she had checked countless times...

"But now we are safe from any intrusion." David's voice brought her back into the present. "Alana, do you want to sum up the content of the scroll, so we can think of some plan of how to proceed?"

"Yes…" Alana said, balancing back to think again professionally. To encourage her, David took out a portable projector and screened the content of the scroll. Laurin's two and half thousand years old handwriting appeared on the wall of this modern-day hotel room.

"I shall tell you what I've translated, and Sofia can relate to it with her memories," Alana began this unusual little conference, which felt like a mystical academy where the author of a historic scroll was — in a new form — but nevertheless present.

"The scroll is divided into two major contextual parts," Dr. Alana began. "The first is about the statute. After Pasión's death, members of the Order — including myself and David at that time — began donating meritorious energy to turn the statue into a portal to Elysium. The idea was that whenever the statue was energetically fully charged, a future incarnation of Laurin would be able to use it as a portal to Elysium at the moment of death. To use the portal, two things are needed: grabbing the intent, and invoking Elysium."

"That is the problem, isn't it?" David interrupted her. "Anyone can use the portal, if they are in its proximity at the moment of death, grab intent, and say the destination of Elysium."

"Yes." Sofia nodded. "In ancient days, we wouldn't have imagined that the Dark Order could ever track us like this."

Alana's face turned dark through suspense.

"So, what could happen if some members of the Dark Order tried to usurp the portal?" she asked.

"There is no precedent." David raised his shoulders. "Hence, we don't know. But we do know that it is the eternal ambition of the Dark Order to destroy Elysium. If they ever find their way in, the consequences could be dire. Unspeakably dire. It is not only artists and mystics who draw their inspiration from those realms — every human on Earth needs to tap into higher mental patterns, which serve as blueprint for our destinies. Without Elysium, humanity would lose its vision and could easily be enslaved or driven to the point of total self-destruction."

All three of them went silent under the gravity of what had just been said.

"What does the second part of the scroll contain?" after a while, David moved them on.

"The second part…," Alana held her breath for a moment, "contains something I was hoping Sofia would understand. It seems to be the description of a deep practice of our Order, which I have never come across before: a ritual that allows for the fusion of two people. Do you remember any of that, Sofia?"

"Yes," Sofia said. "I remember it now because the scroll reminded me. It is the most powerful, the most ancient, and the most unique act of magic I have ever learned, which is preserved only for a certain soul archetype."

"Which soul archetype?" David asked, his curiosity sparked.

"The lover," Sofia said. "We all carry an idea in us, don't we… You, David, live out the helper, and you, Alana, live out the scholar, Pasión and I belong to the archetype of the lover. It's true that I carry some essence of the healer, and Pasión some essence of the artist, but at the deepest core of our beings we incarnate as lovers."

Sofia paused and looked at her two friends, hoping they would understand. She noticed that they did: their hearts were open, and they listened not merely to the words she uttered, but to the eternal essence they carried.

"The lover is an archetype like no other," she continued. "While all others reach liberation once their soul is purified and their potential fulfilled, the lover can only reach liberation together with the beloved. It is for this reason that we ceaselessly search for each other across all time and space: Pasión and I can only reach liberation from the wheel of physical birth and rebirth if we merge our beings."

Alana was listening like a child to a wondrous tale of unheard promises, and asked, "So, the ritual in the scroll will enable you to unite?"

"Yes, but we can only do so when we both have turned our stones into diamonds: once both are purified. Then, at the end, we, Pasión and Sofia, will become One."

The magnificence of these words reached deep into the souls of David and Alana. Members of the Order have always known that no cosmic event was greater than the moment in which a human being reached liberation from the wheel of life and death — to become god: free to create anything by the mere power of thoughts, bringing forth even a new set of physics, new worlds, new universes. Such an event strengthens the good, the true, and the beautiful, and if there ever was a chance for two humans to reach liberation together, nothing would be more devastating to the Dark Order than the lovers achieving it.

"Why did Laurin add this ritual to the scroll?" David asked, as he couldn't recall Laurin ever mentioning such a thing to Diona.

"In case Pasión decided to be reborn before I made it to Elysium," Sofia said with conviction of her memory.

"Pasión to be reborn," Alana echoed her words with softly spoken excitement. "Do you think he would try to do that?"

"Yes," Sofia said. "In fact, we have agreed that he will be reborn."

"Agreed? When?" David and Alana chorused.

"Once we both found our way into Little Eternity: that timeless, mystical space near Laurin's Grove. I've shared with him my experiences about the future, which enchanted Pasión so much, he vowed to come back into my time."

"How are you going to find each other?" Alana wondered at the prospect.

"When he found out that we still have the Olympics," Sofia smiled, "he pledged to be reborn and come to the Olympic Games in 2020 and win a gold medal in gymnastics for exposure so that I can find him. Do you think he can do that?" Sofia turned to David.

"From Elysium, of course, he can do that," David said. "It's child's play once he had reached that level of consciousness."

"So will he be reborn?" Alana echoed the question. "Is Pasión really going to be reborn?"

"Well…" David shook his head. "I wouldn't use the future tense. If Pasión pledged to win at the Olympic Games in 2020, he's bound to be already alive. He cannot win the Olympics as a newborn, after all. Pasión must already be some-where among us."

***

The gala evening came to an end. Thomas Morrison helped his wife back to the car, which he preferred to drive himself and park in the deep garage, like most of the folks. He liked to be known as a simple man: rich, yes, but simple. A man who fits as a Fortune 500 CEO just as famously as a farm husband with lands and horses. Tonight, he hit a splendid image when he handed over a large, poster-sized check to the indigenous people. Oh, those flashing journalists and that handclap-ping, well-dressed audience full of philanthropic sentiments! He almost fooled himself too into believing what a good man he was! No, no, his company wasn't exploiting indigenous medicinal knowledge; no, no, they weren't such biopirates; no, no, they were compensating their informants fairly and justly. They were ad-vancing those primitive people, who previously knew nothing about money and making a profit: now they could go to school, get vaccinated, and buy toys. Yes, tonight was almost as good as the day when he married his wife! That beautiful blonde model who lost a leg in a tragical-tragical accident. Little did Mr. Morrison know on the day it happened what a genius strike of PR that accident would be. Overnight he won the image of the most loyal, devoted, and sacrificial husband. Yes, yes, people learned to like and respect him over time. Yes, yes, that was pref-erable to ruling by terror — which Mr. Morrison always used only as a last resort.

"Wait here, darling," he said to his wife after he opened the car door for her and helped her inside. "I'll just go and check with Harris."

He saw his son, Harris, at the other side of the deep garage and walked over to him. First, he looked around, making sure there was nothing else around, only that smell of fuel in the air, and that his wife was all locked up in the car, out of earshot.

"What happened?" he asked his son and scrutinized him. Morrison didn't like to look at his son. He detested his oily skin and pudgy limbs, but he found his diabolic ways with computers, data manipulation, and all things spying very use-ful. "What happened to that scroll?"

"Unfortunately," Harris, his son, sniffled his nose while he broke the bad news, "the archaeologist burned it just before we got there."

"Do you have a copy of the text?" Mr. Morrison asked in his usual, unshaken voice. His calm was frightening.

"Of course." Harris grinned, believing he won't disappoint. "It was very easy. The archaeologist, smart as she thought she was, threw her memory stick into a bloody bush in front of the building when she saw the police approaching."

"Did you place the stick back where it was?"

"Yes! Yes, of course. They must not suspect we had it."

"Even though they now have the content also."

"They have it anyway. This Sofia woman remembers the content from a previous life, she claims."

"Such thing I'll never understand." Mr. Morrison quietly shook his head, as if he needed to admit for a moment that there were things that disturbed even him. "How the heck can they remember something from centuries ago? We have our chronicles dating back into the fifth century BC, but how can a single individual remember…"

Neither the scientists on his payroll, nor the ones captured in his high-security facilities could explain how this would be possible. Yet, Thomas Morrison had too much insider knowledge about the workings of the world to dismiss the reality of metaphysics. He knew about the Order and knew that ultimately, it was his greatest enemy as it had ways to end his most ambitious projects, bring down his wildest ventures, and jeopardize his final success. He knew that in the end, the Order had to be conquered and could only be conquered through occult workings, which he and his people were not as versed in as they were in the normal psychology of persuasion. Thus, he remained hungry for any magic, no matter how weird or dark, that would help him bring down the Order he feared and hated so much.

"I don't understand it, either." Harris shrugged his shoulders. "But I have some good news. Very good news! The scroll actually contains a simple way to pass through one of their portals."

"What?" the father exclaimed.

"It's a statue through which we can reach their metaphysical home-base and bring it down. If we succeed in that, consider our cosmic takeover done, Father."

Thomas Morrison thought for a moment and allowed himself to smile a little. He was so pleased he wanted to produce a wide grin, but as a dignified and cautious man, he held back. Rightly so, as his son warned him of something else.

"But there is one more thing, Father."

"Yes?"

"There is great danger, also. The scroll has a second part, which contains instructions for the Sofia woman to unite with a cosmic partner. That could be quite devastating for us if they succeeded."

"Yes, I've heard of such things before," the father said. "Occasionally, members of this Order fuse into one: it's like merger and acquisitions of a cosmic scale. It gives them powers that even we cannot comprehend. Think of Buddha or Jesus, and some of the other freaks — they always pull through our calculations big time. Indeed, that is bad news. You must prevent this union."

"Yes, I know. What do you suggest would be the best way to proceed?"

"Well, didn't Einstein say that the best solution was always the simplest one? Kill Sofia and her lover."

Harris awkwardly stepped from one foot to the other. He felt trapped by this order, which he anticipated but could not follow.

"I…" he hesitated to admit, "cannot do that, I'm afraid. We've tried to kill Sofia before, because she always smelled of trouble, but she's proven impossible to destroy. She lived through times in war zones where she should have died even without our intervention. But she is under the protection of a Hierophant." Harris pronounced the word Hierophant as if it was some indecent, shameful thing to say. "As for Pasión, we don't even have the faintest clue of who he is in this present life. All we know is that the two of them are planning to reunite at the Olympic Games 2020…"

"Olympic Games," the father repeated in a snarky tone. "What nonsense! Make sure you prevent that!"

"Prevent that?" the son asked, aghast. "How can I prevent that?"

"Oh, for fuck's sake." Now the father lost his temper. "Work with the PR team. You guys can find something that scares the living hell out of people, can't you? Get a terrorist attack going! Or be creative. Find and spread some virus… I don't care. Just make sure that the Olympic Games 2020 will not happen!"

Chapter 20
Rebirth

The twenty-first century that Pasión was born into, was all but as exciting and fresh as Elysium. It may have lacked the intense, ineffable happiness that was inherent to the Pure Realms, but Pasión's purified, creative mind was strong enough to take him to a time full of joy, full of innovation, freedom of the mind, and technologies indistinguishable from magic. Pasión loved this new space-time and immersed himself fully into it from the moment he was reborn.

His new mother had invited a seer to be present at his birth — as it was quite customary. The seer told her that the soul she was receiving had come straight from a Pure Realm to reunite with his cosmic partner, for which he needed to become an Olympic gymnast and that his name was Pasión.

Both his new mother, who was an artist, and his father, a prominent mind scientist, felt enlivened by this news and pledged to do everything in their power to help Pasión live up to his intent.

From the first time they took him to the playground, they used all the climbing frames and high towers to help Pasión find balance in his new little body. Pasión felt enchanted by the world and his own regained physicality. How different this time was from living in Ancient Greece! Now the cities were clean and green, endless freedom was in the air: no more slavery, no more wars, no more famine! This freedom was like a sweet scent: easy to breathe, good to grow up in. There were no toxic influences, and no one had to hide their true selves.

If there was any drawback to the twenty-first century, it would be the distraction it could cause. Growing up, Pasión hardly ever recalled his Greek past, or even Elysium. He only spoke when his parents were curious. He became engaged in riding his motorcycle into the sun and dancing through nights filled with rhythm and smiles. Although he never forgot his vow to meet Sofia and always trained hard, his aim to arrive at the Olympics and win remained dormant — until there came a day when everything came back to him...

He was seventeen years old and drove to school like on any other day. Still tired from last night's training, he took a seat in the second of the two rows in Ms. Valérie's gigantic, circular classroom and dozed off.

I must have really fallen asleep, he thought to himself as time went by. What is this if not a dream?

All throughout the school year, he was used to seeing impressive, life-like moving pictures in the middle of the auditorium, which was so grand and spectacular it resembled a planetarium. Ms. Valérie liked to use augmented reality in her history class. Yet today it was different. Pasión suddenly saw things that he remembered and had occasionally dreamt of before. He recognized those dramatic, deep-colored rocks sculpted by the volcano, and even the cliff from which he and his dark brother, Moris, had jumped into the blue deep, once upon a time…

"This stunning island in the Mediterranean Sea is called Melos," Pasión heard Ms. Valérie's soft, seductive voice. He wasn't dreaming after all! "It is the home of the Venus of Melos, one of the most iconic statues of antiquity, now to be found in the island's local museum. It is also famous for a piece of intellectual heritage known as the Melian Dialogue. Who has heard of that?"

A slim girl with long, amber-colored wavy hair, sitting right in front of Pasión, raised her hand. Ms. Valérie wasn't surprised: she was the most widely read student in her class — by far.

"Yes, Amber Sunshine…"

"The Melian Dialogue," the girl began in an intelligent, almost adult voice, "occurred during the Peloponnesian War. Athens invaded Melos in 416 BC and demanded that the Melians pay tribute, or else face annihilation. The negotiations between Athens and Melos went down into history as a classic example for justification of war: Athens demanded surrender, not on any ethical grounds, but simply by the power of the strongest. At the end, the Athenians killed every single man on the island and sold all women and children into slavery. During the dialogue — " The girl wanted to continue how the Melians argued they were not the enemy, but she was interrupted by a voice from behind her.

"There wasn't really a dialogue," Pasión's voice traveled, strong and bitter, through the circular classroom. "And they didn't kill every single man, either."

"What do you mean?" Ms. Valérie curiously walked over to him. She was like a fairy: her airy steps made the light-blue, translucent skirt she was wearing fly behind her with every step.

"I used to live in those days. I was one of the Melian men who escaped the massacre."

As soon as they heard this, all the students rose from their seats and came as close to Pasión as they could. Ms. Valérie watched them gathering on table tops and in each other's laps, and she didn't mind. In this modern day and age, mind science was of utmost importance, so it was always worth interrupting a class if a student wanted to share an inner experience. Besides, this was her favorite interaction with students: when one of them remembered a past life in times she was teaching about. Oh, what lively details about bygone days she always learned from them!

"Go on, tell us!" she encouraged him, and Pasión began to tell his tale.

"I escaped the execution: with my brother, we jumped off a cliff above the sea and swam to hide in a cavity under the rocks. Later, we were found, though, and sold as slaves."

How ghastly, a dark murmuring went all around the auditorium. *How insufferable that must have been.*

"Well," Pasión smiled, "to tell the truth: in the midst of that horrendous fate I found my greatest blessing. That is how it all began. That is how I met Laurin, son of Talesander."

All of the other students moved even closer now. Everyone wanted to know what this enigmatic attraction was that Pasión's voice so deeply suggested, and Pasión told them about everything: their love, his initiation into the mysteries behind life and death, and finally, Laurin's sacrifice in order to send him to Elysium. With eyes wide open, some even filled with tears of fascination, the class listened as if Shakespeare had just staged Romeo and Juliet for the first time on earth. If there was anyone among them not yet in love with Pasión, by now they also gave in to his exalted, otherworldly charm and beauty.

Yet, at the end of the class, everyone left except Amber Sunshine. She turned around to Pasión. He seemed, for a brief moment in time, to see a fleeting teardrop in her eyes, reflecting some ancient recognition, sorrow, or remorse, but she quickly camouflaged it with a bright smile and asked Pasión before he could grab his belongings and leave, "Would you go out with me tonight?"

Pasión looked at her incredulously: this wasn't the first time she asked.

"Why... wouldn't you go out with me?" she asked again.

Pasión studied this girl who was unlike any other he knew: she could be infuriating, yet sweet, demanding, but in a soft and velvety dark voice as if inviting to some unknown, subversive adventure. She was always outspoken, never to be held back by any convention.

"You know," she continued, drawing him in a good-humored way, "I always thought you were a Greek god. Today, it turned out that you really are one! So, finally, finally, finally: you must go out with me."

She looked at him like a child, with eyes wide and curious, really amber in color, as was her hair that framed this fairy-like, porcelain face with tiny, ample curls.

"What is," Pasión laughed a little, "the... correlation here?"

"Well, you see," Amber smiled to explain, "if you have a Greek god in your class and he goes out with you, that's heaven. But if he does not, that's such heartbreak, it practically qualifies as torture. You wouldn't want to torture me, would you? Cause me immeasurable suffering..."

"No," Pasión shook his head. "I couldn't stand that."

"You see!" Amber smiled triumphantly. "So, where are you taking me?"

"Taking you?" Pasión looked at her again. "Well... now that you're saying, perhaps I could use a girl on my new Pegasus. Would you like to see it?"

So it happened that Pasión took Amber Sunshine from their history class straight to his family's bright home and opened the garage door to show her what he called his Pegasus.

"An airbike…" Amber looked amazed.

"A Harley Davidson Galaxy King," Pasión corrected her and leaned in close to the girl's face. "I love…," he whispered to her, "machines."

He took her hand and pulled Amber Sunshine to the bike.

"Do you want to try?"

For a moment, Amber rather wanted to return to her library and hide behind shelves of books, but then she reminded herself she had not been born to be a coward. It helped to look at Pasión's chest muscles under the slim-fit, white top he was wearing which were definitely worth…

"… dying for," Amber finished her line of thought out loud. "All right, if you want to die on this thing, I'll die with you."

Pasión swung himself on the bike and invited Amber Sunshine to sit behind him. He could feel her heart beating fast as she put her arms around him and leaned her breasts against his back. Her words and her body felt exciting, and Pasión's blood began to boil.

"That's right," Pasión said before they took off. "Feel the wind and be ready to die any moment! Then you can enjoy life."

With these words, they burst out together from that garage, like two young dragons freshly released from the den and hit the highway.

Pasión's mother watched them from the upstairs window of her atelier. It was an astonishing moment, for she never knew of her son being in romantic company ever before. She assumed it was because he hadn't found his cosmic partner yet. Could this girl be it? Or was this the workings of hormones? she pondered. They looked pretty, anyway.

She saw the aircycle ahead on the road, taking off into flight.

"Hold on," Pasión shouted into the wind, as they lifted into the air. Amber screamed: first, out of fear. Then she felt the wind in her hair, and she screamed in excitement. Finally, she felt Pasión's muscles tensing under her hand, and she screamed of delight. They flew far and wide. Nature was all around them when Pasión brought his airbike down and to a halt in the middle of a pine forest. He lifted Amber Sunshine off the saddle and in the moment he touched her waist, a torrent of unexpected pleasure flooded him.

Yes! This is how it felt. This is how it had been!

For two and half thousand years, Pasión had not touched anyone in a physical body. Indeed, the last time he felt human skin with a human hand he was with Laurin and Diona. Oh, how he had forgotten what bliss a touch could release: this must have been the purpose of creating the whole physical world! For all the ethereal happiness of Elysium, what could create greater extasy than this contrast: in a body that was born out of pain, lived through suffering, and waited only for death, to be comforted by the loving touch of the Other.

Pasión breathed in the pleasure deeply and pulled the girl to himself with a delightful, urgent passion. Like a young god capturing a forest nymph, he chased Amber Sunshine into the woods where he kissed and caressed her until exhaustion and hunger drove them back to find some food. Pasión took them to a place he always liked: it was an eighteenth-century log inn overlooking the Shenandoah River.

They sat at a massive, rustic table in candlelight. Suddenly, Pasión found himself astonished by her beauty: Amber was always pretty, but now that she had been allowed to touch him, she radiated a heavenly glow, which was the hallmark of those being in love.

"What is that?" Amber asked him, first to break the quiet. "That jewel around your neck?"

Pasión grabbed his pendant. This girl had a wicked way to push forward into his core being.

"It's an ancient thing," he said, hoping this would satisfy as an answer, but it only increased her curiosity. She was again looking at him with those irresistible, child-like eyes…

"I'm a member of an ancient mystical Order," Pasión revealed to her, "ever since I lived in Greece. This is our sign."

Amber looked spellbound.

"The stone… so big and pristine. Is it quartz?"

"No," Pasión said, almost casually. "It's a diamond."

Amber looked around in awe and shock: if there was a diamond so large in the world, it must be worth a fabulous fortune. She wanted to ask more about it, but suddenly she found Pasión's gaze transfixed on a holovision screen, which was playing silently behind her back. Amber turned around and saw a sports program running. It didn't look in any way extraordinary: just an interview with some coach, behind her boys and girls practicing gymnastics — yet, Pasión was staring at it as if he'd seen an apparition.

"What is it?" Amber asked, looked at him and the screen again. "Who's that? Do you know her?"

Yes, Pasión knew her: he had recognized Diona's essence incarnated in the trainer of the gymnasts.

"How impolite of me," he apologized to Amber, "to stare at a screen when I could be staring at you."

"Do you know her?" Amber asked again.

"Yes," Pasión said with a minute nod. "I know her — from another time. Seeing her just reminded me what I need to do… Amber! I must make it to the Olympics! I need to start training in earnest."

Amber shook her gorgeous hair in disbelief. How was it possible to train harder? She thought of those muscles she felt while on the airbike…

"You are already training day and night."

"I need to train differently," Pasión said, "set my intent, focus my mind… Amber, do you think I can make it to the Olympics and become a champion?"

"I am sure you can," Amber replied, "do anything you set your mind to."

"She," Pasión pointed at the screen, "is the woman I need to train with." The very same moment, her name appeared on the screen: Coach Diana Carter.

Their food was arriving, and they hungrily and hastily made room for it on the table.

"Then we'll find her" Amber concluded convinced. "And you'll be a champion."

With that, they thanked the waiter and began to eat as if they had never eaten before.

There was no need to go out and find the coach, as the coach went out to find Pasión. A week later, Coach Diana Carter was walking into the principal's office at Pasión's school and introduced herself. She explained that she had been impressed by a holographic training video she saw of Pasión and now wanted him to try out for her Olympic shortlist. The high school principal — a big lady with a big heart — clapped her hands in excitement upon such wonderful news.

"Of course, Coach Diana," she said, "let me have a look at his schedule... Yes, Pasión is now in Ms. Valérie's history lesson. It's in the AURA."

"The AURA?" Coach Diana did not understand.

"Oh!" The principal laughed. "Yes, we didn't have those things when we were kids, did we? Technology is evolving so fast these days, isn't it — I can hardly catch up with it myself! AURA... that is the Augmented Reality Auditorium. Go and check it out; the lesson is on for another ten minutes. It's quite an experience if you haven't seen it before: you'll think you were somewhere else. Afterwards, you can talk to Pasión. The AURA is in the basement, Port Number 7."

Diana was glad that the principal prepared her for what to expect, else it would have been quite overwhelming. Upon entering the AURA, she found herself in the middle of a fully flaming ancient battle: she could see the whole massacre, hear screams and neighing of horses, even smell earthy sweat and boiling blood. It was all rather shocking, as violence had long gone out of fashion in her time and age: people knew enough about mental hygiene to banish it from their minds and entertainments. Only for educational purposes was it important to learn about violence as a historic occurrence and remember to keep it in the unmanifested realm of human potential.

Finally, all the moving, holographic images halted, and out of the silence came Ms. Valérie's voice. Today was the continuation of her previous lesson on ancient conflicts.

"War," she spoke, "was the everyday reality of people living in the ancient world. To us, the battles, the killings, and the immeasurable sufferings it all brought upon humanity, are inconceivable — although some of us, like Pasión, remember past lives in which wars were common. Who can tell me, however, when was it that wars had become a thing of the past? How long has our period of peace been lasting?"

As usual, Amber Sunshine raised her hand, but this time, she was sitting in the second row and put up her left hand, as with her right hand she was holding Pasión's.

"Yes, Amber?" Ms. Valérie smiled at them, happy to see love wherever it emerged.

"The last armed conflict was recorded in the year 47 AD. After that, smaller conflicts may have occurred sporadically, but the general consensus among historians is that war disappeared by the end of the first century. Overall, we now have had a period of planetary peace of nearly 2000 years."

"Yes, that's right. And what started this global peace, Amber, would you say?" asked Ms. Valérie.

"Our lasting time of peace started with the spiritual reign of Jesus, the Christ. He was the one who first taught us that transformation must come from within. Of course, at his time, he was using an archaic language, saying things like the Kingdom of God was within or spoke about the sources of both salvation and damnation coming from within. But during the long — 108 years — of his teaching life, people slowly but surely understood his message: that their internal fears, greed, and unbridled aggression were the main sources for things like war. Thus, humanity began to transform their inner thoughts, sentiments, and energies. Since then, we have learned to go within and transform anger, hatred, hostility, and ignorance into love and learning. And that has made all the difference."

"Brilliant, Amber," said Ms. Valérie. "Brilliant. This is a very complex historical topic, and no one could have summed it up better. Next time, we'll continue with the first century A.D, which we call the age of enlightenment, or the beginning of mind science. For now, class is dismissed. Thank you all for your attention."

As Ms. Valérie finished her class, Coach Diana Carter went up to Pasión and introduced herself.

"Yes. I know who you are," Pasión said with a depth in his voice to indicate that he knew more than this single moment in this life would reveal. To his surprise, the coach didn't register that.

"So, you know I'm an Olympic coach," she went on. "Yes, I have seen your performance on recording and came to offer you a try-out for my qualifying team. Would you like to attempt it?"

"Of course," said Pasión. He held back and did not mention that he remembered their agreement quite well. "I would like nothing more than that."

Amber smiled at him, thrilled, and the coach asked, "When can I look at your moves?"

"Anytime."

Coach Diana looked at him, pleased, as he seemed fearless and ready. She concluded that now was the best time and escorted him to the school gymnasium.

"Diona," with great joy, Pasión said to her, as soon as they were walking alone down the corridor. "I can't tell you how happy I am to see you here."

"Diana," the coach corrected him. "It's Diana Carter."

"Yes, Coach Diana," Pasión said, keeping his voice casual, while he thought it all over in his mind. He remembered the promise Diona made in Elysium to assist him in this life as his Olympic coach, and he had no doubt Diana Carter was the emanation of her consciousness. It was only curious that she did not seem consciously aware of it, even though she was carrying out her soul's original intention. Coach Diana acted in a professional and determined way, and that made Pasión feel in the best of hands.

The gymnasium was grand, and its various sections were filled with student athletes, all preparing for presentations and competitions: some played tennis matches, others practiced martial art katas, but most of them were engaged in gymnastics.

Coach Kalamar, who had been training Pasión so far, stood up in excitement as he saw his most promising athlete walking in with one of the nation's most prominent Olympic coaches! He walked straight up to Diana, who took a seat on top of the podium while Pasión began to warm up.

"What was he last working on?" Diana asked the coach, after he so proudly introduced himself to her.

"The Double Twist Arabian," Coach Kalamar said, pronouncing each word with great import. "Pasión's a very eager student. He's already been nagging me to try the triple! I told him he wasn't ready for that yet, but I believe in a year or two he can start learning it."

"All right." Diana nodded and scribbled something onto a clip-chart she had put on her lap. "Tell him to perform that double."

Coach Kalamar quickly stood up.

"Ok, everyone," he shouted down from the podium, "clear the floor. We have an Olympic coach here today. Pasión! Where is Pasión? Yes, come. We shall see your double twist."

These words flew around the hall like a magical formula: all gymnasts urgently dropped whatever they were doing and took seats where they could see well. Their minds were well schooled: dismissing any trace of jealousy or envy, they tuned in to witness something extraordinary. They focused their combined intentions to help their friend achieve his best, who would, in return, inspire them to do the same.

In the field of such unconditional support, Pasión delivered the Double Twist Arabian as perfectly as everyone had been expecting from him.

Coach Kalamar burst with pride, while all the youngsters were clapping and shouting with joy... but Coach Diana, she didn't move a single muscle on her face. She signaled Pasión to come up to her.

"And now," she said, "I want you to try the triple."

Pasión, in his sudden surprise, glanced over to his old coach, who looked petrified, but didn't dare to say a word.

"Let me see whether you can understand my instructing," Coach Diana spoke to him in a powerful yet soft voice, almost whispering. "Do not attempt to do the routine with your physical body. Rather, aim to do it with your dream body. Do you understand what I mean?"

"Yes." Pasión understood. He still remembered, as if it was yesterday, their first day at the gymnasium with Laurin: how he taught him to hold the flag position with the help of Chairon.

"In a dream, I can do this," he said. "If I believe this is a dream, nothing can hold me back."

Diana nodded, seriously happy on the inside that her new student had passed his first test. Then she watched Pasión slowly walking towards the floor...

With every step, he was bringing to his mind the highest reality he had ever known. He remembered the nights during which he could fly out of Elysium and bring dreams into the world. Now, he allowed his present reality to gradually fade into a dream. As he concentrated, the edges of his vision turned blurry and black, as if he was looking through a tunnel of imagination to the only thing that now mattered: the gymnastics floor. Pasión allowed his perception to lose density and become increasingly more pliable. Like Laurin used to say: as ice can melt into water and water can vaporize into stream, so can the rigidness of physical reality soothe into a dream.

When Pasión finally felt like he was in a dream, he knew he was safe. He accelerated his body into the jump and up into the air, believing again he was flying. Only for a few seconds did he need to hold the dream focus — that was enough. That gave his body time to turn — not once or twice, but three times — while up in the air.

And the joy this brought to him was enough to safely bring himself to the ground and land as smooth and sure as a cat on silky paws.

There was total silence in his mind.

There was total silence in the room.

Only a minute later did those loud cries of celebration break out in the room while Coach Kalamar mumbled, "What... just... happened...," hoping his eyes would quietly adjust to see the impossible. Pasión looked at Coach Diana and silently pleaded with her to look at him, but she just sat there like in stone, taking notes on her clipboard.

"Do I get a tryout now?" asked Pasión, who could not help but walk up to her like a kid waiting for praise.

"This was the tryout." Diana smiled at him for the first time. "Welcome to my team!"

"Really? When do we start training?" ardently, Pasión asked.

"Right now," Diana replied, and quickly gathered her notes.

Like a manager shielding her sporting star from flashing journalists, Diana rescued Pasión out of a crowd of admirers, led by Amber Sunshine and Coach Kalamar. Diana thanked the school coach for all his excellent work and told him that now she would not only borrow, but steal, his best student. His contribution would always be acknowledged, she assured him, but then, Pasión's new coach had no more time left for pleasantries.

"When I invited you for lunch," Diana said to Pasión a little while later, as they sat together in the school cafeteria, "I didn't know I would have to file for bankruptcy," she joked. She'd seen it many times, but it never ceased to amaze her how much young athletes on high intensity training could eat. While Diana slowly picked at her tofu salad, Pasión gulped down lunch for seven right in front of her eyes. He ate piles of vegetables, quinoa, beans, mountains of sweet potato purée, and filets of clean meat — which had now been produced for a hundred years, allowing all butcheries of the world to close down forever. Diana watched him with joy: her new trainee seemed full of appetite, not only for food, but for life and love. That was good: she knew that austerity and discipline alone wouldn't make him train hard, only if coupled with heart and this fieriness.

"In the twenty-first century," Diana began to talk, and Pasión took all her words in like nectar, "winning the Olympics is no longer — like it was in ancient times — just a matter of being the fastest, strongest, and most skilled. Nowadays, the mind plays a much greater role in athletic success than body conditioning — which has to be impeccable, of course. You can count on the fact that the physical conditioning of everyone competing in the Olympics will be as perfect as yours, so training hard is necessary, but it will hardly give you the winning edge. Only your mind can. And I don't have the slightest doubt that it will. You have already demonstrated a level of mastery over your mind that is remarkable. You understood very quickly my instruction about the dream body."

"Yes, to me this is like reverse lucid dreaming. From the waking state, as soon as I make myself believe that I am dreaming, reality becomes more pliable. Especially my body: I can do more things with it."

"That's exactly the way. That is what we need to practice further and take to perfection."

"Yes, but how is this then…" Pasión, the forever curious asked, "if I master this very well, theoretically I could do three, four, five… infinite number of saltos. Since we've understood that it's the mind bringing forth reality, what is the limit, or is there a limit at all for what the body can do?"

"Very good question," Coach Diana said. "I would say there is a limit and there isn't. The mind, at any given moment in time, is bound by 1) its own limitations and 2) by the coordinates of the consensual reality of its socio-biological surroundings. In other words, everyone is only ever capable of bending reality to the extent society around him is willing to accept. The stronger the mind, the more it can influence consensual reality, also. Jesus, the Christ, could walk on water because his mind was so strong that he could draw in whole crowds into his version of reality. We can do that now too, each of us to a lesser or greater extent, because we learned from him. That is how you can do your saltos, too, Pasión: perfect your body, perfect your skills, but first and foremost strengthen your mind so that you can draw in the entire sports stadium and millions of spectators from all around the world. Believe, but make them believe also that you can make the impossible happen."

"This is powerful," Pasión thought out loud. "We live in such a powerful day and age. Now I understand why they taught us so much mental hygiene in school: in a society where the mind of people is becoming so strong, it is important that they only use it for good things."

"Yes," Diana said, "good things or cool things. I'm just a sports coach, not a philosopher. Put this to good use, my friend, so that you come first in the Olympic Games, 2020, in Tokyo. To me, that is the only thing that matters."

After lunch, Amber Sunshine came up to Pasión with open arms and a grand smile.

"You're so amazing," she celebrated him, and while throwing her arms around his neck, covered him in kisses. "You have made such an unforgettable entrance. Now you will really go to the Olympics!"

Then, she calmed a little.

"Will you even find time to come to the prom with me?" she asked him with a bit of theatric sadness.

Pasión sighed. He thought this was time to tell her.

"Amber Sunshine." He turned to her to look into those beautiful, shining eyes of hers. "I will have the time to go with you to the prom, and it will be my pleasure to do so, but I need to tell you something, else it will not be fair."

The girl looked at him curiously, a bit, perhaps, scared of what he had to say.

"I am not going to the Olympics to collect glory," Pasión finally opened up to her. "I am going there because I have a cosmic love, Sofia, and this is how I am meant to meet her. One day, I will be with her instead of anyone else. When I find her, I will not care if she is 102 years old, crippled, or sick. From that day on, I will be with her and with her only."

"I know," Amber said, even looked relieved. "I always knew that. It is my promise to you that I will never stand between your love. I know that a god will eventually find another god to love, as that is the right order of things. Meanwhile, however, a girl like me can have some fun, can't she?"

"She can. Certainly," Pasión whispered, and hugged her to his side. He felt touched that all was going as he had planned for this life. He had made no mistake so far, and he would make no mistakes afterwards either.

Three years later, on July 21, Pasión was the first athlete to board the national team's flight. Lovingly chaperoned by Coach Diana and Coach Kalamar, his parents, and Amber Sunshine, he was flying as a gymnast to Tokyo, the Olympic Games 2020, as he had promised to Sofia that he would.

Chapter 21
Tokyo Olympics, 2020

U nder the new rules of the Olympic Committee, those athletes who had lived in Ancient Greece during their cosmic past had the honor to lead the Procession of the Torches.

Today, on the first day of the Games, they all stood on the shore — Pasión among them — looking out to the sea.

The Sacred Olympic Stadium built for the Games in 2020 was a circular platform in the Bay of Tokyo with a spiraling tower on its top that stunned by its simplicity. Like every modern-day Olympic venue, it was built on water.

"Ladies and gentlemen!" the voice of the Olympic High President rose in celebration over the stadium and the shoreline, where athletes and guests were waiting for the ceremony. "Welcome to Tokyo: the Games of the 699th Olympiad."

All the one billion people of the Earth were watching. In every town and in every land, people gathered at salient spots, in joyful crowds, to watch the holographic broadcasts: in Ancient Olympia and at the Acropolis, at Stonehenge, in Angkor Wat, at the Lindenblüten Gate in Berlin, the Diamond House in Washington City, and — of course — in front of the Potala Palace in Tibet, where preparatory meditations had begun days ago. Many watched from home or in small circles of friends and family. At the event in Tokyo itself, the number of spectators never exceeded that of participating athletes. Being invited to see the Olympics was a special honor reserved for those who had done the most to advance humanity in the last four years, especially in the fields of mind science, evolution of consciousness, and healing.

"The Procession of the Torches will commence," Mercurius, the Holovision presenter, began to comment. "An ancient priestess is now bringing the Olympic Torch, which has traveled all throughout the world from Olympia. With the Olympic flame, she first lights the torch of Pasión el Greco, this year's exciting newcomer in gymnastics. He lights the torch of Kassandra Frey, another promising gymnast." While the athletes are lighting each other's torches, one by one, the guests are beginning to walk across the bridge into the Sacred Stadium.

"Now that the torches are lit, we shall immerse ourselves into the fascinating site, which, year after year, warms the hearts of one billion people all across the world. The athletes, holding their flaming torches, are now beginning to walk on water, towards the stadium."

Sacred music arose the depths, lifting the global community of humans into heights of lofty inspiration and joy.

"As we watch the athletes walking slowly over water," Mercurius continued, "we are reminded of the powerful symbols being evoked in this ceremony. The flames the athletes carry symbolize our heritage from the Ancient Greeks, who stole the fire of passion from the gods, and based upon that, we advance the evolution of consciousness. The water on which the athletes walk is our eternal symbol of Jesus, the Christ, and the deep, archetypal changes his teachings caused in the eternal history of humankind."

Now Mercurius turned to his lady colleague, Agila Verana, the committee's athletic advisor.

"Walking on water is still not an easy feat, is it?" he asked her.

"By no means," Agila Verana confirmed in her friendly, professional voice. "Even after two thousand years, it takes practice, focus, and a great command of your mind over matter. Walking on water is considerably more difficult than a fire walk, but not as difficult as walking on air, which is still considered an impossibility... although rumor has it that there is a gymnast who might attempt it this year."

"Now wouldn't that be something?" Mercurius said with full enthusiasm. "After all, this has been the motto of the Olympic Games for the last two thousand years: Make the impossible happen!"

On the third day of the Games, which the gymnastics competition was scheduled for, Pasión woke up with an excitement he hadn't felt since he last saw Laurin and first saw Sofia. The energy for winning gold was rising in him like the sun.

His intention remained focused and pure. Whatever would happen, this was to become the most significant day of his life, if not his entire existence. Pasión had no doubt in his heart that Sofia too remembered and would honor their eternal agreement to meet at the Olympic Games of 2020. Even if she didn't make it into the audience, she would be here in the city, waiting for him. Even if he didn't win, she would still see him among all the other athletes at the Moment of Silence, since that was an event the whole world watched and participated in. Either way, this would be the day on which they would find each other again. This would be the day when he could hold her, Laurin's incarnation, in his arms for the first time in physical reality after two thousand and five hundred years of separation.

What a day to wake up for!

"You are gliding," Coach Diana smiled at him, "as if your feet did not need to touch the ground while you walk. You don't need to do anything anymore. You are ready. You will perform. You will win. And I will be there."

Diana left him with a hug and the unconditional conviction of victory: her disciplined mind kept the vision of the desired outcome, and nothing but the desired outcome, never allowing any intrusive thought of doubt to sneak in. Pasión, as always, greatly appreciated her support and eternal care. Only the two of them knew about the routine he had been preparing for today — and Chairon, of course, whose idea it was in the first place.

"Ladies and gentleman," Mercurius, the presenter's voice sounded yet again all above the stadium. "We shall commence with the Moment of Silence, the pivotal event we have all been anticipating — by many considered even more important than the Games themselves! Since mind science made a new, industrial scale breakthrough in the late eighteenth to early nineteenth century, it has been proven that the unified intention of large populations can change the course of history. Since, it has been a perennial: once every four years, here at the Olympics, we, the entire population of the entire world, come together to manifest what has been voted the single most important issue of the year."

"This time," the voice of the presenter continued, "we have voted as our utmost priority to strengthen our immune system, train our lungs and hearts, and remember that our will to live is stronger than any destructive force that may want to show up. Let us now, humanity as one, concentrate on the strengthening of our global health. We are one. We are alive. We are thriving. Brothers and sisters, let the Moment of Silence begin."

As soon as these words were spoken, the world fell into a sacred silence during which nobody moved or uttered a word. One billion brains fired thoughts to manifest health, one billion minds connected for this shared intent, forming one global neurological network with unparalleled power.

However, it was also tradition that as soon as the global mind concluded the Moment of Silence, the issue was dropped and immediately forgotten.

The time had come for the athletes!

Gymnastics at these modern Games invariably consisted of a single, rather dangerous act, which all contestants had to perform, but it was left up to them how to execute it in the most artistically beautiful, athletically challenging, and mentally innovative way.

Today, the gymnasts were required to walk up the spiraling staircase to the highest point of the floating stadium. Athletes from other disciplines were standing on the steps. From the dizzying height above, every gymnast had to jump down and find a safe, yet novel way to survive the fall.

"Ladies and gentlemen," Mercurius' voice sounded above the melody of the Olympic Anthem. "Our first contestant in gymnastic is Kassandra Frey, from Athens, who is now ascending the spiral stairs and will shortly announce the intent behind her routine."

Kassandra Frey was a beautiful young woman with a huge hair crown made of a million little curls, dark olive brown skin, and the unique challenge of being born without arms. As she walked up the spiral staircase, with every step she took, one by one, athletes raised their torches in honor. From the top of the stairs, when she called from the top of her voice, everyone in the world could hear her.

"This is Kassandra Frey. I was born without arms. Therefore, I have developed my intent to grow wings."

After her words, the world went silent. Speaking the intent was as important as the performance: it allowed the entire mental field of humanity to tune in for her, helping her to realize it. If she succeeded, it advanced not only her, but our entire species to move yet another step into the unknown, to make the impossible happen.

What Kassandra Frey accomplished on that day looked nothing short of a miracle indeed. She had learned to concentrate her body's internal energy so precisely that she could let it flow out at her shoulder-blades. As she dived into the depth, the flow of her energy did not only look like wings but worked as such. Externalizing her energies also made her body appear ethereal like a fairy: clapping her wings, she saltoed and pirouetted a great many times in the air before she landed on the ground with ease and elegance.

The stadium erupted in applause.

Many more wonderful and splendid athletes followed until time came for the act the world had been hoping for in almost legendary anticipation for years now.

"Could this be the Olympic moment," Mercurius' voice raised with excitement, "we've been waiting for? A moment of sporting history in the making? Ladies and gentlemen, please welcome the most promising routine announced for today: Magnus Elyiah."

As a child of the Nordic fjords, Magnus Elyiah already stunned by his looks: he was strong, his core hard as rocks, but his pliant limbs moved like waves of water. He had hair ice blue like the Nordic Sea.

Magnus climbed up the torch-lit stairs like a god from the Nordic legends. From up there, however, he did not dive into a jump like all the others. He began to descend. Step by step — on air.

In order to do that, he had to learn to collect an unspeakable amount of mental energy to draw in all the athletes standing on the stairs. The mental field they generated together drew in the spectators, and that enlarged mental field rippled out all over the world. Magnus Elyiah had a mind strong enough to extend it to every human. His thought became a new thought of humanity: he began to think that he could walk on air, and as he thought, so it became.

For the first time ever, a human being, Magnus Elyiah, was walking on thin air. He walked for seven seconds. For another three, he performed his jumps and saltoes to show his artistry. Finally, he used another second for his body to land safely, and yet another to lift his arms above the head.

The world had held its breath, and only after his feet firmly hit the ground, in the thirteenth second, did the crowd dare to break out in the most celebratory applause. The score changed immediately. In the unified mental field, humanity had voted for Magnus Elyiah to be the undisputed winner. The moment was historic. To surpass this performance was now impossible.

Only one contestant was left. Only Pasión. And he was in love with this moment. He loved nothing more than attempting the impossible: once upon a time, that was what Laurin demanded of him. (He still remembered his words from the first day they trained together at the gymnasium: "Once you get to know me," he said back then, "you will realize that I'm not expecting you to do your best. I'm expecting you to do the impossible.")

Today, Laurin of the past, Sofia of the present, shall see him doing it.

The routine was one of Chairon's genius ideas. The centaur had brought an ancient episode back into Pasión's awareness, which, albeit important, he seemed to have forgotten while he was in Elysium. It occurred when Pasión returned to Melos after Laurin had freed him and he found his dark brother, Moris, in the house. That day, Pasión could use his spoken words to influence and amend the past, as well as the future. Chairon encouraged Pasión to ponder the workings of the mind and of time: to use his initiation for rethinking the entire concept of linearity.

Even now, here at the Olympics, Pasión could feel Chairon's presence as he began to ascend the spiral stairs. One last time, the athletes raised their torches, and Pasión, the last athlete for the day, walked up. When he spoke his words of intent, he touched the hearts and the souls of a billion people on Earth.

"I lost my cosmic love two and half thousand years ago," Pasión said to the world. "I made one wrong move in battle, and an enemy spear hit me. It was only one moment in time, but it changed the course of eternity. For my sake, my love gave up his entry into Elysium, suffered loneliness and hardship through centuries. My intent has become to break the tyranny of time over my mind. If I break the illusion of time, can I find my love again? I want to find Sofia, that is my intent."

The next moment, the spectators saw the most unexpected thing. Pasión had landed on the ground, without ever jumping off, without anyone ever seeing him in the air. No one knew how he got there. Many stood up or came closer with worried looks on their faces, to see whether the athlete was all right or broke himself and needed help.

But then they saw the miraculous.

They saw Magnus Eliyah's unforgettable routine yet again but backwards in time. Performed by Pasión, first, they saw him having landed, then they saw his body catapulting into the air, doing jumps and saltoes in reverse, slowing down instead of gaining speed, and finally, walking on air but taking every step backwards, until at last, Pasión stood on top of the spiral staircase.

The audience failed to clap. Their shock was too great. People here in this pristine twenty-first century — who all grew up with mind science — knew this feeling: when the boundaries of the mind were pushed, the results could be as scary as they were wonderful. If this one athlete had found a way to move beyond the workings of linear time, so would others soon. One of the solid coordinates — space and time — which their reality was built on, was now altered. It meant that no one could possibly know the type of reality tomorrow they would wake up to. It would be a new world, consisting of the ultimate unknown. Such a thing was fearsome, yet to be celebrated. So, the audience, after their initial surprise was receding, now began to rise to their feet and shout out in acclaim.

The Olympic Committee tuned into the unified field consciousness for the results. It was a fast and straightforward procedure. Unanimously, this last performance won the gold medal in gymnastics.

Pasión stood on top of the world. He did not only win gold, but something infinitely more precious: now, through the unified field consciousness, everyone was holding up his intent.

Everyone now was searching for Sofia.

Any minute now, they would find her.

Any minute… she may walk in… she may message.

They may hear from her…

The whole world wanted to see her.

The whole world held their breath.

And the whole world sank into bewildered disappointment.

No matter how long they waited, Sofia was nowhere to be found. Perhaps she would be at the medal ceremony? But then, she must be somewhere already… Where was she?

Pasión walked out of the sacred stadium. Not on water, for he felt deadly tired. His seminal performance took most of his strength — not seeing Sofia took the rest. Suddenly, he felt fatigued, in mind as well as in body: two and half-thousand years of separation finally overpowered him.

He walked across the bridge, alone in the crowd, without any joy over his victory. How he wished Sofia would be standing there at the end of that bridge waiting for him…

And there was someone waiting for him — but it was not Sofia.

It was the Hierophant.

Chapter 22
Worlds Upon Worlds

V isitors from around the world had been gathering at the cafeteria of the Olympic Village. All were fascinated by Pasión and would have loved to talk, take a holograph with him, or simply wish him good luck, but as they saw him entering with the Hierophant, the enlightened one, they respectfully kept their distance. That way, Pasión could sit down with the Hierophant for a cup of tea and be alone in the great crowd. Sheltered all around by minds who knew consideration and boundaries, they got the privacy they needed.

"Am I in the wrong time?" Pasión asked the Hierophant straight away. There was no need for pleasantries or explanations.

"Yes," the Hierophant said, who came to tell Pasión the very same thing.

Pasión was disappointed and relieved at the same time: disappointed as his last hope to meet Sofia had now vanished, but relieved knowing that the mistake was in the timeline and not in Sofia's intention or desire to come and be with him.

"Was she born earlier or later than I thought?" Pasión asked.

"Neither. She was born at the time you thought she was born, and as of today, the 27th of July, 2020, she is alive here on Earth."

"I don't understand..." Pasión felt puzzled. "Didn't you just confirm that I was in the wrong time?"

"Yes," the Hierophant nodded, "the two of you are in different times — but not in different calendar times, rather at different levels of vibrations within time."

Pasión took a quiet sip of his tea. It was the last one. After that, he never touched his cup again: as the Hierophant's words became stranger and stranger, Pasión's tea slowly turned cold and was forgotten.

"In fact," the Hierophant revealed to him, "you once shared not only the same time but the same place with Sofia. It was at the Shenandoah River Inn — where you were last with Amber Sunshine. The first time you were there, ten years ago, you happened to show up the exact same day, at the exact same hour, even at the exact same minute in which Sofia — who was visiting America at the time, walked in, too. You even sat at the same table."

"I can't believe I didn't recognize her!" Pasión exclaimed.

"Oh, you would have recognized each other, believe me," the Hierophant said. "It was not a question of recognition. You didn't see each other because even though you were at the same time at the same place, you were not at the same vibration."

"Not at the same vibration," Pasión repeated slowly. He wasn't sure whether he understood or perhaps even wanted to understand such things.

"This is one of the hardest things about the mind to understand," the Hierophant assured him, "something even modern mind scientists struggle to fully grasp. Even someone as advanced as yourself may not appreciate the full implications of the mind creating reality. Think about it: your mind, which has spent two-thousand-five-hundred years in Elysium, is bound to produce a qualitatively different reality from someone who hasn't had the chance to leave earthly lives. Look at your pendant: it is a diamond. If your diamond mind creates a twenty-first century, as you did, it'll be advanced, loving, exciting, and good. Sofia — although also very advanced by now — is weighed down by the great grief over your loss that she has been carrying since the days of being Laurin. She is in a world parallel to your time: tougher, darker… She cannot see you, and you cannot see her because your realities do not overlap."

"So, it is true… there are parallel realities," Pasión muttered, thinking back to the many fantastic stories he heard and watched as a child.

"There are and there aren't," the Hierophant said. "Like with many things in the realm of the mind, potentialities become actualized only when the mind is capable of seeing the opportunity. In the world Sofia lives in, experiencing parallel realities is nearly impossible (although even there, the impossible occasionally does happen). Mind science in her world is almost non-existent: it never developed on a large scale."

"How can it be that it never developed?" Pasión objected. "They also had 2000 years, didn't they? Or was it that…" Pasión paused here, as the possibility that crossed his mind was too grim "… that Jesus, the Christ, did not incarnate?"

"Oh, he incarnated," the Hierophant said weightily, and continued after a dark, dramatic pause, "but never got to deliver his teachings fully. He was crucified."

The words came as such a shock to Pasión, he hardly could say anything.

"That is impossible," he tried to conclude. "I know that you… as the Hierophant… know things, but I can feel things, too. I sense this to be an impossibility. This is too ghastly to even contemplate. Why would anyone…" Pasión could not articulate how aghast he felt.

The Hierophant bent closer to him and lowered his voice. He spoke with profound respect, not only for knowing the shock and pain Pasión felt, but for the graveness of the sinister news he was about to deliver.

"It is not only that," the Hierophant said, almost whispering. "Humanity in her timeline did not only crucify its great teacher. Worse, it never redeemed the crime, it never took responsibility. Quite the contrary, it started to worship the cross. Look!"

The Hierophant showed some holographic images to Pasión — of churches and other places of worship — all featuring erected crosses, many with bloody details of the wounds and sufferings of the crucified.

"Take that away from me," Pasión said and turned away, his eyes tearing up. "I haven't seen such a horrendous atrocity since Ancient Greece… Even back then I thought it too barbaric to keep an image like this in my mind. This is poison to the soul."

"It is," the Hierophant agreed. "But the people in Sofia's world have made suffering into their religion."

Although the Hierophant saw that Pasión could not speak because of the shock, he needed to hear more, so he continued.

"Jesus, after he was murdered, had risen from the dead, as you'd imagine that he would. He even took humanity's great sin upon himself for purification…"

Pasión smiled.

He knew Jesus.

He knew his greatness.

He knew he would do such a thing.

"But this is where humanity truly went astray," the Hierophant continued. "Because of this unspeakable generosity of Jesus, they thought the murder was justified — that it even constituted the will of God. They began to think of the crucifixion as an act through which Jesus saved the world rather than facing their own guilt and shame for committing the greatest crime. You see, they saw someone who could turn suffering around, so they began to worship suffering, instead of following Jesus' teachings and turning suffering around."

Pasión was searching for something to say but could only mutter that this was too terrible… Full of anguish, he slowly got himself up on his feet and staggered to the cafeteria counter, hoping to freshen himself up. This time, the behavior of the crowd changed towards him. Whoever he walked by laid a hand on his shoulder and gave him a smile or a hug, as it was customary in this pristine twenty-first century, for moments when someone was in pain. Girls formed rings around him and shared one great embrace, children wrapped their arms around his legs, and some wise old men took his face and brought their foreheads together. Nobody asked him for an explanation nor wanted to deliver any advice, they just offered their support, reminding him that he never ever was alone. At the counter, Pasión grabbed a bottle of blessed water — a fashionable beverage of his time — which was laden with minerals, vitamins, and positive thoughts. Drinking his way back into a stronger mindset, soon Pasión was able to return to the table.

"What happened after his murder?" Pasión asked. He was scared yet burningly curious to know.

"It would be more than a challenge for someone like you, having lived in pure realms for so long, to even imagine the wicked history that followed," said the Hierophant, who sounded like he knew very well what he was talking about. "There's no period of peace in that world, Pasión, there never was. Humans used their intelligence to build more and more effective automated weapons to kill hundreds of thousands on the spot: wars reached an unprecedented level of destruction! Worst of all, throughout history, millions have been killed in the name of Jesus, the Christ, by those who spread the poisonous religion they invented in his name. Do you remember Christopher Columbus from your history class?"

"Yes, of course," Pasión said, unsure where this was going. "The man who discovered America and who also brought on the second wave."

"The second wave…," the Hierophant repeated meaningfully. In his look was deep questioning.

Pasión became even more distraught. It was impossible that the Hierophant didn't know what he meant, nor was it likely that he wanted to test him on trivia…

"Yes, the second wave of SIMS: Spiritual Infusion into Mind Science," Pasión explained anyway, perhaps to cut ahead of any other sinister revelations that might come. "After Columbus discovered America, all the Native American shamans and elders were invited to Europe to share their spiritual wisdom with the students of Christ. Their knowledge cross-fertilized — "

"No," the Hierophant — as gently as he could — interrupted him. "That never happened in Sofia's world. Instead, the Natives were killed by the millions, their lands taken, and their spiritual ways of life marred forever."

"What about the third wave?" Pasión tried to hold on to the good events he knew about, hoping that some of them at least occurred in Sofia's world also.

"Buddha lived and taught in that world, too," said the Hierophant, who knew that the third wave referred to Tibetan Buddhism coming to the West and merging with global mind science. "Luckily, he wasn't murdered or silenced like so many others of the great teachers. His teachings are available to those who seriously seek them out, like Sofia, yet remain unknown to the masses, as Tibet is under ongoing attack: the Chinese Communist regime invaded their land, killed and tortured the Tibetans by the millions, and destroyed virtually all of their monasteries."

"Please tell me…," Pasión pleaded, feeling sick in his stomach, nauseous in his head, and terrified in his heart "… at least… that it is improving for them…"

Pasión was struggling — not only to hold out against thoughts of such a terrible world history, but to accept how strange this was… to let go of ideas that were ingrained in him since school as facts. He had to face a different interpretation of reality now, which was not only horrendous beyond belief, but incredibly different.

The Hierophant shook his head quietly. He looked at Pasión and saw the desperation in his eyes.

"Don't give in to despair," he warned him, before he would reveal any further traumatic details. As the Hierophant knew Pasión's deepest thoughts, he had great empathy for everything he went through this afternoon. He held his hand on Pasión's arm while he spoke. "Don't identify with the world I'm telling you about. Don't let the dark trance of suffering pull you in. You don't need to make that reality your reality. Those who know how to transmute suffering do not need to suffer and must not worship suffering. I'm telling you all of this for one reason only: so that you understand why you did not meet Sofia today."

"But, Master," Pasión weakly raised his beautiful head, "how can I not be touched by all that suffering, especially if Sofia is in that reality?"

"The only way," the Hierophant said with great weight, "for the two of you to be together ever again in physical reality is to make your reality hers, not the other way around. You only need to know about the history of her reality, you do not need to live it."

Pasión nodded. Inside, he started to turn numb. He felt the paralysis of those who experience the absence of love and some shock so great that feelings need to freeze, thoughts need to blur, and life needs to be restrained to go on. If it hadn't been for the Hierophant, whose presence mysteriously suggested to him that everything would be all right in the end, Pasión — the fresh winner of the 2020 Olympics — would have wept.

"I understand," he said to the Hierophant. "Tell me more, please. Can you tell me some better news about their modern history at least?"

"I'm afraid not." The Hierophant shook his head. "The twentieth century was the worst of all: that was the time when hell really broke loose. It was a time of two world wars and authoritarian regimes bringing upon the murder of millions. Atrocities — for you unthinkable — became commonplace. Masses of people were killed in the worst imaginable ways, including dropping of atomic weapons, which destroyed entire cities in a matter of minutes; there was Auschwitz, Buchenwald — "

"Auschwitz." Pasión caught up on a word that, to him, gave hope.

"You know about Auschwitz?" the Hierophant asked, even though he knew how quickly the double-edged sword would cut into Pasión's mind.

"Yes, of course," Pasión said with confidence, even though in his gut he felt the dark trap. "It's a concentration camp," he said, pretending as if he was answering in Ms. Valérie's history class. "It's where Jewish scientists succeeded in concentrating the life force energy in a way that makes today's plants grow seven times faster, which revolutionized agriculture, freeing up even more time for meditation, mind science, and conscious evolution. Research there also started Clean Meat, ending butchery forever."

"A death camp," the Hierophant turned around the sword. "Set up by Nazi Germany to exterminate the Jewish people."

"The people? Exterminate? I don't understand."

"To kill. To kill them all."

"To kill? A whole people? Why? What have they done?"

"Nothing. Nothing at all. Human evil needs and has no reason. You want to ask me: What have the Jews done? Nothing. What was the reason? Nothing. What's the explanation for doing such evil? Nothing. There is none. But the fact is that they have sent innocent men, women, and children into gas chambers and killed them by the millions. They cremated their bodies on the spot."

"I refuse." Pasión jumped to his feet, and with roaring and inexorable, yet sacred and divine anger, he repeated, "I refuse to believe that Sofia has to live in a world so evil."

The good crowd looked at him with compassion: what could possibly have driven this accomplished champion, who just demonstrated superb command over his mind, to lose his temper?

Pasión then sat back to his seat and quietly added, "I refuse to believe that anywhere out there, a world so evil actually exists."

The Hierophant looked at him with compassion and gratitude: he knew that Pasión's rage was of a sacred, divine nature: an expression of the cosmic intelligence no longer willing to tolerate horror of this kind.

"Hell realms do exist," he still had to remind Pasión. "I apologize if I caused you pain by telling you about all of this, but only when you know the truth, you can change it."

A thought fell on Pasión — oh, what an unbearable burden it was! Suddenly, he realized the only reason he did not have to endure this hellish world was Laurin's unconditional generosity as he gave up his keyword to Elysium for him! Pasión's heart sank under the torturous weight of understanding that this would have been his lot. How would he ever be able to compensate for this greatest of sacrifices?

"How is Sofia doing?" he had to ask the Hierophant. "Did she go to the Olympics and suffer the same disappointment as I did?"

"She could not go to the Olympics, as there are no Olympics 2020 in her world. The forces of darkness certainly do not want you to meet her."

"Why?" Pasión did not quite understand. "What does it matter to them whether we meet again or not?"

"It matters to all the world! The cosmic story of the lover that you embody will reach its happy ending when the two of you unite. In other words, through your experience, the cosmic mind will have discovered another way of happiness — that the dark side will want to avoid at all costs. Every time a soul finds its unique happiness, it finds enlightenment and freedom: the good, the true, and the beautiful increases for all eternity."

This thought put a smile on Pasión's lips and helped him face what was coming next: the medal ceremony. Would he have ever thought, even a day ago, that receiving his Olympic Gold could become a burden? How was he now going to stand in front of the whole world without bending over in desperation?

Coach Diana came to accompany him back to the Sacred Stadium. She had brought Amber Sunshine with her too, who looked at Pasión in the most meaningful way, as if she knew exactly what was happening with him.

Also, he found that his contemporaries were even more considerate and empathic than he would have hoped for. It was impossible for the world to share a mental field as powerful as during this Olympics and not perceive Pasión's pain and sorrow.

Still, there was an ocean of joy coming from the amazing achievements of the day: the boundaries of what was possible had truly been pushed like never before at any of the Games. No matter what, as Pasión was walking back to the stadium, accompanied by his coach and girlfriend in that life, he couldn't help but feel the solemn beauty of the moment descending upon him. It gave him consolation that he kept his cosmic pledge to Sofia — that it was neither his fault nor her indifference that prevented them from meeting.

While the Olympic Anthem was gracefully rising one last time above the stadium, it was announced that the Bronze Medal of the Gymnastics Discipline in the 2020 Games was going to the woman who grew wings: Kassandra Frey. Pasión saw her walking up the podium, surrounded by the solemn admiration of her race.

"And the Silver Medal…," the world heard the next announcement of glory "goes to the first man who ever walked on air."

Magnus Elijah stepped up amidst unprecedented cheer and joy in appreciation of making humanity's great dream since Jesus, the Christ, come true. But Magnus did not only receive his silver medal, but also the special honor that goes with it: it was tradition that the first runner-up had the honor of introducing the winner. In this pristine twenty-first century being, second was not seen as a missed chance but rather as the most envied winning position: the silver medalist did not only succeed in making his highest vision come true, above all, he gained proof that reality could be better than that.

So, it came that Magnus Elijah was the one selected to step forward and put the Gold Medal around Pasión's neck.

"To the one who broke through the restraints of time," he said and — as it was customary — he continued with his speech of appreciation.

"We have seen something today," he began, "that we have not anticipated — something beyond anything we could have imagined possible up to now. However, we have also seen what happens when the mind stretches itself beyond hitherto known limits so fast that we cannot keep up with the consequences. We were happy, and now we feel the sadness of the champion as we have learned that Sofia was not among us. Who knows what other unexpected consequences we shall experience if we continue to break the linearity of time? But! Is this a reason not to venture further? Would life be easier if I had won the Gold Medal for simply walking on air? Yes, life would be easier, but we, my dear contemporaries, are warriors of consciousness: we want adventure, not stagnation. I'm infinitely pleased by this unforeseen turn of events — that today we have truly seen the impossible. I only hope that our champion's sadness will soon ease, as I'm sure that soon a new way will manifest through which he can meet the one he wants to meet — "

Nobody would ever find out if Magnus Elijah wanted to say anything more, as his speech was interrupted by a soundless murmur sweeping across the unified mental field of the Olympics.

Over here, over here…

Over here… Some repeated who were standing at the banks of the ocean.

There was a ripple in the water, a ripple in the mind…

A ripple in time and space.

First, it was the people at the shore who turned their heads away from the stadium. Then, one by one, the crowd began to gather to see what was happening in the water below.

A face emerged from the tiny, foamy waves. It belonged to a woman who looked as if she'd been dropped into the water from seemingly nowhere. Her face was bleeding a little, but she didn't appear seriously injured: she swam with powerful strokes and lifted her body to the wooden pier with one swing. As she stood up, she merely looked disoriented, as if she herself didn't quite understand how she got there and where exactly she was.

It was Sofia.

Pasión moved. First, shy and unsure, not knowing himself what was happening, yet following his instinct and the universal mind, he moved towards the bridge.

Sofia began to walk towards the bridge as well.

The world held its breath as it watched them.

On that day, the 28th of July, that fateful, third day of the 699th Olympiad, the modern, consciously evolving society based on kindness, compassion, and mind science, saw two things on that bridge it had never seen before.

It saw Sofia walking towards the middle of the bridge to meet her beloved. The world had never before seen somebody coming over here from another time.

It also saw a dark figure merging from the crowd, who lifted his chubby arm that held something this pristine world had never seen before, either.

It was a gun.

Pasión saw Sofia just a blink of an eye before he would notice the assault. He jumped to run towards her, but in that moment... a bullet hit him. It penetrated his chest, like the Spartan spear did once upon a time. This time, from the front, the shot found its way straight to his heart and left him no time. Pasión, the newest champion of the Olympics, surrounded by the most enlightened society the Earth had ever seen and just seconds before he could reunite with his lost love, fell dead on the spot.

Chapter 23
The Statue of Pasión

3 months earlier

"Will we be able to count on you?" The question echoed in Sofia's mind long after she heard it on the phone.

It was after she had returned to where it had all began: to London. Together with David and Alana, they wanted to secure the scrolls and the statue before Sofia headed to the upcoming Olympic Games. Yet, the more she neared her sacred goal to unite with Pasión, the greater the resistance she had to encounter.

Never before had Sofia felt as conflicted as now, following this phone call from the head of her agency at the United Nations. The old boss personally asked Sofia to interrupt her sabbatical year and join the international humanitarian fight against the new pandemic of 2020. Yes, he begged her to come without delay! Various agencies were scaling up their virus response operations in refugee camps and other ultra-vulnerable communities — where Sofia's expertise in handling mass medical emergencies would be urgently needed. He explained the dismal prospects of places where people were already facing crises due to political conflicts, natural disasters, and climate change. Sofia knew the buzzwords, but she also knew what they really meant. If she denied her duty as a doctor because she chose to meet her cosmic partner instead, others may not be able to meet, and someone else's soulmate may die. Sofia knew the real humanitarian tragedies were not in the numbers: they were in the loved ones never to be seen again… in the cuddly toys lost over barbed wire fences… in dates lovers never could attend… in stillborn dreams… fires of passion extinguished while trying to escape the brain-pounding madness of the human race…

Sofia noticed how people in her world were becoming scared. The air was buzzing hot with rumors that were more frightening than any cold facts could ever be. Was the virus to be feared most, or did its strange RNA of unknown origin indicate something even more sinister? Were politicians and doctors to be trusted to have goodwill, or was it high time to look at the bottom of some conspiracy theories?

What was worse: the thought of death or the new emergence of dictatorships… getting ill or giving up our rights of movement and assembly, giving up our natural habits to touch and to love body to body… how much should we halt life for trying to avoid death?

Without a doubt, Sofia felt something wasn't right, and things were not as they appeared. Still, she received an intuition not to dwell on questions arising out of the growing confusion. By trying to understand the chaos, she would only be swallowed up by it. Earth now resembled a gigantic alchemical cauldron the cosmic intelligence was using to separate gold from lead. Sofia wanted to stay in her highest calling to ensure that her existence contributed to the consciousness of gold and not to the fear, ignorance, and destruction of lead.

Yet, her high intention brought upon Sofia a terrible moral conundrum. She had taken the Hippocratic Oath, and her soul carried the eternal essence of a healer — how could she deny helping the emergency teams? Their way to cure was far from ideal. (After all, most modern physicians did not know more about the mind and subtle energy flows than the caveman knew about electricity.) Still, they could bring relief with life-saving technologies and heroic efforts. To join them sounded right, but at the same time, it required Sofia to abandon her own quest. Facing this dilemma, Sofia had been trying to reach David and Alana all day long, but their phones remained silent. In the end, on her own, Sofia decided to take up the assignment and took a taxi to the airport.

For the first time since she had seen the statue, Sofia was not doing what she truly wanted.

David's phone call stopped her in her tracks while the taxi was still fighting its way through the late afternoon traffic in downtown London.

"Sofia." David's voice sounded urgent. "We've been trying to reach you all day… You must join us immediately."

"David! I'm on my way to the airport. They called me on an official UN mission to the refugee camps to fight the vi — "

"Sofia…," David interrupted her in earnest. "Sofia, don't let all this madness avert you from finding Pasión."

"Finding Pasión..." she muttered. It was so peculiar to say his name while wearing a gun and UN-badge over a white suit: it felt like some forbidden magical formula. "David! I already know, even if the public hasn't yet been informed that the Olympic Games won't happen this year. It's decided. So, now I have no other way to find Pasión but to use the statue — and I can only do that is when I — " Here, she suddenly quieted her voice, becoming conscious that someone else — the taxi driver — may be listening.

"... When you die," David finished the thought for her at the other end of the line. "So that you can go to Elysium..."

"Yes."

"But... this is the reason for you having to turn around immediately..." David did not know how to break the terrible news with finesse, so he just said it. "The statue has been stolen."

The phone fell into Sofia's lap.

The taxi came to a halt at a red light. Sofia stared out of the window. She tried to hold on to some impression of normality: watching the crowd of men and women in business suits going out for after-work drinks and dinner, as the news she heard was too sinister to fully grasp.

"Sofia," David's voice came to her help, "there is also good news."

Sofia put the phone back to her ear.

"Alana learned the lesson from being spied on by the Dark Order: she let her team install a hidden tracking device inside the sole of the statue. This morning the statue was missing from the museum, and all signal was lost, so we feared the device had been discovered. But! About twenty minutes ago or so, we got hold of it again: it seems the statue is moving now. It is heading towards Silvertown Quays at the Docklands!"

Sofia commanded her attention to come back fully.

"Turn around," she ordered the driver. "We need to get to Silvertown." But he refused.

"I'm sorry, ma'am, limited access there today... can't drive you there."

Whatever it takes... Sofia quickly thought to herself, got out of the car, and walked around to open the driver's door before the lights would switch.

"United Nations." She showed her badge and waved the gun. "Get out of the car, sir. I need to borrow it."

Hypnotized by the badge of authority, the driver bought into the bluff and sleepwalked out of the car.

Sofia put away her empathy, as well as the gun, and jumped into the driver's seat. She turned the car around while the traffic started to move again.

"I'm driving the car now," she told David on the phone. "Where shall I go?"

"We actually lost signal at Raleigh Street, Millennium Mills — but that is not necessarily a bad sign. They might have arrived at their destination and driven the statue into a sealed place. If so, it is there right now. You'll arrive there before us... Sofia, you will need to use your intuition to find Pasión's statue..."

"I will find it," Sofia said with sudden conviction. "Have no doubt, I will."

"All right. Be careful!" David said, relieved, as he heard the strength back in her voice. "You know, of course, that this is not an ordinary theft of art... Who knows how close the dark forces are following you right now... Try not to draw attention to yourself."

"I shall not," said Sofia, yet she took a sharp move to the right to overcome three cars in one and gain speed like a gangster.

As she drove, Sofia noticed that the world was changing around her: dark clouds of cinnabar red and crimson color flying above like dragons to accompany her into a great battle. But the powerful clouds had fused into darkness by the time she arrived at the docklands. The setting felt surreal as Sofia was walking along in the twilight darkness of the waterfront, towards an abandoned warehouse, like being on a film-set, arranged by the cosmic director for the greatest impact. Like an indigenous hunter, she did not need to know where she was going, brave intuition and eternal love guided her every step, attracted by a beauty that also held great peril.

First, she had a glimpse of the statue.

It wasn't being shipped or flown away by some private airplane from behind the warehouse, as she feared it might be. It stood there in the middle of this soulless, derelict building, yet its beauty shone brighter than ever before. How Sofia wished she would be dying now: all she would have to do would be to put her arms around that exquisite marble chest, whisper her intent to enter Elysium, and right away she would be transported by centuries of magic to be with him forever.

Instead, she was all too alive and all too alert: without delay she noticed two figures coming out from behind the statue. Two ancient enemies of the Order! Sofia had not seen them in this lifetime, but she knew immediately who they were: from the left came Moris, and from the right, his dark father.

They both held a gun and pointed them at Sofia as they saw her walking towards them, but she was not to be fooled. She knew these two had no scruple about committing suicide and were not going to miss or even delay their only chance to travel up to Elysium. Now that the statue was in their possession, they only needed one moment, and they were ready to take it.

But Sofia, for her part, was not ready to let it happen. She fired her shot as quickly as the two moved their arms to aim — at each other. Sofia's gunshot came with such precision of the ancient warrior that it hit Moris' gun out of his hand. But the father's shot! The father's shot hit Moris and wounded him. Sofia only hoped the wound would not be mortal as she took another shot at the father and hit his weapon away from his hand too.

Yet, the worst doom she could have imagined was already happening: Moris was dying, but with his last strength he stumbled forward. The father, the horrible father, just had enough time to step in, lift one of the guns, and tuck it into his son's pocket. Moris reached the statue and put his pudgy arms around its pristine shoulders. Unlike Sofia — who would have given the statue her most beautiful embrace if her final hour had come — Moris was clinging to it like a rapist. Ugly. Desperate. Looting.

Unfortunately, this was the weakness of the otherwise brilliant, ancient plan: the portal had been set up to simply open upon focused intent in the moment of death, regardless of who was uttering the word.

And Moris had just enough time to say his intent out clearly: "To Elysium."

In the very moment of his death, the magical procedure irrevocably commenced. The statue itself began to dissolve as if it wasn't made of marble, but some dust turning into light projected into this world from somewhere else. The father instantly backed away from the scene as such light was unbearable for a creature of utter darkness like him. Sofia, with her precious sapphire consciousness, held out much longer: she even ran towards it, hoping to pull Moris away, but there was no flesh and blood to grab any more. The vortex had already come into motion. With tremendous force, it lifted Moris up. He was now ascending into Elysium, and there was nothing Sofia could do to prevent it.

The same force threw Sofia — because she lived — off its track. She flew across the room, hit her back against a column, and fell to the ground, unconscious.

***

Fast, so fast as only thoughts can travel, Pasión passed through the Cinnabar Gate yet again and returned to Elysium with the naturalness of a man who simply came home after an honest day's work. This time, he had found his way back to the Pure Land on his own merit: in his last — short but glorious — life he had beautifully contributed to the advancement of consciousness and not committed any unwholesome actions.

Unbeknownst to him, however, he had brought great peril to the sacred realm. It was for his sake that Laurin gave up his entrance into Elysium, and a new portal for him had to be created.

Pasión saw it as soon as he arrived back in the Valley of Ideas.

It looked like a beautiful nightmare.

A spectacular, spiraling vortex of light was open, creating a crater into the below. Around it were all the diamond souls, standing in a circle, holding hands, and staring ahead towards the depth with primal fear and confusion written on their faces. The spiral was not only omitting light: it was contaminated with a dark infusion from the inside. Amidst the wonderful energies that were moving it, a dark, sticky mist brought up something else also.

Al'Om, the ancient Hierophant, was the first to notice Pasión. With a wave of his hand, he invited him over to stand next to him.

"What is this?" Pasión whispered, looking at the crater of light.

"The portal has been activated."

"I don't understand," Pasión said faintly. "Pardon, I just died. I've been murdered and feel still... a bit... confused."

"Your statue," Al'Om said gently but firmly, "which you crafted once upon a time and was turned, in the last twenty-five centuries, into a portal into Elysium, has now been opened."

"Not by Sofia...?" Pasión voiced his fear.

"No, not by Sofia. By the dark forces that are now finding their way into Elysium."

Pasión looked at Al'Om. To his horror, he saw the same pervasive fear in his eyes that had grabbed all his diamond brothers and sisters standing in the circle. How could it be that the one who had seen the beginning and the end, the Alpha and the Omega of consciousness, was afraid, too?

"What happens if the dark forces reach Elysium?" Pasión asked carefully, sensing that something unspeakable and sinister was arising as a possibility.

"I don't know." The answer Al'Om gave was truly disconcerting. "There has never been a precedent."

But Al'Om knew it would bring the evolution of consciousness to a halt if a member of the Dark Order penetrated the Pure Realm. Elysium would lose its purity, not only by its mere presence but also in any attempt to fight it.

"Come, Pasión," Al'Om said, and opened the circle of hands to his right to let Pasión in.

To everybody's astonishment, instead of joining the circle, Pasión stepped into its very middle, and the others closed the chain of hands behind him.

He stood on the edge of the vortex crater.

Pasión was the only one daring to gaze directly into the vortex, using an emotion that was all too human, ever so useful, envied by the gods, and his very own favorite: curiosity. It helped him to see what others were too afraid to glimpse.

Looking into the vortex was like looking into a cosmic volcano, which was not only bringing up the brightest of light but from long-forgotten depths of human existence, all the burning lava of old violence and molten mud of history's every hatred. Fantastically, the space inside the vortex looked as vast as only galaxies would be, but at the same time, it seemed infinitesimal, like peering into god's microscope. At the bottom of the vortex, he saw an old warehouse, in the corner of which lay — Sofia.

Pasión was also the first to see who was inside the whirl, riding the energy of ascent: Moris!

Nothing could have troubled Pasión more than this sight.

"What would happen if I jumped?" in his despair, Pasión asked Al'Om. He was contemplating whether he could travel down, perhaps wrestle Moris back or change the movement of the vortex...

"Don't even think that," Al'Om warned him. "Yes, the portal is open in both directions, but it would destroy you if you attempted to go down there! You would not only fall back into hell. During the fall, your body would become denser and denser and the impact could kill you — both your physical body as well as your diamond etheric body. Your consciousness would remain trapped in the darkness of those lower realms, unable to find your way back here."

Following these words of warning, Pasión could hear the entire Elysian circle raising their voices in unison:

> *Dear One, you must not kill yourself,*
> *You must not give up your advances,*
> *You belong to us. Brother, do not forget:*
> *Self-sacrifice does not advance the mind.*
>
> *Do not descend. Do not descend. Do not descend.*

Pasión gazed again into the depths and contemplated how Laurin was not afraid to do the same. He did give up his advances for him!

Suddenly, Pasión could not only see Moris, but also hear him, which made the experience even more petrifying.

"Wait, you glorious crowd," Moris came shouting. "Wait in your silky paradise until I get there! You shall not think that I do not belong where you belong! You shall not dare to think that I am different from you. I know magic as you do, and I know you better than you know yourself. Be ashamed that you think you are better than me! You deem me unworthy of your compassion?! Wasn't I the one who worked in the mines for your silver to buy you time for noble philosophy? I've seen you: how you have created your peace by stepping on the suffering of others. Yes, I have seen you! I have seen what you have done!" Moris let out a diabolic cry, which shook the very foundations of Elysium from below. "I've seen you all. I've seen you, Pablo, how you raped that maid... I've seen you, Albert, how you enslaved your wife... I've seen you, Thomas, how you locked up Sally in the basement... I've seen you, Rinpoche, fucking your students... I've seen you Athenian dogs... I've seen your naked body, Mahatma, touched by those young girls... I've seen you all... you hypocrite crowd... who dares to throw the first stone at me?"

How maddening this was! How sinister! Moris kept addressing everyone in Elysium by their names, exposing what seemed to have been their greatest sins and weaknesses. All his evil words reached the Pure Realm like bad seeds, to set off the ultimate contamination by self-doubt, guilt, and shame.

As Pasión saw how great the threat was, he hesitated no longer. He gathered all his valor and vigor — and accelerated. Pasión, who never wanted to become a martyr, but even less so wanted to see Elysium destroyed, jumped into the vortex, holding on to his highest hopes and best of luck.

He fell with a speed that blew his mind, regardless of how powerful it was — he could hardly see, or later remember, what exactly happened and went wrong. He saw Moris and steered towards him in a heroic attempt to grab his shoulders and wrestle him back. In this speedy cosmic confusion, he failed to do the impossible. He only succeeded in grabbing the leg of Moris and pulling him off the upward spiral. But Moris swung his body and broke loose so that Pasión could not bring him down with himself. Somehow, somewhere, Moris tore himself away, and at the edge of the vortex, flung himself out.

The ground came so speedily that Pasión hardly had time to focus. Too quickly, his body was becoming dense again. Still, every move he ever trained for the Olympics came now to his advantage. Every thought he ever practiced toward manipulating time came to his advantage. His iron discipline training with Coach Diana came to his advantage as it allowed him to take his attention away from the growing panic and focus his thoughts on time instead: how time was but a perception... How perception followed intention. So, he grabbed the intent to slow down time to make every second count for a minute, and he tried to make every minute count for more... Even so, he barely had time to take a few steps back in the air, to make one single leap backward in time, before he crashed through the rooftop of the warehouse like a fallen angel and hit the hard ground of the Earth.

The pain was immeasurable! Nothing hurt Pasión like this in twenty-five centuries. At least he was alive! Only his body, freshly condensed through the fall into physical form, immediately reminded him of all the sufferings in lower realm existence — and there was not only physical suffering. When Pasión opened his eyes to keep himself from fainting, he saw the other of his ever-greatest tormentors: not Moris, but his father... their father from the time they lived in Melos.

The father extended his arm towards him, and for a moment, Pasión thought he wanted to help him stand up — so long in Elysium, kindness had been the only natural way for him. But the father did not want to help. He wanted to take away from him, using his chance to steal the diamond pendant!

Once upon a long time ago... when Pasión was sold at the slave market, he thought the pendant was the only thing he had — which they wanted to take away from him. This time, he knew it was the only thing he had. All any of us ever had is the sum of our experiences that purified our hearts, advanced our consciousness, and helped us to create happiness.

This is all we have — and this is all the Dark Order wants to take from us.

Pasión tried desperately to stand up and defend himself, but his bones were broken, and his body so devastated by the fall that it was astonishing for him to even be alive.

The dark father had nothing more to do than step and forcefully tear the pendant off his neck — but he was interrupted.

"Don't touch that pendant!" a voice behind him said.

He turned around.

It was Sofia.

The father of the Dark Order did not make a mistake about it: he knew she was not merely a lady in a white suit, nor even a woman with a tough military background. He was facing his most ancient enemy, someone who had accumulated power to combat him over a long cosmic past. Yet, he attempted to seize the pendant, nonetheless.

Sofia became fast like a single bolt of thunder as if Zeus himself had moved her body, lifted it up to form her leg and torso into a horizontal weapon that kicked him away from Pasión. Sofia landed next to him, strategically in the right place, from where she would be able to kill him in the next move with one hand strike only.

"See, you see! After all this… development," the dark father said mockingly from the ground, "centuries of… conscious evolution or what you call it… you still don't have a better answer than us — you still only want to kill your enemy. It is only human."

Sofia knew this was dangerous. Still, at least fleetingly she had to look at him. What a sight! What an incredible, horrible-beautiful sight she had now, right in front of her eyes.

After twenty-five centuries of waiting, many thousand-and-one nights of dreaming, there he was in his physical form, the man she had been longing for: Pasión!

He also was covered in blood, his face distorted with pain and scars. But she could be there with him, in a second, if she only killed this dark figure lying between her and him.

Pasión met Sofia's eyes: he warned her and, of course, he was right. If she killed the dark father now, she would lose twenty-five centuries of advancement with a single act of murder.

"If you preach compassion," the dark father accused her further, "why do you have none for us left? You were taught and loved by advanced masters; we were not. Why is it that you were given to wear the sacred signs and we are not?"

So, here I am, and I have dropped my pen while writing this. I'm looking at Sofia like I have never looked at her before. Already, I know what she is about to do, but I am curious whether she was fully aware of the consequences of her action or merely trusted the universe regarding what she was about to do. I like to believe that she knew exactly what was to happen, when in the silence of her heart, she made the decision that would change the course of the world.

"You are right," Sofia replied in a soft voice to the dark, broken figure lying at her feet. "You have never been given the chance. Here is the moment for this to change."

Even Pasión gasped as he saw what she was doing. Slowly, thinking deeply into every minuscule movement of her hand, Sofia began to pull the silver ring off her hand. As she pulled, its color slowly but visibly began to change. The sapphire stone in the middle of the silver lyre form began to lose its purple color. By the time Sofia removed it from her finger, it was utterly clear. It had turned into diamond.

"It is yours now. Take it!" she said and handed the ring over to the father, who greedily grabbed it. Immediately, he put it on his hand.

Never in their lives will Sofia and Pasión forget the scream they heard the moment the ring got itself tight around his finger. The diamond stone had instantly turned back into black obsidian and cut with its razor-sharp essence through blood-vessels and nerve-endings, straight into the brain and the heart of its new bearer to cause the greatest of pain known in the entire universe.

It is the pain that is felt when evil recognizes its own nature.

In vain did the father try to pull the ring off.

"Free me!" he screamed in indescribable agony, like a man on fire. "Free me from this curse."

"Only you can," Sofia said silently. "Only you… the pain lessens as you purify yourself."

"How long will it take?" The question came amidst the greatest of agony.

"Eons, it will take eons," Sofia said as a matter of fact, but the man in pain no longer heard her. He was running out of the warehouse, all through the docklands, all through the world… trying to run away from something he would never be able to run away from any more.

Sofia glanced after him. It was a good moment, albeit a painful one. She knew that pain and suffering were always the necessary first steps for evolution to commence.

She then stepped towards Pasión, who by now had lost consciousness. Sofia lifted his broken body, drenched in blood, onto her lap. Her white skirt turned red. She said a silent, forever prayer. Her hands traveled through the beloved landscape of Pasión's classical forms: she felt the pain, she felt the damage, but slowly, as she felt more, she began to smile… even laugh a little… and her tears began to fall down from her hot cheeks onto Pasión's chest. Tears of joy.

Sofia smiled, laughed, and cried because by now she had felt all his injuries: his bones were broken, and his tendons torn. But this time, his wounds were not beyond healing, this time the damage was not beyond repair… one night in her healing touch… and by the next morning, Pasión would be mended.

This time, Pasión would live with her — for sure.

Chapter 24
True Gods

X enocrates used to teach a profound thought at Plato's Academy that both Laurin and Pasión would have appreciated, but this was some while after they were all gone: Pasión had died in battle, Laurin left Athens for good, and even Socrates already had to empty the hemlock cup. Only Plato, despite the friends he lost and the terror he witnessed, stood his ground. Undaunted, he continued to treasure his dream. After he had built the Academia, Xenocrates arrived there one day and told all the sophists that the Olympian gods were not the true gods.

He insisted that in all the universe there were only two real gods: unity and separation. All the others were mere spectators; even the Elysian messengers and the various demons, who brought ideas and inspirations to the mortals, were but derivatives of unity, which desires separation, and of separation, which desires unity. Those two alone set the cosmic play into motion once upon a time, and continue still: breathing out and breathing in the world, forever again and again.

Today, twenty-five centuries later, the truth of Xenocrates was coming back like a beast resurrecting in Sofia and Pasión. It moved in such curious ways that time was needed to acquaint it.

Initially, Sofia noticed nothing unexpected. Hour by hour, moment by moment, joy kept sweeping through her like evening waves of the Mediterranean gently washing its moon-lit shores. All night long she was holding Pasión in her arms! This night, she was in one person every king holding their every crown, every alchemist holding the elixir of life, every adventurer holding the greatest diamond they had just brought out from the barrels of the earth — in one person she was holding every joy of humanity. She felt Pasión's pain also and the torment he suffered from his injuries, but she gave him prompt relief through her healing touch. Watching his magnificent face by the glow of a single candle, she could tell he had drifted into a peaceful sleep. Sofia was even glad that she had him simply lying there, without moving or saying a word. How else could she have adapted to the immeasurable bliss of being with Pasión again? Just as someone who was lost and starved first must take small bites of food not to burst the stomach, so did Sofia need to breathe in carefully, breath by breath, Pasión's powerful presence.

It was only in the morning when she decided that she needed to stretch and prepare a coffee to stay awake that the curious became apparent.

In the kitchen, as she took out a mug and filled the coffee-maker, slowly the counter began to turn, around and around her like a whirl. She felt like Alice suddenly back in the rabbit hole, flying in a vortex that grew larger and larger every minute, and inside of which she wasn't alone…

Moris must not reach Elysium, grab him at any price, pull him down, yes like that, now Elysium is safe, but oh no, no, no, no, he is escaping through the vortex wall; he has a gun, the beautiful crowd at the Tokyo Olympics is in danger because of this portal, because of the statue we created now falling, falling, falling…

Sofia fell hard on the kitchen floor as if from great heights. Yet, she got quickly back on her feet with the velvet jump of a tiger and rushed in to see Pasión.

Startled, she saw that Pasión was awake. He had just jumped back on his own legs too, after having fallen from the bed. His body was wonderfully healed and recovered, but his face looked distressed, like after a nightmare.

Still, Sofia felt an immense joy seeing him — at the same time, an immense joy of seeing herself. Pasión moved, quick and nimbly, to take her into his arms too — at the same time, his jump moved Sofia's body also. As a result, she spilled her coffee and dropped the mug on the floor. When she bent down, reflexively, Pasión's body bent, too!

Perplexed, they froze their movements in time.

What is happening my love … Everything that is happening to you is happening to me … I feel overwhelming love for you, I feel your overwhelming love for me… I have never known that I was treasured so much throughout centuries… tune into me if I move my limbs, you move too; we move each other's body now, we share every move now, we share every feeling now, we share every thought…

We are sharing one consciousness.

With careful, slow movements, Sofia and Pasión began to get closer to each other. First, it all looked like some imitation pantomime: whenever Sofia moved, Pasión moved with her, whenever Pasión moved, Sofia moved with him. It seemed as if they were seeing each other in a living mirror, reflecting themselves in another body. It was infuriating — they did not want to mirror; they wanted to touch each other.

Soon, however, they realized what was happening: their bodies moved in unison because they shared a unified consciousness. Unified, they had to learn that they no longer had a pair of arms and a pair of legs, but rather, they had a pair of feminine arms and masculine arms, a pair of feminine legs and masculine legs. Also, they could see the world from two different vantage points. As soon as their brains became accustomed to processing this, they derived immense pleasure from the experience. They could separately move their female and male parts, yet, as soon as they touched, they both felt each touch given as well as received. When Pasión touched Sofia, his body reacted as a man, which she could also feel, and so laughed with impish delight. From previous lives, she remembered the male body's pleasure and missed it. Pasión too felt charmed and enchanted, as he felt never-before known erotic currents inside her body. Both of them felt not only their love for the Other but also the love of the Other. Unconditional. Forever. Infinite.

They threw themselves on the bed, eager to make love in a way out of this world — but halt! An all-pervasive question formulated in their shared mind:

We know what will happen if we unite our purified consciousness… to make love like this means we fulfill our purpose together… we would leave the world behind… but it is not quite time for that yet… we cannot let Moris run amok… do you see my love… he had brought a gun committed murder in a place where there is no police no gun control no military because none of these things were ever needed… until now…

we must undo the harm our statue has brought into the world... before we unite for-
ever.

With these thoughts, Sofia and Pasión slowed down and sat facing each other, to begin a ground-breaking new experiment.

They touched to find out how to move their limbs separately. In the beginning, whichever thought fired first, moved a limb, regardless whose body it belonged to. If Sofia thought about Pasión's arm, it moved. If Pasión thought of Sofia's arm, it moved. They could touch themselves with the hand of the Other, and it would have been easy to be carried away by pleasure if they hadn't known discipline and determination. So, they learned that they could separate the gender lines: any moment, either of them could choose to feel feminine or masculine respectively, control the masculine body or the feminine body, become Sofia and Pasión again, but they could also merge and become one complete being who was both a man and a woman. From that moment on, they touched to learn how they could perceive everything in unison: each other's thoughts, feelings, sentiments, and all impressions from the environment. An entirely new way of being opened up to them: any moment, they could be in unison, or at will, they could be separate again. They could be in unison and feel the Elysian bliss that came with it, or they could separate in order to function in this world of duality.

To put their new ability to test, after breakfast, they left Sofia's apartment for a little stroll on the street. Although they felt confident that they would be able to move their bodies and minds respectively, even a little walk proved to be unexpectedly burdensome as Pasión entered the world that was not ready for his level of purity and excellence.

Pasión dived into his new surroundings with his eternal curiosity, moving and taking in everything with the sensitivity of an artist, the stamina of an athlete, and the heart of a diamond consciousness.

Straight away, he could tell this wasn't a pristine place. It resembled ancient Athens much more than the other twenty-first century he came from. Back was the noise, the dirt, and the separation, back was the inherent threat of violence. Even though the streets were cleaner than in Athens — at least there were no piles of corpses like after the war-time plague — this was not a natural cleanliness: everything seemed sterile and sanitized. Pasión could see how the people were wearing masks, like actors in a Greek drama, hiding and socially distancing their faces and their souls. He knew that such a thing was a sign of a world with inhabitants not free to be fully themselves.

Still, there was life: people walked around, and there was even some laughter and screams of children to be heard.

One little boy, proudly riding his toy motorcycle, came screeching with joy towards Pasión, who immediately tuned into the innocent, open enthusiasm of the child. So, when the boy stumbled across a stone and fell off his bike, Pasión reacted faster even than his mother. He quickly picked up and comforted the toddler, who began to cry as if the end of the world was upon him. Pasión began to turn around with him, urgently to restore the child's happiness, spinning and spinning around with him. Soon, the little boy was laughing and giggling again, as Pasión commenced to run, holding him up above his shoulders at the height of the trees, ready to fly.

But then, suddenly, Pasión heard some people screaming at him.

"Put down that child!" They sounded demanding and bullying. "Put your hands behind your head where we can see them!"

A hasty blink back revealed to Pasión that there were two dangerous, armed men. Worried about the safety of the little one, he ran faster. The men, both slightly overweight and not so fit, tried to catch up with him but they had no chance against Pasión, the Olympic athlete.

However, in a second, a car with sirens blaring pulled in right in front of him, and two other uniformed men jumped out of it, pointing their guns at Pasión.

"Put the child down!" they yelled. "Hands up."

To his surprise — he wanted to continue to protect the boy — Pasión's body followed the command.

Why are you doing this, my love? he asked Sofia in thoughts.

Beloved, he heard Sofia thinking to him, *these people are the police, similar to what the city wall guards were in Athens. If you resist them, dozens and hundreds will come into their place and will eventually overpower you. They won't harm the child. Only, they thought, you were running away with him. Here, they are afraid of kidnapping.*

Certainly, as soon as Pasión's arms put down the child, the policemen also lowered their guns. The little one, however, didn't go over to them or even back to his mother by his free will. He was clinging to the fun young man's legs until he was pulled away.

"Your papers, sir," one of the policemen told Pasión, who remained perplexed, looking after the boy, who cried again when his mother gathered him.

"Papers?" Pasión broke his mind over what this could mean... He understood little about papers, but he understood all the better that this was a game designed to cause global guilt and intimidation.

Sofia came to his aid.

"I've got his papers," she said to the police. "He... he is my brother."

Hastily, Sofia pulled out an ID from her bag and handed it over to the policeman.

"Dr. Sofia Erato," the policeman read out loud. "United Nations." His voice by now gained respect. "But that is your ID, ma'am."

"Oh, excuse me," said Sofia. Pasión was watching her from the inside: it was clear to him that she was buying time. Why? Who were these men? How come they were harassing them?

Our truth is stronger than their truth, he thought with powerful intent to remind himself and Sofia that they need not allow the poison of mistrust apparently inherent in this system to penetrate their world.

Whatever we believe in, is the way it is. Sofia understood and joined in with her powerful intent. She then found something in her bag — it was Alana's business card — and handed it over to the policeman.

Whatever we believe in, is the way it is. Sofia and Pasión both echoed each other's thoughts, and together they created a powerful field of intent.

"This is not an ID card, is it?" the policeman said, confused, as he began to read the name on the business card, but Sofia, calmly, gently, yet with utter conviction replied.

"Oh, but it is. If you look more carefully, you can see that it is. You can read his name here…"

Anything is possible, Sofia thought, and Pasión echoed the thought.

Anything is possible.

"There is no photo on the card," the policeman said as he tried to object and fight an impossible feeling arising in him; suddenly, he wasn't sure whether he was awake or dreaming.

"Look," Sofia said softly, deeply penetrating the part of her mind that she shared with this man she was talking to. "It is here, the photo you wish for. It is the photo of… my brother."

What a beautiful voice this woman had! The policeman couldn't help but be seduced and mesmerized by it. Suddenly, it felt as if she had the voice he wished for his whole life that his girlfriends, lovers, and wife had, but they never did.

As Sofia whispered into his ear to look at the photo, so the policeman marveled at the photo, which wasn't there.

"Anything is possible," she whispered into his ear.

Yes, her voice was so alluring that there was no need or wish to resist it — a voice suggesting that there was more to life than all this fraud you've been subjected to… all through school and work… television shows and peep shows… it was the perfect voice to wake you up within your deepest hopes and most personal fantasies. The policeman didn't want it to end.

He nodded to the ID card. It was perfect to him.

"Dream on," at the end, Sofia whispered to him. "Life is a dream. You can live it beautifully. Tomorrow morning, wake up. Quit this job that you've hated your whole life."

Home again, Pasión had a shocked look in his eyes. Sofia — perhaps out of respect, perhaps to find some comfort in the old ways — withdrew her perception and let him be alone for the moment. She understood that he needed some time to adjust; for him, this was not only a shift in realities, but this was also a descent to hell.

He had tears in his eyes.

"When I held that boy," he spoke out loud, "I recognized he was one of us. He was like me, once upon a time. He can hear colors, see melodies; he can feel the invisible movement of energies — and he is ready, so ready — not only to ride his good little machine, but to grab... no, not the chisel, more the calipers. He is not a sculptor; he is more of an architect and an industrial artist: that treasure within him is clearly rising. He himself is already aware of it. Yet, he's being treated as a mere toddler, some immature being. His unknowing mother and these ignorant policemen, as you call them, were more concerned about his bodily safety than his soul! They are utterly blind to his wonderful daemon and so neglect his talent, which will wither away if not nourished. When we lived in Ancient Greece, I saw the individual being sacrificed for the collective, but it was changing. Individuality was on the rise. I may have been a slave, but you, as Laurin, granted me freedom by giving me the marble. You validated my soul, my daemon, my centaur — you allowed me to ride on the back of danger and fly on the violent wings of freedom.

Now, I see the individual being sacrificed for the sake of the individual's body, only permitted to crawl on the ground like an insect. The eternal daemon is being sacrificed for the safety of those transient bones and skin..."

Pasión spoke these words with the sadness of the one who saw the deep and returns to find a shallow, superficial world of humans full of lies and half-truths.

"This is frightening to me," he continued, "because it means that this reality that surrounds us now is too dense, too rigid, too petrified to let anything or anyone change it. Yet we must go back to the reality I came from in order to stop the menace caused by Moris! We must cause a shift in our dimensional perception to do that. But how will we able to mend this reality when we are alone here, not surrounded by anyone or any kind of energy that would support it?"

Whether it was an answer or an interruption, they heard the rattling of keys at the front door. Sofia glimpsed to the corridor and relaxed. It was only Cynthia: normal for her to come cleaning on a Monday morning. But when Pasión saw her, his agitation grew even worse.

"What is she doing here?" he asked, in a voice surprisingly stern, even hostile for someone who came from Elysium. It was a voice of noble anger, unwilling to tolerate evil and ready to fight injustice. Sofia understood his reaction, as she knew it was because he remembered the old woman's ancient essence.

"Once upon a time," the housekeeper now said, "I used to torment you all in the house. This time I came back to rectify things."

"It's all right," Sofia told Pasión with her eyes and moved herself again closer to him, not merely physically, but allowing her thoughts and feelings to merge into his, embracing and soothing him from within.

"Medea is no longer Medea," her thoughts revealed. "Now she is Cynthia and she set herself up to help us. She was the first who told me about you. She predicted and prepared me that I would meet you on the day when I saw your statue again after twenty-five centuries."

Pasión switched his look from her to the housekeeping woman, as if to gauge whether she was friend or traitor, but soon Cynthia said words in a way that allowed him to open up to her.

"I came to tell you about a dream I saw last night," she said, opening her eyes wide like an owl, as always when she reported sensing something from the invisible world. "I saw the two of you, finally united in soul. But it wasn't here…"

That caught Pasión' attention.

"If not here…," Pasión urged her to speak more, "where were we?"

"Oh! You were in a magical forest," Cynthia said, lost in reverie. "A forest so pure and pristine, it still carries the original vibration of the earth. This magical forest is in a land where profit, prestige, and power matter little; a land where sacred energies are directed towards the happiness of all sentient beings, not the growing of production; a land where all warrior energies are directed towards assistance, not destruction."

"Are you talking about Elysium?" Pasión asked, unsure about the meaning of these words. Cynthia was speaking, but these were not her words: they came from a source higher than her consciousness.

"No," the old woman answered. "I am talking about the Land of the Dragon King."

"A fairytale kingdom…," Pasión murmured as he was hoping for a real place from where they could transition into the other timeline. If only there was a kingdom like that: yes, then they could use its land to go into deep contemplation, break the prison walls of their current reality and travel back to Pasión's twenty-first century.

"It's not a fairytale kingdom," Sofia suddenly said. She then stood up and walked over to her bookshelf. She took off a weighty tome, which contained maps and colorful images of all countries, and laid it on the table.

"Yes, this is what I thought," she said as she found the page she was looking for. "The Dragon King… this is how the King of Bhutan is traditionally referred to. The country Cynthia refers to really exists! The country where Gross National Happiness is measured instead of Gross National Product, where the military is trained to rescue in case of emergency, and the major aim of the state is to spread the teachings of the Buddha. Even if it's not a perfect pure land, as nothing at this level of reality is… this country may be the place closest to it. It makes sense that Cynthia had this dream. Yes, why was I not thinking of Bhutan?"

Sofia was reaching back deep into the past. She smiled.

"I went there as Laurin… Yes, believe it or not, I made it that far, all the way from Greece, on foot! There, behind the Himalayas, is the ancient motherland of our Order, it is where the Original Monastery stands. Yes, that is where we must go!"

Pasión saw Sofia's thoughts running fast. She was contemplating how they would get there, with worldwide pandemic lockdowns and closed borders. Now that there would be no Olympic Games, no international travel, now that the forces of darkness were using sickness and fear to suppress evolution, how could they reach this far-away land? It was one thing to fool a single policeman, but how could they fool entire airports and border agencies?

Sofia's questions sounded severe, yet they were not born of desperation, rather in the spirit of inquiry: she was searching for cues on how to make the impossible happen.

"You can't do it alone," Cynthia said. She spoke decisively. "You are not meant to do it alone, either."

As soon as Cynthia said this, Sofia and Pasión began to tune into something. A sacred shiver went through their shared eternal memory. Like an electric current shooting through the cosmic web of consciousness, their thoughts traveled from the oldest, deepest recesses of the cosmic order all the way to future connections in the making. They felt, coming from the past, going into the future, there was something invisible, yet very real. All throughout history, there were hidden righteous ones, who had developed a higher level of consciousness that others were not even aware of. At times, they formed the Invisible College of the Rosy Cross, and when needed, they formed the invisible world government. Those who penetrated the mysteries could always recognize each other for a shared purpose and the darker the times became in which they lived, the brighter they let their invisible light shine.

Pasión and Sofia tuned into their current reality. In the midst of all the chaos, whipped-up fear and ignorance, there was something magnificent they could set into motion. There was the potential for some cooperation of a new and higher order. What it was, exactly, was still unknown, even to them: nothing but a vague potential. Yet, they could already sense it coming towards them from the future.

"Are you saying…" Sofia tried to put into words what they were sensing, talking to Cynthia.

"Yes…"

"Yes," Sofia echoed her. "In order to overcome all obstacles in the physical world and fight through every resistance, we must…" She paused.

Pasión — who now understood everything — finished the sentence:

"… activate the Network."

Chapter 25
The Original Monastery

Y ou are the same consciousness that created the universe. You are of the same essence as I am, as Pasión and Sofia are, or Plato and the Hierophant — for consciousness is a singularity. Your ability to manifest ideas into being is the only creative force there is. It is primary and fundamental: it has always been, always is, and always will be — everything else is derivative of it.

Only consciousness can construct reality, and only consciousness can deconstruct it. Yet, deconstructing reality is by no means an easy task. Everything that ever happened: every thought, every object, every dynamic ever brought into being has long become a brick in the edifice of reality. Its walls are held up by the mortar of persistent belief in natural laws and are well plastered by the fear of change and the unknown. What a painful prospect: to tear down this familiar building, our only home! A single atomic moment of enlightenment can detonate the entire edifice, but Sofia and Pasión needed to remove only parts of it, brick by brick to give themselves more space and freedom.

They needed to find their way back into the pristine twenty-first century and free it from the menace of Moris.

Sofia and Pasión sat together, facing and holding each other in the dark. Despite the fear inherent in the human form, which they still felt, and the burden of the responsibility they took, the beauty of their mutual presence was indescribable. They leaned against each other like two beams constructed at a perfect angle to create a tensegrity strong enough to hold up a whole building.

Their strengths were remarkable.

Pasión knew how to bend reality when the conditions were favorable, and he knew how to deal with the limits of the limitless mind. He had experienced the power of curiosity and love: surrounded by purity and compassion, he had been brought to great heights. Sofia knew bravery. She knew how to work through hardship and adversity: over vast centuries, she had accumulated knowledge of how to fight resistance. With no-nonsense endurance, she had learned to keep going in whatever hell she had ever found herself to be in.

Pasión brought his curious, unbridled passion, which he learned to expand all across space.

Sofia brought her unstoppable, committed wisdom, which she learned to keep through all time.

Too modest to realize, together Pasión and Sofia were invincible: as they focused their intent, they formed the most powerful force there was currently on this earth. And their aim was simple: they did not seek to walk on air or turn back time, only to find a safe passageway to Bhutan, despite the dystopian roadblocks and border controls, which were set up in every country.

Enter the dream! Pasión thought, as he had learned to do while he was training for the Olympics with Coach Diana and let the thought enter their shared consciousness. *We shall enter the dream of a higher vibrational world, in which external movements support our internal resolve. Everything from now on will be dream-like. Every event will come to our aid. And we will allow for every event to unfold, no matter how unlikely, impossible, or even too good they may appear.*

The world reacted as soon as Pasión and Sofia finished sending out their intent.

The phone rang.

"Dr. Erato." On the line was Sofia's old boss from the United Nations. "Are you still in London?"

"Yes."

"Good, that's really good," he said. "I'm glad you have received intelligence on time. Greece is full. We need you on the Indian-Bhutanese border."

"I'm on my way," said Sofia and jumped like a predator who sees movement.

"We have sent a private jet for you to the docklands," the UN boss — amazingly — said. "It will bring you to our Vienna headquarters, from where you will need to take a commercial airplane to India."

India is bordering on Bhutan. That is all they needed to know.

Next, the doorbell rang. It was David, and he brought Alana with him.

Sofia and Pasión had seen David in many forms, over many lives. They had seen him in Ancient Greece, when the same consciousness was the slave girl of Laurin: Diona, the warrior; Pasión remembered her from Elysium and in the form of Coach Diana who helped him win the Olympics, but neither of them had ever before seen Diona's consciousness as eerily beautiful as on this day.

"We are taking you to the Docklands," he said.

As they were on their way, neither David and Alana, nor Pasión and Sofia spoke a word. There was nothing more to say, as they all knew they were in the dream that was real and that would take them to the ultimate destination. They passed by the warehouse where Pasión's statue exploded into light not so long ago. Sofia and Pasión entered the jet and flew to Vienna. Their spirits were high, and they felt that nothing could stop them. Sofia and Pasión reached the strange, half-moon buildings of the UN headquarters, from where they were transported to the International Airport.

There, the situation suddenly seemed as impossible as turning back time. Sofia had a diplomatic passport, an airplane ticket, a gun, a firearm permit, and a UN mandate; Pasión, however, did not even have a birth certificate. Here, at the airport, they also began to see the virus. They saw it in the lounges, later, on the airplane, they saw it in India, they saw it at the border to Bhutan. It was not the virus that attacked the lungs. It was another, much more dangerous pathogenic agent, spreading globally, causing a crisis of the worst kind.

It was the disease of fear that they saw spreading.

It attacked every human being who did not have the antidote, and it attacked where they were the most vulnerable: the ones who feared illness and death were now afraid of getting infected; the ones who feared the loss of freedom and their rights were now afraid of rising dictators; the ones who feared loneliness and depression were now afraid of the curfews; the ones who feared themselves and their families were now afraid of being locked down with them. The world had changed. Everyone's personal fear was brought out into the open. The cauldron was boiling.

In their perceptive, twilight state between waking and dreaming, Sofia and Pasión noticed the fear swarming in and out of people, like myriads of insects biting into the soul flesh, into ambitions, hopes, and dreams, rotting away people from within while still alive. It took discipline and determination not to give in to the all-pervasive fear around them. Instead, Sofia kept their minds and eyes alert, and Pasión brought in his memories of how they were to change reality from within.

My love, he thought, *my love.*

My love, we are neither awake nor asleep.
We are neither here nor elsewhere.
Like sleeping beauty, we are amidst the roses.

Watch as the old walls crumble down.
Watch as the grumpy old time goes to sleep.
Watch as the future braves through the thorny deep.

Walls crumble down.
Old time goes to sleep.
Future braves through.

Crumble down.
Time goes to sleep.
Future braves through.
Future braves.
Future.

Pasión repeated these thoughts over and over again, each time more slowly, each time more quietly. Eventually, everything they saw all around — the thin crowd at the airport, the cues at the coffee shops and sandwich bars, the check-in point and the computer displays — every movement began to slow down. Eventually, the steps of the people, the typing on the computer keyboards, taking a sip of a coffee or a bite of a cake — it all came to a halt. Nothing moved any more. The old time, the old reality, stopped.

People were frozen into living statues.

The world was not only frozen; it was different. A barely audible, yet infinitely beautiful music diffused throughout the air. It calmed the nerves so wonderfully: fear and agitation were soon long forgotten memories. Colors began to shine brighter, and the human heart felt brave enough to escape the ribcage and connect to everything there is.

"Pasión! Sofia!" they soon heard a kind yet alert, female voice calling them. They saw it came from a young lady. She was not only pretty and agile, she had a glorious luminosity all around her that was more to be seen by the heart than by the mere eye. She rushed to the nearest passport control terminal. "Come over here, please."

As soon as they reached her at the terminal, she was already printing out two boarding cards for them in the midst of a sleeping, static world.

"Go through here. You can trust everyone you encounter," she said. "Everyone who is still moving is part of the Network. We will escort you to the airplane. Have a safe journey."

Sofia and Pasión walked through the same airport at which they were sitting before, yet it was a different one. With its brighter colors, silent, yet uplifting melodies, it belonged to a reality of a higher order. Someone arrived at every checkpoint they had to pass through, someone who knew their names and let them through like royalty on a supreme mission. They were all luminous members of the Order, but they were even more than that: connected to a higher intelligence, they all knew what they were assisting with.

The magic of the Network was needed until they arrived inside the aircraft. As soon as Pasión and Sofia took two seats, the passengers, who had already boarded but were locked into immobility, resumed their actions. They finished putting their handbags in the overhead lockers, found their places, adjusted their safety belts… remaining unaware that something had just happened outside of horizontal time.

Once they reached Bhutan, Pasión felt more at home again. The path they were following was invisible — invisible to anyone outside of the Network. It was nowhere to be seen among the mountains, valleys, and rivers, and it was not among the many routes marked on maps for expeditions and hiking. Here in the mountains, many searched for gold, rubies, and diamonds, but so few ever found them. Many also searched for the miraculous and various spiritual treasures, but most of them failed, even disappeared forever. For the resplendent Original Monastery, the ultimate repository of all wisdom coming from the higher realms to Earth cannot be found without a call. Only a few ever reach the holy place, only if they are already purified, and only if the fulfillment of their mission requires them to find it.

On their way, Sofia and Pasión passed by many hot springs: small geysers would erupt wherever they walked: piles of water vapor danced in the air like escaping earth spirits. At the beginning of their track, they saw many warm, crimson-and ochre-colored monasteries, but at greater heights the signs of human civilization — prayer flags flapping in the wind and some last stone offerings — became more sparse.

As they arrived at the peak of their path, there was nothing other than a rock shaped like the face of an eagle. There were no more plants, no more animals, not even birds to remind them that they were on a planet that had life. Somewhere else. Not here. Here, there was nothing.

Still, their unified consciousness knew that they had arrived.

There was nothing else to do but wait. They laid down on a flat rock, which reminded them of the large stone in Laurin's grove, where in ancient times they liked to lie together, watching the stars.

And this is what they did now too. They waited for the darkness to come and light up the stars.

What great cosmic dream, what great cosmic pain is in the moment when human beings look up to the starry sky! Those who do not know eternity may be overwhelmed by feeling so small amidst vast, inaccessible galaxies. Those who remember eternity may be taken by awe into the midst of inconceivable mysteries.

Sofia and Pasión knew eternity. As they took their glimpse of the stars that night, they remembered Pasión meeting Sofia during his celestial flights. So, they reached up to heavens, and it happened that the sky began to collapse — far became close, space drew back into their eyes. The starry, starry sky came close, and it formed a dome: inside, the fallen stars formed a circle of fires all around them, the sky poured into a sacred lake in the middle of the sanctuary.

The heavens, as it all collapsed, became the Original Monastery.

Sofia and Pasión were now inside of it.

They were alone, yet they were not alone.

The Hierophant came walking around the sacred pool towards them.

He looked young, as in Ancient Greece where he was born as the son of Pasión and Diona, raised by Laurin, but he carried the wisdom of centuries in his eyes and the charisma of the enlightened.

"Welcome," he greeted them. "You are a soul who has arrived almost where it began. Only almost. For the moment, you remain split into the lover and the beloved. You are purified. Yet, you have set actions into motion that prevent you from uniting. As for you, Pasión, you know that you have to find Moris and prevent him from infiltrating further the higher and purer realms. This is the right place to do it from. This sacred pond is filled with the Water of Memory; it is the same water you have tasted in the caves of Greece, but here it is in the most pristine state. If you immerse yourself into it, you can relive any memory and change it. You, Pasión, have to change a single moment in time to ensure that you don't die after the Olympics. As for you, Sofia, you have to make sure that you do not miss the Olympics and meet Pasión there. For that, you have to correct the gravest mistake of twenty-five centuries. That is your sacred obligation still."

Sofia looked at the Hierophant seriously, with full awareness and knowledge of what they were talking about.

"Walk, Sofia," the Hierophant continued, "into the Water of Memory, and as you do, it will reverse the lives you lived. Walk until you arrive at a point in time where you have to make your one amend. Pasión will follow, and the two of you will meet again on the other shore."

Sofia stood fascinated, yet aghast.

"How long will it take?" she had to ask. "Will I have to walk all these centuries backwards, relive them all backwards in order to reverse some lines of action? Will it be centuries again until I reunite with Pasión on the other shore?"

"The water of the pond," the Hierophant said soothingly, "belongs to eternity. In the essence of eternity, time does not exist. Yes, you will go through all the centuries backwards in time and relive every moment. You will do what needs to be done. Yet, it will only take a glimpse. A blink of an eye after Pasión has emerged on the other shore, you will emerge as well. Go first, Sofia."

She looked at the Hierophant; she looked at the beloved.

"There is no need to say goodbye to each other," the Hierophant assured them. "In a blink of an eye you will meet again. While every individual soul fulfills one cosmic dream, it may also make one, a most powerful, amends. You will have good luck."

The words came as a wish, as well as a prophecy. Sofia began to walk into the water, slowly, steadily deeper. Pasión looked after her for what felt to him, an eternally long time. He knew he would immediately have to follow her, and when he emerged on the other shore, he would immediately have to reverse time, only for a minute, but to the best of his abilities.

Before he did so, however, one more time, he looked at Sofia.

He saw her immersing into the water, surrounded by the spiraling fire of the stars. He smiled, for he knew.

Sofia won't hesitate and will use the power of the water to reverse things. At a certain point in time, Sofia will choose another salient rebirth. This time, Sofia will not be reborn as the son of Pontius Pilatus. This time, Sofia will be reborn as the governor himself. This time, he will not allow for the crucifixion to commence.

***

One moment later, Sofia emerged from the water. She was somewhat confused as the sacred pond felt more like a mist in which twenty-five centuries happened again outside of time and space, but now she was in real water. She had to swim in order to move and not to drown. She swam with strong, sturdy strokes but soon hit her arm on something when she realized that she was at a pier. She held on to a wooden jetty and lifted her head out of the water to breathe again.

The world around her was filled with celebration. She only saw the wooden planks in front of her, but from the buzzing sounds in the air, she could tell a huge crowd had gathered all around the shore. People saw her, too. Hands reached into the water and lifted her up. This is when Sofia, wet and bleeding a little, saw the circular platform with the spiraling stadium on its top, which she recognized from Pasión's memories. This was Tokyo. This was the time of the Olympic Games held in the pristine twenty-first century.

The atmosphere was incredible.

Sofia saw that all people around her were surrounded by that luminosity, the same that she saw all around the members of the Network. Here, the luminosity was so strong; it caught her right away, like a beautiful current of warmth, and she no longer felt alone. She felt the impulses of the others, and they felt her thoughts, feelings, and sentiments. Yet, she wasn't exposed; she was sheltered and protected as part of a global network of minds all dedicated to the advancement of consciousness. What an amazing, spectacular thing this was: Sofia had just gotten used to sharing consciousness with her beloved, and now — albeit in a less intense form — she was sharing consciousness with one billion human beings. An immense joy swept through the shared field when Sofia was found. She felt welcome like never before. But there was no time to marvel at this miracle as she had to find Pasión. Immediately, she perceived his thoughts and feelings and knew he wasn't far away. Yes, up there on the bridge! Sofia began to walk towards him.

Pasión stood on the bridge and struggled for a moment to balance his consciousness having returned to the pristine twenty-first century. He had to alert his attention to reverse this very specific moment when Sofia had risen from the waters and the shot was fired. Fully alert this time, Pasión saw the attacker! Knowing what would come next, he only needed to step to the side to avoid being hit. And yes, this way, this time, he got himself out of harm's way just in time: the bullet flew by, missing his left shoulder, leaving him unharmed.

But how naive, how careless, how silly was it of him not to think that surely, Moris would have a second attempt at shooting him! Perhaps, his urge to reunite with Sofia after twenty-five centuries at a place that was physical but pure was so strong that he forgot everything else. From the moment after he avoided that bullet, Pasión only saw Sofia. He saw her clearly, coming towards him on the bridge, and with a beautiful smile erupting on his eternal face, he took a step, and the next, and the next towards her... walking, running, shooting... when Moris, still hiding in the crowd, fired a second shot.

It came with the precision of an act only the devil could have accomplished: straight and unhalted, the bullet traveled towards Pasión's heart.

But when the bullet impacted, it was not Pasión's chest that it hit. The woman who loved him saw what was happening, and followed a decision she made in no time, without hesitation. She jumped in front of the bullet to save Pasión.

This was but a single moment, yet as every single moment, it was infinitely precious and crucial, as every single moment is eternally a pivotal point in every human heart. It makes no difference whether that single moment is of great historic significance or a solitary, private experience. If attention is shifted and a decision made towards increased evolution, consciousness, and vitality, the history of the entire world will shift. Yes, true power belongs to the single individual who makes a single decision in a single moment in time — it is the axis of change. Even if only one individual resolves to find enlightenment for the benefit of all sentient beings and never gives up on that intent, the entire world finds liberation through that one decision. And so does the entire world change if one decides not only to live, but also to die for the beloved.

In horrendous desperation, when he realized what had just happened, Pasión turned. Before she could fall to the ground, he caught the mortally wounded body of Amber Sunshine.

At once, Sofia was running towards them through the crowd. Shocked, she quickly glimpsed at Pasión and then kneeled down beside the wounded girl.

"I'm a healer," she urgently said to her. "Let me hold you and give you life force energy, I hope this is not beyond — "

"No, Sofia, it's all right," Amber said. "Let me die, please."

"No!" Pasión objected in horror and remorse for having let another shot in another careless minute cause another deadly wound. "Sofia is a powerful healer, and we have the intention of a billion minds behind us — "

"No." Amber looked at him in earnest but still smiling. "I needed to do this. Really. I needed to do this before I could find my peace and my own access to eternity."

The world held its breath. Pasión and Sofia looked at her with fearful compassion. She labored as she spoke, so Sofia laid her hands on her to ease the pain, at least.

"I needed to do this now," Amber Sunshine repeated, "because once upon a time, I was an ignorant fool. Back in those days, I didn't know what I was doing. And now that one unfortunate, evil deed has been keeping me from reaching the higher spheres. Back then, I thought I was doing it for valor, honor, and the fatherland. Of course, it was just another act of murder… But I separated you… Pasión and Sofia… when I was… the Spartan… throwing that spear. I caused you a mortal wound… it separated you lovers. Now it is right that I take this mortal wound… to unite you again."

"Everything is all right." These were her last words. "Everything will be all right."

Chapter 26
Eros

Z igzagging through the crowd, Moris felt befuddled and disoriented. The more he walked, the harder it became for him to move his limbs.

He knew he had to get out of here, for he committed murder, even though he missed his aim and killed someone else. Who was that girl, anyway, who jumped out of nowhere? And what was this place and time, he wondered, which made him so dizzy as if there was some nerve poison in the air? The crowd was creepy, too: it felt like walking among some strange mentalists. Moris couldn't explain why he had an inkling that everyone wanted to reach into his brain, but it made him paranoid. He tried to run, yet he could hardly move or even keep his eyes open: he was slowly becoming so, so sleepy… His body was going numb… Now he needed to lay down for a moment… It wouldn't matter… if it's just on the pavement… Let it be… He'd go on when he had a little rest… a necessary little rest…

As Moris collapsed, he did not crash on the ground: countless hands grabbed underneath him and gently laid him down. In a way, he was like Gulliver, shipwrecked in the land of the dwarfs. Even though Gulliver was a giant compared to them, a regiment of little people managed to bind him with tiny ropes — rope after rope — while he was unconscious. Now Moris, the giant evil, found himself stranded in a realm too pristine and vibrant for his body-mind to assimilate. No one put shackles on him, yet nerve by nerve, he found himself bound as he was unable to move with the higher vibrancy of a much faster world speeding up all around him.

By the time he fainted, many people had gathered around him, the sleeping evil son of an unfortunate world. Pasión, Sofia, and the Hierophant came rushing by. Without having to say a word, they immediately nodded at each other, knowing what had to be done.

"May I?" The Hierophant stepped toward Pasión. He took the chain from which the pendant hung around Pasión's neck and wrapped it around their fingers.

It was the same chain which in ancient times, Melaneos, the smith, fused around Pasión, the slave's neck on the order of Laurin. Pasión, who remained immortal in his Greek form, had been wearing the pendant around his neck ever since: in every time, in every realm of reality. Now the Hierophant used the hot, powerful life current flowing in their fingers to separate the chain.

He laid the pendant on the chest of Moris.

"His evolution will be a lot more gentle than that of his father," the Hierophant said as he fused the chain around Moris' neck. "He is lucky that this moment has come upon him at a place as pristine as this. He's gently asleep. Of course, he will still have to undergo his own long, hazardous journey of purification. His sleep will last a thousand years, and as many times yet another thousand years as needed. While he is asleep, he shall dream a dream within a dream, in which he'll live lives upon lives, die deaths upon deaths, at other times, in other spaces, wherever the wanderings of his consciousness shall take him. He will suffer, he will sin. But wearing the pendant on his sleeping body, he will always be guided. He will always have an underlying, inexplainable hunch that there is something good for which he must search, something worth fighting for in the end. We all have started like this, in the dark, once upon a time."

By the time the Hierophant said these words, he had fused the chain around the neck of sleeping Moris. With that, Pasión's diamond pendant turned back into black obsidian. Moris showed no sign of pain, yet powerful vibrations swept over his body, which deepened his sleep.

The Hierophant's words fell like seeds on the ground. Softly, rain began to fall, washing away the heat of all lives Moris lived in evil. In weeks, months, and years to follow, thorny vines grew from the seeds, bringing forth roses fragrant of truth. The kind and gentle people of the pristine twenty-first century had built a chapel around sleeping Moris to protect him from the elements. And the rose vines grew and grew, farther and farther, to shelter his thousands of years of sleep from any intrusion or disturbance.

One day, he will awake, at another time, in another land, and on that day, we will hear from him again, as the youngest new member of the Order.

***

Sofia and Pasión took a walk away from Tokyo, away from the city, away from civilization. The time had come for them. They gained no more from being part of humanity and from being involved with matters of the manifest world. Only one place was there for them to go: to the stars, as their souls were now purified and free to leave this world behind.

Even so, while walking their path of light, Mara, the shadow servant of darkness, began to follow them. Mara was clever. He knew it was futile to tempt Sofia and Pasión with things like beautiful lovers, as they were the most beautiful lovers to each other. It was to no purpose tempting them with thirst and hunger, as they were accomplished warriors, resistant in mind and body. They couldn't be tempted with hatred, either, as they'd just sent their enemies on their way to freedom with their best wishes.

No, Mara had to be more clever than that — and he was. He conjured up an ancient dread, which none of the cosmic lovers could ever withstand. Throughout all times, this wicked strategy worked so well because this sorcery was the harder to break, the more the lovers loved each other.

In the twilight, as darkness fell, Sofia and Pasión were advancing on their path, suspecting little that anything could hinder them. They saw the first stars illuminating the highest mountain peak, on top of which the Original Monastery awaited them.

Despite the Monastery in sight, the dread gained on them. The slopes of the mountain turned steeper and steeper, until they became nearly vertical and a cosmic abyss opened up all around. Suddenly, their path shrank to a narrow plank, bridging above a bottomless void.

Pasión found himself walking ahead, feeling ill at ease, as step by step the abyss grew not only around, but between them. The void swallowed up his thoughts and severed the conscious connection he hitherto had with Sofia and the Network.

The last thought Pasión received from Sofia was a warning: *Don't turn back.*

After that, all he could hear were her footsteps.

What a diabolic display: the abyss was so deep and endless, it seduced one to jump! Now that Pasión was disconnected from Sofia and the Network, there seemed no incentive not to. Walking alone, nothing was holding him back from jumping, from falling, and nothing was moving him forward. Disconnected, his own thoughts came to a standstill, and he forgot who he was, where he came from, and where he was going.

Only the footsteps he still heard from behind kept reassuring him. He could not forget that those footsteps were important since nobody could erase his deepest longing for the beloved.

This is how Mara found his ultimate desire.

All he needed now was to make Pasión turn around for them to lose their balance and fall into the final void forever. All he needed to do was to cut off the sounds of Sofia's footsteps.

Pasión heard Sofia slipping back.

The demons of the void made her voice cry for help.

And it was impossible for Pasión to refuse that call, for love makes it impossible not to turn back when the beloved is in peril.

But heaven knows that there is a secret that makes one more than one could ever be. The secret lies in what is before us and what we do not know until we succeed.

In front of him, Pasión saw the Hierophant rowing down the river of time. His coming was an invitation, to relate with hopeful expectancy to the possibility of a future salvation — a victory of the good, the true, and the beautiful — and to resist turning back in fear of the possibility of evil. The Hierophant lifted an arm towards the waxing light of a future moon. Pasión glimpsed the moon and saw that it was a mirror, and in the mirror of the future he saw the Truth: Sofia was walking steadily behind him. She was neither crying out for help nor was she slipping back.

With utter conviction, without ever turning back, Pasión continued walking, and in three easy steps reached the Original Monastery with his beloved.

When up at the highest mountain peak, the Monastery opened up for them. They discovered that the inside of the temple was laid out with silk. It resembled the place they had the fondest shared memories of: Laurin's master bedroom with the cedarwood four-poster bed and Pasión's frescoes on mythic seductions painted on the walls. Everything was arranged in the same way as on that fatal night when the Spartan attack prevented them from reaching the stars together.

By now, the Spartans and their spears were gone, Moris and his father were gone, Mara and his temptations were gone.

Sofia and Pasión sat down together in cross-legged postures: belly to belly, heart to heart, throat to throat, forehead to forehead. They were facing and embracing each other. As they slowly started to merge into each other, all separation was dissolving; when Sofia kissed Pasión, she kissed her own lips, when Pasión drove into Sofia, he was penetrating deep inside himself. Their bodies were still apart, but their shared consciousness soon realized they were like two hands, holding two pencils, drawing themselves. They realized they were making love to themselves, creating the lover and demolishing the lover with every move they made. The truth of their creation revealed itself to them as they softly spoke the word into their own ears:

I created you. You created me.
All I ever wanted to do is make love to you.

At the same time, somewhere in the Theater of Consciousness, the Wizard of Separation stepped in front of the curtains and took a bow. He smiled at the audience he created on a stage, in a world that was the product of his imagination. Grabbing courage, he dared to remember how it all began: that he was alone in the universe. Consciousness was the one and only magician, holding the power to conjure up the separate lover in a separate world.

In their ultimate moment, Sofia and Pasión reversed all separation. While united in body, they let the serpent power rise high up their spines and higher up still. That created an eternal moment of highest bliss, for which it was worth wandering for centuries, but so powerful that neither the human body nor any manifested reality could survive it. There was no need, either.

Their enormous bliss erupted in a cosmic climax, which came with the power of an almighty explosion: it destroyed their bodies and all the physical reality that they ever knew.

Their consciousness was back in the void.

> *Gods! We are coming!*
> *they shouted into the Kosmos.*
> *We are passion. We are wisdom.*
> *We are bringing you our human story.*
> *All our experience, at the end of our journey.*
>
> *We offer you ten thousand songs from around ten thousand fires*
> *hear of our tribes, heroes, and bravery.*
> *We offer you ten thousand children from ten thousand births*
> *hear of our sons, daughters, and poetry.*
> *We offer you ten thousand crowns of ten thousand kings,*
> *raised by dragons of the holy struggle.*
> *We offer you ten thousand hearts of ten thousand lovers,*
> *hear of their letters, roses, and affections.*
> *We offer you ten thousand anthems of ten thousand throats,*
> *hear of our hopes, deaths, and victories.*
> *We offer you ten thousand sights of ten thousand stars,*
> *learn about the Muses, in the skies of Elysium.*
> *We offer our Sacred Connection to you:*
> *despite the ten thousand times*
> *you sent titanic destruction upon us,*
> *we never lost sight of you.*
>
> *We claim back our seats amongst you.*

At the end, there was silence.

***

Silence filled the primordial emptiness, pregnant with all the possibilities of creation. From here and now, their consciousness could take any form.

They appeared for the last time in their human form at a place halfway between the earth and heavens.

Sofia and Pasión returned to where their soul and story began, and where their story shall finish: a place they set up eons ago, when their journey began, to return here last for answering the ultimate question.

They were back at the Eternal Library.

This was the time when I found myself back at the Library also. Thus, I came to learn that this place hovering among the stars was not only an etheric collection of the world's finest books, scrolls, and scripts ever to be written, it was also a rare meeting point between realities. Inhabitants of different realms, who had that particular ability to travel, could meet here and talk to each other.

I must have been the last person from Earth who saw them in their old forms as Sofia and Pasión. Sofia's wisdom appeared shining from heights greater than any human, but it saddened me, as I already knew she wouldn't linger on here to talk with me. Pasión's beauty blinded me and pained my heart, as I already knew I would not be seeing him for much longer. They smiled at me as if to meet and greet, but I already knew they were soon to leave, never to return in the form I had learned to love them.

I believe I wasn't meant to speak, for something emerged before I could say a word. First, I only noticed a bookshelf. Soon, though, its colors at certain spots gained depth and texture. A contour began to vibrate and move, and out of the image emerged — the Librarian. How relieved I was to see her! If she was here, I wouldn't remain alone when it all ends.

The Librarian noticed me there, yet she went straight to Sofia and Pasión, letting me only observe things. This was not a prohibition, rather convenience. The things I was about to see were so strange and miraculous that I would have found it impossible to comment. All I could do was to sit in one of those flying easy chairs, watching in awe.

"Old soul," the Librarian addressed the unified consciousness of Sofia and Pasión. "As you have completed your history on Earth and brought your love into eternity as your contribution, you now have the choice."

A magic motion took control of the Eternal Library: it was a spiraling whirlwind, which slowly solidified into a whirling staircase. It led upward to the sky and downward back to Earth. No one said it, but we all knew this was the stairway to take Sofia and Pasión into eternity. Which way they would go — upward or downward — that was the ultimate question.

"You may now leave our planes forever," the Librarian said. "You have unlimited freedom to create whatever, whenever, wherever you want — or would you choose to return and help all others to reach liberation?"

The Librarian, as was customary, left them time to think.

Now, she turned to me.

"You know, of course," she said to me, "that every soul can make this decision at the end of their time. It would be best if you already prepared yourself for the same. Think: Would you come back, into this world, if you had the chance to leave it? For the sake of others? Do you have what it takes to commit that you shall not leave until you helped every other soul to purify — the last scoundrel, the greatest dictator?"

She raised the question without expecting an answer. It was a paradox, as I sensed it: if consciousness was a singularity, as we, members of the Order, understand it, this is not a choice but a necessity, an inevitability even.

"For now, I can only hope that I'm evolving. I adore the idea that one day, I will transcend this human form also and become something higher," I only said carefully.

"You most certainly will," the Librarian said, and enigmatically added: "I can personally vouch for that."

"You know about my future?" I exclaimed.

"Yes, more than anyone could ever know."

Naturally, I felt most intrigued, yet could not ask further because Sofia and Pasión returned from their contemplation. I could no longer see them, as they were no longer in a human form. Their consciousness only had a voice, not a form: it was Laurin's pristine, magical voice, which reverberated through time.

"We have our answer," their voice said.

In anticipation, I was not the only one holding my breath, so was the Librarian. Together we were listening to the divine words, which drifted into music all across the spheres:

> *We have seen where our soul may go now.*
> *We have seen the land without limits.*
> *We have seen the forces of enlightenment victorious.*
>
> *We have seen highest happiness without pain.*
> *The future holds our highest hopes.*
> *All our efforts were and will be worth it.*
>
> *Yet we think of the world we are leaving behind.*
> *We think of the old darkness still on the rise.*
> *We see Diona, we see Alana, and we see you.*
> *And for you, our heart shall remain human.*
>
> *We do not wish to leave you abandoned:*
>
> *For as long as time endures,*
> *For as long as space remains,*
> *So long shall we too abide,*
> *To power you with all our love*
> *And dispel all misery of the world.*

"We are choosing to be reborn," Sofia and Pasión's divine voice said at last, "and we have a message to share with the world."

The words no longer even came to my ears, I could not see anything either. If there was light, it may have been too bright for me to stand. The Truth felt so close that my perception gave way to knowing.

"What is the place you choose for your rebirth?" the Librarian asked, and immediately came the answer by Sofia and Pasión's unified consciousness.

"We shall be reborn in Greece."

"What is the time you choose for your rebirth?"

"We shall be reborn in the year 404 BC."

"What is the identity you choose for your rebirth?"

"We shall be reborn as Dion, son of Diona, raised by Laurin."

***

Silence fell upon the Library. The noise of a thousand trains departing and the uproar of a thousand airplanes taking off, which accompanied the descent of the Hierophant, eventually all came to an eerie quiet. Out of whirling stardust, bookshelves appeared, surrounded by pleasant fairy lights. Soft blankets fell on the flying easy chairs, inviting the cosmic reader to engage in forever stories yet to come.

"The Hierophant!" I murmured out loud, grateful that the Librarian was still around, listening to me. "How is that possible: Sofia and Pasión becoming the Hierophant, going back into their own past, helping not only others but themselves? Can they really go back as one person into their own past?"

"Of course." The Librarian assured me that this was a most natural thing. "Don't think that it is only the past that is causing the future. It is the future that is causing the present."

"How?" I asked with an urge that reminded me of Pasión's sense of curiosity.

"Causes that come from matters of the past are driving the world towards increased chaos, uncertainty, and randomness," the Librarian explained. "That is all what the past, that is all what matter is capable of. Consciousness, however, counteracts this chaos. It is working from the future towards increased levels of love, harmony, and happiness. Like an acorn carries the idea of the grown oak tree, so do we all carry the seed of enlightenment. It is our future, not our past, that shapes us to become better — it was the idea of the Hierophant that shaped Laurin and Pasión to become better — for it is always your future highest self that is your one and only authentic guide."

"Do I also have a future self?" I asked.

"Of course you do."

"Who is that?" she drove me to ask. "Who is my future self?" My passionate curiosity reached its peak.

"I am," the Librarian said, while she looked at me with her serpentine eyes, and for the first time since our encounters, smiled heartily.

I was too stunned to say a word and she gestured towards my lap.

"But now, before I can become your future, you must take care of that."

Only now did I notice that there was an envelope sitting on my lap: its material looked like old parchment, and the beautiful black letters written on it reminded me of Laurin's handwriting. It said:

Message from the Hierophant

"It is not only for you," the Librarian pointed out. "It is for everyone who followed the story of the woman who one day walked into a museum and fell in love with a statue. The message is for them, as the consciousness of the future does not belong to any single individual. Earth now requires, and is now ready for, group consciousness to emerge."

As I opened the envelope, a hitherto unknown force emanated from it.

"Learn the message by heart," the Librarian ordered me. "Remember each word, so tomorrow you can write it down and share it with the world."

So, now I came back to give you the message of the Hierophant: Sofia and Pasión's legacy for us. Thereby I had to leave the Eternal Library — the place where I would have wanted to stay forever.

Epilogue
Message from the Hierophant

Our Beloved,

If you have come so far reading our story — of Sofia and Pasión — we have one more request to you: Burn this book!

Burn the words you are reading, silence the sentences. Ours is but a story, and as every story, it must come to an end. We shall not even remember our names anymore.

All that matters is what we have achieved: witness that we have purified our mind, and we have found each other in love. However, we vowed not to quit here. Therefore, we want you to know we are out there again, and we shall not give up until we find you, too.

We will search all across the skies and the earth, we will climb the mountains and we will crawl back into the depths of the caves. We will come into the cities taken over by muck and madness, if needed, and we will penetrate the matrix. We will risk our brains to twist, our hearts to break, and our soul to tremble, only to find you. Because it is true: we are one consciousness. We created you. You created us. All we ever wanted to do and want to do now and in the future is to make love to you.

We see you. We see the madness and the darkness into which your world is plunging. We saw the Tokyo Olympics falling victim to the curse, and we see the pandemic of fear rising. This is the time of the twilight, after which comes utter darkness.

Yet, behind the madness of your world, a higher order is emerging.

It is against the utter darkness that stars can begin to shine. It will be human stars. Those of us who will resist being swallowed up by the darkness, by shining our own light, will shine brighter than any human has shone before.

We are the ancient order of Hermes Trismegistus.

We are bringing forth a new consciousness.

It is the consciousness of the Network — like a sacred spider web woven of our deepest hopes and most personal dreams — it spans above the darkness and does not let anyone who is linked to it fall and disappear into the gloom.

Join us! We have not told you our story in vain. We call you: no longer allow suffering and fear to govern you. Let your highest vision guide you instead! Find what you want, what brings you true joy, and do that. Against the darkness of the world, shine your light. Against the noise of the world, turn your music louder. Against all the resistance you encounter, train your mental muscles to become stronger. Renounce fear; do not get infected by it, strike it from your mind.

We now want to tell you how to become part of the Network.

Find a handful of magical people — three, four or six, seven beings closest to you — who resonate with your heartstrings. Find something you can share — not merely your mind to share, but your heart, your soul, your blood. Dancers may dance together, singers may sing, painters may paint, warriors may train, dreamers may dream shared dreams, lovers may love, the wise may meditate, the curious may study, the wanderers may hike off into the mountains. Whatever you do together, penetrate deep into each other's souls, for the connection is sacred and you aim to share your consciousness. We learned to do that, when we were Sofia and Pasión, and so can you learn it. Practice with your soulmates, practice regularly, and practice until there is unconditional cohesion between you.

Do not let each other go!

It is a global neurological network you are becoming part of this way. Through your sacred, wonderful, intimate, and magical personal connections, you are linked to others, like brain or nerve cells are linked to each other through their synapses. Once our Network is strong enough, thoughts will fire through it that are of a higher order than our individual thoughts.

None of us may yet know what those thoughts will be like, just as a cell in the body cannot anticipate the ideas of the whole. Still, we must trust it, as the unified human consciousness of the Network is our next level of evolution.

Your access to the group consciousness is through your individuality. Whatever you practice with your soul friends will depend on your personal talents and passions — and there will be as many types of practices as there are member pairs in the Network — but there also must be a unified intention that directs all activity to raising consciousness. It is an intention beyond the fields of right doing or wrongdoing, towards increased vitality, to counteract the paralyzing effects of the fear pandemic.

There is a spiritual war going on. Nonetheless, make no mistake and do not seek out to find an enemy, for there is none out there. It is up to each and every one of us to choose love over fear, and thus to strengthen the Network and not give in to the gloom. Avoid polarizing and dividing yourself, especially in view of the ignorant, illusory battles of power. May all our efforts be dedicated to the benefit of all humanity and every sentient being.

We are the forces of evolution set into motion. We have thought, felt, and created the tribe, the cities, and the kings. We are now moving beyond the tribe, the cities, and the kings. We are children of the stars, walkers on the highest future path, ambassadors of a better world. We are seeking you, as much as you are seeking us. Do not be afraid, we will find you.

This is not the end, this is…

THE BEGINNING

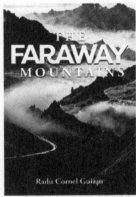
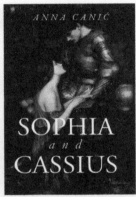
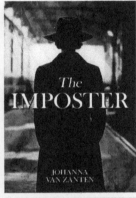
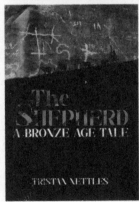